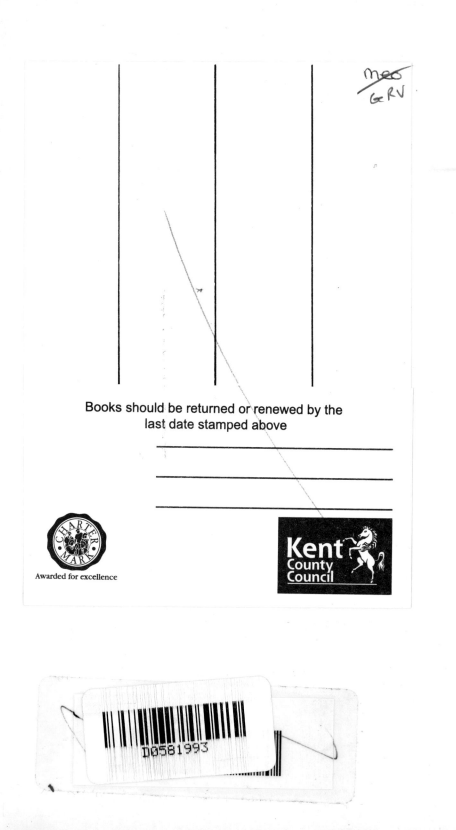

meo
GRV

Books should be returned or renewed by the
last date stamped above

Awarded for excellence

Kent
County
Council

D0581993

Vampyrrhic Rites

Also by Simon Clark

The Night of the Triffids
Judas Tree
The Fall
Vampyrrhic
King Blood
Darker
Blood Crazy
Nailed by the Heart

SIMON CLARK

Vampyrrhic Rites

Hodder & Stoughton

A CIP catalogue record for this title is
available from the British Library

ISBN 0340 81940 5

Typeset in Plantin Light by Palimpsest Book Production Limited,
Polmont, Stirlingshire

Printed and bound in Great Britain by
Mackays of Chatham plc, Chatham, Kent

Hodder and Stoughton
A division of Hodder Headline
338 Euston Road
London NW1 3BH

For Janet

Here terrible portents came about over the land of Northumbria, and miserably frightened the people; there were immense flashes of lightning and fiery dragons were seen flying in the air.
ANGLO-SAXON CHRONICLE, AD 793

We use them every day, but few know the true meaning of the days of the week. One can only guess how ancient their pagan origins. So, hereafter, are our common-or-garden days with their ineffably exotic translation: –

Sunday – the day of the Sun god
Monday – the day of the Moon goddess
Tuesday – the day of the god Tiw
Wednesday – the day of the god Odin, sometimes known as Othin
Thursday – the day of the god Thor
Friday – the day of the goddess Freya, leader of the Valkyries
Saturday – the day of the god Saturn
A VERY PAGAN FOUNDATION by the Countess of Bedale, 1929

One sign of the vampire is the power of the hand
Joseph Sheridan Le Fanu (1814–1873)

Navel, septum, labret, tongue,
Purple, black, lace, leather,
Chains, collars and candy necklaces.
Stoker, Lovecraft, Poe.
Poetry, painting, rain, and death by architecture.
All these we want. All these we need.
MIDNIGHT'S FAIR, Anonymous

I have a personal dislike to vampires, and the little acquaintance I have with them would by no means induce me to reveal their secrets.
Lord Byron (1788–1824)

DARKNESS RISING

1. Electra's Room. Hotel Midnight.

She lay on the bed. Her hair of beautiful gunmetal blue splashed outward as if it had exploded across the pillow. Hotels at midnight are other-worldly places. They house strangers who sleep under the same roof. They are a rendez-vous for lovers. Places where marriages are consummated. Where individuals of a certain nature may indulge their secret passions away from their own homes.

The weight of darkness pressed down on her naked body. Sometimes she willed that sensation into the mental image of a lover pressing her tight against the bed. A lover with long hair falling in soft curls across her face. This lover wouldn't hold her with arms but with a pair of vast black wings. Bat wings. They'd have the shine of patent leather. Through them would run veins that pulsed with warm, rich blood. They'd rustle as they encircled her. Aromas of clean hair and skin would rise deliciously into her nose. She rested her hand on her face, her fingers splayed, forming a cage across her eyes.

I see my lover. I see the wings that will hold me. They beat the air above my bed. Now my lover swoops . . .

A soft chime shimmered on the midnight air. Electra Charnwood blinked the fantasy away.

No.

There is no lover there, hovering on outstretched wings above the bed. I'm lying awake, as I do every night in this forbidding Gothic horror of a hotel in Leppington. There never is any lover. The town's dead. It's snowing. It's just the same as always . . .

Electra climbed from the bed and stood there for a moment, feeling the chill of midnight air on her naked body. Normally, she'd slip into the silk kimono with the gold dragon winding down the back but she'd grown to enjoy the cold against her skin. Lately, she'd even taken to turning off the heat in her room. Now there was something delicious about the way the chill night air slid through the part-open window to roam across her shoulders, breasts and thighs.

The musical chime sounded again.

Two e-mails in as many minutes? *Your popularity's bursting through the ceiling, girl.*

She crossed the room to her desk where the computer screen burned with a cold blue light in the darkness. The first message ran a heading: *Meet Thursday?* She recognized the e-mail address.

'Only in your dreams,' she murmured, then deleted the message without reading it.

The next one caught her breath. Shivers tingled across her back and arms. A mass of tiny ice feet invading her skin.

This one was headed: *Please.*

Sight of the e-mail address filled her mouth with the taste of something metallic. *That's the taste of fear,* she told herself. A mere glimpse of this e-mail address always had the same effect on her. She sat down at the desk, straightened her spine in a way that signalled 'OK, I don't want to do this, but I won't be frightened . . . *I won't be frightened* . . .'

Even so, the feel of icy insectile feet now pelted down her spine. Her heartbeat quickened.

OK. I don't have to do this, she reasoned. *I can read it in the morning, or next week, or even delete it; never read it at all, but I—*

No. He needs me.

Before she prevaricated any more, she went for it. Skimming the cursor across the screen, she struck the highlight bar that contained a single stark *Please*.

Electra,
Thank you for your message. Those kind words meant so much to me. Please know that they carried me through some difficult nights. Those terrible sounds come again. They came through the walls. I'm convinced that if I opened the—

Electra stopped reading. The sound of footsteps in the hallway startled her. It was the sound someone makes when they approach stealthily across carpet. Now they were just outside the door. There they paused.

Clenching her fist on the desk and half turning, she spoke in the direction of the door. 'Yes. I know you're there. I know who you are . . .' Her heart pounded in her chest, her ears buzzed with the force of blood being driven through her veins. Louder, she repeated, 'I know who you are. But I won't let you in. You can't hurt me . . . not if I don't let you.' With a sudden fire in her voice she called out loudly, 'And you can tell that to whoever sent you!'

A necklace of black beads lay on the desk beside the computer. Picking them up, she flung them at the door where they clattered against the panel. They'd not even come to rest on the floor when she heard the footsteps backing away. Closing her eyes, she saw in her mind's eye those bare feet. They'd run, making nothing louder than whispering sounds, away along the carpeted corridor to the stairs. Then down the staircase, moving faster and faster.

And they'd be the strangest feet in the world. Back-to-front feet with the heels pointing forward and the toes back. Moving ever faster, they'd race across the lobby, past the reception desk where Electra spent so much of her working day, then past the kitchen to the basement door. Without pausing, the runner would speed down the steps into the basement. They wouldn't pause to switch on the light. They didn't need it.

No, she saw them plunging down into darkness to race between ancient shelving, empty bottles, junked bed-frames and broken mirrors. Not even solid ground would stop them now. She pictured them plunging through the brick floor into the earth beneath Leppington town. There they'd swim deeper down through layers of clay, the foundations of medieval houses, Viking feasting halls, Roman villas – tiles, bricks, potsherds of terracotta and blood-red Samian ware. Further down through flint arrowheads and axes. All this and more, blended with the bones of Leppington's ancient dead.

At some point the runner would find its master.

Electra Charnwood got another message.

'That's right,' she whispered as she returned to the computer screen. 'That's right. I did. And I know you're trying to start it all over again.'

Electra read the e-mail.

2. Rowan's e-mail. Twenty past midnight.

Electra.

Thank you for your message. Those kind words meant so much to me. Please know that they carried me across some difficult nights. Those terrible sounds came again. They came through the walls. I'm convinced that if I opened the door I would see something out there. And, believe me, I don't want to see. The noise is terrifying. To see what makes the sound must be beyond imagination. But I can 'feel' their presence – if that makes sense, Electra. I feel waves of cold – absolute cold – rolling into the house. I feel dread. If I were to open the door nothing would ever be the same again.

Electra, I'm frightened. I want to go home.

Only I know I can't find my way home. I don't even know where I am. You asked questions and requested information. How did I come here? To describe my surroundings. To try and remember.

I do try. All I can say for sure is that my name is Rowan. I'm not an old man. I'm sure I am young. There are no mirrors. But if there were I know I would scream at what I saw.

Now . . . why did I write that? Why should I scream into the mirror? What is it that's so wrong with me?

It's those sounds. They infest my ears . . . they move like worms in my brain.

I'm sorry, Electra. I know I should stay calm. You have asked me questions. I will supply answers. Right:–

FIRST. HOW DID I GET HERE?

Easy, Electra. I don't know. I just found myself here. I didn't even wake to find myself in this place. It happened over a long period of time. As if I lay on the bed for days while a mist slowly . . . ever so slowly . . . cleared around me. In short, not only don't I know how I arrived here, I don't even know how long I've been here. Now, how crazy is that?

SECOND. WHAT IS THIS PLACE?

That's easy, too. An old house of some kind. The walls are bare stone. There's not much furniture. A sofa, an armchair, a few framed prints of seascapes on the walls. Three bedrooms on the first floor; another bedroom in the attic. In the kitchen . . . if I can bring myself to venture into the kitchen, which isn't often, because that's where the trapdoor to the well is . . . there's an old-fashioned-looking cooker, a table and chairs, a dresser with plates, a microwave, a refrigerator; a big Belfast sink.

*But I don't know **where** this is . . . out in the countryside, I guess. The reason I'm not sure where – and you're going to laugh out loud at this, my dear Electra – is because I dare not look out of the windows. I daren't. As simple and as stupid and as crazy as that!*

*The windows terrify me. When I was in this fog of not being fully wide awake I knew people looked in at me. No, not looked but **STARED**. Frightening faces. Electra, this was the worst part. I was paralysed. All I could do was look at the faces staring in at me. Inside my head I was screaming. But I know I couldn't even murmur aloud.*

And during that time everything seemed monstrously distorted. The doorway was an ugly hole that constantly changed shape. The dimensions of the room moved from being as tiny as a box that pressed against me, to expanding into something as vast as a cathedral where the ceiling light was only a dot in the distance. Sometimes I felt as if my head was swelling. It would keep swelling until it was bigger than the room itself. That's impossible, I know. But that's how it felt. And it was such a terrifying and sickening sensation.

But that's over. Only you might understand now why I daren't look out.

After I emerged from this mental fog I searched the house. I found a hammer and nails and nailed down the trapdoor in the kitchen. Wasn't I the man of action?

And now I have this sensation growing inside me. A sense of wanting. Needing. It's a hunger, but not a hunger, if you know what I mean?

No? It doesn't make complete sense, does it?

*But I guess it's what birds **feel** in their hearts when the time comes to migrate. They don't KNOW what they want, but there is this instinct – this God-almighty overpowering instinct – that possesses them; that drives them to gather into flocks, then to fly south.*

Some instinct's growing like a clump of weeds inside me. The pressure's enormous. Sometimes I wonder if my heart's simply going to grow and grow until it bursts my ribcage.

I need you, Electra. I believe that only you can reach out to me. So each night I find myself sitting here at the computer.

There is no telephone but I can send these e-mails to you down the line.

I could send messages to other people. Is that what you're thinking as your gaze glides across these words? But everything else on the computer screen is a fog. Only this link through your **Hotel Midnight** *site is clear. When I wake I find myself sitting here, so I type. After that, I walk from room to room in this lonely house until it's time to sleep.*

If you do read this, if you do believe what I'm saying is the truth (and, God help me, it is) then please will you try and find me? You can't imagine the terror this life holds for me. Please help me before those sounds grow louder than I can bear. Please try to

Electra leaned back in the chair; she massaged the tight muscles in her neck, sighing. That was all Rowan had written. He had even finished mid-sentence. That had been the eighth message, and probably half of those had finished suddenly, as if fear had smothered his senses. It was all he could manage to hit the 'send' icon.

So how can I help Rowan? Whoever he is? Wherever he is?

There'd be no answers tonight. Electra saved the e-mail message in the *Hotel Midnight* file. After that, she washed her face and arms in cold water before lying down on the bed. There she closed her eyes, and imagined that a bat-winged lover was gliding above snow-covered mountains to be at her side.

LAZARUS DEEP

1. Lakeside. Midnight.

The sign had so many bullet holes in it that he could see the starlight burning through.

LAZARUS DEEP

DANGER

DEEP WATER

The glacier – a river of ice a thousand miles long and over a mile high – had carved Lazarus Deep out of heart-rock. Back in a time when men and women lived in tents made from animal hides and mammoth tusks.

Now, seven thousand years after the ice had retreated northward, the lake remained. Lazarus Deep – six miles long, more than three miles wide. Deeper than anyone knew. In 1945 a B-17 bomber had crashed into it on Christmas Eve. The crew's bodies were never found. In summer teenagers who were foolhardy enough swam in it.

It was a cold lake in a remote valley hidden away in England's North Yorkshire Moors. Perhaps the only thing that ran deeper than its waters were the legends surrounding it.

Fable had it that its depths concealed the ruins of a lost town, Kirk Fenrir (meaning Church of the Wolf). This had been home to Viking warriors who had looted Christian abbeys from Lindisfarne to Whitby. The story was that they slaughtered so many priests, monks and nuns that when they returned home the sheer weight of their clothes, heavy with the blood of their victims, caused Kirk Fenrir to sink beneath the lake. It was also said that now and again, on a still moonlit night in winter, the lake bed yielded up a blood-red stain that floated on the surface for an hour or two before being slowly reabsorbed.

There were plenty of other legends, too. Local children collected them for the school website where there were photographs of ancient stone heads that had been found on the fringes of the lake. These were known as the Lazarus Heads and were permanent reminders of the severed heads of the Vikings' enemies. As such, they were used as symbols of fertility and military power. The stone heads with their flattened faces and glaring eyes also had hollow crowns. Archaeologists speculated that they were used as receptacles of some sort.

In the local museum, a painted door panel from a nearby medieval church showed a demonic figure with blazing eyes supping from such a stone head; his blond moustache was slick with crimson liquid. This was blood: the drink of LIFE itself. The entity seemed to drink with passion, his body swollen with the strength drained from his countless victims. A guidebook historian had captioned the figure 'vampiric'.

Ancient legends accessed by the click of a computer mouse.

But not all legends were ancient. Not all legends were safely confined to the deepest parts of cyberspace on a website created by children.

The owl flying high over Lazarus Deep could see the lake in its entirety. In the moonlight the lake was shaped like a human skull; against the pale vegetation the water had no colour, appearing merely as black shadow. With uncannily sensitive eyes the owl saw shapes stir beneath the surface of the lake. Fish darted away from man-shaped figures that rose from the cold heart of the lake. The figures moved with slow churning motions, limbs outstretched like the wings of the ravens that had once adorned Viking shields. These figures were a deeper black against the darkness. Impossible to see with the human eye.

The owl's nerves sparked a psychic red as it sensed danger. Instantly, the bird swooped in order to pick up speed. Above the need to find food now was the overriding instinct to leave this place. It plummeted downward, the steep angle of the dive increasing its velocity, until the slipstream tore away a breast feather. A figure rose in front of it at the water's edge. In the moonlight the face seemed to blaze. A huge distorted thing with wide, staring eyes.

Screeching, the owl flapped its wings, hurtling away from the lake in the direction of the valley over the hill.

2. The North Shore. Beyond Midnight.

The screech came through the bullet holes in the sign. *DANGER – DEEP WATER.*

Startled, Dylan Adams flinched as a pale object hacked a path through the air just over his head, then soared away over the fields to vanish as quickly as a ghost. Dylan reached out a hand to take a piece of moonlit froth from the air.

Owl's feather, he told himself. From an owl that had been in such a hurry that it had nearly collided with his head. He looked at the fine fibres of the feather catching the moonlight as it lay there in the palm of his hand, before a breath of air took it away from him, losing it among the bushes at the side of the lake. He shivered. There was nothing like this breeze coming off the lake on a midwinter's night to turn your blood to ice. He could almost feel it moving through his veins. A freezing slush that crawled toward his heart, making it hard to breathe.

Come on, you idiot, why aren't you at home? Why aren't you warm in bed? Why aren't you having hot, steam-driven dreams about Vikki?

But no, you have to drive out here at midnight. You have to stand here at the edge of the lake, freezing your noodles off. You have to come out here, you great drama queen, to agonize over your conflicting emotions.

'You're eighteen,' he muttered to himself, smiling wryly. 'That's what you're supposed to do. Haven't you ever heard of teenage angst? You've got a chance to leave home. You can pack your bags and walk out of a town that's got less life in it than a cemetery. You can get on the train. Go to London. Never look back. For pity's sake, Dylan – this is what you've always wanted . . .' He picked up a stone and hurled it out across the lake. 'Only you haven't got the guts. You're scared. You're scared about leaving home . . .' The stone landed with a splash that sounded uncannily loud, breaking the night-time silence. 'Yeah . . . and what's this really about? You're scared that some farm boy's going to muscle in and steal Vikki while you're gone.'

Ripples from the splash lapped the shore. They made sucking sounds against the stones. As though the lake itself had liquid mouths that fastened leechlike onto the dirt bank, trying to drain the life out of this desolate place that had been Dylan's home for the last twelve years.

For Heaven's sake, he'd been raised for the first six years of his life in York. A city that bustled, that was vibrant, where *life* didn't just happen, it buzzed. Then his parents had had what could only be described as a lightning fit of insanity and had moved out here to the heartlands of NOWHERE. For twelve boring years he'd lived in the market town of Morningdale. (Yes, it was a pretty name; yes, it had stone cottages; yes, it had an inn with log fires and ceiling beams low enough to crack a jockey's skull.) The downside was that Morningdale had a population of two thousand (multiply that by twenty if you wanted to include the sheep that roamed the damn moors). It was quiet enough to make the dead yawn. And it was so far from civilization that a trip to the supermarket was considered an exciting day out by the locals. And as for a night in a town that had music and young people – you might as well plan for that like you'd plan a journey to Las Vegas.

But now, thank God, he'd got the chance to make his GREAT ESCAPE. The chance had appeared like magic, though he still hadn't finished the photography course at college (well, at a rural annex of a city college in yet another market town not much bigger than Morningdale). It had been one of those bleak Sundays in January when it never even got light. After prowling round the house like a bad-tempered bear (made even more bad-tempered because Vikki had escaped to her student friend's house in Manchester for the weekend) he'd sat down to write a blazing letter to a photographic studio in London.

'I'm wasting my time. I'm wasting my time,' he'd growled as he stabbed his fingers at the computer keyboard, like he wanted to kill something. 'I'm not qualified. I've no experience.'

But by that time on a lousy winter Sunday, after falling out with his parents . . . (Over *his future*; naturally, they'd nagged him to build a 'nice' safe foundation of academic qualifications before he followed his heart as a photographer – 'which sounds a risky business,' his father had said. 'Very risky.') So before his head exploded. Before he kicked holes in his bedroom wall. Before he threw himself into Lazarus Deep – anything to break that straitjacket of monotony – he wrote the letter. Then he emptied cornflakes into a plastic tub so he could use the box to parcel up a selection of photographs from his portfolio. After that he'd sat on his bed, glaring at the cornflake box wrapped in brown paper and bearing the address of the photographic studio. And he'd hated it. *It's a waste of time*, he told himself, *they won't even look at it. I've no experience. They haven't heard of me. They're going to chuck it out without even looking at the first photograph.*

The same emotion flared the next morning when he took the package to the post office, stood in line for what seemed hours, then endured the smug comments of Brian behind the counter about sending brown-paper parcels to London.

Hell, by that time Dylan wished he'd thrown the thing into Lazarus Deep. Even the postage costs had taken what little money he had. He exchanged what would have been a rare cinema trip with friends (with a miracle or two it might have included the beautiful Vikki) for the outside chance of showing a photographic studio his work.

A waste of time, he'd told himself again as he'd left the post office. *They won't even bother sending the photographs back. That means printing up a fresh batch. And that means finding yet more money to buy a pack of expensive photographic paper. You crazy idiot, Dylan. You might as well have fed the cash to the goat in the field over there.*

Then a week later he got the telephone call. The head of the photographic studio wanted to talk . . .

The sound of water stirring made him look up.

You've been away inside your head again, he thought. *You get so wrapped up in your thoughts that you even forget where you are.*

He looked out across the black water of the lake. It didn't reflect moonlight. For all the world, it didn't even look as if there was water there. It was a blot of shadow on the landscape. Nothing but a vast crater into which total darkness had seeped. His breath came out as a mist when he breathed into his hands. He pulled the coat collar up against his ears.

For the first time he felt vulnerable in this remote spot. His car stood a little way off behind him at the side of the track that led to the shore. There were no houses nearby. There wasn't even a main road. All there was here was—

The lake. Lazarus Deep. A blot of darkness.

On the far side of the water the valley rose to bleak moorland wastes. At this side there were clumps of brooding trees that formed a boundary line between the lake shore and fields of spiky grass.

Water swirled again. Ripples sucked at the shoreline. This time Dylan could make out bubbles whitening the surface maybe twenty metres out.

Did fish feed at night? Or maybe it was an otter, or even a swarm of water rats? They could probably see him standing there on the shore.

This is stupid.

No, you*'re stupid. You could be in bed. Freezing your hide off out here isn't solving any—*

A voice.

He tilted his head. He could hear a girl's voice. It was distinct enough and it came from his right. From a fringe of woodland that hugged the shore.

There's something not right about that voice.

He didn't know why he reached that decision about the voice, only that there was a certain inflection to it. He couldn't hear words as such. It was just a sound. But that sound managed to convey a blend of fear and protest. With it came the mental image of a woman being dragged into the bushes.

He listened.

Nothing.

He stared into the darkness beneath the trees.

He could see nothing.

Dylan glanced back at the car parked on the track. In thirty seconds he could be closing the door, starting the engine, playing music loud enough to drown out any unsettling sounds from the lakeside.

It might have been an animal, he reasoned. After all, it was unlikely that anyone else would be wandering beside Lazarus Deep in the middle of the night. He convinced himself enough to start walking toward the car. Then he heard the sound again. A voice that was quickly cut short, as before. His imagination supplied vivid images of a woman crying out before a hand clamped down across her mouth. The sound wasn't loud; it wasn't even a whole word.

He glanced at the car again. Right then it seemed like an extension of his own home. Somewhere safe and warm to retreat to. He saw himself driving away, feeling the welcome rush of hot air from the heater across his feet, chasing away the damp chill of the lake.

Oh . . .

Now he heard that clearly enough. It was close.

The thought flashed through his mind: *You've got a choice, Adams. Go home, then read a story in the newspapers that's going to haunt you for ever . . . or go find out what's happening in the trees.*

3. In the dark wood. Long past midnight.

Dylan thought: *There's a torch in the car. And a hammer.*

Light and a weapon. Those would be two good friends at a time like this. But this couldn't wait. He'd have to grit his teeth, then go into the woods and see who was there.

Dylan walked quickly and quietly, leaving the shore for the grass path that ran beside the lake and into the wood. In front of him, trees bulged rather than grew from the ground. They were ancient birches with smooth, pale bark that made him think of skin.

His chest tightened. The blood quickened in his ears. This felt *wrong*. The sense of wrongness that comes when you know you're acting against what your instincts tell you. That you could get back to the car. You could drive out of here fast. Not look back.

But it wasn't going to be that easy. He had to check the source of that female voice. If he thought it through he knew that his imagination would serve up hell for him in the form of all kinds of nightmare scenarios. Instead, he forced his *self* to sidestep somehow inside his head, to keep reality at a distance. And what a reality. A deep lake. Dense woods with trees forming grotesque phantom shapes. Bare branches lunged down at him. Knotty contorted limbs nourished by water drawn through roots from Lazarus Deep itself. He moved fast, weaving round the thick trunks. All the time he expected a face to thrust suddenly out at him from behind a tree, or maybe he'd meet a figure blocking the path.

Dylan expected that now.

By expecting it, perhaps he'd be ready to deal with it?

Expect the worst. If it happens it won't be such a shock.

But it will be, and you know it.

He pushed his *self* harder. Moving it to the back of his head, trying to armour himself with psychological detachment. It helped if he imagined that he was watching himself on tele-vision – far away from this reality of the woodland at midnight where a woman had made those frightened sounds.

There he goes . . . walking along the frozen path in the wood. Dylan Adams, eighteen years old. A denizen of a little town that holds no interest for him. He's six foot two. He has light hair that was blond when he was eleven years old but has been slowly growing darker. A pair of blue-grey eyes that look large in the darkness. Moonlight falls on his hand as he pauses with his arm raised to push aside the branches of a bush.

This is frightening. This is the most frightening thing he's ever done. Only he's not frightened for himself. He's scared someone is going to suffer before he can stop it. He's afraid of finding a dead human being stretched out on the frozen ground . . .

As he pushed his sense of self further back, he found himself moving faster, determined to find whoever had made the sound. To his left, he saw glimpses of water beyond the tree trunks. Above him, branches reached over his head like so many goblin hands. While all the time the cold witch-fire of moonlight poured down from the sky, illuminating clumps of grotesque toadstools or glinting against frost that formed thousands of watchful eyes. The breeze came in waves of ice that slid across his face. Fingers of dead children choked by the evil lake.

Dylan shuddered. His imagination wouldn't give him an easy ride. Already it was conjuring sick-looking toadstools as faces with staring eyes. There they were, squeezing through splits in tree trunks . . . leering at him. The darkness wasn't just an absence of light but some toxic matter that swelled from the lake to flood through the forest.

His heart thudded in his chest. He was going to walk until he came face to face with something here in this deep, open grave of the night. He knew that now. It was inevitable. A *terrible* figure. His imagination projected it – there, just beyond the next turn of the path in this forest, where there oozed a cold and a silence that poisoned the air he breathed. Branches ran their cold talons through his hair.

The voice came again. This time there was no distress but a teasing chuckle. It came from someone who knew it had lured him here.

Such a cheap trick. Dylan Adams, so easily led into this place. He couldn't shut his sense of self out any longer. That sense of detachment vanished with the shocking suddenness of a tomb door bursting open to reveal the leering face behind.

Waves of cold swirled around him. Those dead fingers reaching inside his collar to slide down his neck – down his spine. He shivered. Then shivered again. A deep shudder that sent waves of cold blue fear rolling down through his veins, deep into his bones.

The female voice came again. Higher this time. Expectant, as if it knew he was close. He plunged through darkness, eager to end this, even if it meant encountering the monstrous face his imagination told him would be waiting at the end of the path. He couldn't take the wood any more with its dead, swollen roots bulging from the soil.

Night winds groaned down from the moor. Ominous, broken-hearted, a monotonous note sung by a being with no heart and no lungs.

The female voice in the dark became laughter. A sharp coughing laugh that didn't so much enter by his ears as drive itself like spikes through the back of his neck.

'I know what you're trying to do. I know what you're trying to do.' He panted the words as he moved at a near-run.

The laughter turned into something else. He shivered. Cold froze his nerve endings.

That barking sound . . . he knew now.

Dylan ran toward it. Seconds later he burst into a clearing among the trees. The bark turned into a high-pitched cry. There on the ground in front of him lay a shape. He didn't pause now, closing in on it.

A pair of eyes burned up at his in the moonlight.

He paused only for a second to take in what was there – and what had been making the sound. When it opened its mouth, showing teeth and a white, bloodless tongue, he heard a female-sounding cry pour from its throat, followed by a snapping bark that sounded like vicious laughter.

He stepped closer. A gleaming-eyed stare locked onto his face. Unblinking.

The fox wasn't merely injured. It went beyond that. Its whole rear third had been torn, its back legs mutilated. Its red tail was flattened and wet-looking.

The sound coming from the vocal cords of the fox veered from near-human to animal. Its head quivered as it struggled to lift it, yet the eyes were still bright. Despite its terrible injuries their stare was still unwavering.

Dylan Adams seized a rock from the water's edge.

When he was certain that the animal was dead he returned to the car.

He drove home, Lazarus Deep behind him. When he glanced in the mirror he noticed wraiths of mist blossoming on its dark waters.

Later, the image of the fox came to Dylan as he lay in bed. As it do so, a question suddenly occurred to him and brought him fully awake. *The fox was mutilated – its entire hindquarters torn open. But why wasn't there any blood?*

3. The Mouth of Horcum. Two a.m.

All drunks can find their way home. This, then, was business as usual for Stony Waters. He could get home: no problem. It was the time it took that was a source of grief. He'd left the gang of boozers at around one in the morning. Now the church clock over in Castleton chimed two and he still wasn't home. Maybe it was the booze that slowed him down? If he could persuade the drinks syndicate to switch to vodka after the home-brewed beer that might be the answer. Might make him lighter on his fifty-year-old feet.

When Stony reached the eastern end of Lazarus Deep he followed the road that took him over the bridge at the Mouth of Horcum. Here, one of the mountain streams fed the lake. It was about that time when he felt the urgent need to relieve himself. God, it happened often enough here. Had to be the sound of all that water tumbling into the lake. Come to think of it . . . he rubbed his jaw. It happened every time these days. Just here as he crossed the bridge with the water pouring creamy-white over the rocks. The sound of all that running water. Thousands of gallons of the stuff. Millions . . .

Dear Christ. He had to go. A familiar sense of urgency gripped him. Those bladder muscles weren't as tight as they used to be. The idea of walking any distance in this cold with wet trousers didn't appeal one bit. Even so, Stony didn't relish the idea of relieving himself on the bridge. He'd done that once years ago. Of course, a patrol car had just happened to be passing. The sharp-eyed cops had witnessed his tasteful sprinkling of a signpost and they'd taken him to the police station.

Despite – or perhaps because of – the amount he'd had to drink he'd found he was mortified. He'd never felt so embarrassed. He'd wept like a ten-year-old caught shoplifting lollipops. He'd sat wiping his streaming tears with tissue after tissue as he'd told the cops through bleating sobs that he was sorry, that he'd never do it again. And no, he wasn't an alcoholic. He did possess self-control.

Perhaps it was Stony's non-stop weeping that had made the cops decide that it would be easier on their ears to send him home with a verbal warning rather than make an official charge. They'd shown him the police-station exit pretty quickly. Ever since, even though he hadn't had to endure the shame of facing a charge of urinating in public, Stony Waters wouldn't pee in open view. Even at this time of the morning. Even in the Mouth of Horcum, which was miles from the nearest house. His own included.

He didn't stagger as he retraced his steps to the start of the bridge where he knew a path led down to the lakeside. (Now, he'd used *that* one plenty of times before – his fifty-year-old feet could find their way in the dark all by themselves. Clever feet, those fifty-year-old feet.)

When Stony steadied himself on the steep path by resting his hand against the supporting wall of the bridge, he found his gaze lingering briefly on the fingers of his left hand. Three of the fingers had no nails.

What had happened to those nails?

They'd got burned clean away. Never grew back.

And why did they get burned?

That dull clang sounded deep in his chest. The interrogation sequence always fired up when the alcohol at last began to be filtered out by his big old ripe melon of a liver. And why did the fingers get burned, Stony Waters?

They got burned because someone forgot to check whether there was a power cable under the road before we started digging.

Which someone was that?

It was me, Stony Waters. The cable plans were in the site office. That was a long walk . . .

Why do they call you Stony?

When I started drinking, I'd telephone people and say 'It's Tony'. Only it got a bit slurred and came out as 'S'Tony'.

Stony Waters, what happened when Clayton chopped through the buried cable with the pneumatic chisel?

What do you think?

I'm asking you, Stony.

Flash, bang, smoke. He burned.

You tried to save Clayton?

I tried, all right. The arc had been so hot that it ignited the fat under the man's skin. He was a fireball.

That's when you burned your own hands?

Yes.

The fingernails never grew back?

No, sir.

So Clayton won a modicum of revenge, disfiguring your fingers with his burning body . . . even after he was dead?

I suppose you could say that.

You regret your incompetence?

Yes, sir.

To his surprise Stony Waters found he was weeping by the time he reached the water's edge. The tears left trails that irritated the skin of his face. He rubbed hard with his knuckles, erasing the tickling sensation that he hated so much.

River water boomed as it hit the surface of the lake.

Get it out, then get home, he told himself. It was dark and slippery down here. All he needed was to slip onto his backside and he'd be walking in messed trousers after all. Stony Waters reached the slab of rock that formed the bank of the lake at this point. The water lay flat, undisturbed and as black as road-tar. Above him, the moon shone brightly enough. There was no reflection. Stony found himself thinking that Lazarus Deep wasn't only greedy for the mountain streams that it sucked gluttonously into its body. It drank moonlight, too. No light bounced back from the surface. It sucked it all in. The starlight, too.

Did it do that with reflections?

Suddenly he was curious to see his own reflection in the water.

Stupid.

Stupid Stony Waters. What the hell did he want to do that for?

Just relieve yourself, then get home before sunrise. Those fifty-year-old feet should be good for that. But even though he told himself to clear off, the temptation had lodged now. *Maybe it's a whisky thing*, he thought. *Just one of those peculiar drink-induced fancies.*

So, just a little peek into the lake. See my oh-so beautiful whisky-chiselled face. He chuckled. Maybe the booze hadn't completely relocated to his bladder just yet. This absurdity of gazing into the lake in the frozen early hours of the morning tickled his funny bone.

'If a mermaid I should spy,' he muttered, 'then a merman I should become.' The chuckle crackled in his mouth again. Stony Waters lowered himself down to his knees to look into Lazarus Deep.

The rock glistened with ice crystals. The cold sank itself into his hands so deeply that the bones of his wrists and forearms ached darkly. For a while he stared at the surface of the lake.

There was no reflection. The hungry water swallowed every glimmer of light. Even the rumble of the falling torrent at the Mouth of Horcum a few metres away didn't sound so loud now. He lifted his head to look out across the lake. It lay flat and black and still. The hills rose from the far bank, their covering of bracken revealed as a dull amber. Above that was a night sky glinting with stars that shone as coldly as the ice crystals beneath his bare hands.

The cold ache had wormed its way up his arms to his shoulders. A supernatural cold that gnawed at his joints and thickened his blood. He looked down into Lazarus Deep.

The face looked up at him from beneath the water. The glaring eyes were wide.

He knew this wasn't a reflection. This was—

'A drowned boy.' The words whispered from his lips. 'I've found a drowned boy.'

The face in the water had a dead, grey pallor. The wide eyes had no colour. The irises had bleached white. In the centre of each eye the pupil formed into a hard, black spot that stared into his. The hair on the scalp had all gone. From the state of it, the body must have been in the lake for weeks.

Stony knew what to do. Pull the body out onto the slab of rock. Cover the face with his jacket. Call the police.

He reached down to the lake, extending his own scarred and nailless fingers to just above where the face hung suspended mere centimetres below its surface. His own face descended toward the water as he bent down.

Lower.

Lower . . .

He would have to reach down, grip the corpse under the arms. Pull it out. It would be heavy. He kept his own stare fixed on the face of the drowned boy. Those eyes with the black dots in the centre were terrible to look at. His stomach muscles clenched painfully. If anything, this was worse than what had happened to Clayton.

Stony's fingers broke the surface of the lake with barely a ripple. Slowly, his hands glided down through the water, reaching out to where the body had to be, under that seemingly disembodied head that floated there.

The speed of what happened next caught him by surprise. A pair of arms erupted from the lake, encircled his head, and dragged it down. His face slapped against the water. Then his head was beneath the surface.

The water blurred his vision. But he could see enough. The face of the boy jerked forward, the cold eyes staring into his. The mouth gaped open. He saw it as a dark chasm lined with teeth. Then the dead face struck the side of his head like a slap. Through the intense cold of the water Stony felt a burning pain rip into the side of his face.

Now he saw nothing as he fought. Bubbles creamed the water. Hands gripped the back of his neck, pulling him down. Teeth crunched the skin of his right cheek.

Twisting, hearing his own scream underwater, Stony wrenched himself backwards. He wasn't sure if he blacked out but the next thing he knew he was lying on his back on the stone slab. His breathing came in shallow gasps. His heart hammered. The side of his face burned. When

he touched it the moonlight revealed blood on his fingertips.

Coughing, he pulled himself up until he sat on the rock,
his outstretched arm supporting the upper half of his body.
He looked at the lake. The surface was still again.

There's something down there, he told himself. Something
like fish moving just below the surface. White shapes, flitting.
Fast as sharks.

Only they weren't fish. Quickly, smoothly, as if they'd been
crouching just below the surface, figures rose from Lazarus
Deep. With the water coming up to their thighs they moved
to the bank. Their stares locked on Stony. That was all he
was aware of. Burning eyes. They had no irises. No colour.
Just the hard dark points of the pupils that glared with a fierce
hunger.

He pushed himself to his feet, then stood swaying dizzily.
He struggled for breath; the water must be in his lungs. The
lack of air hurt his chest. His heart beat in hard knocks against
his ribs. His sight blurred.

But he could still see the outlines of those predatory figures.
The pairs of burning eyes. The hunched, powerful shoulders.
The naked, muscular arms.

Above his own breathing that crackled wetly in his throat
he heard water pour off the bodies.

The first figure reached the water's edge. Stony knew they
were here for him. Something about him fascinated them. Still
light-headed, he spun around. He remembered the way well
enough by now. He lumbered back to the narrow path that
ran up the slope by the bridge to the road. If he could reach
the road surely he could outrun them? He had a good start.
Adrenalin flushed his veins now, powering him up the steep
incline. And coming down from his right in the distance was
a car. He'd *make* it stop for him.

He glanced back. The white bodies of the things had left

the water. They stood on the slab of rock he'd vacated. There, they looked up at him. Crowded together, they were a mass of hairless, butter-coloured heads with blazing dark eyes.

They moved toward the path: a block of solid bodies, with heavy naked shoulders. He could outrun them. The car must be only seconds from the bridge. He was going to make it. He was free . . .

Free for another ten thousand nights of home-brewed beer and whisky? Another ten thousand nights interrogating himself about Clayton?

Suddenly Stony laughed out loud. He was FREE all right. Because he realized that this was the time and the place to meet what he had always wanted.

He turned on the steep slope and stepped to the edge of the path.

He heard his own voice come roaring from his lips. 'If you want me, take me!'

Stony Waters stretched his arms out like a bird and leaped from the bank. Through fascinated eyes he saw the faces expand to fill his field of vision. Then he plunged into the mass of cold, naked skin. Muscular arms caught him, preventing him from striking the ground. Then open mouths darted down, teeth crunched through skin.

The fifty-year-old man felt no pain, only a wonderful sensation of melting release.

Above him, he watched the moon drift away into the sky; a magical silver balloon, growing smaller and smaller until only a silver speck of light remained. When he closed his eyes he found he could still see it. It only faded to black when they drew him into the water for the start of their journey to the heart of Lazarus Deep.

CHAPTER I

I

From **Hotel Midnight**:

My name is Electra. I am not revealing my full name or my home address. You know why. Three years ago I encountered vampires. I've talked about my experiences before on this site and many have flamed me for being so candid. But if you wore this skin of mine, believe me, it helps me sleep at night if I unburden myself. After all, haven't you ever had to carry a secret? And they are an uncomfortable burden, aren't they? Here I can bare my soul. So yes, boys and girls, I have encountered vampires. And for those who claim there are no vampires, you're not opening your eyes.

Haven't you ever seen a pair of lovers whose lovemaking energizes one partner but seems to weaken the other? Or a husband who bleeds his wife's bank account white? Or ever met a pair of twins, one of whom is twice as cheerful as the other? You see, my dears, vampires come in many different guises. The ones I encountered would never call themselves that. But vampires they were. And they took from me my only chance for real love.

2

Dr David Leppington took the short cut from the A&E ward where he spent his days and nights assessing and diagnosing followed by suturing, cauterizing, excising . . . in fact, the whole deal when it came to being a doctor in urban life's front line. Even though it was barely evening, frost was taking hold on the grass that flanked the path linking the hospital building with a dozen satellite annexes. After hauling round a wad of folders containing patient records he was now carrying a wad of birthday cards.

The card senders' modes of address had run from the formal *Dr Leppington, A&E* to a more friendly *David*, and to a new nickname that he'd earned from the team in the pathology lab when he'd turned up once with a bad case of sunburn – *Leppers*. Now *that* was a nickname he hoped wouldn't stick. It had been bad enough to see that someone had taped a yellow Geriatric admittance form to his locker door with prominent ticks on the 'incontinent' and 'confused' checklist. Across it in large print were the words: ***30 TODAY. IT'S ALL DOWNHILL TOMORROW!***

Gee, thanks, Spiro. He'd extract his revenge on the squash court for that one.

Paul and Soraya in the path lab saw him from the brightly lit windows and waved. Paul pantomimed drinking, then pointed at his watch. David grinned and gave a thumbs-up sign. After a shower he planned to meet the usual crowd from work for birthday drinks in the pub where a well-known surgeon had been known to take a shot or two of the hard stuff to steady his hands before scrubbing up for theatre. Even more than the drinks David was looking forward to the meal afterwards. He'd arranged to meet Liz from Radiology. On the face of it, it was just two friends going out to murder a Thai banquet.

But there's something in those beautiful green eyes, he told himself. *There's definitely a twinkle.*

The Robinson boy was wheeling his mountain bike from the back door of the mortuary as David passed. The Robinson *boy*? David wondered why he thought of him as a boy. Matt Robinson was an experienced mortuary assistant. Maybe thirty *was* old when you start thinking of mortuary assistants as boys.

Come on, old man Leppington, he told himself. *Time to stow your Zimmer frame and crack a hip on the town tonight. After all, there's Liz. I wonder – if I ask her back home, will she accept?*

But what's that about keeping work and pleasure separate?

Come on, David. You only die once . . . No, the phrase is: you only live *once. See, thirty years old and you've started rambling away to yourself.* He smiled as he ran down the grass banking to the car park. By this time his fingers were tingling with cold and his breath was forming white clouds. Already rush-hour traffic had started to clog the roads out to the 'burbs. Luckily his home was in town. Loft conversions in town-centre commercial buildings had their merits after all. You always found yourself beating the rush hour. They were going in as you were going out . . . and you were going in when they were going out. *Capisce?*

Apart from the cars that stood there in new coats of ice the place was deserted. In the sky above David stars burned bright. Even so, he kept his gaze focused on the ground, avoiding frozen puddles. He'd diagnosed enough fractured wrists today, due to Londoners slipping on ice, to be wary of where he put his feet.

Staring down at the asphalt, he was nearly within touching distance of his car before he realized that a figure was leaning against the door. Surprise turned to shock when he looked up into the face.

'What's the matter, Dr Leppington? Aren't you going to greet me with a kiss?'

3

Bernice Mochardi opened the louvred door.

'All those boots are yours?' The electrician's eyes widened. 'There's dozens of them!'

'Call it my only vice.' She felt her shoulders give a shy hop.

'And I thought my wife had a lot of shoes.'

Again Bernice made the shy shrugging gesture. 'With me it's boots.' She was wearing a pair now. Black ankle boots with a slender heel. She saw the man's stare slide over them from toe to ankle before gliding up her calves sheathed in black fishnet stockings.

Probably guessing what I do for a living, she thought. *Now he's quickly coming to a conclusion.*

'I'm going to a party,' she said.

'Oh.'

God, why did I say that? When I get embarrassed I start answering questions before people ask. Probably thinks I'm a head case.

'Fancy dress?' He looked at her short leather skirt and black lace top.

'That's it. Fancy dress. It's a house-warming party. They wanted it to be different from the usual . . . you know – cheese, wine, sausage rolls?'

There I go again, offering more answers than he ever wants to know. Just let the man do his job. She bent down to point under the shelves full of boots. 'There's a twin power point under there.'

'In the wardrobe?'

'It wasn't always a wardrobe. When I moved in this was just an alcove. I put in the shelves and hung the louvred door—'

'For your boots?'

'Yes.' Bernice smiled, feeling nervous and foolish all at the same time. 'The apartment hasn't been modernized. That's the only power point in the bedroom.' She shrugged. 'I have to sit down there in the doorway to dry my hair.'

'In the wardrobe?'

'Almost. Would you be able to put in another power point by the dressing table across there?'

'I can do that,' the electrician said, assessing the distance by stretching out his arms. 'I can put extra points in your kitchen as well.'

'I only need one in here. Thanks.'

'I noticed you were running appliances from an extension cable. That's not a safe way to go about it, you know.'

'I'm on a bit of a tight budget.'

'You're the boss. So – one in the wall by the dressing table?'

'Please.'

'You have to take your boots off.'

'Pardon?' Startled, she glanced from the electrician to her feet. Her heart thudded.

'Take the boots off, young lady.'

Startled, Bernice said the first thing that came into her head. 'I'm going out.'

The man unbuttoned his jacket. 'You need to take the boots off those shelves before I come to do the job. I have to cut through the plaster in the wall behind the shelves. There'll be some mess, I'm afraid, but that can't be helped.'

She drew a relieved breath. 'Oh, yes. No problem. The carpet's old, anyway.'

'I don't make *that* much of a mess.'

'When can you do the job?'

'A week today?'

'That's fine.'

'It won't . . .' He pulled a pen from his pocket and used it to gesture at the room. 'It won't interfere with your, er, line of work?'

He does *think I'm a whore.* 'No. I'll be at the office. My neighbour's going to let you in.'

'I see.' He wrote something on the back of his hand. 'Can I have your name again. Mock . . . eh?'

'Mochardi.'

His face didn't crack a smile. 'Can you spell that for me, please?'

'Yes . . . M-O-C – *Oh God.*'

This time his cut-from-stone expression did break. 'Jesus, look at the size of that.'

The thump at the window had made Bernice start. She looked through the glass. A bird flapped against the glass as if it was trying to break through. She had an impression of black feathers, vast beating wings and an eye that glittered right in at her.

'Now, I've never seen one that close before.' The electrician sounded awed. 'Crow, isn't it?'

The bird's bright yellow beak clattered against the glass. Then, beating its wings one last time so hard against the window that it sent a thunderous pounding around the room, the creature flew away. She watched it go. The bird's wings flapped, slowly, almost leisurely, carrying it across the night sky.

'Crows are big buggers, aren't they? And I never knew they flew in the dark, either.'

'It's not a crow,' Bernice told him in a voice that sounded strangely flat to her ears. 'It's a raven.'

4

From **Hotel Midnight:**

Electra here, boys and girls.

Wicca Man, you asked the significance of the Raven in connection with the vampires I encountered. During that time I began to notice that a large raven was constantly wheeling over the town. In Norse mythology the Raven is the eyepiece of the gods. I guess it was to Odin, Thor and the others what spy satellites are to the military today.

Cheyla, you wanted to know the purpose of **Hotel Midnight.** Well, my dear, think of it as the place where we gather to share our secret stories. Imagine we sit together beside a crackling log fire in a cosy hotel bar. Tell me those inexplicable things that have happened to you. It doesn't matter if people believe. It doesn't matter if it's true, fiction, barefaced lie or urban legend. Share it. It helps us feel as if we're not alone in the world.

Rowan. If you're reading this, write soon. I'm worried . . .

5

The raven soared away from the building where the girl dressed all in black looked out of the window. Frightened eyes. Yes . . . It recognized frightened eyes. Now it beat its blue-black wings, gaining height over the ancient cemetery at Highgate where London's dead lay by their thousands in burial pits that were ninety feet deep in places.

Its eyes were the same lustrous black as beads of jet set in a funeral brooch. With an unimaginable acuteness of vision it scanned the ground, matching the positions of trees, mounds, buildings with the positions of stars above and processing this information through the powerful guidance centres in its brain. In the moonlight it saw tombstones and statues of weeping angels in the cemetery. It saw the cemetery's sunken Cedar of Lebanon complex that housed Highgate's crypts. And when the raven called, the sound plunged vertically to the ground where it ghosted down through frozen earth into the coffins themselves. It was the same cry that had sounded through forests in ancient times: after the great battles that had left Viking warriors and foes alike lying in the fallen leaves with their bodies broken open and their blood soaking into the loam. The raven's call had the power, so the legend ran, to get fallen warriors back on their feet to do their master's bidding.

Beneath the bird modern London bustled. Along its tarmac arteries cars, buses and bikes streamed. House and office lights blazed, furiously holding primeval night at bay.

The bird called again. Its cry pierced the graves to strike the skulls of the dead. Dry bones twitched. Skulls by the thousand turned as if to look upward at the raven.

Now the bird saw the lights of the hospital. It dived, swooping down with wings outstretched. Two figures stood by a car. Ancient instincts triggered thought that flashed through bundles of neurons containing the race memory of the creature's species. The bird didn't process thought patterns into anything so clumsy or imprecise as words. If it had, those thoughts would have shaped the word **LEPPINGTON**. The bird flew low over the cars, wings outstretched. Its sharp eyes fixed intently on the taller of the two figures.

David Leppington ducked at the sound of an object slicing through the air just above his head. He half-glimpsed a dark shape that glided smoothly away to vanish into darkness.

'A bird,' the girl told him, as she appraised his face with unblinking eyes. 'Even I don't believe birds can harm you. Not any more.'

David straightened. 'Katrina. What are you doing here?'

She smiled. 'Come, David. You don't think I climbed over the wall of the lunatic asylum and rushed here all breathless to confront you, do you?'

'No, of course not, it's just a—'

'Shock?'

'A surprise, that's all.'

'You certainly didn't expect your ex to come calling on you, then?'

'How did you find me, Katrina?'

'You're not in hiding, are you?'

'No.' He smiled but it wasn't an easy one.

What is Katrina doing here? The last time I saw her she was in a hospital bed. Schizophrenia had got its hooks in her so deeply she could barely talk. Now she's—

'I've obviously caught you at a bad time, David.'

'No, it's not that.'

She tilted her head as if to say *I expected that you wouldn't want to see me.* She gave an apologetic smile. 'I only wanted to bring you your birthday card.'

'You remembered?'

'Do you think I'd forget?'

'It's been a good many years, Katrina.' He smiled again, trying to look at ease. *If that's possible,* he thought. *Unexpectedly encountering my schizophrenic ex-girlfriend in the dark.*

'You were my first love, David. For years you were all I thought about.' She smiled as if to lighten her words. 'As the old saying goes: You were my world. So, no, it's unlikely I'd forget your birthday. Here's your card.' She handed him a red envelope. 'You'll see it's not a big one in a box.' She gave a light laugh.

The sound sent a trickle of electricity through his stomach. *Her 'bedroom' laugh,* he told himself. He'd loved the musical sound it made.

He took the card from her. 'Thanks. It's . . . very kind of you to remember.'

'No worries. Oh, and it doesn't sing to you when you open it, and I haven't written anything gooey.'

'And good of you to go to so much trouble to—'

'To find you?'

Hell, he felt so awkward about this. He sensed a stammer creeping into his throat. 'Well, to find me . . . and to come out all this way—'

'Don't worry about it.' Her voice was resolutely cheerful.
'I live closer than you think.'

'Really?'

'And I have a confession, David.'

'Oh?'

'I was visiting a friend in the maternity ward, she's just had
twins of all things, and I cut through the staff car park to catch
a bus on the road across there when I happened to see this.'
She nodded at a notice fixed to the wall directly in front of the
car. '*Reserved. Dr D. Leppington.* I figured there can't be that
many Dr D. Leppingtons in Britain so I bought the birthday
card and took my chance.'

'Thank you. I appreciate it.' *God, that sounds so lame,* he
thought. *But what now? Do I edge away, while thinking of an
excuse to leave?*

Katrina pushed back a strand of hair with her fingertips.
'And I've another confession.'

Dear God, here it comes.

'I do have an ulterior motive, David.'

What did I tell you? The madness starts.

'I've been thinking about it for months.' She gave a shy
smile. 'Well, "vacillating" would be a more accurate word.'

'Oh?'

'And the bottom line is I just wanted to say hello again and
show you that I'm well . . .' She stepped back and held her
arms out from her sides. 'Da–dah.' She sang it like a fanfare.
'I'm better.'

'You look better.' David winced at the humouring note in
his voice.

She registered it but he saw that she let it pass. 'Of course,
I mean that in a relative way,' she said, smiling. 'I'm better
than I was. I still take the funny little tablets. They've got the
side effects under control. And, hey presto. Da-dah. I'm a
functioning human being again.'

'I'm pleased to hear it. No, honestly, that's great, Katrina.'

'Thank you. Of course, I don't think I get the sane-woman certificate yet.' She laughed.

Bedroom laugh again. He shivered.

Katrina squeezed his forearm. 'The sane-woman certificate was a joke, David; don't look so serious. See, to make a joke about oneself requires insight and humour. And as untreated or unreformed schizophrenics tend to lack both a sense of humour and insight then it shows my medication must be doing some good up here.' She tapped her temple with her finger.

He felt a warming sense of relief spread through him. 'It *is* good to see you, Katrina. You do look . . . *so* well. It's just so—'

'Hard to believe?'

'A surprise. You're so different from—'

'From the dribbling wreck babbling delusions?' He saw that she flinched at her own words. 'Sorry,' she smiled. 'That was a rough-and-ready description, wasn't it?'

'Just a bit.' David smiled. 'Are you living in London now?'

'Living – and working. I'm doing computer stuff for a ticket agency. Theatres, concerts, that kind of thing.'

'And you live close to the hospital?'

'Just up the road by the cemetery . . . not that I'm suggesting an ironic link.'

'Heaven forbid.' He found that the smile on his face was the real thing now. 'How're your parents?'

'Fine. Travelling the world and being frivolous with my inheritance . . . Say, David – *this* is the insane thing, isn't it?'

'What is?'

'We're standing out here chatting . . . it's cold enough for polar bears.'

'Do you want to go for a drink?'

'I'd like that. Thanks, David.'

'There's a coffee shop just by the entrance to A&E.'

'A hospital café?' She wrinkled her nose.

'Bad choice?'

'Truth is, I've had enough of that hospital smell to last me a couple of lifetimes.'

'That was insensitive of me. Sorry.'

She raised her finger as if having an idea. 'I know a quiet little place. We can catch up on old times.'

CHAPTER 2

I

Dylan Adams expected it.

As they all ate supper together in front of the television his parents were perfectly reasonable, they weren't hostile, but they gnawed away at his good news until he wished he hadn't told them.

'Well done,' his father said. 'So they like the photographs?'

'That's what the head of the photographic studio told me.'

His mother repeated her first question as if his answer hadn't registered the first time. 'And this studio is in London?'

Dylan nodded as he chewed the pizza.

'London's a long way from Morningdale,' she commented.

His father smiled. 'That's probably part of its appeal. Escape the one-horse town for the bright lights.'

'Topaki are a good studio,' Dylan added, knowing what was coming next. 'They handle a lot of big commercial contracts.'

His mother frowned. 'For what, exactly?'

'Photographing products for magazine advertisements. Architectural photography. All sorts.'

'Not your average wedding-day photographer like Betty Danby.' His father switched channels. 'Film's just starting.'

'London's a long way.' His mother retraced the flow of the argument. 'It'll be expensive to find accommodation there, won't it?'

Dylan gave a no-problem shrug. 'They've got other trainees at Topaki. They're always looking for people to share rents.'

'And there's travelling?'

'APEX tickets don't cost much.'

'But you don't know anyone in London.'

'I'll soon get to know the people I'll be working with.'

'But you don't know what they'll be *like*.' His mother's tone darkened. 'They won't be like *us*.'

And who are people like us, *exactly?* Dylan bit hard into the pizza crust to stop himself asking the question. *Us* were the people of the village of Morningdale; they didn't venture much beyond Whitby if they could help it. For them this remote valley enclosed by moorland was the whole world. Everything beyond it was at best suspect, at worst poisonously corrupt.

'When would you start?' His father added this as if it was an afterthought.

'I haven't been offered the job yet, Dad.'

'Photographic assistant.' Adams Senior ran his fingers across the short grey hairs on his chin. 'And they didn't say how much it paid?'

'No. I've still to go for the interview.'

'So you've decided to go down to London for the interview, then?'

'They won't give me the job without it.'

'Dylan.' His mother looked as if she was going to start talking to him like he was ten years old again.

His father came in quickly. 'Why not, Fay, it'll—'

'He's only eighteen.'

That's it, talk about me as if I'm not here.

'It's good experience. Dylan'll have job interviews at some point.' He smiled. 'This'll break him in good and young.'

She pressed her lips together. Then: 'So, when *would* you start . . . if you got it?'

'In July, when I qualify.'

'You've still to finish the photography course yet, remember,' she said, seeing a way out. 'Don't get your hopes up about moving to London until you pass the exams.'

His father smiled. 'Your mother's just being protective.'

'Protective, my foot. I'm just being realistic. It doesn't do anyone any good, chasing rainbows. Besides . . .' She wiped her mouth on a tissue. 'Going to London is a big move. It's completely different from round here.'

That is *one of the attractions.*

'Dylan, I thought you planned on staying on at college for the HND in photography and video?'

'That's another two years, Dad.'

'So?'

'I'm ready to get some real experience in a photographic studio, rather than all theory.'

'You don't want to rush these things.' Again his mother's dark tone, as if he was careering toward disaster.

'London's not the dark side of the moon, Mum. If things don't work out—'

'But when you get older you can't chop and change, Dylan. You have to commit yourself to a job.'

'It's a career, Mum.'

'What?'

'A career, rather than a job.'

His father played the diplomat. 'Let's not argue about it. I don't see a problem in Dylan going for the interview. It'll be good experience.'

Dylan put the half-eaten pizza down on his plate. Cold now, it had become as pleasant as the cardboard box it came in. 'By that, Dad, you mean you think I won't get it?'

'We don't want to see you disappointed,' his mother said. 'It can't be easy, becoming a photographer.'

'The competition will be hot, you know that?' His father sipped a glass of beer. 'There'll be dozens up for it.'

'I know.' Dylan picked up the plates. 'I'm going out.'

'Besides . . .' His father put the glass down. 'This isn't the career you wanted, is it?'

'I want to be a photographer.'

'But I thought you were aiming to be a photojournalist on a music magazine?'

Nice one, Dad. Shoot the good news down in flames. Watch this smile crash and burn.

'Eventually,' Dylan told him as he moved toward the kitchen door. 'But this would be a start.'

He went into the kitchen where he ran water onto the plate. From the window he saw the valley bottom in the moonlight. The River Esk, little more than a stream at this point, wove a tortuous path down toward the sea at Whitby. Sheep showed as pale clumps in the fields.

Yeah . . . Good place for sheep, this. Not for much else. Dylan felt a sudden surge of anger toward his parents. They were going to spend the next few days chipping away at his plan to attend the interview. When he'd spoken to the head of the studio and heard that they were interested and the guy had said great things about his photographs he'd felt so bloody good. Now that bubble of euphoria was deflating.

His parents could be so infuriating. They both loved Morningdale and the valley. For them it had been a dream come true to leave York and return to their home town to live. His mother taught at the local school. His father managed a rural branch of a bank in West Aisleby. They weren't bad parents, but if you could have looked through their eyes they'd still have seen their only son, Dylan Adams, as a ten-year-old. Hell's teeth. He was eighteen. He needed independence.

He glanced up at the window, this time seeing only his own reflection looking back at him. He saw that he was frowning, with his head lowered. The dead weight of this lifeless valley was pulling him down. If he even thought about it too much he felt tightness in his chest; it became hard to breathe.

Now that's a symptom of claustrophobia, he told himself. *You need out!*

2

The Goth party in the Jack Black room at the Station Hotel, Leppington had really started to come alive. The music grew louder. Alcohol buzzed in the veins of the guests. The dance floor seethed with a mass of black-clad bodies topped by white faces with blood-red lips.

Electra Charnwood, the hotel's proprietor, checked that the bar staff were in control; that there'd been no fights so far; that no one was taking things to extremes and starting to bite necks (it had happened before); that there was no *open* evidence of drug taking – although she noticed two men dressed in deep purple sharing a spliff. She let it pass.

For a second she stood in the doorway, enjoying the pulsating beat of the music. The heat generated by the crowd's excitement ran through her gunmetal blue-black hair. People travelled miles to the Goth Communion (as she billed the gatherings). She relished the dark electricity created by the revellers. The music, the odours of body heat and heavy perfumes washed through her nostrils. Her skin tingled with the energy unleashed there in the room.

I want to join you, she thought as she watched thirty people sway on the dance floor – all Goth kohled eyes, blood-red lips, grave-white make-up. *I'd love to jump into the flow and be carried away. I long for release. I want to lose my sense of self. To dissipate in the music. To melt away into the walls, the tables, the resin statues and darkly romantic figures.* The magnetic pull of the revel drew her into the room.

OK. She'd stay a little while. But although she loved to watch she knew she could never be part of it.

Something got broke three years ago. It never got fixed.

Hearts are like that.

But then, she'd always felt like an outsider. Even though she'd grown up in this little town dominated by its massive slaughterhouse she'd never felt as if she belonged. *Admit it. Electra. You and the cuckoo have a lot in common. You were born into the wrong family, in the wrong place at the wrong time.*

'We're starting now – come on.' A man dressed in white Christ robes took her arm and dragged her toward the stage. 'I'm first!' His face blazed with excitement. He put his arm round her shoulders, giving her a hug that nearly cracked a bone. 'Stay right at the front . . . I'm going put my mark on you.'

'I'm sorry,' she began. 'But I'm—'

'Luke, if you're first I'm second.'

'All right!'

'Ben! Do it while I'm hot! I've been working out back there.'

'Keep it going. Hyperventilate. Like this.' The one called Ben panted: short shallow breaths.

Electra looked round. She'd been swept to the stage by a dozen newcomers. They were here for the party – only they were dressed in white.

So what's happened to Goth black? Maybe white is this year's black? No. That's absurd. Goth fashions haven't changed that fast. I'd have known. Unless—

Suddenly she had an inkling.

'No.' She pulled at the white dress that swathed a beautiful red-haired girl who was around nineteen. 'No. I don't allow this at the parties. You've got to stop—'

The girl grinned at her, then pointed at her ears. *Sorry, I can't hear you.*

The DJ racked up the volume. The song Electra recognized as 'Puncture Wounds' pounded the air so fiercely that wraiths of tobacco smoke vibrated in time to its demonic beat. As the room lights dimmed the footlights on the raised dais grew brighter. A hard, white light. The kind of light found in operating theatres.

And Electra knew why.

3

David Leppington brought the drinks to the table in the corner of the bar. Katrina had slipped off her coat to reveal a blue denim shirt and jeans.

David's medical training was too deeply embedded for him not to notice the small scars on the backs of her forearms. Old bite marks where she'd tried to mutilate herself in the throes of the schizophrenia that had taken her from him when he was twenty.

The man in him noticed the downy hairs on her arms. He remembered lightly running his fingers across those.

'Hairy monster, aren't I?'

'Oh, on a scale of one to ten?'

'Must be pretty bad.'

'A level six, I'd say.'

'Sounds serious.'

He'd smiled. 'That's a werewolf, at least.'

Now Katrina smiled at him. A bright smile. Nothing doped about it. Those new anti-psychosis treatments suppressed the schizoid symptoms to levels that had to be considered normal behaviour.

Stop that, he thought. *Stop looking at her as if she was your patient*. But if he looked at her through objective eyes he still saw an undeniably attractive woman. She had none of the collateral clinical effects of bloating, skin blotches or lethargy that were the side effects of the old pharmaceuticals with which the medical world had once bombarded mental patients. She was a young woman. She was vibrant. She was how he remembered her when they'd been planning a future together.

'Thanks,' she said, raising the wineglass. 'I'm allowed one of these a day.'

David smiled. 'I'm sure I could prescribe another. Two glasses of Chardonnay won't set the alarm bells ringing in your doctor's surgery.'

'Thank you, Doctor.' She sipped it. 'Hmmm . . . that's good medicine.'

He took a swallow of beer. The coldness felt wonderful in his dry throat after a day racing around the A&E department. 'How long have you been in London?'

'Almost six months.'

'Do you plan on staying?'

'You mean making it my home town after the wilds of rural Cheshire?' Katrina shrugged. 'It's a case of suck it and see.'

'It can be lonely if you don't have friends here.'

'After spending the last ten years being lost . . .' She tapped the side of her head. 'Lost in inner space, I mean, I've got some catching up to do.'

What David said next was meant to be light-hearted. 'Well, don't overdo it. Weekends can get a little crazy.'

'Crazy?' She looked him in the eye. 'You don't think I can handle it yet?'

'I didn't say that. That's what I'd tell anyone coming to live in London for the first time.'

She still held him with her gaze. Her eyes had an unwavering directness to them now. A penetrating quality that they hadn't had in the past. *An effect of the medication, maybe . . . a morbid desire to stare . . . Dear Christ, I'm playing the doctor again. Don't.*

Katrina leaned closer, still looking into his eyes. 'David. Be honest with me. Do you think I'm here to ask you if we can pick up where we left off?'

For a moment he didn't know what to say. His gaze travelled along the gold chain round her neck. It ran in a shining trail down her chest to disappear where her shirt was buttoned.

She clicked her tongue. 'No. That would be delusional on my part.' A smile turned up one side of her mouth. 'You'll be married with three bonny children and a dog that lies snoozing by the fire all day.'

He shook his head.

She put the glass down on the table. 'So you haven't got round to it?'

'Not yet.'

'You were always one for putting off until tomorrow what you should have done today.' She drained her glass. 'Another drink? No, put your money away. It's my shout. Beer?'

David glanced at the clock on the pub wall. At that moment he knew he was going to miss that birthday drink with his friends.

As Katrina stood up she looked at him and said, 'Do you want another drink here, or shall we go somewhere else?'

4

'Stop it! This is my hotel. I don't allow this!'

Thundering music drowned out Electra Charnwood's voice. The party-goers, all in their teens and twenties, pushed forward to watch the performance. She saw white-painted faces framed by wild manes of black hair. They were all excited . . . no, more than that: their faces blazed, their emotions fuelled by adrenalin, alcohol and hours of erotic dancing. They applauded the white-clothed people on stage. The men were dressed like Christ. The women wore loosely belted garments that looked like the gowns of Egyptian priestesses.

'*I'm telling you NO!*'

But the whole crowd was shouting at the stage. By default Electra had become one of them. She looked like them, with her black clothes and her long black hair. Faces crowded alongside hers. People even rested their hands on her shoulders, believing she was part of the audience.

'No!'

I'm wasting my breath, she thought, angry now. *If what happens next goes wrong I'll have the police and ambulances here. Then I'll lose my licence. The hotel will go bankrupt soon after that. Damn them. This is my livelihood.* And then the Leppington coven of gossips would relish Electra's downfall. They'd always talked about her behind her back. Ever since she'd been a child her neighbours had singled her out as something alien, an outsider – even though she'd been born in this godforsaken town! How they'd love to see the bailiffs take possession of the hotel and throw her out into the street. Electra's blood burned in her veins. Sheer fury made it hard to breathe. She wanted to scream at these reckless idiots to stop.

The audience cheered as the white-clad people bowed, grinning. And, ye gods, were they ever hyper! Their faces were flushed, their pupils dilated. They hyperventilated to make their hearts race; blood would be pounding through their arteries.

The DJ started to laugh. A pounding theatrical Vincent Price kind of laugh, so amplified that it made Electra's ears hurt. From 'Puncture Wounds' he switched to a recording of a cathedral organ. Great booming chords that sounded as if they were roaring across time and space from some vast carved Gothic vault.

Electra winced at the volume level of the DJ's voice: '**LET THE BODY PENETRATIONS BEGIN!**'

If I can't stop it, I'm sure as hell not going to watch it!

Furious, she tried to move back but the crush of bodies had driven her hard up against the stage. Then the needles appeared.

No, not needles, Electra thought, feeling the body heat of the crowd sear through her clothes to her skin beneath. *Not needles. Meat skewers.* They were as thick as knitting needles. Almost as long. Shiny steel skewers, wickedly sharp.

The guy called Luke held out his arms like a crucified Christ. His face flamed red. He shouted something she couldn't hear. The woman with copper hair lifted his head, placed a skewer under his chin. Pushed hard. There was a moment of resistance, then the skewer smoothly entered the skin below his jaw and passd through the floor of his mouth. The woman pushed up until the point emerged from between Luke's lips.

The crowd roared. Now *that* Electra could hear, even above the cascading notes of the organ.

Luke had flinched when the spike broke flesh; his knees buckled; his arms dropped. Then he recovered to show the crowd the skewer.

The rest followed fast. It had all the frenzy of long-parted lovers tearing off one another's clothes, frantic for the head-long rush toward penetration. The girls slipped off the plush cords from their waists so that they could open their gowns.

Electra couldn't stop this now. She couldn't even move. Instead she was forced to watch, seething with fury, as more slender needles penetrated the flesh behind nipples. Male and female nipples alike. Ben worked on the red-haired girl. He pushed skewers into the taut skin across her chest until the area of flesh between her small breasts, following the line of the breastbone, was full of metal. He'd created a criss-cross pattern that looked as if the right and left halves of her chest had been laced together with surgical steel.

Electra knew why they had been hyperventilating. That, plus a good many shots of vodka to thin the blood, had quickened the flow. Now the red fluid ran freely from puncture wounds. They'd chosen white clothes rather than black so it would show the blood in shocking contrast. The girls danced, their naked breasts bouncing softly. Blood dripped down their bodies, stained the white cotton. Dripped onto the stage.

A guy at the front of the audience jumped forward so that his top half fell across the stage. He wiped his fingertips across the blood drops, then licked his fingers. The music pounded. One of the guys having his penis pierced fainted. Another one was walking with a swaying walk; he wouldn't be far from following his friend into unconsciousness.

Damn! Electra slammed her hand down onto the stage. *They're going to get me closed down for this. I'll probably end up on a police charge. Damn them, the idiots!* She slammed her hand down again, palm first, more in frustration than hoping to attract anyone's attention. Already she could picture herself walking away from the boarded-up hotel, suitcase in her hand, a one-way train ticket out of Leppington in her purse. And how the townsfolk would gloat over her misery!

But the tall youth with softly curling blond hair noticed her pounding the stage and smiled at her. Electra remembered his name. 'Luke!'

He kneeled down beside her. Blood ran down his throat and chest. Now she could see that the wound under his chin tightly encircled the steel skewer. Hardly any blood was leaking from there. Instead it filled his mouth.

'Hello, my beautiful lady.' He spoke clearly enough despite the metal spike protruding from his lips. *Boy, oh boy. He's done this before.* 'I promised I wouldn't forget you.' He leaned forward, smiling bloodily at her, his gaze fixed on her eyes. 'Promise is a promise.'

He kissed the end of his index finger and touched her cheek, drawing it down along the line of her jaw to the point of her chin. She felt something wet on her skin.

Luke's smile broadened. 'Beautiful lady, can I talk to you after the show?'

5

Leppington town lay dead. It went hand in hand with the dead winter's night. Cloud had swept down from the hills to blot out the stars.

Electra stood in the rear courtyard of the hotel. She pulled hard on a cigarette. In the reflection of a van window she saw the smear of blood on her cheek that formed a chevron pattern.

Ice had formed on the cobblestones underfoot. The air itself was so cold that it cut like a knife. But she was glad to be out of the hotel: away from the insanity of the body-piercing act. The music, the smell, the press of bodies had been—

What? Exciting, Electra? Did you nearly break your arctic shell and let yourself go? What if you had woken in the arms of Luke, the youth with the metal spike through his bottom jaw? What if you'd loved those sensations of him caressing you? How would you have reacted when he stroked your thigh? Kissed your hips? Run his tongue between your legs? Would you have protested if he'd made love to you?

But no, you have to force yourself to keep remembering what happened three long years ago. You keep the memories humming inside your head as if you're singing a tune day and night. Can't keep that up for ever, you know? You've got to relax or you'll crack right down the middle.

But deep down she'd got used to the idea that somehow, if she could keep remembering what she had encountered –

what had nearly destroyed her body and soul three years ago – it would prevent it happening again.

Now that is crazy. Admit it, Electra. That's what Dr Leppington would call 'obsessive-compulsive' behaviour.

Dr Leppington? She imagined him saying to her, *'Don't worry about this, Electra. It's in the past. We won. We destroyed those things. The town's free of them. They won't come back.'*

But suddenly Electra found it difficult to picture him. Was his hair black or dark brown? He had a nice soft voice. But lately she'd imagined it burred with a gentle Scottish strain. But David Leppington wasn't a Scot.

In the deserted yard she looked round in sudden panic. Why couldn't she remember what he looked like any more? Or even remember his accent?

Shadows oozed out from the walls. The cars became dark, deformed creatures lurking there; headlights glinted with witch-fire. They seemed to watch her with monstrous eyes. While above her loomed the evil bulk of the hotel. Windows reflected the witch-fire, too. The cold came at her in chilling waves.

Why couldn't she remember David Leppington? She evoked Bernice Mochardi in her mind's eye. Her fair hair. Her passion for black clothes and boots – sultry little ankle boots with chains and stiletto heels. How they'd joked together about her shoe fetish. But now Electra envisaged Bernice as a younger version of herself, not a true image of the girl who'd stayed in the hotel. True, there was a passing resemblance. When Bernice had lived here she'd developed a taste for Electra's style of clothes.

'Black, dear. Always choose black. It flatters the figure and inflames the male libido . . .'

Now, Jack Black. With his tattoos and muscular arms he was altogether unforgettable. The shaved head looked as if it had been hewn from rock. But so often now she blended his form with the bat-winged lover of her imagination. But that was just amusingly whimsical on her part. A way of easing away those sleepless hours before the sun showed its face above Leppington. Only now, when she pictured him, she saw him with black leathery wings unfurling from his broad back.

A shape swooped by her head.

For a second Electra found herself thinking: *Jack Black. He's here . . .*

Membranous wings beating the night air; they're as glossily black as patent leather. They can wrap around me; hold me tighter than any arms . . .

But as the object glided into the light thrown by street lamps she saw that it was a raven. The bird revealed itself as a blot of darkness against the deeper darkness of the night sky. It soared over the roof of the slaughterhouse. She heard it calling.

I've seen her, I've seen her, I've seen her. Her imagination formed the bird's cry into those words, but she sensed that was its meaning. If she got hold of the evil thing . . .

Electra drew a breath. Then glanced at her reflection again. The breeze blew her hair away from her face. Once more her attention was taken by Luke's blood, drawing the pattern along her jawline.

A sudden urge drove her back to the hotel. Music still pounded from the Jack Black room. The Communion would go on for hours yet before people made their way home or climbed the stairs to the rooms they'd rented for the night. At least the live body-piercing was over. She'd be up early before the cleaners arrived. She'd have to wipe away the bloodstairs herself or talk might reach the police.

With the time creeping like death to midnight Electra walked quickly through the reception area to her office at the back of the hotel. There, CCTV monitors showed the car park, lobby and main bar (now empty apart from a lone glass-washer). She unlocked a steel filing cabinet that contained neatly marked videotapes marked 'Archive'; each one bore a date, too. Trembling now, as if she wanted to move faster than her hands would allow, she snapped a tape into the VCR, pressed the button, lit a cigarette and then sat back to watch the monitor. The hand that held the cigarette shook badly.

Now she was here she didn't want to watch the footage. Not for a million pounds did she want to watch it. But she knew she had to.

CHAPTER 3

I

Even though it was past midnight and the Goth Communion party would be ending, Electra sat in the back office, watching the CCTV videos. The recording made on the hotel's security cameras ran the time and date along a black bar at the bottom of the screen. For security-camera footage the image burned surprisingly hard, with a diamond-bright sharpness. On the screen she saw the hotel lobby. The date revealed the footage to be three years old. There'd been some decor changes since then. The pine reception desk, flowered wallpaper and drab carpets had gone. Electra had recently vamped up the interior to its original Victorian splendour, even drawing from period photographs of the place in 1888.

Now she found herself looking at the old pine desk on TV once more. Walking into shot came Bernice. (*Notice the boots*, Electra told herself. *Always she wore stunning boots*.) These had such a high heel that she balanced on her toes. Bernice stopped at the desk and looked back over her shoulder as if she'd heard her name.

She had. Coming into shot was David Leppington, dressed in jeans and a fleece jacket. They talked earnestly together. Electra heard nothing because the security system didn't boast microphones. Even so, the image seemed strengthened by the silence. Instead of listening to words she saw how the two figures made eye contact. The way they moved their hands in those gestures that are often so revealing. They were calm, yet serious. This was the time when they began to understand the nature of the danger that lurked in the town of Leppington.

Electra watched as David put his finger close to his face, a gesture that clearly said, '*Don't say anything more, someone's here.*'

That someone had been Jack Black. Smoking a cigarette, he walked with that swaggering walk of his. Electra marvelled at the tattooed bluebirds hovering at the sides of his eyes. His shaved head reflected light beneath the artificial illumination. He didn't say anything to David or Bernice. He stood and stared at them. There was nothing discreet about him, or anything hesitant about the way he told people what he thought of them. At that point there had still been strong mutual suspicion. Neither Jack nor David liked each other.

They didn't know then what they shared at a deeper level and what bound them together.

Then there were four. Electra watched the image of herself that was three years younger glide from the office to join them. She didn't look that much different. She had the same long gunmetal blue-black hair. She was still dressed in black. Perhaps her face was a little fuller then. Certainly she'd lost weight since those events of three years ago. Who wouldn't? In fact, who would still be sane after what those four had endured?

Now Jack Black was dead. The other three had gone their separate ways as if the unseen forces that had brought them together now drove them apart. The last she heard, David had moved to London. Bernice was back in Manchester. To her knowledge neither of them had contacted each other since their last meeting.

Electra ran the tape in slow motion, concentrating on faces. Familiarizing herself with their features. She'd forgotten how one of David's eyebrows seemed to rise as if about to leap over the other when he was anxious. Or how Bernice would rock one foot as if acutely conscious of the sense of constriction the boots produced around her calves. Jack Black didn't move his hands when he talked. He masked his body language entirely. His face could have been carved from stone. When the four of them were together there was an electricity present. She even felt it sparking from the television monitor. There was power there. They could feel it back then, only they didn't know how to use it, never mind explain it.

The footage showed them speaking – that was all. At least, it nearly always did. *But there's the strangest thing,* she thought; *there have been times I've revisited it over the past few months and there's been something extra. An image in the background. It doesn't move. It might be a patch of reflected light, or even dust on the camera. But every so often I can see a figure there. One that watches the four in the hotel lobby. It's so indistinct I'm sure it's just a trick of the light. Other times I'm not so sure. Then I tell myself that when we talked we had an eavesdropper. One that, although it was quite close, we could not see.*

2

Status? Alone.

Bernice Mochardi sat in her apartment with the job-application form in front of her on the kitchen table. It was late but she didn't feel like sleeping yet. A restlessness had crept up on her over the last few weeks. Suddenly she wasn't content with her career. Nor her apartment, nor the way she looked. She'd taken to painting her nails in increasingly darker shades of purple. When she looked in the mirror she felt the urge to pluck out her eyebrows.

I want to change my appearance. I want to change the layout of the living room. I want a new job . . .

Why did she feel so unsettled? It was as if she sensed that some huge change in her life was imminent. Somehow, on an instinctual level, she was preparing for it. But what kind of change? Bernice looked down at the application form again. Where the item *Status* had required her to enter *Single, Married, Divorced* or *Widowed* she'd automatically written *Alone.*

Is that it? she asked herself. *Does the girl pine for a new love in her life? Is she tired of living alone?*

Sighing, Bernice laid the pen down. More than anything, she wanted to take a long walk to try and push this edgy restlessness from her body with sheer physical exhaustion. Only walking without a companion at this time of night wouldn't be wise.

But to hell with wise, she couldn't sit still any more, never mind sleep. For a moment Bernice eyed her boots by the door. Black leather, sharp pointed toes, needle-thin heels. She imagined easing her feet into them and feeling the tight constriction around her calves. Boots like that could take a girl a million miles . . .

With a hiss of frustration she tore up the application form and rammed it down into the pedal bin.

'So what's it to be, Bernice? Walk away the tension, or . . .'

No. Not this late at night.

'But I've got to do something.' The sense of restlessness troubled her. She didn't know what was causing it. Worse, she didn't know how to deal with it.

'Gotta do something, girl, or you're gonna go crazy.'

First she channelled the restless energy into useful work. She polished her boots until they reflected the kitchen lights like glass. Then she went into the bathroom to stare into the mirror with a growing conviction that she needed to change the way she looked. *After all, if you change your appearance, you'll change your life, won't you?*

With that thought in mind, Bernice took her tweezers from the wall cabinet and began to pluck her eyebrows until they bled.

3

Everything had gone spinning out of control. Everything was wrong. David knew this. But he couldn't do anything to stop what would happen next.

It was Katrina who said, 'You don't have to do this. We can stop right now.'

'I don't want to.' *There, I've said it. There's no going back.*

He kissed her hard on the mouth. Blood roared in his ears. He felt her fingers digging through his hair to his scalp; they seemed so cool against the heat of his skin.

This is insane. I shouldn't be doing it. But when they'd reached her flat the years had vanished. Right then it seemed as if Katrina had never been ill. And all that time between her breakdown and the present had never happened. He could have been nineteen again and simply visiting her at university as he'd done so many times.

He lowered her onto the bed, kissing her on the lips, then down her throat, allowing his lips to sweep down across her chest. He unbuttoned the denim shirt, then slipped off her bra. Her breasts were just as he remembered them, right down to the position of a freckle above her right nipple. The scent of her was just as it always had been.

'David, I've missed you . . . I'd lay awake at night and imagine you back with me again . . . just like we had been . . . oh!'

He kissed her nipples, then sucked deeply on them, pulling hard until her back arched. She crushed his face against them, then caught hold of it and guided it up to hers. He kissed her full on the mouth and it felt so good. His body sang. He'd been in the wilderness and now he was home again. It felt so right to hold Katrina.

'Will you make love to me . . . please, David? Will you make love?'

His heart melted. She'd asked so politely. As if only just daring to ask a great favour.

'Of course I will.'

She unbuttoned his shirt; her cool lips raced across his chest. In a blur he shrugged off his clothes, then turned his attention to the beautiful woman on the bed. She smiled up at him, her hair cascading out across the sheet. He slid her jeans off. Her skin had such a beautiful sheen to it; beneath it, here and there, he saw the delicate pattern of a vein. Even her pubic hair possessed such a downy lightness. Helpless now, he couldn't stop himself from burying his face between her legs, his hands sliding up the back of her legs to cup her small firm buttocks in his hands. He lifted her effortlessly so he could work at her with his tongue.

She moaned, squirmed.

'Thank you . . . that's so lovely . . . oh, yes. I wanted that so much . . . I wanted it . . . oh . . .'

Moments later, he kissed a pathway back up her stomach, up between her breasts until he was kissing her neck again. She tilted her head backward, stretching her throat so it looked long. His lips worked against her bare skin. Her perfume intoxicated him. Before he even realized it she'd raised her knees at either side of his body. Now he knew all self-control had gone from him.

He pushed down into her. She gave such a shout of surprise and pleasure that it seemed as if she couldn't believe what was happening to her. She gripped his head and pushed his face from her throat.

She wants to see my face, David told himself. *She can't believe it's really me; she needs to reassure herself.*

But then, he felt the same way. After ten years apart – now this. It seemed as if they'd only been apart for days and that the evil schizophrenia that had ravaged her mind had never been there at all. He pounded into her, shaking the bed.

Katrina panted 'Yes, yes, yes!' into his ear. She curled her fingers round his hair, then pulled his head down to the side of her bare neck. 'Bite me,' she whispered. '*Bite me.*'

4

When the radio alarm showed one in the morning Dylan Adams realized that sleep just wasn't coming. He pulled the light cord. He lay for a while with his eyes roving to the 35mm Nikon camera that had cost him a summer's wages from working at the farm. The camera was his ticket out of Morningdale.

Well, that was his plan. But he knew his parents were going to chip away at his enthusiasm for the job in London. Only it wasn't even a job yet. It was a lousy interview. What had started to get under his skin was the fact that his father had been right. His real ambition *was* to work for a music magazine. Three months ago he'd have laughed at the idea of photographing soap or hamburgers. But now there was a real chance of using the Topaki studio to escape to London he'd jumped at it.

Now that smacked of desperation. Maybe he should wait a couple of years . . .

See? Good old Dad. Dylan began to doubt that the job was for him after all. *Damn* . . . Morningdale still had its talons in him. It wasn't letting go yet. And if he let it, it would drain his lifeblood right out of him.

5

David Leppington woke in a strange bed.

Katrina . . .

Even though it was still the middle of the night, traffic rumbled on the road outside the window. Vehicle lights sent silvery phantom shapes sliding across the walls of the bedroom. His gaze followed one.

He started when he saw Katrina kneeling by the side of the bed. She watched his face. She had no expression. Her hair tumbled down over one breast.

'You'll be warmer in here,' he whispered and reached out to caress her arm.

Her skin was like ice. So cold that he jerked his own hand away. Katrina didn't react. She didn't even move.

Uneasily, he whispered, 'Katrina. Is there anything wrong?'

Without any expression, or even any indication that she'd heard him, she continued to stare.

David noticed that something had changed. One of Katrina's eyes was dead. The dead eye seemed to look into his eyes, while the other one, which appeared normal enough, gazed over his head. The dead eye – that sickeningly lifeless eye – had a large, vacant pupil that pushed the white almost back under the eyelid.

The dead eye stared. He stared back, not sure what to say.

6

Another e-mail:-

Electra, this is Rowan. I woke on the sofa in the middle of the night. The cottage was dark; no lights. I think they've cut the power.

They?

They! I don't know who they are but there are men outside the cottage. There must be dozens of them. I can hear their breathing through the doors. They turn the handles. That rattling goes right through my head. When I looked through the curtains there were faces looking in at me. White faces, a strange blue-white. And their eyes? *It sickens me even to try and recall them. All I remember is shouting at the faces. What I was shouting I don't know; I just kept shouting, maybe trying to frighten them away – who knows? I can't think straight any more.*

Electra. I need you more than ever now. Even an e-mail will help. I feel so isolated. And I know they're out there. But what do they want from me?

7

"'A vein runs through her.'" She looked at the disc as she sat in the front of the car. 'What's this?'

'A song I've been working on.'

'I didn't know you were a musician?'

'I'm not, I play bass.'

'Pardon?'

'It's an old band joke. The guy with the least musical ability always plays bass guitar.'

'Oh.'

She read the label on the disc. '*A Vein Runs Through Her* by Luke Spencer—'

'That's me.'

'And Dylan Adams.'

'That's him.' Luke pointed to the picture sleeve inside the case.

'Dylan Adams. He looks familiar.' She clicked on the car light so she could see the photograph. 'I'm sure I've seen him on the Whitby train.'

'Yeah, he's a local boy, too.'

'I didn't know two rock stars lived in Morningdale.'

Luke smiled. 'They don't.'

'So you just flew in for the Goth Communion from LA.'

'No. The song's a demo. I recorded it at a studio down in Scarborough. Dylan's a good guitarist but he's in more in love with his goddamned camera. But he did a good job with the mock-up inlay card.'

'To impress the talent scouts?'

'Something like that.'

'So how goes it?'

'Do you mean have we got a million-dollar contract? And a luxury penthouse?' Smiling, he shook his head. 'We're ahead of our time.'

'Pity. I always wanted to be a rock groupie.' She kissed him. 'Doesn't that hurt?' She touched the underside of his jaw where the steel spike had punctured the flesh.

'Would you believe me if I told you no?'

She shook her head, smiling. Lightly she touched the sticking plaster that covered the seeping wound. He winced.

'It hurts,' he told her. 'It *really* hurts.'

'Then why do it?'

He shrugged. 'Maybe I'm an attention seeker.'

'You got *my* attention, you mad man.'

'Mad must be the word.'

She ran her hand along his bare arm. 'Are all these body-piercing scars?'

'Sure. Did you think I was really spiking myself with heroin?'

'You never know.' She kissed the puncture scars on his arm.

'No . . .' He let out a sigh of pleasure. 'Pain's the real narcotic. Heroin, cannabis, E – it's all piss-weak compared to a good solid white-hot bolt of agony ripping the top of your skull off.'

'You *are* weird.'

'Morningdale's so boring you've got to do something.'

'But hurting yourself?'

'Believe me . . .' He tapped his head.

'Mel.'

'Mel . . . Believe me, Mel, pain is one of the things that's in inexhaustible supply. And totally free.'

'Weird.'

He nodded, grinning. 'Damn weird.'

'So, you won't be interested in sex?'

'Sex is good, too.'

'Free. Super-abundant.' She slipped her hand into his jeans and found his penis. 'It can be exciting, too.'

Sighing with pleasure, Luke leaned back in the car seat. *Now that feels good*, he told himself. The sensation of her rubbing his cock ran like fire up his nerves to the puncture wound in his jaw that still filled his mouth with blood. Sexual excitement complemented the buzz of pain in his skin.

She freed his penis. Kissed it. Ran her tongue down the shaft to his testicles. 'You've got piercings everywhere, haven't you?' she whispered.

'I'm half man, half steel.'

'Nipples, scrotum, ears, nose, lips, lovely cock . . .'

'Other places, too.'

'You going to show me?' Mel moved her mouth over the end of his penis, swallowing the head into her throat.

Luke closed his eyes. This was bliss. She took it so deep that her throat muscles spasmed around his cock, nipping the head: a delicious sensation. He moaned. As she worked at it, he reached up to rip the sticking plaster from the wound. He dug his thumb into the exquisitely tender split in the skin.

This was heaven. Right here in the front of his car. In the middle of the night. At the edge of Lazarus Deep.

The girl . . . Mel. That's it, remember her name. He said it aloud to embed the name in his mind. 'Mel . . . Mel . . . Sweet Christ, that feels good . . .'

The girl had been right at the front of the crowd in the Station Hotel tonight. He hadn't seen her at first. The tall woman with blue-black hair had grabbed his attention. She was older than the rest of the Goths there. She might have been in her mid-thirties. And there was such a look of experience in her eyes; an electricity there that was so erotic that he'd felt his body tingle when she'd looked at him.

After the spike had gone in, he'd marked her with his blood. He'd hoped that would be enough to snare her. *Hell, squit happens* (as his mother was fond of saying). Squit had happened and she'd vanished from the room. Later he'd found out that her name was Electra. *Shit, she even owned the hotel.* But that was – ah – academic now.

Back at the Goth party Mel had reached up to take his blood on her fingertips. With his trade-mark priestly gesture he'd rested his hand on her tightly curled black hair, then signed an inverted cross on her forehead in his own blood. That had delighted her – she'd beamed a huge smile up at him. Then she'd leaned forward to show her breasts plumping up over the top of her corset that was a lustrous black veined with purple. She'd traced a line of blood along her cleavage, right in the valley between her large breasts.

She'd appeared by his car when he'd left the hotel, his white clothes still glorious with blood.

Now she – hell – she knew what she wanted . . . And, good Christ, this was hot. This was hotter than fireworks. Luke pushed his hands against the roof of the car as Mel's mouth gorged on his cock. Licking, sucking, lipping the stud.

'Talk to me,' she whispered. He glanced down. His cock was silver with her saliva. Her eyes blazed at the sight of the purple head, as if it mesmerized her.

'What do you want me to say?'

'What you really want.'

'Fantasies?'

'Yes.'

Mel went down on him again. She was full of vitality. This could have been an Olympic sport for her. She burned up physical energy. The car windows began to steam on the inside. Light-headed, Luke let his head roll. Beyond the windscreen lay Lazarus Deep. It looked like a pool of blood in the dark. It was completely still. Even though it glistened it didn't reflect the moonlight.

'Scream if you want to go faster.' She mouthed the words along his hard shaft; her breath tickled his groin.

'Oh, wow. Oh, Christ.' His body burned. The wound in his throat pulsed to the same rhythm as the blood pumping through his veins. It felt as if he'd burst from his skin at any second.

So good, so fucking good. So fucking wonderful . . .

'You're not talking, Luke . . .'

'Ah, you're too good . . . too bloody good . . .'

'Talk fantasy and I'll get even better.'

Mel sucked. The lubricious sound brought Luke to the verge of exploding into her mouth. He dug his thumb into the wound under his chin, shifting the centre of physical sensation from his groin to his head. Now he played with it, not touching his jaw, allowing that synapse-crackling sensation to slide back to his penis where nerve endings vibrated to the touch of her dancing tongue. Then he'd nip the broken edge of the skin. Those powerful sensations would shift again to the upper part of his body. He ran the fingers of one hand through her curling hair. The fingers of the other hand played with the ring piercing his right nipple.

With practice you can move sensation round your body like you can move a piece around a chessboard.

'Fantasies,' he panted. 'You want fantasies.'

'I want it all. Then I want you inside me.'

'You'll get that . . . believe me.'

'Talk me hotter.'

'Fantasies.' Luke cupped Mel's skull in his hand, eased himself deeper into her throat. 'Fantasies . . . Castration. For –

oh, Jesus – for years I've fantasized about castration. I wanted to cut myself there first. Yes, bite. Use your teeth a little . . . Uh . . . My fantasy . . . Castration . . . I wanted a woman to appear like a shadow in my room. I dreamed I could see her face. Her hair pours down almost to her knees. Covers her face. I can't see her. As I lay there naked on the bed I don't move. She pulls back the sheet. She takes hold of my testicles in one hand . . . uh, God, yes . . . She squeezes, pulls at the same time. Hands as cold as ice. Did I tell you that? She's got a hand that feels like it's been buried in ice . . . only she's – uh . . . Then she shows me a knife. Holds it right there in front of my face. So I can see the blade. I don't move. But I feel myself grow hard. Then she takes the knife away. I feel it touch my balls. The edge is sharp; it's the same as a nettle sting. Burning, prickling . . . Then POW! She slices them off with one . . . oh God . . .'

The girl's body heat poured over his penis like a fluid; a burning rush that fired up his nerve endings. Made his heart beat harder.

Luke turned his face to the side.

'***God damn it!***'

'What's wrong?'

'There's some bastard looking in.'

'Oh, shit.' Mel wiped her mouth. 'Pervert!' She flicked a finger at the white face staring through the car window.

Luke looked at the face that would almost have been touching his if it hadn't been for the door window between them. It might have been the obscuring effect of condensation on the window. But there was something about the face. Especially the eyes. He couldn't see an iris. There were only black pupils. They were fierce, hard-looking; they stared right through his face like it was made of glass, too.

'Pervert!' Mel was shouting. 'Fucking pervert! Luke, you ought to go out there and break his face. All I wanted was—'

'Mel.'

'Aren't you going to hit him?'

'Mel. Don't open the door!'

'Why? He deserves a—'

'Leave it.' Luke pressed a button. The central locking activated with a click. Something about the face. Something wrong. But a wrongness he couldn't put his finger on.

'It's just some pervert,' she said, annoyed that he was chickening out. 'Aren't you going to chase him off, or are you scared?'

'Listen. There's more than one of them.' He jerked his head back.

Through the misted glass Luke saw more figures moving round the car, coming to the side doors. He heard one pull lightly at the handle of a rear door.

Mel changed her tune. 'They're trying to get in.'

'I know that.'

'Luke—'

'Don't worry, we're getting out of here.'

'Perverts!'

'Leave it,' he told her. 'We'll just go.'

'There's more of them. Where are they all coming from?'

'Who cares? We're leaving.'

He turned the key. The motor started first time. Then he hit the lights. More figures were caught in the glare. This time they fell away as if the intensity of the halogen lamps hurt their eyes.

Something's not right . . .

He couldn't see clearly; the glass still carried a misty film of condensation.

But there's something so strange about the figures, he told himself. *The shape of them. The body language is all wrong. They move too slowly. There's a sluggish deliberateness about them. They don't move like highly strung pervs who like to watch couples make out in cars.*

Luke gunned the engine. Hands swam out of the darkness. One pressed against the window, palm to the glass, fingers splayed out. *The shape of the hand's all wrong,* he told himself as he slipped into reverse. *Not that it matters. We're gone. Leave the creeps by the lake.* No doubt they'd got something planned for themselves later. The car lights streamed across the surface of Lazarus Deep that lay just a dozen metres away, catching the water with a ghostly glimmer. A mist congealed on it. A couple of rotted tree branches emerged at the water's edge like a pair of muscular arms.

He engaged the gear. Reversed. The car bucked but didn't move.

'Shit.'

Mel shot him a frightened look. 'What's wrong?'

'Tyres . . . they're slipping.'

'But you parked on the track, not the grass.'

'I know . . . don't worry. I'll run it forward, then back.'

'Luke, you're right at the edge of the water.'

'There's plenty of space.'

'Christ.'

'Put the music on.'

'What?'

'Switch on the CD player. If we make a lot of noise it'll make them scoot.'

To emphasize his statement Luke punched the horn. The sound bleated across the lonely waters. At last Mel found the play button. Instantly the sound of Dylan Adams's soaring guitar slammed from the speakers. Hell, his friend could play. It sounded like flights of angels gliding through the heart of God.

He eased off the handbrake, then touched the accelerator pedal, bouncing the car forward. Now that it was free of the mud he'd be able to reverse back to where the track was wider. Pull a quick U-turn, then *go*.

Only he heard a thumping sound as if dozens of fists were punching the car's bodywork. Mel screamed, her breasts heaving against the restraint of the corset.

Why's she screaming like that? We're getting out of here.

But she'd realized first what was really happening. The sound was indeed that of hands hitting the car. But they were purposefully pushing, not blindly striking it. Luke slammed the car into reverse, then floored the pedal. The engine screamed. The vehicle slowed its forward motion.

Only it didn't stop, let alone reverse. Whoever the strangers were they were still pushing the car forward.

'Hey, enough! The lake's right in front of us!'

He shouted as if their assailants were just some guys pulling a prank. Only it didn't seem like that now. Dylan's guitar powered searing notes from the car's sound system. The steering wheel vibrated under Luke's palms. All the time he was pumping the pedal. The engine bellowed; dirt sprayed from the tyres to shine in wild silvers and golds in the beams of the car's headlights. Transformed into fountains of precious metal.

Mel's screams grew piercing.

He pumped the pedal, hoping pulses of energy surging along the drive shaft would force the car back against those crazies who were pushing it toward the lake.

But that was when it stalled.

Luke froze in the seat. His lips formed the words, 'Oh my God.'

Then those dozens of hands pushed against the back of the car once more, this time encountering no resistance from its engine and reverse gear. On wet turf now the wheels didn't grip. It didn't help when Luke crushed down the brake pedal. The car glided forward, down the shallow banking, across the shore of crackling pebbles and into the water. The car's nose dipped. Its headlights still shone, but this time they were underwater, flooding the lake bed with submarine light. The music continued. His best friend's guitar played on with supernatural grace.

Beside him the girl stopped screaming. Instead, she gasped as she gazed through the windscreen as the surface of the lake slid up and over it. The car's lights flickered now as water rushed into the engine, finding the battery, the cable contacts. And still *A Vein Runs Through Her* pounded through the pocket of air in the car.

But out there, beneath the lake that still glowed with the light of the dying head-lamps, he saw men and women. They hung suspended. Arms outstretched, faces gazing at the car. Their eyes, with their hard black pupils, fixed on its occupants, piercing them as surely as the point of a blade.

The girl's hand gripped Luke's just as the windscreen crumpled inward. Cold lake water gushed through the opening. The figures weren't far behind.

CHAPTER 4

I

Four in the morning. A winter's night as black as Bible ink. Sheep shivered in their pens. The breeze blew from the moors, down into the valley bottom, stirring the dogs. A fox yelped. The houses were transformed into gravestone shapes by the darkness.

In Skagg's Cottage Dylan Adams dreamed of screaming people. They screamed up at him from the bottom of a gloomy pit that grew darker by the second, drowning their faces in shadow. They screamed his name.

Dylan opened his eyes. His clock radio burned with the intensity of a single staring eye. 4:02. Riding on the night air from far away, the howling of dogs came through the partly open window A phantom shimmering sound that sent a shiver across his skin. Suddenly, the curtains were blown back hard by the breeze. They stood horizontally from the curtain rail, revealing the block of night sky shaped by the window frame. A carved African primitive figure tumbled from the windowsill. It rolled across the table beneath the window, knocking over a stack of compact discs.

Rubbing his forehead, he climbed out of bed. The faces in the dream stayed in his head. They were screaming in terror. He remembered the look in their eyes. He rubbed the sides of his head harder, as if to erase the dream images that still lingered there.

Dylan switched on the light before pulling the window

closed, shutting out the night air. Then he picked up the discs.

'Damn.'

One of the cases had been chipped in its fall from the table. He looked at the ball of his thumb where the jagged edge had nicked the skin. He sucked the blood away. The CD was the demo he'd recorded with Luke in Scarborough eighteen months ago in a tiny four-track studio that looked out over the harbour. *A Vein Runs Through Her* didn't tear open the music scene for them. Although it got plenty of play at the Goth parties that drew Luke like a moth to a flame. They'd even played it live at the Masquerade Ball at Whitby Pavilion during the annual Goth week, when Goths and vampire-lovers flapped into the little seaside town from all over the country.

Beneath the light Dylan saw that his blood had smeared the plastic case, forming a red veil over Luke's face in the photograph. He licked his finger and wiped it. He looked at it again.

That's odd, he thought. *The plastic must be porous. I can't get rid of the stain on Luke's face.*

2

The raven swept over Skagg's Cottage where Dylan Adams switched off the light and went back to sleep. The raven's long glide, its wings outstretched, carried it like a glistening, dark missile over the fields. Over Lazarus Deep where bubbles still rose from the car lying on the lake bed.

The bird sped over moorland heights that were gouged by deep valleys. In one place houses clustered, gathered tightly together as if clinging to one another for protection. Then, once more, hills pushed up toward the night sky. Fields became moorland heather. Here blisters of turf told where there were ancient burial mounds. They held bones that had been old centuries before the Vikings landed their longships on the coast just fifteen miles away. A cruciform shape lunged from the night. The raven screeched at the old stone cross that marked the burial site of some long-forgotten saint within the walls of a ruined abbey. It wheeled round, then flew inland.

Minutes later it swooped down a valley side. Below it lay a railway track that drew a silver line into the town. In the town's centre stood a formidable block of cold brick. The sign above its door read:-

STATION HOTEL
Prop. Electra Charnwood

A light burned from an upper window. Hovering on the updraught of air the raven hung motionless, its outstretched wings trembling as air currents played through its feathers. Through the uncurtained window it glimpsed a figure on the bed, sleeping.

3

Electra Charnwood slept with the light on. The sheet had slipped down to expose her naked back to the draughts as she lay face down. Her hair spilled over the pillow, its ends reaching the floor. A dark eyebrow formed a question-mark shape as she dreamed.

From the computer screen that still glowed coldly blue a soft chime announced that a message had arrived. The sleeping woman merely murmured in her sleep.

Electra,

This is Rowan. Why don't you reply? Don't you believe me? It is true. They're here tonight. Just outside my door. I can feel them. They're pressing at the walls. They want me . . .

In the dream Jack Black opened the door to her room. Still naked, she pulled a sheet around her shoulders like a cloak.

'I've called you every night,' Electra told him. 'Why did it take you so long to come back to me?'

He raised his chin and she saw the cavernous void in his throat. The teeth that had done that had been both frenzied and sharp.

'I've dreamed you here.' She stepped toward him. 'I can dream you to speak to me.'

The shaven head gave a single shake. His eyes burned at her from the tattooed face.

'So, why have you come here?' She stretched, arching her back slightly. 'To make love to me?'

Again a shake of the head.

'Then why, Jack?'

He lunged forward at her, his arms out, huge hands spread wide. This time there were no bat wings unfurling from his back. This dream was going to be different.

He grabbed hold of her, gathering her up into his arms as easily as most men would pick up a child. Then he turned and ran with her. He passed through her bedroom door, down the corridor.

Fascinated, Electra fixed her gaze on his torn throat with its profusion of severed arteries looking like the complex forking of tree roots. When she could force her stare away from his neck she looked into his face. A hard, brutal face moulded by a thick mask of powerful muscle beneath the skin. A tattooed teardrop clung to one cheek. His eyes looked forward above her head. Electra closed her eyes for a second, drawing comfort from his arms that held her to his chest so effortlessly. *This is the dream I wanted,* she told herself. *I wanted to dream he carried me away for ever.* Then she opened her eyes to see that he was running down the main hotel staircase. he raced across the entrance lobby, past the reception desk to the cellar. The sheet around her rippled in the rush of air. He burst through the cellar door. In a few massive strides he was down in the underground chamber. There were no lights. Darkness swallowed them – *vanished* them. She sensed the thousands of tons of hotel masonry above them. She divined the barrel shape of the vault that enclosed them like a tomb.

But I feel safe, she told herself. *Even though he's running in the dark he will not strike any obstruction. He won't slip. He will not fall. I'm safe. He won't let me go. I'm completely safe.*

Electra Charnwood felt warm, even drowsy, in the sheet that wrapped her body. And through the sheet she felt the strength of his encircling arms. They'd protect her from anything that lurked in the dark. Death had only made Jack Black invincible.

She didn't even wonder where he was taking her. After all, it was her dream. Her beautiful, sensual dream. Maybe soon she could run her fingers across his arms with their tattoos. The delicious bristle of hairs. Muscles would bunch like hand grenades beneath his skin. All that latent power, just waiting to erupt from his veins. His booted feet moved silently across the floor of woven brick. From the darkness loomed the iron door that sealed the basement from the labyrinth of tunnels that swarmed beneath Leppington town. He didn't stop.

They hit the door. Passed through it with only the faintest whisper of atoms in her ears. Then they were in the night-black tunnels. There was no light here but Electra knew that they were moving through them at colossal speed, Jack Black holding her tight, her hair spilling back over his shoulder, her arms and legs gathered tightly into her body against his chest and stomach. She felt tiny against this powerhouse of muscle.

But then, it's my dream. I can dream it as my subconscious self chooses.

They passed beneath grates set in the road that admitted

columns of light from street lamps. Water dripped down; diamonds of falling light. As they passed through pools of illumination she glimpsed tunnel walls lined with brick. There were clumps of toadstool grown into the shape of long faces with lightly closed eyes.

My dream . . . my dream of dark magic . . . Gothic fancies . . . immortal love . . .

Jack Black moved with the speed of a bullet flying through a gun barrel. He took her across subterranean streams, his feet splashing through water. Past underground waterfalls; through cathedral-sized caverns that had been carved from the living rock.

'What are you showing me, Jack?' she whispered in his ear. 'What's down here?'

Three years ago she'd been here when the labyrinth beneath Leppington town had swarmed with those ugly vampires. Jack and Bernice and David had defeated them. The creatures were gone now. The tunnels, she saw, were empty.

What was more, there was a sense of abandonment. Even her instinct told her that nothing larger than a rodent moved down here. The vampires were gone.

So why has Jack Black brought me here? But then dreams are strange things . . . maybe there is no reason. That isn't the case, though, is it? He's brought me here for a purpose. It's important. He wants to show me something.

That sense of dark forces gathering returned to her.

Jack carried her faster. He plunged into a natural cavern deep inside a hill. Seconds later he burst through a curtain of water to emerge on a hillside. The waterfall rumbled behind her. Darkly thunderous, deep liquid voices telling her to beware.

'What is it, Jack? What's wrong?' Still in his arms she gazed up into his face. He didn't look at her, but over her. She followed his line of sight.

At the bottom of the hillside she saw a lake in the darkness. Its waters were calm. Mist shapes ghosted across its surface. His cold-eyed stare searched it.

'What do you want me to see here, Jack?'

A light breeze stirred the sheet around her. She felt suddenly cold. The dream was feeding all her senses. She heard the sound of the waterfall. Saw the lake. Smelled the peaty earth beneath Jack's feet. Felt the cold night air creeping under the sheet.

But why this place? The dream made no sense.

God, yes, she'd had plenty of that sort. Never with this level of detail, though. She even saw a tuft of sheep's wool clinging to a thorn on a tree where the animal had brushed against it.

So what? It's just a dream about some lake in a valley.

Then she realized it wasn't a nameless stretch of water. Surprised, she murmured, 'That's Lazarus Deep.'

That, it seemed, was as much of the dream as Jack Black needed to wait for. Lazarus Deep. She'd identified it. The visit was over. He turned with her and loped back into the waterfall. Once more they burst through the curtain of water. Back they raced across the cavern, through tunnels of raw rock that gave way to brick-lined passageways. The iron door of the cellar exploded into her field of vision. A split second later they were through.

Into the cellar. Up the steps. Into the lobby, Jack's feet blurring across the carpet. Then up the main staircase. When he reached the bedroom, he laid her down on the bed.

'You're going to come back to me,' Electra told him softly. 'I'm going to make it happen.' She took a deep breath. 'Kiss me goodnight, won't you?'

He leaned forward. She forced herself not to see the broken-ended white-grey tubes that were his bloodless arteries. They swayed as he loomed over her.

Then she knew why they were swaying. They had a life of their own. Like snakes they writhed, driven into motion by a life of their own.

Then they darted forward, punching through the naked skin of her throat and chest. Burying themselves deep into her flesh. Driving down to her own arteries, rupturing blood vessels, penetrating her heart.

'*Jack!*'

She shouted herself awake. The bedroom was still lit. The computer screen glowed, forming a single oblong eye in the corner.

Dear God. What a dream. I felt his veins inside me. That had been so vivid. *Biting through my skin.* She ran her fingers across her chest and throat, even cupping a breast to look underneath where the skin continued to tingle.

Not a mark. But then, when did a dream leave tangible evidence of its existence?

Wait a minute . . .

On impulse, Electra swept her silk kimono from the hook at the back of the door and slipped it on. In seconds she'd hurried along the corridor, down the staircase to her office. The security monitors revealed night-time images of the yard, bars and entrance lobby. She located the VCR among the bank of machines that covered the lobby with a high-angle camera. Hitting the rewind button, she ran the tape back. After a moment, she pressed 'play' then turned to the monitor. It took some time but eventually she saw it. A huge figure – a man with a shaved head running through the lobby. She saw herself in his arms, hair spilling out, the sheet flapping around her.

She rewound the tape to play it again and again. Outside, cars started to pass by in the street as the sun climbed in the wintry grey sky.

I've got proof, Electra told herself. *I'll send copies to David*

Leppington and Bernice Mochardi. She'd tell them to come back. This was important. And what she would tell them would centre on Lazarus Deep.

Quickly she made copies of the tape. The cleaning staff were arriving when she checked the copies on the VCR before putting them into the padded envelopes.

They were blank.

She replayed the original master tape. It showed the entrance lobby, lit by a single night light on the wall. The tape counter reached the point where she'd seen the speeding image of Jack Black pass across the floor to the cellar door beyond the reception desk.

She kept watching. The tape showed no such image. Not even the ghostly flicker of one.

She put her face in her hands and wept.

4

Bernice Mochardi woke to the sound of the weather report on the clock radio. Cold, with the threat of a coming storm.

5

David Leppington opened his eyes to look up at the unfamiliar light shade hanging from the ceiling. A purple ball, forming a Chinese lantern.

His first waking thought was: *Where's the dead eye?*

Uneasy, very uneasy, he turned to look at the pillow beside him. Bedclothes formed a humped shape that looked barely human. For a moment he watched it. Knowing what he *should* do but understanding also that he didn't want to. In the end there could be no more putting it off. He reached out to the quilt, gripped the edge, pulled it back so that he could see Katrina in the cold light of day.

He sat up, surprised, his gaze roving across the other side of the double bed. It was empty. No Katrina. The bedding had simply been rucked into a mound when she'd climbed out while he was asleep. Even so, he saw the deep depression in the pillow. Her head had lain there. Once more he thought about waking in the night. How she'd kneeled, looking at him. One of her eyes was dead. There was no more accurate way of putting it.

She'd had one live eye that gazed into space. And one dead eye that stared at him. *Into* him.

He glanced round the unfamiliar bedroom. A photograph of Katrina's family stood on a shelf. Books stood on the shelf below that one. On a dressing table close to the bed was a greetings card. *Congratulations on your new home.*

The sound of a door closing reached him.

Katrina? Climbing out of bed, he pulled on his clothes.

David Leppington would go and find Katrina. Nevertheless, he still found himself thinking about her single dead eye.

CHAPTER 5

I

David Leppington shivered. This wasn't much better than walking into a tomb. The windows were open. An icy wind stirred the blinds. The sofa was still shoved hard against the wall. He'd been in the grip of such passion, kissing Katrina, that it had rolled back on its castors. One sheet of newspaper, detached from the rest of the journal, fluttered round the room like a bird trying to escape. Traffic bellowed in the street. David looked at the clock on the mantelpiece. 7:35. He'd have to leave for the hospital soon for the start of his shift. In the mirror he saw his stubbled jaw, the dark shadows under his eyes. Signs of a night on the tiles.

But with his ex?

What had gone through his mind? He'd lost all self-control. Katrina had only recently got her life back on track after years in a mental hospital. The schizophrenia had been so deep-rooted, so overwhelming, that she hadn't recognized her own family. Most of the time she'd been gripped by delusion. She'd believed that her boyfriend, a medical student by the name of David Leppington, was going to hurt her. Drink her blood, for God's sake. Now, within a couple of hours of meeting her again, after almost a decade, he'd fallen into bed with her.

That's not smart thinking, David, he told himself. *Not smart at all. You don't know the extent of her recovery. You might have done more harm than good. That dead eye. Staring. Hell . . . I'm an idiot.*

'I shouldn't have done it.' He spoke to his image in the mirror. So he was startled when he heard a reply.

'Shouldn't have done what?'

'Katrina . . . good morning.' Nice try, but it sounded forced.

'Good morning to you.'

'Sleep well?'

Katrina looked bright. Fresh. God, she looked beautiful.

No sign of the dead eye. Both eyes were bright and so twinkling with life that she could have been a teenager, one with a lean athlete's body at that. She was dressed in black trousers and a lime-green top. Good God, she was amazing.

'I thought I'd let you sleep,' she told him as she picked up the sheet of paper. 'You looked exhausted.' She smiled. 'Gosh, you must be frozen. I'll close the windows.'

'No, I'm fine, honestly.' David smiled back. 'It'll wake me up.'

'Ever since I got out of the –' she gave an impish smile '– the fun factory, I've become a fresh-air fanatic. I sleep with the windows wide open. I walk to work rather than using the bus.'

'Good idea.'

'Breakfast?'

'I'd love to, bu—'

'You've got to dash to work?'

'Katrina, I'm sorry if I'm giving the impression of—'

'Loving me and leaving me?'

He looked for a sign of anger – rejection, possibly – in her face. But she had an unshakeable air of cheerfulness. Excitement, even.

'David.' She took his hand. 'Last night took us both by surprise.'

'You can say that again.'

'So those words were an expression of regret?' She repeated what he'd confessed to the mirror. '"I shouldn't have done it."' Her eyes shone. 'Shouldn't have made love to me?'

David felt shitty. 'Katrina, that sounded terrible. I'm sorry, believe me I am, but . . .' He squeezed her hand. Did it feel good? He wanted to hold both her hands. 'My God, I'm sounding like an embarrassed child. Last night was wonderful. It's been amazing to meet you again after all this time.'

'But it was too much, too quickly. I agree.' She smiled. 'We just went a bit mad, didn't we?'

'I think we did. But – and I don't know how you felt – but it was as if we hadn't been apart from each other for ten years, more like just a few days. It was so natural to pick up where we left off.'

'I felt that, too.' She touched his cheek, her eyes limpid. 'We really did love each other, didn't we?'

'We did.'

'And it was the real thing?'

'Absolutely.'

'It won't work, you know.'

'What won't?'

'Trying to get back together again.' Katrina squeezed his hand, smiling. 'Call last night animal passion.'

David laughed softly. 'I think I'm going to have mental flashbacks for months to come.'

'Good, so we enjoyed ourselves. There's no regrets?'

'None.'

'Now we've got what you medical types call closure.'

When he started to talk she touched his lips. 'No. We've got it out of our system, David. It's time we moved on with our own lives.'

I thought I was going to be the one to suggest we cool things. Now she's telling me we really are over. God damn it, this really hurts.

'Now, David.' Katrina stepped back, still looking up at his face. Almost formally, she clasped her hands together in front of her. 'Now, I'm going to ask a favour . . . a big, big favour.'

'Ask away.' *What's coming next? Will she suggest we see each other as friends?* David's heart pounded. Emotion overrode common sense now. He wanted her to confess that she still needed him. *Friends is okay.* He could handle being friends with her. *Take it one step at a time . . .*

'Will you give me a hug?'

He smiled. 'Is that the favour?'

'Nope.' She stepped into his arms. David wrapped them round her. Even as he told himself to keep it a friends-only kind of hug he found his face drawn down to the top of her head. He rested his cheek against her hair. It felt incredibly soft. Smelled wonderful, too.

Dear God, what's happening to you, David?

It's Cupid's arrow, you fool. His own answer didn't take him by surprise. He'd known it deep down within minutes of meeting her yesterday.

LOVE.

Say it loud, say it proud, David.

'David?'

'Yes?'

'I don't want you to be late for work.'

'It's only a ten-minute drive.'

So it was twenty minutes but he'd tell any lie to keep holding her like this.

'I'm sure it's further.' Katrina's breath was warm on his chest through his shirt. 'But it's sweet of you to say that. It makes me think you're not wanting to rush from me in blind terror.' Her voice was light with sheer good nature.

Marry her.

He tried to suppress the wild thought.

'David. London's a big enough place. We're not likely to bump into each other by accident.'

'We can swap numbers.'

'No, it's time we moved on.'

'Oh?'

'But it's important for me to know that when we go our separate ways in a few minutes we have only warm thoughts for each other.'

His heart fell suddenly. 'We can do that.' The words came woodenly.

Katrina put her arms round him, squeezing him tight. 'I mean it. Call it part of my therapy, and know that you have helped my recovery.'

'I didn't do anything, Katrina.'

'You did. And it means a lot to me.'

'But if you did want to—'

'Ah, ah. You're going to be late for work, Dr Leppington. You've lives to save, babies to deliver.'

He smiled. 'More like boils to lance and drunks to suture.'

'Have you got everything? Watch? Jacket? Car keys?'

'Yes.'

'I'm going to grab some toast and coffee, then I'll get off to work.' She kissed him on the cheek.

Not a kiss, a peck. And I'm getting the bum's rush.

'Goodbye, Katrina. It was nice to see you again. Honestly.'

'Honestly. You were always one to mean it, too.' She gave him a sisterly hug, patting him on the back. 'Look after yourself.'

And that's it. No 'See you around'.

Seconds later David found himself sitting in the car as if he'd walked there in his sleep. Buses and cars streamed by. Vicious blasts of cold air tugged at the trees. Pedestrians hurried by with their heads down. Everyone scowled like they hated the world.

He started the engine. Gripped the steering wheel with both hands so tightly that his knuckles turned white.

Dear God, the car is cold as ice.

He glanced at the passenger seat. One of Katrina's hairs glinted against the grey fabric of the headrest. Damn . . . he was annoyed that he'd let his emotions get opened up like this. Yesterday morning? Fine. This morning his nerves were so tender that everything reminded him of Katrina. And it hurt to remember her face.

Doctor! Doctor! What can you give me for a broken heart?

That was an old medical school joke. He couldn't even remember the punchline. He looked up at the window of Katrina's flat in the Victorian block across the road. The ground floor consisted of a row of shops. These were the inner-city kind. A dry cleaner's; a travel agent's; a grocer's; a newsagent's with paper boys and girls returning with their now-empty satchels.

David looked at his watch. 'Time to go to work, Leppington.'

His gaze was drawn back to Katrina's second-floor flat. Lights burned in the bedroom. Probably changing the bedding. Chasing away those clues that he'd ever been there.

He looked at his eyes in the rear-view mirror. 'You should have asked her to marry you when you had the chance.'

He slipped the car into gear and flicked the signal. It ticked loudly as he waited for a break in the traffic. Once more his gaze went from Katrina's bedroom window to the rear-view mirror where his eyes shot him an accusing stare.

'OK. What's stopping you going back there right now? You idiot, go and ask her to marry you.'

It happened faster than he could think it through. He switched off the engine and climbed out of the car. Then, slamming the door shut behind him, David crossed back over the road to Katrina's flat.

2

Electra Charnwood does a great recovery job. Make-up smoothed on so the cracks don't show. Hair brushed. Look at that beautiful shine! Clothes neat. Figure trim. Wonderful waist, darling! How does one retain that hourglass figure? Wow! Thirty-eight years old and still sweet enough to eat.

Electra pursed her lips and turned her head to reassure herself that the fine jawline was still there.

'No jowls yet, girl.'

This was ritual. Every morning she picked up the pieces from her emotional crashes. They occurred most nights. Last night's had been especially catastrophic. The dream journey with Jack Black to Lazarus Deep. Then finding that the image had been caught by the security camera. Elation at being able to share the incident had been followed by a plunge into depression when the image of Jack Black carrying her had dissolved from the tape.

'But of course you probably dreamed that as well, dear. There . . .' She smoothed down her long black skirt. 'You'll do, Miss Charnwood. You'll do nicely.'

Today she'd work on the Hotel Midnight website. Oodles of unread e-mails. Loads of stories submitted by vampire hunters and ghost detectives worldwide. You might not have found that many haunted houses out there any more (electricity massacred ghosts), but why were there so many haunted people? *Why do we have so many personal demons?*

'Ooops, blood,' she reminded herself. First she'd have to clean away the bloodstains left by the body piercers from the night before. 'I can't leave the Jack Black Room looking like a slaughterhouse, can I, now?'

More and more Electra found herself slipping into the caricature of a spinster schoolmistress. She'd done it for

years as a way of cheering herself up. Now the act seemed
to be sticking fast. Briskly, she left her room to sweep down
the hotel's broad staircase.

*Now, Miss Charnwood, let's see what this sparkling new day
has to offer. Surprises . . . pleasant ones, I hope.*

3

The single rail track curved away into the distance. It carried
one train an hour through scenic countryside. At the moment
the only traffic was rabbits, nibbling the shoots that grew
between the sleepers. At one side of the track the River Esk
foamed over stones on its twenty-mile journey to Whitby.
Here it was little more than a stream.

Dylan Adams stood at the edge of the platform. Nearby,
backpackers were talking about how picturesque the one-
hundred-and-fifty-year-old station was. One went outside to
take photographs of it and the medieval church nearby.

Dylan considered photographing the brass plaque next to
the ticket office that commemorated railway men who'd died
fighting in the First World War. It would form part of a
photographic brief he was working on at college. His lecturer
had titled the brief *Life, Death & Yorkshire Pudding* and had
added a guideline in brackets: *(Student, employ your formidable
imagination to represent two profound themes in a homely – and
down-to-earth! – way.)*

So, here was a railway station with the names of eighteen
men who'd joined the army. They were probably teenagers
just like him who'd lived in the cottages in Morningdale (just
like him). They'd gone to the trenches in France where more
teenagers from German towns had killed them. He glanced
at the station clock that was set in a vast confection of Gothic
ironwork. Still another twenty minutes until the train arrived.
Plenty of time to grab those photographs. The brass memorial

plaque had been so vigorously polished that it had the lustre of rose gold.

Dylan slipped the camera from his shoulder as a girl of around eighteen, wearing a long cream coat, walked up. She had a thing about Luke Spencer.

She nodded at Dylan. 'Morning.'

'Morning.'

'Has your friend rolled in yet?'

'Luke? Should be here any minute.'

'He was going to collect me in his car this morning.' She was pretending she wasn't miffed but she was. 'He was going to drive me down here so I wouldn't have to carry that.' She pointed to a suitcase behind her on the platform.

'Going on holiday?' Dylan asked, carefully drawing the camera from its case.

'I wish. It's full of shoes I'd collected for some display or other he's making at the college.' The girl sounded hurt. 'He was going to collect me in his car,' she repeated.

'He went to one of those Goth Communions. He's probably stopped over.'

Ouch. That had been tactless of him. The girl's eyes widened.

'The one in Leppington?'

'I think so.' *Double ouch.* Maybe Luke was dating the girl in the cream coat. If so, Dylan had just gone and dropped his friend in it up to his neck. 'He's probably just a bit bleary-eyed, that's all.'

'You know, Luke only thinks about himself.'

Dylan gave the kind of shrug that committed him to nothing.

The girl looked at him. 'You're Dylan Adams, aren't you?'

He smiled. 'Guilty.'

'You don't know Luke's mobile number, do you?'

'I haven't got it with me.'

'Blast.'

'Don't worry, I'm sure he'll turn up. He's probably just running late.'

'I'll bet.' She made it sound ominous.

Dylan knew what the tone meant. He wasn't surprised. Luke had a different girlfriend every other week and had probably met someone at the Goth Communion. In whatever secret hideaway he'd found Luke was probably having the time of his life.

4

Three miles away from Morningdale Station, where Dylan was talking to the girl, was Lazarus Deep.

A heron had an easy meal of it. Dead fish floated on the lake's surface. The bird ate in such a lazy fashion that it hardly bothered to identify fish from flotsam. One piece it plucked from the water was an inlay card from a CD. When it realized it couldn't eat it, it tossed it aside.

The card floated for a few moments on water that was as flat as glass and as black as ink. Printed on the card in Gothic script were the words: *A Vein Runs Through Her*. The photograph showed Luke Spencer and Dylan Adams standing in the ruins of Whitby Abbey. The bird began to flap its wings. It flapped harder, struggling to leave the surface of the lake.

A hand that was as white as grave marble burst from the water and seized the heron by its long neck.

Dragged it down.

5

The entrance to the apartment building was behind the shops. David Leppington had to cut down an alleyway and then double back into a yard where a van was delivering sacks of potatoes to the grocery store. He walked in through the communal entrance and took the stairs two at a time. A woman closed the door of her flat with one hand while holding a baby in the crook of her other arm. He stood back to let her by.

His heart beat faster as he climbed to the next floor. He struggled to find an opening line. Even though it had only been ten minutes since he had last seen Katrina he was planning a light-hearted, 'Long time no see.'

Then what, David? Launch right in. Tell Katrina that she's never left your mind for the last ten years. That you've grieved for her while she was in the mental hospital as if she was dead. Now, a miracle. She's back.

Marry me.

He knew she'd sounded firm just a few minutes ago when she'd told him that they should never meet again. That their lovemaking the night before had just been a way of closing an episode in their lives. Only he doubted that she'd really meant it. Katrina didn't want to impose on his life again. She was telling him what she *thought* he wanted to hear. Cold air blasted upwards from downstairs. The woman with the baby must have managed, one-handed, to open the door to the building. Air currents gusted around his ankles, moaning in the stairwell like an unhappy child. They rattled the doors that led off from the landing as if they wanted to go inside the apartments.

One door, though, the breeze didn't rattle. Katrina's door was already open. The draught pushed it wide before David could touch it.

The breeze was blasting right through because all the windows were wide open. It snatched up the newspaper again. This time half a dozen sheets were flapping round the room.

'Katrina . . .' He stepped into the room. A sheet of newspaper blew against his face, wrapping itself around his head. He dragged it away. The wind rose to a shriek.

'Katrina?' An instinctive realization hit him before he could put the feeling into words.

She's gone . . . she's not coming back.

6

The carriage doors closed in front of Bernice Mochardi. Gravity pulled at her as the Tube train accelerated away into the tunnel.

These tunnels – hundreds of miles of them beneath London – were the arteries that pumped liquid shadow beneath the streets. Bernice had only to allow her eyes to focus on the tunnel walls beyond the train's windows and it all came back to her. She saw herself in the labyrinth beneath Leppington. *It's three years ago. I'm with Jack Black and David Leppington as they use chainsaws to cut the heads off those* things.

Only just in time she stopped herself using the word: *Vampires.*

'Excuse me – have you the time, please?' She'd asked the man in the business suit at random.

He glanced at her wrist on which her watch was plainly visible. Then he gave a knowing smile as he said, 'Yes, I've got time.'

7

David checked the bedroom, then the rest of the apartment. His instinct hadn't played him false. The place looked more deserted than if Katrina was merely absent from it. It had an air of downright abandonment. As if, just moments after he'd left, Katrina had walked away from it for good.

After a moment wrestling with his conscience, he pulled open the dressing-table drawers. Hollows among the folded clothes suggested that she'd taken clothes for a journey. That made him uneasy.

The remaining folded clothes made him uneasy, too. Sweaters meticulously arranged with the sleeves gathered in a cross shape over the breast. Just the same way he'd position the arms of a dead patient across their chest before the hospital orderlies came to take them to the mortuary. David winced when he opened a wardrobe door. Above a rail of empty hangers was a shelf. On the shelf he saw blister packs of pills. Katrina had laid them out in meticulous lines.

He checked them quickly. All full. None used. The dates on the labels showed that they'd been prescribed weeks ago. The labels also gave him the dosage and the type of medication: Zyprexa – standard treatment for schizophrenia. It didn't cure the illness. It damped down the symptoms. At best it gave schizophrenia sufferers a fighting chance of leading a normal life.

David looked at the full packs, closed his eyes and breathed the words:

'Oh, Katrina, what have you done to yourself?'

CHAPTER 6

I

From **Hotel Midnight**:
OK, boys and girls, Electra's in the house tonight. Now, my dears, some thoughts on that question so many of you have been asking: –

Meditation on a Vampire

How do you identify those people who have become vampires, or at least vampiric? Cinema gave us the screen vampire that didn't reflect its image in mirrors, that would recoil from a crucifix, that would be seared by holy water. In truth, it is rarely possible to identify a vampire until it makes a move against you. Obviously, by that time it is often too late. Whatever you are in life becomes immaterial then, because you are now the victim. And once that happens you are lost to this world. From your e-mails I now know that many of you are waging your own secret battles against certain individuals who, although they might not comfortably fit into the definition of a vampire, are most clearly 'vampiric'. They might not want your blood, as such, but these vampire-like men and women might be hell-bent on draining you of your money, or your happiness, or your self-esteem, or even your love. So good luck to Rico in Naples, to Rachel in Portsmouth, and to Sylvia in Boston. Don't give up! Our thoughts are with you.

2

'Hello . . . Julia Thomas?'

'Yes, speaking.'

'Hello, this is Dylan Adams. I'm phoning about the vacancy for a photographer's assistant at the studio.'

He moved further away from the main entrance to the art college. Sod's Law. You make an important telephone call and suddenly there's a splurge of chattering students.

'Sorry?' He pushed the earpiece of the mobile hard to his ear while covering his other ear with the palm of his hand. 'I didn't catch that. Yes, I can make March the first.' He moved further away to the wall that separated the campus from a churchyard. 'Nine o' clock? I'll be coming down from Yorkshire by train. Is it possible to make it – yes, 11:30's fine.' Dylan eased a pen from his jacket pocket and, nipping the phone between his shoulder and the side of his head, wrote down the appointment time and date. 'Do I need to bring my full portfolio to the interview?'

'Hey, Dylan . . . Dill!' A guy with blond dreadlocks waved to catch his attention. 'Have you seen Luke Spencer today?'

Dylan shook his head. Then, pointing at the phone, he mouthed: *Important phone call.*

Its importance or otherwise skated past the guy. 'Luke's got a meeting with the principal today about his course application. Do you know if he'll be in this afternoon?'

Dylan shrugged in a way that said *Why ask me?* During this he wrote down directions to the studio that Julia was spelling out to him. 'Cornwall Way.'

'No, Cromwell Gate,' repeated the voice in his ear. 'The nearest Tube station is Shadwell. I'll spell it for you.'

Oh, great. Because of Goldi's interruption he'd missed half of what she'd said. Already the woman (no doubt a key member of staff at the photographic studio) would have dismissed him as some backwoods doofus who couldn't even spell his own name. Hell, if she was conducting the interview . . .

He finished the telephone call, doing his best to sound bright and personable. Meanwhile, Goldi made a circling motion with his finger. *Wind up the phone conversation.*

Hell, Dylan would wind the idiot up into a ball and kick him over the churchyard.

When he finished the call he pocketed the phone. 'That was an important call, Goldi.'

'Girl trouble?'

'Job interview.'

'No!'

'Yes, Goldi, and you nearly blew it for me, you—'

'Hey! You should have phoned from somewhere quieter.'

'This *was* quieter.'

'What? Have you been hassling the *Gazette* for an interview?'

'No.'

'Good, because everyone from your course does that.'

'I don't want to be a photographer on a local newspaper.'

'You wouldn't get in, anyway. They got an old girl snapper who's going to be there until they nail her in her box.'

'I know.'

'So where you going, then?'

'A studio in London.'

'London, huh?'

'That's if I get the job. After that call they'll probably be chucking my application form through the window.'

'London's expensive. You'll never be able to afford accommodation, you know?'

The whole world conspires against me. Dylan started to walk away.

'Bye, Goldi.'

'Hey, if you see Luke Spencer tell him that there's only one place left on the graphics course. If he doesn't get the application in before the end of the week, he'll lose the place.'

3

David peeled the latex gloves from his hands. The blood of a man who believed he could fly had smeared them a rich strawberry colour.

'Drugs screw you up.' The surgical registrar grinned at David as he started to scrub his hands.

'They screwed that guy up, all right.'

'Someone should have told him that airline tickets aren't that expensive these days.' David worked the soap into a creamy lather. 'What's more, they bring food and drinks to your seat.'

The anaesthetist came in. 'Did the guy say where he was flying?'

The story of the airborne junkie had spread fast

David binned the gloves. 'New Zealand. He's got a sister there.'

'All that way.'

'Damned hard on the arms.' The surgeon shook his head. 'OK, David. What have I got to do to put Humpty back together again?'

'He's lucky. A double-decker bus broke his fall. It's mainly a stitch-and-tape job. But he's got a greenstick of the left femur.'

'Realign and pin the iddy-biddy pieces. Bang goes my nicotine break.'

'Looks like that, but he's your baby now.'

'Hey, David, why did you stand us all up last night?'

'Yeah, we were standing around that bar like lemons, waiting to sing you happy birthday.'

'It's a long, long story.'

'In other words, Rob –' the anaesthetist winked at the surgeon '– it's intensely personal.'

'And no doubt intensely erotic. The blonde beauty from radiology, I presume?' Rob worked his fingers into the latex gloves. 'God, I love to hear the snap of rubber against skin in the morning.' He nodded at a nurse waiting by the operating theatre door. 'Our bird hasn't flown the nest, has he?'

'He's all ready for you, doctor.'

David took ten minutes to grab a coffee. After working the shift system for so long he could often miss an entire night's sleep without feeling even remotely drowsy. After last night's passionate encounter with Katrina – and its bizarre aftermath – his mind was sharp enough to deal with what A&E could throw at him. Besides, he'd snatched a couple of hours' sleep, even if it had been interrupted by Katrina gazing at him with that weird dead eye of hers.

Now she'd exited from his life. That should be that.

But he felt responsible. She was no one-night stand. He'd gone steady with her through most of his teenage years until her schizophrenic breakdown. If she had quit taking the medication the paranoia and the delusions would come roaring back at her. She was unlikely to be a threat to others but she'd become a danger to herself. Damn . . . life could get complicated.

In the staff lounge David poured himself a large coffee. A pair of orderlies hunched over a magazine in the corner. He glanced at a wall clock. Seven hours to go until the end of the shift. On a weekday one in six admissions would be alcohol-related. Weekends, the figure rose to eight out of ten. Smelling stale booze on patients' breaths as he assessed broken limbs and lacerations should have been perfect aversion therapy. But come evening he'd be more than ready for a beer or two.

But between shift-out and the pub he knew he'd have to return to Katrina's flat.

4

Riding the train home that evening Dylan telephoned Luke's mother.

'Hello, it's Dylan. Is Luke there, please?'

No, he wasn't. Yes, he'd gone out last night but he hadn't come back. Had Dylan tried Luke's mobile?

'Yes, but it must be switched off. All I'm getting is the answer service.'

'Well, I don't know what to suggest, Dylan. You know what twenty-year-old students are like; they don't tell their mothers much.' She sounded easygoing about it. 'I expect he's staying with a friend.'

A friend? Yeah, he'd hooked up with another girlfriend. He might be gone for days.

'Thanks very much, Mrs Spencer.'

'I'll tell him you phoned, Dylan. When I see him, that is.'

After he'd finished the call Dylan sat back to watch the passing scenery. The train followed the bottom of the valley. At either side of him fields enclosed by drystone walls climbed up to the moors. God, in February they could be the bleakest places on earth. The rays of the setting sun picked out lone farmhouses. Sheep showed as white flecks against the deepening green of the fields.

Dylan closed his eyes. In six months he could be returning home from the studio by Tube. After he'd showered and changed his clothes London would be his. And what a playground. Nightclubs, bars, restaurants, cinemas. He loved the thought of simply strolling along city streets that would buzz with the excitement of all those people. Young people hungry for fun. More than anything he wanted to be part of it.

5

Electra sat at the computer, pasting new material into the Hotel Midnight site. It was an open forum, so she didn't make editorial decisions about what went in and what didn't. Hotel Midnight was a website for the entire world. Anyone could contribute . . . no questions asked. Even so, she hesitated about adding the latest e-mail from the man who called himself Rowan. A troubled man at that.

> *Electra, I know I am under siege in this house now. For some reason I'm still lost in this mental fog. I don't know where I am. I don't know who I am. All I know is that at night people come to the house. They're trying to get in. What they'll do to me I don't know but I live in absolute terror. I'm pleading with you: PLEASE FIND ME. No one else will believe me, but after reading of your own experiences I know you will.*
>
> *I've been thinking. Maybe I've been ill or I've been injured in some way. It has damaged my ability to think clearly or to remember. But please do your best to find me. If I describe my surroundings it might help. The house stands alone in woodland. I only dare look through the bedroom windows during daylight hours. Through a gap in the trees I can see a lake. A white road leads to the front door . . .*

And just what makes you think I've the wherewithal to rescue you? she thought. *I'd grown used to the idea that I was the one who needed rescuing.*

Even so, the e-mail interested her. Lately, she'd started to wonder what Rowan looked like. After all, he'd written to her so often that his e-mails were beginning to form part of the fabric of her life.

'That's one of the dangers of living alone, honey,' she said softly to herself, trying to muster her old flippant tone. 'You're easy prey for any man who shows an interest in you. It doesn't matter how barmy they sound. You start imagining beginning a new life together.' She lit a ciga- rette and leaned back in the chair. Her reflection coolly regarded her. 'You're right, honey . . . I'm just a gullible woman . . .' She blew a smoke ring at her reflection. 'A desperate one, too.'

Over in the station a train sounded its horn. The mournful sound called to her. Something deep inside her answered it. She should be on that train. She needed to get away from Leppington for a while. Only she couldn't. 'I'm standing guard here,' she told her reflection.

But against what she could not say.

6

'Dylan . . . Dylan. Wait.'

He paused on the platform as people streamed off the train behind him. He saw Vikki Lawton step down from a carriage. 'Dylan. I've been wanting to see you.'

'If it's about Luke the answer's no. I haven't seen him. I don't know where he is.'

'Sorry?'

'Everyone I meet today wants to know where Luke's gone.'

'Not me. It's you I'm chasing.'

'Me?'

They walked from the station together. A cold wind blew down Morningdale's Main Street, a road broad enough for shepherds to drive their flocks to market. It was flanked by stone cottages and an assortment of butchers, greengrocers, coaching inns and touristy cafés.

Smiling, she gave a grimace. 'You haven't forgotten, have you?'

He clicked his tongue. 'The photographs? Oh, hell, I'm sorry, Vikki.'

'I expect you were busy.'

'No, I should have taken them. Is it too late?'

'It's my mother's birthday at the end of the next week. If you can get the photographs to me by Monday I can still get them framed in time.'

'I'll take them Saturday.'

'Thanks – that'd be a life-saver.'

'You want both dogs in the same photograph?'

'Please.'

'They'll sit together?'

She grinned. 'We'll glue their heads if need be.'

'Or use a couple of six-inch nails.'

She laughed and touched his arm. 'Thanks, I do appreciate it. My mother's infatuated with those dogs. It'll make her birthday to be able to sit and look at a dirty great photo of them.'

'It'll be a work of art,' Dylan promised.

'Let me treat you to a drink at the Fox.'

'I can't. I'm on a mission tonight.'

'Oh.'

He noticed that she looked embarrassed. No doubt she was thinking he was on a date. And the truth was that Dylan had thought about Vikki for years, ever since they'd been at school together. He'd used to call her Funny Face, but that face had grown into something striking. She had a froth of dark hair that, although it wasn't long, formed a deep feathery halo around her head.

'See you Saturday, Dylan. I'll give you a ring when I've got the dogs all prettied up. If that's all right by you?'

'No problem.'

'Night.'

'Vikki?'

'Hmm?'

'I need to drive around tonight . . . some of Luke's haunts. I've got to find him or he's going to lose his place on a design course.'

'Oh, I see.'

'Places are like gold dust.'

'Well, good hunting, then.'

'If you're not doing anything do you fancy coming along?'

She shrugged. 'Why not?'

'Pick you up in an hour?'

She started to walk away in the direction of her house by the village green. 'Fine.'

He stared after her.

My God! I never thought she'd say yes.

CHAPTER 7

I

When David Leppington had finished at the hospital he drove through the rush-hour traffic to Katrina's flat. After he'd found it empty that morning he'd taken a spare key that was hanging on a hook in the kitchen, locked the door, and gone to work.

Instinct told David that Katrina wouldn't be coming back. When he finally reached the flat he saw that instinct hadn't steered him wrong: she hadn't returned – and she hadn't been back during the day, either. It was an old trick but he'd closed the door, jamming a fragment of a matchstick between the door and its frame. If someone had opened the door the sliver would have fallen out without the person noticing. David saw that the matchstick was still in place at knee height, nipped tight between the two wooden surfaces.

Technically this is trespass, he told himself as he entered, but he didn't see that he had a choice. Katrina couldn't have been taking her medication for weeks. When the schizophrenia erupted again – as it surely must – she'd become a real danger to herself.

David checked Katrina's address book beside the telephone, copying down the telephone numbers of family and friends. When he returned home he'd have to work through these until, he hoped, someone would be able to tell him where she was. Her parents would be worried sick. They had to know, however, that their daughter needed medical help. There was no avoiding it. Before he left it occurred to him to check the waste bins.

Quite the detective, aren't we? But he had to help Katrina. His conscience wouldn't allow him to skip this one. In the kitchen swing bin, each empty food can had been wrapped in its own individual plastic freezer bag. Compulsive cleanliness, paranoid fear of contamination by germs . . . dear God, it smacked of the early symptoms of impending psychosis.

When he found no other clues he locked the flat. It was time to go home and start making telephone calls.

2

At six o'clock sharp Electra opened the side door of the hotel that led into the public bar. Business as usual. A cold breeze slid through the town, stirring the fabric of her skirt, chilling her ankles.

'If you can hear me, Jack Black, come home.' She murmured rather than called the words. But it was a call to the dead man all the same. Even after all this time, despite her head telling her Jack Black had died, her heart told her even more loudly that one day he'd return to her.

Electra switched on the lights behind the bar, then waited for the first customer.

3

'I hope you've got a broad mind,' Dylan told Vikki as she climbed into the car beside him.

'Broad enough. Why, what have you got planned?'

In the light from the dash he saw that she was smiling. A beautiful smile at that. She wore make-up now. Her scent filled the car. He breathed it in, taking pleasure from the thought that her body heat gave the scent wings.

He pulled away from the house. 'What I plan to do is call at some places where I know Luke goes.'

'Sounds mysterious.'

'You could say that.' The car's lights flashed against the cottages as he accelerated. 'He has a few places where he can take girls when he needs privacy.'

'What? He owns houses?'

'Not quite. His parents are caretakers for some holiday cottages. Luke soon realized that these are vacant for most of the winter so he made copies of the keys.'

'Devious little devil.' Vikki laughed. 'So he's got a string of love nests?'

'There's eight that I know of. He chose the ones that are out of the way.'

'So he wouldn't get disturbed?'

'And his parents have copies of the booking forms so he knows which ones are vacant.'

'Ingenious. So where first?'

'Leppington.'

'That's a bit of a haul, isn't it?'

'There's a house overlooking the town there. He sometimes uses that when he goes to the Communion.'

'Communion? He's a churchgoer?'

'Luke? Hardly. No, it's the Goth Communion. They have Goth parties at the Station Hotel. It's famous for them.'

'Luke's a Goth? That would explain the black coat and riding boots.'

'You should see his bedroom: purple walls, black ceiling, incense.'

'You think he might still be partying?'

'It'll just be a party for two now, if you know what I mean?'

'You're very loyal to Luke. Most people wouldn't go driving all over the moors looking for him.'

'We're friends. He's all right, we've always done stuff together.'

'I know, I remember when you and Luke put up those posters of teachers playing nude volleyball.'

'Ah, we had photographic talents even back then. I told the teachers we were taking photographs of them for the school magazine.'

'Then you pasted their heads onto photographs of naturists.'

'We were thirteen.'

Vikki laughed. 'And it made the pair of you famous in school.'

She chatted about the funny things that had happened in the past. She smiled as she talked. Dylan found that he was noticing details on her face. Her lips had suppleness to them, changing constantly from broad smiles to the kind of shape a girl would make if she were about to kiss someone. She did this unconsciously when she was recalling a past event or name. All the time her gaze flicked from the road to his eyes.

Dylan had not been looking forward to hunting for his absent friend until Vikki had agreed to come along. Now he was enjoying it a lot. She was good, lively company. From hitting the memory trail she turned to talking about her job. He knew that just a few weeks ago she'd started work for the local tourist board office. With her enthusiasm and intelligence he'd always anticipated that she'd move away from Morningdale, but he was surprised to learn how committed she was to this line of valleys, strung like pearls along the course of the River Esk. Her role was marketing the area to tourists. Lately, she'd been instrumental in winning European Union funding for a campaign advertising the area.

'We're targeting Japan,' she told him. 'Most tourists from overseas follow the route from London to Edinburgh without stopping off anywhere in between. We're trying to siphon some of them off halfway and bring them here to North Yorkshire.'

'Where the air is fresh and the night life thrilling.'

'You don't like living here, do you?'

'Oh, it's a beautiful place. There's no doubting that. Only it's *sooo* quiet.'

'Visitors come for the tranquillity.'

'Great, they can have my share of it if they like.'

Dylan saw Vikki fix him with a look. 'I heard that you were planning on moving to London?'

At least that proved there was nothing sluggish about the neighbourhood gossip.

'It's not certain yet. I've got an interview with a photographic studio.'

'Oh . . . it'll be an adventure after living up here.'

He smiled. 'That's what I'm hoping.'

The drive to Leppington took them along a narrow road that snaked through the valley, first hugging the line of the railway and the river, then winding up to the moors. In the dark it was a wildly desolate place. Here winds buffeted the car. Heads of cloud rose over the horizon to scud across the starry sky. On the valley floor Dylan saw the skull shape of Lazarus Deep. It looked as if part of the earth had fallen away to reveal a starless void.

'It's beautiful,' Vikki breathed. 'You know, I never get tired of it.'

'It's . . . striking.' Enjoying her company, Dylan didn't want to disagree with her. He glanced at her eyes, shining in the reflection from the dashboard lights. This had been a long time coming – being alone with Vikki. He didn't want to blow it by pouring ugly words on the valleys she loved. He drove up the steep incline, the car's engine fighting gravity as the vehicle's nose pointed toward the stars. At last it levelled out on the high moorland plain. There, three ancient burial mounds marked the summit.

Amused, Vikki named them. 'Don Brow, Don Flint, Don Nether Adder.'

Dylan glanced at the bumps rising from the heather as the headlights swept over them. 'Don Nether Adder? Why did they give them such bizarre names?'

'They're probably not the original ones. The real names will have become corrupted down through the centuries. But the first part of each name, "Don", means a clan of Celtic goddesses.'

'I remember the history teacher telling us they were five thousand years old.'

'And that Don Flint contained the skeleton of a horse and what was left of a chariot.'

'And the bones of a giant female warrior.'

'Ah, that's the legend part. No human bones were found when archaeologists excavated it.'

He nodded. 'She's one of the undead, then. Never buried with her chariot and horse, she roams the moors when the moon is full. Searching for a bus ride home.'

'You certainly like taking the piss out of Morningdale, don't you?'

'Just habit.'

'A bad one, Dylan.'

He looked at her. She was frowning.

Ouch, you're treading on toes, son. Even so . . .

'I don't hate Morningdale,' he told her.

'You could have fooled me.'

'But there's two issues I've got with the place.'

'Oh?'

'One. It's just not the place for me.'

'You're a city boy at heart? Good for you.'

'Maybe. And two—' He held up two fingers from the

steering wheel, then quickly folded them back down in case she got the wrong idea. 'Two. Morningdale lives in the past.'

'How come?'

'Look at it. When we boast about the place we go through the same old list. There's dozens of *ancient* burial mounds. It has the *oldest* stone bridge in Yorkshire. The *oldest* abbey ruins. The landlord of the White Horse Inn tells visitors that the fire in the bar was lit the same year Columbus discovered America and it hasn't gone out since.'

'Charming tradition.'

'Christ, Vikki. I've been in the White Horse dozens of times and seen when the fire wasn't lit. But every tourist who goes in, Mine Host stands there and says, "Madam, see that log fire? It's been burning for hundreds of years."'

'Cynic.'

This wasn't going well, Dylan realized. For the next twenty minutes they drove in near-silence. In fact, he was relieved when they reached the road that took them down into Leppington. He tried to think of something complimentary to say about the place. All that came to him was the old joke: 'The only good thing to come out of Leppington is the train to Whitby.'

No, not diplomatic. Think of something else. He was still thinking hard when he pulled up outside the Station Hotel.

4

Electra idly sipped a vodka and lime in the bar. She sat on a bar stool, chatting to her barman. Thursday nights were generally quiet. Tonight wasn't going to take anyone by surprise. A few regulars had drifted in. It was a far cry from the Goth Communion nights when the place pulsed with music and the building was full of men and women clad in black with their hair dyed darker than raven feathers.

Close on eight a couple came in. They were in their late teens, she guessed. They had interesting body language.

They're in love with each other, she mused, *only they don't know it yet.* Electra lit a cigarette as the tall young man pulled out his wallet. He had a handsome face and his hair was longer than was considered the norm round here but he had a local accent. *An individual*, she decided. *Not your conventional Leppington teenager. I've not seen him before. Or his friend. Not girlfriend, though, she's not that – yet.* The girl was pretty, with a high forehead and curly hair. She wore a long woollen coat that was a subtle shade of honey. Very elegant. And it was very touching how, when one of them wasn't looking at the other, the unobserved one watched their companion closely. Almost anxiously. *They* are *in love with each other*, Electra thought. But neither dared to make the first move.

Electra pulled on her cigarette, feigning interest in the menu chalked on the board at the back of the bar.

The young man was talking to the girl. *Maybe he's an artist of some sort*, Electra thought. *Musician? Painter?*

'Vikki, what would you like to drink?'

'White wine, please.'

He ordered the wine and an orange juice for himself.

'Dylan?' the girl asked. (*The girl's called Vikki*, Electra told herself.) 'Did you find Luke's car?'

'No. Nothing.'

'He could have parked it in a side street.'

'Not Luke Spencer. He loves that car. He'd want to keep it as close as possible to him.'

'Could he be staying in the hotel?'

'He might be. But there's no way of telling.'

'You could ask at reception.'

You can ask, dear, Electra thought, *but I won't tell. We respect client confidentiality. But then, you shouldn't be eaves-dropping, Electra dear. Now, isn't that another sign of rampant loneliness?*

The two took their drinks to a table. It became harder to hear their conversation. They looked shy and ill at ease with one another. Even so, a powerful magnetism drew them together.

Yes, indeed, love is like that, Electra told herself, sipping her drink. *It picks you up and throws you into the arms of people you couldn't possibly have dreamed of even liking – never mind surrendering your body to them – and sets you adrift in the other physical and emotional waters that go with it.* Electra let her gaze stray to the mirror where she could see the pair's reflection. The girl, Vikki, took sips of her wine. She seemed calm but whenever the young man, Dylan, looked away from her, she watched him with a nervous intensity that suggested she was startled by, even afraid of her own thoughts.

Yes, you've got it bad, my girl. Now you're wondering if he's feeling those same emotions – those same powerful and disturbing emotions as you. For a moment Electra toyed with the notion of going across to introduce herself. She could chat with them, gain their confidence.

And what? Play matchmaker? Wait until the young man returned to the bar for another drink and whisper to Vikki, 'You do realize that he's crazy about you?' The scenario appealed to her. As well as brightening a dull evening, she'd be doing the pair a favour, wouldn't she? She turned her head a little to catch a few stray words of their conversation.

'. . . Best check the cottages.'

'You sure Luke will be there? He might have driven through to . . .'

Electra didn't hear the destination.

'Vikki, you can bet your bottom dollar that he'll be with a girl in one of the cottages.'

Vikki said something that Electra didn't catch.

'Luke's desperate to get a place at college. If he misses out, he'll have to find a job.'

The girl mentioned something that included the words 'design' and 'illustration'.

Ah, so there is *an art connection somewhere in there.*

Dylan said, 'It won't be what he's wanting to do. He'll wind up helping his dad on the farm.'

'Well, we'd best find him, then.' Vikki drained her glass, leaving a blush of her lipstick on the rim. Dylan finished his orange juice in a couple of hefty swigs.

So they were leaving in search of the elusive Luke. A pity; Electra stubbed out the cigarette. *I'd have loved to play the role of Aphrodite for the evening.*

The couple walked out of the bar. Dylan, smiling charmingly if shyly, made a point of opening the door for his friend.

Good luck. I hope you find a way to light the flame.

Setting her glass down on the bar, Electra nodded at the barman. 'Same again, Tony.'

5

They ticked off the list of Luke's love nests pretty quickly. Most of the cottages were in darkness, with no sign of Luke's flame-red Ford parked nearby. Winter kept most tourists away, but there were a couple of cottages with sturdier tenants. Although one glance at the car parked outside each of those was enough for Dylan to shake his head and say, 'No, not this one.'

He worked his way back along the narrow country lanes to Morningdale. After a while, he clicked his tongue. 'It looks as if Luke's going to end up working on the farm by June.'

'You've tried his mobile again?'

He nodded. 'Switched off. Whatever this girl's got it's dynamite.'

'You don't think something's happened to him?'

Dylan concentrated on the steep descending bend. 'If he'd had an accident we'd know by now.'

'Maybe he's got married.'

'Luke!' He laughed. 'He'd only get married by accident. Or at gunpoint.'

'Where next?' Vikki looked at the list Dylan had pencilled on a notepad.

'It's on the far side of the valley. Out near Lazarus Deep.'

6

The earpiece pressed against David's ear felt hot. When the person answered he ran through the same words he'd used more than a dozen times before.

'Hello, my name's David Leppington. I'm a friend of Katrina West. You haven't seen her today by any chance, have you?'

He was getting used to the reply, too. Either the person was understandably wary of talking to a stranger on the telephone or sometimes they were more relaxed. 'No, I haven't seen her lately.' Or a work colleague: 'No, it's strange because she was supposed to be at work today and she hasn't phoned in sick.'

7

The pub in Bloomsbury was pretty much like any other London pub with its tables and chairs and bar in dark brown wood that bore the beer-patina of over a hundred years of use. The second you walked through the door your nostrils were filled with those unmistakable odours of tobacco and alcohol. Bernice Mochardi preferred the lighter and airier bars of the

West End but the upper room of the Princess Louise drew like-minded souls.

Ignoring the stares of the middle-aged men leaning against the bar, she bought a glass of red wine and took it upstairs. She found herself smiling. Wondering how long it would take for her friends to see through her disguise.

Well, hardly a disguise, she told herself. *I've given myself a make-over.* She'd got rid of those troublesome eyebrows and drawn in more symmetrical dark lines with a cosmetic pencil; then she'd gone mad with purple eyeshadow and nail gloss, and with head-to-toe black clothes. What was more, she'd dyed her hair a deeper raven black that now glinted subtle flashes of indigo; add to that white face make-up, crimson lipstick, kohl for her eyes (applied in the traditional Arabian way by placing the powder by brush directly onto the eyeball so that the moisture would naturally distribute the black dust around the edge of the eye – yes, uncomfortable as it sounded it looked a hundred times better than eyeliner). All in all, she was pleased with the effect that her afternoon spent in the bathroom had produced. She'd radically changed her appearance, and the new boots she'd bought that morning added just the right level of frisson to her Goth-erotic chic.

Bernice slipped into the pub's upper room without any fanfare. She wanted to see how long it took for anyone to recognize her. Inwardly she was smiling, yet outwardly she kept a straight face.

Even though it was early evening the room was swarming with people – most dressed in black and with a super-abundance of leather, lace, corsetry and jet jewellery. This was the in place for people who were into outsider fashions and arts. It was a place where Bernice could talk to her heart's content to fellow footwear fanatics. Straight away she recognized the four men and a girl who were in the Goth band Cuspidor. There was also a smattering of writers and artists.

One of the band pulled from a case a small stringed instrument; it was something like a lute or balalaika, and he began to pick the strings with his black glossed nails, playing an exotic-sounding melody. It wasn't meant to be a formal performance – he was probably just showing the instrument to his friends – but most people stopped to listen. They smiled and nodded their heads, enjoying the helter-skelter of notes that evoked Arabian sunsets.

Bernice relaxed, listening to the music. A few people she knew glanced her way but she could tell from their expressions (or lack of such) that they didn't recognize her under all the Vampira make-up. Now her smile was hard to conceal. She'd intended to walk across and reveal her identity (no doubt to their shrieks of surprise), only now she found herself enjoying her new-found anonymity among all these people she'd known for months. Besides, she was sure someone would recognize her in a moment.

So she sipped her wine, listened to the music and watched her friends drinking, smoking and chatting in what amounted to their club. In fact, Bernice began to feel increasingly like some phantom that, although it was present in a crowded room, couldn't be seen.

Yes. I'm invisible. I see you, but you don't see me. A secret smile reached her lips. This was an unusual but strangely enticing experience . . . even a little voyeuristic.

There's Rachel, Eleanor and Thomas sharing a joke, and Joel showing Ben his sketch for a CD cover . . . they glance at me but don't know who I am.

Surely I've not changed my face and hair that much, have I? I was in here only last week. Joel bought me a glass of champagne to celebrate his first commission; so why doesn't anyone recognize me?

They don't recognize me because I'm not really here. I'm a ghost.

A shiver of such icy magnitude crawled up Bernice's back-bone that the wine glass jerked in her hand, spilling a few blood-red drops onto her bare wrist.

A ghost? Come on, Bernice, your head's playing tricks on you. They don't recognize you because you look like Dracula's tart, sitting here in all that make-up.

Even so, she felt an eerie sense of unease now. It was as if her friends really couldn't see her. What was more, she didn't feel as if she belonged here any more. Even though she was physically present in the room it seemed as if she'd been sealed off somehow in her own little sphere.

The sensation of separation from this familiar and friendly place struck Bernice with a chilling power. Her blood ran cold beneath her skin; she found herself trembling. She knew that she could break the spell if she sashayed across to Joel and the rest and made some joke along the lines of 'Guess what I've come as?' but now she could hardly breathe, never mind speak. Instead, wave after wave of panic and dread swept through her.

What's happening to me? Am I going mad? First, I'm so restless that I can't sit still and want to change my career and how I look. Now this. I'm in the same room as my friends, yet they can't even see me. I'm invisible. I'm a ghost. I've been dead for years and no one remembers me . . .

No, stop this, she told herself. *You're letting your imagination run wild. Just get outside for a breath of fresh air, then come back in again and da-dah! Say, 'Look at this. Bernice Mochardi as you've never seen her before!'*

Only when she got outside into the cold night air she couldn't face going back into the pub. She didn't know why, but the experience of not being recognized was more deeply unsettling than she could say. Instead she walked home, intent on a hot bath and an early night. Even though Bernice walked so fast that the heels of her boots clicked like a frenzied heartbeat, she couldn't shake off the question that stalked her.

*What if I had gone back inside to my friends, cried out 'It's me!' and they **still** hadn't recognized me?*

8

Marnie Loftus drove along the road that skirted the north side of Lazarus Deep. She was pushing the old car hard as music pounded from the speakers. There was a Chinese takeaway in the carrier bag looped over the gearstick. (Boy, the times she'd got home to find the cartons tipped up and the sauce pooled out in the bottom of the bag.) She kept the speed up along the country lanes so that she'd get the Chinese meal home still hot and steaming . . . and, by heaven, that garlic and black bean sauce smelled good.

The car's lights shone dazzlingly against drystone walls. Every so often they sent a shaft of silver across the dead flat surface of the lake itself. Rabbits scuttled away in front of her. Once she saw the sly eyes of a fox glinting emerald from the grass verge. Frozen puddles bounced light away to illuminate grotesquely deformed trees.

'Come on, baby, come on, baby.' Marnie nursed the car round sharp bends, over humpback bridges, down under railway lines, then back toward the lake again. That took a cool nerve as well. The road appeared to run directly to the water's edge. Tourists often feared their car would plunge into the lake but at the last moment the road flicked back on itself.

A pair of figures stood at one side of the road. For all the world it looked as if they were waiting for her. They even stared into her face as she passed by. She glanced back through the rear-view mirror at the two peculiar-looking forms.

'That's Luke Spencer,' Marnie said aloud, surprised. 'Why isn't he wearing any shoes?'

CHAPTER 8

I

From **Hotel Midnight**:
My name is Electra. I fought vampires. If I don't write that
at least once a week my head will explode. At least, that's
what it feels like. 'Vampire' is a convenient term for those
creatures that crawled like maggots under the town where I
still live. Those vampires lusted after more than blood. They
lusted after power. They had a craving to dominate human
beings. In life they were driven by their Viking obsession to
conquer. In death that obsession was fused into their bones
and muscle tissue.

My friends and I won. We destroyed the vampires. At least,
that was what we were allowed to believe . . .

2

'Is that it?' Vikki's eyes widened.

'That's it. The last one. Lazarus Wake.'

'If ever there was a haunted house, that's the one. Just look
at those ugly windows. They're like eyes.'

'Don't you love the house name? Lazarus Wake.'

'Yeah, who said that they didn't have a sense of humour
in . . .' He saw her look at the carved stone slab above the house
door. '1727,' she read the inscription. '*Lazarus Wake. Raised by
Magnus Leppington, a True Believer. Dedicated to my god. To his
FURY, and to the*—Uh, I can't make out the rest.'

Dylan Adams peered through the car's windscreen. The house gleamed in the glare of the headlights. Its stone walls were as white as skull bone. Vikki had been right about those windows, too. Gigantic eye sockets that glistened darkly with antique glass.

You better be holed up here, Luke, old buddy, or you can kiss that college place goodbye.

'Lazarus Wake . . .' Vikki said, looking at the house as if it would suddenly lunge forward and bite her. 'Why call it Lazarus Wake?'

'Lazarus was raised from the dead by Christ. And just through those trees you can see Lazarus Deep.'

'Sounds pretty morbid.'

'Like the inscription. Do you think the guy who built it was making a point when he wrote "god" with a small *g* and "his" with a small "h"?'

'He must have had a hell of a sense of humour.' She shivered. 'He doesn't say "built by". He writes "raised by".'

'Maybe it was considered the height of wit in 1727.'

'Maybe.'

Dylan smiled. 'People probably came from miles around to see it and have a really good belly laugh, just where we're sitting now.'

'Beats sitting in front of the television.'

'Of course, old Magnus Leppington would have thought they were laughing at him so he'd come running out of the house to rip out their lungs.'

'Dylan . . . don't,' Vikki warned. 'It's scary enough as it is.'

'This? It's just a holiday cottage.'

'Just a holiday cottage to you, but I'm going to have bad dreams about this tonight.'

He touched her arm. 'I'll protect you.'

'Hey. Where are you going?'

Dylan opened the car door. 'I'm just going to check if Luke's here.'

'There's no lights.'

He smiled at her. Her hair glinted in the glow of the courtesy light. She did look good. 'Luke's probably doing whatever he's doing in the dark.'

'And no car?' Vikki sounded nervous. She really *didn't* like being out here in the dark.

'There's a garage round the back. He might have put the car out of sight.'

'Dylan . . .'

'Don't worry. Stay in the car where it's warm. I'll be back in a minute.'

'Come running if you hear me scream, won't you?'

He saw her eyes; they were large and luminous-looking. 'If you need me, just pucker up and whistle.'

'Pucker up and whistle? Don't worry – I'll make sure you hear me, all right.' She pointed at the house. 'Now, find Luke and let's get out of here.'

Dylan reached into the side compartment of the car door and pulled out a hefty flashlight. *Morningdale's that kind of frontier town*, he thought wryly. *Everyone carries flashlights, shovels and Wellington boots in their car.*

'OK, Magnus Leppington. Let's take a peek in your windows,' he muttered. *My God, it's freezing!* Dylan's face and fingers burned with the cold. He could imagine the atmosphere itself sliding across the ground in a miasma of icy blue. Chilling spikes of air passed through his clothes as if they weren't there.

You owe me for this, Luke, he thought crossly. *You owe me big time.* He switched on the flashlight, pushing back the shadows. The front door loomed in front of him. A massive thing, banded with iron, with black studs and huge Gothic hinges.

Welcome to the ghost house, he told himself. *Who'd ever want to stay in this monstrosity? Especially on a bleak winter night.* It was in the middle of nowhere. There were no other houses out here. Lazarus Deep, away through the trees, looked as inviting as a slab of ice. Dylan clenched his fist and pounded on the door.

From inside came the sound of running feet.

2

Dylan stepped back when he heard the noise of footsteps in the house. It sounded odd. *That's not someone merely hurrying, that's someone moving at a full-blooded run.* The sound of running feet grew louder; they were coming toward the door, but then they suddenly *receded* into the depths of the house. He knocked again, half expecting to be confronted with some irate tenant demanding to know who was damn well hammering on the door at this time of night. But the footsteps retreated deep into the heart of the house. Then they fell silent.

Dylan leaned forward, his head turned to one side, trying to catch any sounds coming through that formidable door. There was nothing now so he stood back to scan the deep-set windows. No lights. No movement. No one twitching a curtain so they could peep out to see who was belabouring the door.

Nothing.

'Luke,' he called. 'Luke, is that you?' The breeze carried his voice away. He glanced back at the car. Vikki sat watching him, an expression of anxiety on her face.

This place did have an aura . . . a bad aura. His instincts told Dylan to get back to the car. Drive away. There was time to find a pub with a roaring fire. What he wouldn't give for a beer and to sit hip to hip with the gorgeous Vikki. Not this. Trailing round the countryside for his AWOL friend. Luke had gone off on some erotic frolic of his own. *Leave him to it. It's not your fault if he loses the college place. You did your best.*

Dylan was ready to quit this search. Return to the warmth of the car . . . and the heart-warming company of Vikki. Only—

Only he knew that his conscience would nag him ragged if he didn't at least check the garage. If the car there wasn't Luke's then no doubt Dylan had just gone and disturbed some winter holidaymaker. Maybe the tenant liked to hang around the house naked; or maybe they were dabbling in marijuana hocus-pocus. That was probably why they'd scuttled upstairs where they couldn't be seen. *And that's certainly none of my business,* Dylan told himself. *Once I'm done checking the garage I'm away from here. Then maybe I can spend some time with Vikki.* He shrugged in Vikki's direction, miming that he couldn't get a reply at the door, that he was going round the back.

With the flashlight's beam swinging away in front of him, he followed the path round the house. The driveway ran down the steep slope to a garage built into the hillside a good thirty metres from the house. Dylan had been here last summer. A late cancellation meant that Luke had had the place to himself. He'd thrown a party that had gone on for two whole days. Totally crazy days.

Now, in midwinter, the back of the house looked no better than its facade. The same ugly windows glowered from beneath heavy stone brows. He shone the flashlight at the walls. Like those at the front, they could have been built from bones. They were a glistening white. Three hundred years of frost and rain had eaten holes into the stonework. The building's surface looked as if it was suffering from a rash of ulcers. Dylan stepped up onto a garden bench, shining the light into the windows. He saw dead rooms haunted by shadows that slithered across walls as he moved the flashlight from left to right. More shadows thronged the ceilings when he shone it upward. They formed the illusion of fluttering bat wings. Those shades swarmed inside the house. An infestation haunting the rooms, smothering furniture, climbing up over cupboards and shelves.

A cold gust struck Dylan in the back and from there it ran ice fingers through his hair, slid round his neck and chilled him deep into his bones. The winds found the house and screamed at the windows with savage blasts of frigid air. When he swept the flashlight's beam across the windows they seemed to blink back at him. As if they were noticing him at last.

The man who'd built the place had long since gone to bones in his grave, but he'd reflected his malignant personality in the house. This was a place that could tell evil tales. Whisper about ugly things that had been done inside those walls. Dylan's heart thudded.

When he looked at the house his imagination flooded his head with mental pictures that seemed to have leaked from the lower depths of his brain. Those pock-marked walls sucked them in like so many ulcerated, gluttonous lips. His mind's eye raced through rooms just as those running feet had done. Speeding through the darkened corridors, up the stairs, through total absolute blackness that blossomed darkly with purple blooms of deeper shadow. The dust of people long dead floated down from where it had rested on ceiling beams and in the cold timber joints. This was the epidermal dust of men and women who'd lived here. Who'd mated in eighteenth-century and Victorian beds. Whose passions had been powered by the malignant trace left by Leppington.

They mated ferociously; women gave birth in tsunamis of blood and pain. Then the men fed their sons and daughters to the well in the kitchen. Because the stream flowing through the well flowed into Lazarus Deep. At night they rose . . . up from the depths . . . up the well stream . . . migrating night creatures, with bodies cold as eels . . . they needed to feed on the warm, sweet blood of children who were kicking in the water at the bottom of the well.

Daddy fed him to the pit. The little boy's screams and his frantic thrashing in the water brought them to—

The gale smashed into the back of Dylan's head. He stumbled forward from the bench, unable to stop himself. A raging torrent of air, cold as grave dirt, gripped him. His arms windmilled to keep his balance, making the flashlight's beam slash at trees that stood in grim Gothic columns, the grinning face of a statue . . . Magnus Leppington frozen in stone. *His bones rot in a grave but he preserved his likeness here . . .*

Damn. The force of the gale sucked the air from Dylan's lungs. He gasped, trying to capture that cold blue air. Wind groaned through the trees; it screamed from the house. Terrible screams. As though someone was being murdered in there.

The force of the wind shoved Dylan face forward against the house. His face slammed against a pane of glass.

On the other side a face looked back. The eyes were wide. Two splinters of glistening yellow. The mouth yawned in a vast 'O' shape. He saw teeth, the dark well of a throat. Skin that was as white as milk. He even saw the delicate tracing of veins around the eyes, as if a spider's web of blue had formed there.

He recoiled from the face at the other side of the window. Simultaneously it drew back into the pool of deep shadow inside the house.

Dylan forced his way through the storm. An overwhelming sense of danger gripped him. Someone was here. They would attack if he stayed. The very air pulsated with threat. That same sense of menace oozed from the sucking mud beneath his feet.

The gale changed direction, pushing at his back. He found himself blundering through bushes that swayed drunkenly.

Tree branches swept down toward him, goblin hands with hooked claws that scratched at his face. He swung round a clump of bushes to see a figure. It lunged forward, arms outstretched. Its teeth were bared.

Using the flashlight like a club he slashed at the shape.

'*Dylan!*'

At the last minute he turned the blow so that the flashlight slashed through a thorn bush by Vikki's head.

'Dylan. Are you all right— *What's wrong?*' He saw Vikki's hands seize his arms, only now the action seemed distant, as if he was watching events from the house. 'Dylan!'

Then his mind snapped back into focus. He sensed the cold air on his face and the way she gripped him. Dear God, what on Earth had been going through his mind?

I went mad back there. I was completely out of it.

He shuddered as he recalled the images that had flown past his mind's eye. Parents dropping their children down the well inside the house. White figures in the water at the bottom of the well, lunging at the screaming children. Hell, it had been so blisteringly vivid, like—

'Dylan. Do you feel all right?'

He took a deep breath. 'Fine. I lost my balance back there . . . It's blowing a hurricane.'

'Any sign of Luke?'

Dylan remembered the face at the window.

He shook his head. 'I'll check the garage, but I'm sure he isn't here.'

But someone is. Someone with a face that's as shocking a corpse's . . .

Vikki looked at him. He saw concern there. 'Lucky I shouted. You nearly knocked my head off with that bloody torch.' She gave a strained smile. 'I don't look such a monster, do I?'

He grimaced. 'I'll check the garage.'

Within two minutes he'd opened the door for her to get

into the car. The gales threatened to tear it from the hinges. A moment later he'd climbed into the driver's seat. He put his hand on the key to start the engine. Vikki rested her hand on his to stop him.

'I have to tell you, Dylan, I was scared out of my wits, sitting here alone in the car.'

'You should have whistled.' He smiled, feeling easier in his mind now.

'I did.'

'Sorry, I didn't hear.'

She looked at him. He saw her purse her lips and whistle softly.

Dylan found that the smile on his face came naturally. 'You don't have to whistle now. I'm here.'

'But you said I should whistle if I wanted something.'

'What do you want?'

'This, for a start.' She leaned toward him.

He felt her lips touch his. Everything else in the world seemed hard and brutally cold. Everything except her lips. They were soft and warm. Beautifully warm.

3

Katrina wrote the letter to her ex-lover on the train. She posted it at her destination station.

Dear David,

You are an intelligent man. Somehow you will know by now that I have stopped taking my medication. It made my head muzzy. I think far more clearly without it.

Thirteen years ago you stole my heart. I know you brought it here to hide it in your secret place. It is my heart, Dr David Leppington. I want it back. When I have it back I know my head will be all straight again. They will take 'schizophrenia'

*– that ugly, ugly word – from my medical file and throw it
from the train.*

*Train drain. That sounds right, doesn't it, David? Train.
Drain. Brain. Schizoid lady brain.*

*See, David, stealer of hearts, my mind is unchained. I'm
free of you and the other bloodsuckers.*

Yours, with profound affection,
Katrina

For a moment she'd wondered if there were savage teeth
behind the slot of the postbox; she was afraid they'd bite
her hand when she posted the letter. But she was too quick
for them.

She'd have to stay quick. All those biting, bloodsucking
mouths that lurk in wait for you in bathrooms, bedrooms,
postboxes, cupboards, coat pockets, hiding behind lovers'
lips . . .

Still reciting the list of dangerous places, Katrina walked
across the station forecourt to the road. There, swelling out
of the ground to blot out a quarter of the night sky, was the
Station Hotel. She looked up at the forbidding towers that
stood at each corner of the building.

*I've come to your town, David. The town that has the same
name as you. Leppington.*

Leppington holds all those stolen hearts.

The church clock struck ten.

4

David had an early night. Lack of sleep, plus the telephone
search for Katrina, had left him shattered. He closed his
eyes as the radiant numbers on the clock radio flicked over
to 10:01.

That night was the first time in years he'd dreamed about

Jack Black. The man stood beside him on the edge of the lake. He reached up with those tattooed hands to the open wound in his throat. He seized the bloody flaps and pulled them wide open, stretching the skin apart until it formed a void as wide as an open doorway. Blood-red layers of flesh slid back to expose a face with lightly closed eyes.

Revolted, David saw that it was Katrina's face.

Her eyes snapped open. 'You've been looking for me, David. I was here all along.' She smiled. 'Kiss me.' The face lunged forward from the grotesque wound.

The dream images exploded into dazzling fragments. Those fragments, he realized, were stars. They streamed overhead. He flew through the night sky. Instead of arms he had the long black wings of a raven. Beneath him lay a lake. Not far from it stood a house on a hillside. A lonely, ugly house whose appearance frightened him more than he could say.

He plunged down toward it. Now he could make out windows with heavy lintels that formed forbidding brows in stone that was as white as bone. Moonlight shone on the slate roof in a mass of eerie lights. A face peered from one of the windows. In a car on the driveway a couple were kissing.

The dream raven sped downward, plunging *into* the roof, on down through the rooms (those dark and terrible rooms where men and women had screamed at things that had stirred from the shadows), down through the floor, through foundations, down into the caves where subterranean rivers flowed. Even in the dream, shadows deepened so that the sleeping David Leppington could not identify what moved through the labyrinth that was as dark as heart-blood . . .

5

Dylan was the one to break the kiss. The clock on the dash read 10:02.

Vikki grimaced. 'I shouldn't have done that, should I?'

He smiled. 'It's not that.'

'What, then? You're seeing someone and I've just put my foot in it?'

'No.' He nodded at the bone-white house visible through the windscreen. 'There's someone in there. They might be watching.'

'Oh, my God.' This time she couldn't help laughing. 'I thought the house was empty.'

'It has a guest. He looked – I don't know – odd.'

'Let's get out of here, then – pronto, pronto.'

Despite the shock – that weird, weird shock – of a few minutes ago he found he had a wild grin across his face. 'Drink?'

'Love one.'

He started the car, turned it, then sped through the wood toward the gates that belonged to Lazarus Wake.

'Don't look back,' he told Vikki as she twisted in the seat to watch the house retreat.

She smiled. 'Why not?'

'You might turn into a pillar of salt.' He said it in a jokey kind of way, but even so . . .

Dylan drove for five minutes, long enough to put a couple of miles between the car and that godforsaken house (with its weird tenant). Then he pulled over at the side of the road where fields fell away to his left, while to his right moorland sloped up toward a starry sky.

'What's wrong?' she asked.

'Nothing.'

'Why have we stopped, then?'

'No reason.'

'No reason?'

'No, no reason.'

Dylan realized the truth. They were talking nonsense.

Because it wasn't what they said that mattered, it was the way they looked at each other. Her eyes were shining, her face lit by a succession of beautiful smiles.

'Wotcha stopped for, then?' Vikki asked again, with a shoulder-scrunching giggle.

'I'm going to kiss you.'

'No . . .' She laughed, turning her head away from his, her hand stroking her hair back. 'No, you're embarrassing me. Look, I've gone all shy.'

She turned her head away to look out of the side window. After a few seconds, she slowly turned to look back. His gaze was drawn to her mouth. The smile told him what he wanted to know. He slid his hand through her hair to find the back of her neck. At the same time she rested her palms against the side of his face, stroking it gently.

Then she tilted her head as if to say, *'Well, what are you waiting for?'*

He leaned forward and touched his lips against hers. She opened her mouth. When he kissed her he forgot all about the search for Luke, the college, the job interview, Lazarus Wake . . .

6

It was nothing out of the ordinary. Automatically, Electra noted the time of the new arrival. 10:03. The woman must have arrived on that evening's last train into Leppington.

'You'll find it pretty quiet here tonight,' Electra told her. 'There's a Chinese restaurant just outside to your left if you're hungry. Or I can bring a sandwich up to your room.'

'I'm fine, thanks.' The woman smiled. 'I'll be happy with a cup of hot chocolate and bed.'

'There's everything you need for a hot drink in the room.

Now . . .' Electra indicated an open page in the register. 'All I need is your name and address.'

Electra noticed the woman write her name, Katrina West, followed by a London address.

Katrina?

Katty? Kitty? Even Trina?

Electra always ran guests' names through her mind like they were musical notes. She imagined what their loved ones called them. *Katz? Kat?*

She's beautiful, Electra told herself. *Mid to late twenties. Hard to tell, really. Tightly curled hair. Looks natural rather than perm. High cheekbones. Almost as tall as me. She could be a catwalk model taking a break from the maelstrom of London life. No wedding ring. Does your boyfriend miss you tonight? Or is the relationship over and you're here to simply let the wind blow that man right out of your hair?*

Her eyes did have a certain lustre. Had she been crying on the journey up here?

This one had a certain strength in that aristocratic jaw. She'd hold her chin up while gazing out of the window. The tears would come but she wouldn't crumble . . . *My God, Electra, why do you always imagine yourself into other people's lives?*

Electra smiled as she handed the woman (Katrina, Katz, Katty?) the hotel room key. 'Welcome to the Station Hotel. Do you know Leppington?'

The woman flinched as if Electra had made some overly personal comment.

Strange. Guilty conscience?

'Oh, the *town*.' The woman picked up her holdall. 'No, first time I've been.'

'Leppington's very quiet, very peaceful. Some might take that as a euphemism for dead boring, yet it has its subtle charms.' Electra winced. 'Goodness, I sound like a tourist board video.'

'I'm sure Leppington's just what the doctor ordered.'

'Well, if you need anything for your room, or want any directions to places of interest, please don't hesitate to ask.'

'Thank you.'

'Don't mention it, we always take care of our guests.' Electra smiled. 'All the details about breakfast and other snippets of useful information will be on the card on your bedside table.'

'Oh, there *is* one thing.'

'Yes?' Electra smiled her bright receptionist smile. Again, years of practice had gone into perfecting that one. *She's going to ask how to work the shower or order a newspaper; the same old—*

Instead: 'Leppington. Do you know how it got its name?'

Strange question. Electra maintained the smile. 'It's an old Viking name. It became Anglicized down through the years; originally it was called Leppingsvalt.'

Katrina gave a pleasant smile. 'I'm always curious about place names.'

'Leppingsvalt was the name of the Viking chieftain who conquered the whole valley. He claimed he was the son of the god Thor.' *Damn, Electra, she doesn't want the whole lecture.* 'Sorry, local history's my weakness.'

'Isn't that men all over?' Katrina's eyes twinkled as she smiled. 'Their egos are so big that they can't even bring themselves to believe they're merely mortal like the rest of us.'

'Oh, how true,' Electra said with feeling.

Good heavens, she told herself, surprised. *Fate might have just brought me one of life's spiritual allies.*

7

10:04. Bernice dreamed of Jack Black. She hadn't dreamed about him for years. He led her through trees to the edge of a lake. He looked back at her with those powerful eyes that had frightened and fascinated her so much. He beckoned to her, then pointed into the water. When she saw what was there she shouted herself awake.

Her neck muscles were stiff because she'd dozed off in the armchair. On the television screen a man was loping after a woman along an alleyway. It was night; a mist drifted between the woman and her pursuer. Bernice turned off the television quickly. She didn't need horror films to give her more nightmares, especially after the unsettling trip to the pub that evening, when even her closest friends hadn't recognized her. No, it was time for bed.

My lonely bed, she thought. *Why can't I find myself a man?*

She switched off the light and lay watching shadows chase each other across the ceiling. It was only the reflection of car lights outside but she didn't like them. Too spidery by half.

A moment later she switched the light back on and slept with it burning all night.

8

The church clock chimed the half-hour over the frosted rooftops of the town. Electra switched on the computer in the corner of her bedroom. Ten-thirty. It was that time of the night again. The morning was many, many long hours away. *So what to do, old girl?*

Vodka?

That stuff doesn't work any more.

Those brightly coloured tablets in the medicine cabinet?

Too many side effects. I've lost interest in watching my face melting away in the dressing-table mirror, anyway. And don't even mention the constipation those things induce. No, it has to be your constant friend. The Internet.

She checked her e-mails. *One's from your mystery buddy,* she told herself as she saw the name Rowan appear with his e-mail address. 'Here goes . . .' She took a deep breath and clicked the mouse.

Dear Electra,

They came back tonight with a bright light that they shone at me through the window. I'm ashamed to say it but I hid myself away in an attic room where there were no windows. I'm not too proud, either, to admit that I wept like a child. But this fear is like a fist brutally crushing me. I can't think. All I can do is run and hide, then cry so much my eyes burn.

But tonight, dreadful though it was, I made a discovery. No, call it two discoveries. In the attic – in the corner that I hid myself in – I found a padded envelope. It had been sealed with tape and from its position, right under the eaves where the sloping ceiling met the floorboards, I figure it's been deliberately hidden there. Inside the envelope was a computer disk. On the disk itself someone has written the words

READ ME

And get this: there is a scrap of paper inside. Someone seems to have scribbled down an address in a tearing hurry. You know, in a way it scares me, but I wonder if the address is the location of this house where I live in the grip of this amnesia or lunacy or whatever it is. Please, Electra, if you are willing to make the journey, come to the address. I'll write it in full below. Somehow I know that you can help me.

The address is:-

LAZARUS WAKE
MOOR TOP LANE
MORNINGDALE
NORTH YORKSHIRE

CHAPTER 9

I

'Well.'

'Well?'

'Well, what?

'What now?'

As Dylan drove Vikki home they found themselves exchanging smiles. He loved the way her eyes twinkled in the light from the dashboard.

Something's happened, he told himself, his heart beating hard. *Something powerful.* They could hardly string a sensible sentence together. But it didn't matter what they were saying – it was the looks and smiles and glances that were significant. Either life had suddenly got better or it had got madly more complicated. The future had become a whole kaleidoscope of possibilities. Vikki. The interview in London. Exam finals.

'This is my stop,' she said. The smile on her face lit Dylan up inside.

'Will you be on the eight o'clock train tomorrow?'

'Not tomorrow. I'm up at the visitors' centre in Danby. We're making a presentation to some councillors.'

'Good luck with it.'

Damn. He was surprised by the depth of disappointment he felt at the prospect of not seeing her at the station in the morning.

As he stopped the car she opened the door. 'I enjoyed it tonight, Dylan.'

'Trailing round the countryside looking for Luke Spencer can't have been much fun.'

'You know what I mean,' she told him. Then she paused. 'So, what now?'

'I planned on going to the cinema tomorrow night to see—'

'Great. Pick me up at seven?'

'Wait.' He laughed. 'You don't know what the film is yet.'

'Doesn't matter. See you tomorrow night.'

Dylan watched Vikki go up to the house where she lived with her parents. Just as she let herself in through the front door, she shot him another of those cheerful, eye-twinkling smiles. Then she closed the door behind her. For a moment he sat in the car. Blood roared in his ears. His heart still pounded.

At last he found the word to express what he was feeling. *'Wow.'*

With the time nearing eleven Dylan made the five-minute journey home and parked the car on the drive. He noticed the raven sitting on the roof above his bedroom window but the memory of the evening with Vikki still filled his head and he didn't give the bird a second thought. The raven watched him as he walked up the path to the front door. It gave a cry that echoed over the village. Then it stretched its wings and shook them before flapping away above the rooftops. A night-black shape that, just for a moment, blotted out the moon.

2

Electra Charnwood heard the chimes of both eleven o'clock and midnight pass. A haunting sound that shivered on the air. The town of Leppington lay dead to the world outside. Buildings became crouching beasts in the dark. Ice crystals formed on her windows. They refracted the view, so that the distorting effect created beyond her room a ghost world where mysterious shapes prowled the nightlands of the surrounding moors and winged creatures slid through the sky toward the hotel with ominous intent.

This happened every night. The threat of danger oozed out of the earth. High on the hills the Iron Age burial mounds bulged obscenely. In her mind's eye she saw dead hands clawing their way through a membrane of roots of grass, nettles and wild hemlock. Everything that was dead in the world rebelled against its own absence of life. Deceased beings lusted for a vitality they could not have. They craved the warm blood of the living. Down in coffins in the graveyard men and women who'd passed their own blood down to Electra along the biological line of Charnwoods beat on the undersides of coffin lids with bone knuckles.

The bloodline isn't a gift. It's a loan. They need it back. Her dead forebears had given their children life – now they wanted their descendants to give life back to them. The dead Leppingtons would be restless, too.

Electra, go to the graveyard. Cut open a vein in your wrist. Pour it onto the graves. Give it back before they—

'Damn!'

These long night-time hours were a curse when she couldn't sleep. She wrenched open a drawer in the dressing table and pulled out a bottle of vodka that was nestling among some silk scarves. Gripping the top between finger and thumb she spun it loose and splashed some clear liquor into a glass tumbler.

'Come on,' she whispered to the spirit. 'Work your magic for me.' As she raised the glass to her lips musical chimes sounded softly from the speakers.

Electra, you have mail! Thank God – anything to stop her hiding in the damn vodka bottle.

'Oh, so it's you again,' she murmured as she read the e-mail address. 'He's going to ask me to come to the rescue . . . cue tall lady on white charger.' *Yes, Electra. Can't you just see yourself driving across to Lazarus Deep at this time of night? Out on the lonely moors in the dark, looking for a man who might simply be trying to tempt you to his house . . . a lonely house where screams wouldn't be heard.*

She gave a grim smile. 'Ever one for the melodramatic turn of phrase, aren't you, Electra dear?' But then, she knew the area around Lazarus Deep reasonably well.

For God's sake, Jack Black had even taken her there in her dreams.

Again, she felt the grim smile form on her face. It would break the stranglehold of this boredom, though. Driving across the moors in the depths of the night. Searching for the writer of these pleading e-mails. *Think of the excitement.*

Yes, think of the danger, too. He might be a nut. Plenty of those *stalk the Internet.*

Maybe she could just drive out and find the house. Then she could park at a safe distance and watch. Where was it now? She checked the address that she'd copied down: Lazarus Wake, Moor Top Lane . . . (*See, you* are *curious, aren't you? A curious cat, wanting to find out more about the mysterious correspondent.) There you go again. Loneliness makes you do funny things. Funny-bizarre, that is. So do I take a night-time drive to the wonderfully macabre-sounding Lazarus Wake? Ah, the delicious dilemma. Do I risk danger to life, limb and virtue . . . ?*

A sudden snort of laughter escaped her.

Or do I stay here? Where my loneliness is as enduring and as unyielding as the walls that surround me.

Enough of the purple prose, Electra. She took a breath and straightened her back. 'It's decision time, baby.' *Of course, you could just read what he has to say in the e-mail, you idiot.*

She popped open the mailbox.

Dear Electra,

I had to send this to you straight away. Remember how I told you I found a computer disk in the attic, together with the address of this house?

Pow, like lightning . . . like black lightning it nearly tore my head apart. Lazarus Wake. I remember the house now. I remember seeing it, with its peculiar little windows, as I approached along the driveway. There's a weird inscription above the door. I can't remember much about the details, only that the house was built in the seventeen hundreds and that it belonged to someone with a strange name. I can't recall it now. Began with L, I think. But that's beside the point. Electra. My wonderful Electra, who's stayed with me. when I've bombarded her with e-mails. Bizarre e-mails, no doubt. But I'm beginning to remember again. What happened to me – illness, an accident? I don't know, but it's starting to come back. You know, when you're walking through a thick fog and everything's indistinct around you? Trees are just blurred shapes, houses are patches of shadow without edges? Well, I feel as if I'm coming out of a mental fog. Everything's becoming sharper. I do know that my name is Rowan. I know that I had to leave my old home in a hurry . . . but the reason why escapes me.

Wonderful, wonderful Electra. I feel upbeat. I feel alive again. Deliriously alive at that! The weird thing is that I'm not alone in what has happened to me. Strangely, knowing that makes me feel even better. Now, I'm racing ahead of myself. That disk I found. I tried it in my computer and discovered that it contained a document.

It makes astonishing reading . . . Frightening reading at times. But it echoes my own experience so closely. It describes what happened to a family who rented Lazarus Wake. I'm attaching the document to this e-mail. I should warn you, if your responses are anything like mine, you will find it disturbing. You may want to read it in the company of someone you trust, someone to whom you can talk to afterward.

I trust you can open the file on your computer. It's called The Broxley Testament. *As far as I can make out, it details what happened to a family by the name of Broxley who rented the house for Christmas a decade ago. Rick Broxley is a musician. He was using the break to write song lyrics for a new album. It seems his band had enjoyed some success fifteen years before his stay at Lazarus Wake. This was going to be his last chance to make a successful comeback. It was putting a strain on the family; his marriage was suffering. But he staked everything on the new album being a success. If it were, everything would come right again for the Broxley family . . .*

I beg you to have the courage to read The Broxley Testament. *It is important. You'll see what's happened to me in a new light.*

Yours,

Rowan

Not tonight, Electra told herself. Her imagination was active enough. It didn't take much to picture sinister figures lurching along the street toward the hotel. She might read the Broxley document sometime in the future. When her nerves were strong enough to take it.

Then she made her big mistake. When she noticed Rowan had tagged a sentence at the bottom of the e-mail she knew she would have to read about what had happened to the Broxley family.

PS: Electra, my memory is coming back. I can remember the name of the original owner of the house. The name carved in the wall above the front door . . . it's Magnus Leppington.

Oh, my dear God.

A cold breath of wind slid up from the ground over the facade of the hotel. It caressed the carved heads above the room windows before crying into the chimney pots. The sound carried down to her to echo from the fireplace. A shiver ran through her bones as though a ghost had just passed through her, bound for some distant grave.

Now Electra did take a drink of vodka. A deep one. Followed by another. Then, her veins pulsing with dread, she opened the computer file and began to read.

THE BROXLEY TESTAMENT

A Vampiric Lament
by Rick Broxley

MONDAY

This is how it should end. At the edge of the lake with this simple act.

How was I to know it wasn't a way of killing the past? No. It was a beginning.

'*Dad . . . Dad. Stop it!*'

My name is Rick Broxley. I'm standing knee-deep in the lake in midwinter. Lazarus Deep, a name as cold as the water.

'Dad, what are you doing with the guitar?'

'It's called burying a ghost.'

'Dad—'

'Rick . . . Rick, don't you dare—'

There's Dain's mother. She's coming down the hill from the house at a run. She's not even paused to put on her coat; it's still in her hands.

'Rick, come out of the water. *Please!*'

'Don't worry, I know what I'm doing,' I say. 'I'm burying the ghost.'

'Dad, don't—'

It's too late. I won't be talked out of this. I hold the electric guitar in my hands by its neck, with its ivory-white body above my head. Then I swing it as hard as I can.

I hear Abby give a gasp. 'Oh, Jesus.'

The guitar goes end over end, tumbling against the cement-grey sky. Then it's falling. It lands in the lake with a splash; ripples race outward in ever-expanding circles. The water swirls furiously. I see bubbles surge up to whiten the surface. But the guitar's gone. I hope it's taken his ghost with it.

A cold breeze glides across the lake. It makes a bleak and mournful cry among the skeletons of trees. A cry that makes me think of dead things waking in darkness.

Dain can't believe her eyes. She doesn't know whether to laugh or be shocked. But then, she's twelve; minute by minute she swings between giddy laughter and hormonal rage.

'Dad. You idiot! That was Ash White's guitar . . . it's worth thousands!'

Abby stops running. She glares at me. 'Rick, you could have sold that.'

'Call it a rock-and-roll impulse, honey.' I smile but it's no time for smiling. 'And you know we musicians are a crazy breed.'

'Rock-and-roll impulse? Hell, Rick. Don't you realize we need the money?'

'Not that much.'

'Yeah, the car's going to pay its own repair bill. Like the fairies are going to make the overdraft disappear. *Jesus, Rick.*' Her native New Yorker accent grows stronger the angrier she becomes.

'I've told you, Abby. I'll get the car fixed.'

'What? So you can run it into the wall again. I expect we'll get a bill for that as well.'

'Abby, I thought I saw someone standing in the middle of the road.'

'Yeah, I know. Ash White.'

'It looked like him.'

'So you often see people who've been dead ten years?'

'*Missing* ten years.'

'Missing. Dead. What does it matter?'

'Abby—'

'Oh, come out of the lake before you catch pneumonia.'

I wade out of the water, back onto the shore. Lake mud glistens darkly on my legs.

'Dad, your shoes!' Dain's eyes blaze. 'Mom, look at his shoes!'

'Don't worry, Dain. He can buy another pair when we go to Whitby next.' Abby's eyes glitter. She's furious. 'We only have to make money appear out of thin air first.' Sarcasm barbs that New York accent now. 'Or maybe you can swim out there and find the guitar? We might get some cash for it. After all, it did once belong to Ash White—'

'The rock legend. Don't worry. I won't forget it.'

I look back at Lazarus Deep. The lake owns the guitar now. I hope it's deep enough to swallow up Ash's ghost, too. I consider trying to explain to Abby, but she's so angry with me she won't listen. Dain looks from me to her mother. She's expecting fireworks. One of those rows where things get thrown. Maybe another walking-out?

I walk from the shore onto the grass field that runs up to the house. It's best to just head back indoors and change my clothes. If I don't say anything maybe Abby's anger will evaporate. 'I'll cook dinner,' I say.

'Stew again.'

'Casserole.' I do my warmest smile. 'I'll put red wine in . . . make it taste posh.'

Abby comes at me. I think she's so angry that she's going to strike me. Instead, she puts her arm round me. 'Why don't you tell me when something's bothering you?'

'Nothing is now.'

'Then why throw Ash's guitar into the lake?'

'Call it a rite of exorcism.'

She looks up at me. I know she's trying to understand the things I do. She's probably remembering last summer when I went on the brandy-and-pill binge. I'd said the same thing about exorcising ghosts then. Story of my life, huh?

Dain walks ahead of us. 'I don't want any of Dad's stew again. I want to go for a hamburger.'

'Dain, we have to drive miles—'

'Drive miles, then. But I hate those fucking stews.'

'Dain.'

'Makes me want to go *ugh!*' She mimes vomiting onto the ground.

The anger I expect to be aimed at me volleys in Dain's direction. 'You're ungrateful, you know that?' Abby rips into her. 'Your Dad spends hours in that kitchen.'

'With the brandy.'

'He does not. He's cooking perfectly good meals. It's something he enjoys doing.'

'I don't *enjoy* eating them. They taste like shit.'

'Dain, you're getting a filthy mouth, you know? And another thing, you should see the state of your room. Why can't you put anything away?'

'It's a horrible house. I hate it.'

Dear God. They're away again. My muscles clench tight under my skin. There's a bottle of brandy at the back of the pantry. I can see it in my mind's eye. A full bottle of Courvoisier in its sexy bottle.

Those hormones are flooding Dain's arteries, I tell myself. They drive my daughter into a white-hot rage. Just this morning she confessed that she wanted to shout her head off at the lake. This is the big thing in our lives at the moment, whether I like it or not. Dain's building up to her first period. Then she'll be over the menstrual hurdle into womanhood. Her mood swings from blood-red fury to something like giggling hysteria every few minutes. Like her mother, when *she*'s premenstrual, Dain's chosen red clothes to wear. I don't know if it's unconscious symbolism, or a conscious message to the world at large, that soon the blood-tide is going to sweep from her body. Right now I sense that pressure of blood inside her. From the tension on Dain's face, and the bloating of her stomach, I know that it's straining to be unleashed. It depresses me to see her like this.

Dear God. It sounds selfish and uncaring, but this isn't easy. She's gone from affectionate daughter, always ready with a cuddle or a sweet smile, to something close to a raging beast. She slams doors; she throws plates into the sink. Food she's always enjoyed suddenly tastes like shit, she says.

And all I want to do is to sit in front of the computer and write those lyrics. But it's impossible to concentrate when I can hear those stand-up rows between Dain and her mother downstairs. Of course, Abby is so wound up that the slightest thing triggers an explosion of frustration in her. They never tell you when you marry that family life can become a battleground . . . no one takes prisoners. No one gets out of here alive.

Dain picks at the casserole I've made. She's eating the carrots but not touching the meat. Abby has finished and sips her wine before reclining on the sofa, eyes closed. She's thirty-four but already premature lines have formed above her eyebrows. I know that a tension headache has begun to gnaw at her, only she's said nothing yet.

'I'll wash the pots,' I say.

'You don't have to do it yet.' Abby makes herself smile.

'It doesn't matter. I'll listen to the demos again while I do it.'

'OK. And thanks.'

'Don't mention it.'

Abby shoots an eloquent glance at her daughter. 'Rick. *I* appreciate your hard work. The meal was delicious.'

Dain doesn't notice. She uses her fork to pull a pea from under a piece of beef.

Abby sighs, shakes her head.

Dain isn't looking. She's transported herself into a world of her own where her parents can't interfere. Where they can't criticize.

I mouth the word. *Kids*.

Abby nods. She looks exhausted.

'Put your feet up on the sofa,' I tell her.

She nods again and swings her legs up onto the cushions.

I go to the kitchen. My footfalls on the stone floor send echoes bouncing off the walls. It's an odd sound. As if people are running around the kitchen, only they're just beyond the walls where you can't see them.

There's a tape machine on the worktop. I plug it in and press play. The band's backing track starts. As always, Olly's drumming is too prominent. Not that it matters – these are only the rough mixes we laid down in the studio at home. What's missing are the lead guitar and the vocals. Since I've been here at Lazarus Wake I've played the demo tapes as often as possible. Rather than impose lyrics onto the music, I want the music to suggest the mood of the song. The lyrics I'll write will flow from that.

So the theory runs . . . But it's slow going.

Abby's disillusion with the band. The way the money's dried up. That and the cocktail of hormones in Dain's body that crank her up to screaming pitch.

I'm scraping what's left in the pans into the bin when Dain appears in the kitchen. She uses her knife to flick the food into the bin. The knife catches the plate with a squeal that hits the nerves in your teeth.

'Ouch.' I say it good-naturedly but she doesn't take any notice of me. From there she goes to the cake tin where she takes a slice of Christmas cake.

I look out of the window. It's dark now. Even so, I can see the glistening surface of the lake with the line of hills above. Snow clouds bear down on the landscape. The breeze tugs at the trees. They're monstrous things; they roll forwards, straining to reach the house. Branches like claws shake furiously at me. Leaning further toward those absurd little windows, I see light spill onto the grass. I'm looking for the first snowflake. It's cold enough. Jets of air blow up from between the stone slabs in the floor. They freeze my ankles. Bone-cold breaths expelled from fleshless lips of rock.

For a moment the sight of the slab of light on the grass holds me there. I watch, feeling a cold wash of dread as a figure runs into the light. He runs in the way I've seen many times before on stage. Only a long time ago.

His face looms out of the darkness. The skin of his face is as white as his hair. His eyes are vast pools of green that blaze with eerie lights. His mouth is open; his teeth crowd between his lips, jagged blades of enamel that slice the night air. The mouth slides wider into a leering grin. The pupils of his eyes contract into fierce points of black.

He runs straight at the kitchen window. Leaps up at it, his stare still fixed on me, his mouth still grinning. He slaps the glass with the palm of his hand, then disappears into the night. The bang is colossal. An explosion of sound that crashes around the kitchen.

Dain gives a startled cry. Her eyes are wide and frightened. 'What was that?'

For a second I nearly tell her.

That was Ash White. He died ten years ago. But just a moment ago he came running out of the shadows to strike the window-pane. As if to say, 'Remember me, Rick? Now I've come back for you.'

'Dad, what was it?' Dain asks again. Her eyes are frightened child eyes now. I put my arm out and she slips under it to hug me, her gaze still on the window.

'Don't worry.' I kiss the top of her head. 'It was just a bird, that's all. It flew into the glass.'

Winds surge from out of the darkness again, forcing their way under the back door with a thin-sounding scream. I feel Dain shiver against me.

Tuesday

I'm writing song lyrics in the attic room that has no windows. I listen to the band's demo tapes; they're raw-sounding instrumentals at this stage. I listen to them over and over again. I'm trying to open my mind to the emotion in the music. I'm also opening myself to the feel of this old house. This is what a psychic does, I imagine. They say that they tune into the vibrations ghosting from the walls.

Lazarus Wake is a house born ugly, that's for sure. If some-one told me its bone-white walls were built from human skulls I could believe it. Its windows are deep-set, with forbidding stone lintels that seem to hang right over them. The lines of the rooms aren't square. None of the walls are straight. They slant inward. Floors slope, so when you walk from one end of the lounge to the other you find that you're walking uphill. Pens roll off tables because nothing is level. There are cavities under the house. When the wind blows draughts jet up through gaps between the stone slabs, lifting carpets by an inch or so. You sit at night to watch rugs rise and fall. It mimics the motion of the chest of a man deep in slumber.

I struggle to open myself up to the weird personality of the house. Even the carved block above the door reveals that this is no ordinary home. It reads:-

1727

Lazarus Wake

Raised by Magnus Leppington, a True Believer.
Dedicated to my god. To his FURY and to the
LIFE BLOOD of his sons.

When we first arrived Dain noticed the inconsistency straight away.

'Dad, it refers to God having sons – plural: isn't He only supposed to have one?'

Now for the songs. I sit tapping pen against paper to the beat of the music. This is a solemn piece. Mick Allsop, the new guitarist, calls it funeral music. I'm trying to use it as a key to unlock a way back into the past.

In your teens don't you feel emotions more keenly? Excitement is a vibrant pulsing energy that electrifies your body. Love is palpable. Anger is an erupting volcano of red-hot fury. It's not so easy to unlock those strong emotions these days. I'm thirty-four years old. As Abby points out, that's ancient for a pop star. Although I've never been one of those. When I close my eyes I see myself when I was twenty. I've got the clothes and the cascade of hair. I'm with the rest of the band in the limo. There's Olly Gurvitz, drums, and Pete Thurstan, keyboards. I play bass guitar (the least glamorous quarter of a rock band; always the most forgettable, too). And there too is the star of the show, Ash White. Ash has been his nickname from his schooldays. He's an albino (it runs in the White family, maybe that's how they got the name). His hair isn't just white. It's hair without any pigment at all. It's like snow. His skin's the same; he doesn't have so much as a freckle to mark it. All his colour is centred in those striking eyes of his. They're a luminous green. With looks like that he had to be the band's front man. So Ash White plays lead guitar – a beautiful ivory Stratocaster – and sings our songs.

We're in the limo because we've just picked up the Best Newcomer Award at the Brits. We're all young – Ash is the oldest at twenty-one – we're on a high, we're drinking champagne . . . we feel as if we've conquered the world.

Our first album, *Found Wanting*, roared into the top ten on both sides of the Atlantic and stayed there for the spring.

We walked on air. We were applauded. We were treated like princes.

For a bunch of lads from Manchester this was something else. Like anyone else we love attention. And that's what we got. Shedloads of it. The *exhilaration*. It's hard to describe. After a day of interviews in television and radio studios I'd return to the hotel room alone and it would seem as if my whole body was vibrating with that exhilaration, *pure exhilaration*. When I sat on the bed, somehow I seemed to be floating above it.

North of West – the band's moniker – had hit the big time. We'd all composed the first album's songs together in what had been the old coal cellar at Ash's family home where he lived with his mother. So when the royalty cheques started coming in we were all suddenly out buying London apartments and fast cars.

What destroyed it all? Not drugs. Not women. No . . . just one song. Ash White had spent the Christmas with his mother and her sisters at a house on the North Yorkshire moors. There he'd composed a song, 'Night Whispered'. We liked it so we absorbed it into the band's set. This was before we signed to the label. When we did, we all agreed that any songwriting credits would be shared equally. It seemed democratic. We all contributed to songwriting ideas anyway. Even Ash White didn't mind.

But then the record company released 'Night Whispered' as a single. It hit number one. It got airplay like you wouldn't believe. And, Lord, the money became an avalanche. We were all ready to crack on with the next album when Ash suggested that we should take a couple of months off to enjoy ourselves and to acclimatize to the reality of being successful and wealthy and famous.

Meanwhile, I'd fallen in love. Abby was two years older than me, a New Yorker, glamorous as a princess, and worked as a reporter on the evening newspaper back in my home town. It started with a local-boy-does-good interview and wound up with us living together. When Ash White suggested the two-month break I rented a house in San Tropez for the summer. If I remember rightly, Abby and I did a lot of shopping and making love.

In September the band met up in a London hotel, the kind with chandeliers and uniformed doormen who touch their top hats as you come and go. Ash had rented the most expensive suite, where we could meet in style and talk about the follow-up album to *Found Wanting*. I'd got some ideas for songs. I saw Pete, the keyboard player, tugging folded sheets of paper from his back pocket where he'd jotted down some preliminary music notation.

Ash White breezed in, a winning smile on his pale face. He produced a spool of tape from a leather briefcase and held it up so we could all see it. Then he laid it down on the coffee table in front of us with all the dignity of a priest setting down a crucifix on a church altar.

'*Voilà.*' A self-satisfied grin spread across his features. I've never known anyone look so pleased with themselves.

'What's that?' Pete asked.

'The new album.' Ash announced the fact rather than said it. He even made a grand gesture with his outstretched arms.

We laughed as if he was pulling our legs.

'What? Don't you believe me?'

'But we're going to discuss the new album now,' I said, still grinning. 'That's why we're here.'

Ash leaned back in the armchair. He had this expression of cool contentment on his face. 'While you were away roasting your flesh in the sun, I recorded these.'

The drummer frowned. 'What are they?'

'My songs.'

'I guessed that,' I said. *This can't be right*, I remember thinking. *He's up to something.*

Pete shrugged. 'But we've always got together – as a band – to write the songs.'

'I've saved you all the trouble.'

'This is all about "Night Whispered", isn't it, Ash?'

'Yeah.' The drummer sat up. 'You're pissed off because it was a hit and you figure you should have got all the credit.'

'And all the royalties,' I added.

'Aren't you even going to listen to them?' Ash had a face of stone now.

'OK, Ash, if it makes you happy we'll listen.'

'But there's a catch, isn't there?' Pete Thurstan had a head for business. 'You haven't spent the summer writing all these songs for the love of it.'

From the same leather case Ash eased out sheets of paper crowded with hard black print. 'This is a rider to the contract we signed. All the songs from this tape –' he tapped the spool on the table with his finger '– that are used on the next album will be credited exclusively to me.'

'So you'll keep all the songwriting credits?'

'And the royalties.'

Ash shook his head, like he was trying to get through some simple fact to idiots. 'Listen up, guys. Which song made the most money on the album?'

'They were all jointly written—'

'No, they weren't. *I* wrote "Night Whispered". No one else.'

'Pete suggested using a piano to carry the melody—'

'But it was my bloody song.' Ash looked angry. 'I sat in a bloody farmhouse in the middle of bloody nowhere and I wrote that song on my own.'

'We agreed—'

'Well, look at it from my point of view,' Ash snapped.

'I write the song. It tops the singles charts in ten fucking countries. But I only get a quarter of the fucking royalties.'

'So you want to write all the songs on the next album?'

'It makes sense.' Ash looked each of us in the eye, challenging us to disagree. 'I've got the talent to produce massive hits when I write songs *by myself.*'

'Give us time to talk about it.' I went with Pete and Olly to the bedroom where we talked it through. Minutes later we were back.

'We all agree,' I told him. 'We want to continue working together as a team. We decided we should all write the songs together.'

'So, I'm outvoted.' I'd expected Ash to throw the coffee table through the window but he just shrugged. 'If that's what you want then we'll all write together.'

We rented a rehearsal room in Highgate. There we composed songs as a foursome. Only now, according to Ash, the compositions were never quite right. I'll give him this: he was strong-willed. He blocked every song. He persuaded us that what we wrote as a team always had some weakness; that the tunes or the lyrics – or both – weren't good enough for the album.

And this was where the rock-and-roll madness set in. *We* wouldn't relent and record the songs he wrote solo. *He* wouldn't pass a group composition as worthy for the new album. To really fuck everything up, we'd written a term into the contract specifying that we ALL had to vote a song onto an album. And any 'yes' vote had to be unanimous, obviously. Ash steadfastly voted against every group composition.

Looking back, we should have kicked Ash White out of the band. But he had written a great song that went platinum. Also, his albino looks meant that he got his face onto magazine covers. He'd become a cult figure in the music world. We couldn't bring ourselves to chuck him. So the madness continued. We were supposed to record the new album by the following spring. Next spring came and went. We still sat in the rehearsal room writing songs and eating all-day breakfasts from the café across the road. Twelve months down the line the record company fired us. We found another company. They paid us an advance (although it was quite a bit smaller than the first deal); we carried on working – writing song after song after song . . .

Rock madness is legendary madness. This went on for *three years* without us even going into a recording studio to cut a final take of a composition. All we had were piles of cassette demos and hundreds of songs. We even stopped playing live so that we could concentrate on the next BIG album.

The music press was curious. They spun legends about us. An album three years in the making . . . then four years in the making . . . this was going to be so special.

But as is the way in the music industry new bands came along: new sounds; new faces; the press lost interest in us. If we were mentioned at all it was as a has-been one-hit wonder. And still, the band members were locked into this love-hate relationship. Money continued to flow from the first album. We kept our cars and big houses. I married Abby. Then Dain came along. With a new family I wasn't even keen to start touring again. OK, right, I was getting used to an easy life. I enjoyed lazy afternoons in the garden. The focus of my life shifted from the band to my family. I'd go for days without going to the rehearsal studio. After all, it was always easy enough to pick up where I'd left off. Strangely, the members of the band were still on good terms with each other. We were relaxed about work. We continued writing music that no one would ever hear (and that would earn nothing). We still ate the all-day breakfasts brought in from the café across the road. Band members would take holidays or, like me, just not bother turning up at the studio for a week or two.

Then one morning I was sitting with Olly and Pete round an electric piano, reworking an old song that had never made it to the first album. (You see? Easier to polish old songs than invent new.) All of a sudden Pete looked up as if he'd only just noticed something.

'Hey, has anyone seen Ash lately?'

'I haven't seen him in a couple of weeks,' I said.

Olly shrugged. 'The last time I saw him was coming out of Sounds Factory in the King's Road. He'd just had his guitar repainted.' A smile came over Olly's face. 'He said it didn't look *white* enough.'

We'd shaken our heads, laughed, then got back to polishing the melody.

That had been the last time anyone saw Ash White.

Eventually we heard that his mother had reported him missing to the police. Using his credit-card transactions, they tracked him from London to a house on the North Yorkshire moors. It was the same house where he'd written 'Night Whispered'. It was this house: Lazarus Wake.

Wednesday

Outside, the mouth of the wind sucks at the house in the darkness. A dead cry sounds in the chimney breast. And cold jets of air stir cinders in the hearth where generations of men and women now long gone to bone in their graves had tried to warm their hands. The night has us in its implacable grip once more.

We are here in the house known as Lazarus Wake. It stands a few moments' walk from the lake. Lazarus Deep.

'Rick, didn't you ever think about selling Ash's guitar?'

'Are you still angry about what I did?'

'Not angry. Surprised. Perplexed. It was the only thing of Ash's you inherited.'

'It seemed the right . . . no, what's the word?'

'Impetuous? Ridiculous?'

'No . . . symmetry. There was a sense of symmetry about the act.'

Abby lights a cigarette and lets out a lungful of blue smoke in a gush. It looks as if she needs it, I tell myself. Then I remind myself she needs more than that by way of a chemical support system these days. Nicotine, sure. Plus those herbal relaxants that she makes into teas or steeps herself in when she takes a bath.

'Well, there *is* a symmetry,' she tells me. 'There's a bizarre symmetry to this vacation.'

'You needed a break.'

'But why come here?' She steams on, eyes flashing. 'You bring us to this creepy old house in the middle of nowhere – at Christmas, for Christ's sake.'

'Abby, I—'

'A house that Ash White rented so he could commit suicide.'

'No one knows that.'

'But that's what everyone suspects. He rents the house for a month. No one hears from him. The police break in, the food's gone rotten on the table and they find the place deserted.'

'But no suicide note, remember?'

'Oh, Rick, don't keep avoiding reality. Ash White went through that door and walked into the lake – that's all there is to it.'

I shrug. 'I guess I'm coming to that conclusion.'

'So you threw the guitar into the very same lake.' She shakes her head with a wry smile. 'So the great guitarist could be reunited with his instrument.'

I look out of the window.

'Rick, how romantic.' Sarcasm runs thickly in her voice. 'Yes, there's a symmetry there.'

'I thought that if I came here it would help me write better lyrics.'

'What? You believed you could invoke the magic?'

'If you want to put it like that.'

'Oh, yes, I remember. This is Lazarus Wake, the oh-so-famous house where Ash wrote "*Night Whispered*".' Abby stubbed out the cigarette. 'I dare say you can pick daffodils here in the spring but I don't think you can pick hit songs in the same way.'

'Very witty, Abby.'

'I only wish it paid the bills.'

We're not rowing. We just do what we've done for the last couple of years – throw prickly comments backwards and forwards to one another.

'Does Dain know that the pop quiz is starting soon?'

Abby shrugs. 'I don't know. She didn't say anything about watching it.'

'Dain?' I switch on the television and walk through into the hallway where the stairs climb up to the darkened landing. 'Dain, the programme's starting . . . Dain?'

'She's still in her room as far as I know.' Abby lights another cigarette.

'Do you think she's ignoring me on purpose?'

'Your guess is as good as mine. Those mood swings are making my head spin.'

'Dain!' I switch on the light for the stairs. They go twisting up above my head toward the attic room. An ugly spiral of timber like the spine of an arthritic giant.

I run up the stairs. Dain's bedroom is empty. An icy breeze tugs the curtains. I see that the window is wide open. Her magazines are scattered on her bed; the breeze flaps the pages, turning them over as if frantic invisible hands are searching for secret truths.

Ghostly waves of unease pass through me. Dain wouldn't go out for a walk, would she? It's nine o'clock. The December night's black outside. There are no street lights. I run back downstairs.

This time Abby's on her feet. Her expression must mirror mine. That invasive unease. A chilling sensation.

'Where is she?'

'I don't know, Abby. She must be outside.'

'Outside? In this weather?'

I glance at the window. Snowflakes stream past. 'I'll check.'

'Get your coat. You'll need it.'

But suddenly there's no time to find a coat. I sense a new urgency, feeling it in my bones. 'There's a switch for the garden light in the kitchen. Turn it on.'

I pull on a pair of shoes and open the door. A smack of cold hits me in the face. I push through the blast of air, closing the door behind me. Working through that maelstrom of icy air and spitting snow, I walk along the driveway to the gate. Maybe Dain planned to walk to the main road to find a bus stop. She complained how boring it was here. Could she have caught a bus into the nearest town? That can't make sense, though, can it? She doesn't know the bus times, she doesn't know the area.

The cold is brutal. I turn my back against the gale to catch my breath. The wind's so strong that it sucks the air from my lungs. Glancing back, I see the house in the bleak darkness. The building forms a malignant presence overlooking Lazarus Deep. It swells from the ground, its ghostly windows staring at me. Snowflakes wrap it in a billowing shroud. My heart beats gravely; I feel nothing but dread. Here, all those years ago, the house swallowed Ash White. Now it sits there, coldly sinister. Dain had been in that bedroom with the sick yellow light bleeding from the window. Now she's gone.

But in this? The night air cuts me to the bone.

I move as far as the main road. Snow crusts the trees, forming patterns of grinning faces. Branches clatter evilly. The whole countryside oozes menace. It spills from the ground to smear the air itself. It turns trees into monsters. Bushes into humped goblin shapes. Grass into dark tangles of witch hair.

I run back along the driveway to the house, cold wet flakes stinging the back of my neck. Patches of snow stick to the ground; they're man-shaped. They form the outlines of murdered men and women . . . with outflung arms, faces contorted with pain . . .

No, it's your imagination, I tell myself. You're worried about Dain. I glance at the upper window. I see a face there; it's shouting at me.

Dain!

No, it's Abby. I wipe splinters of hail from my eyes. She's pointing.

Behind the house . . . *behind the house!*

I nod. Then I run harder, taking the path through the bushes. They lunge at me, whipping my face. Something grips my ankle. I fall forward, onto all fours, but I don't stop. I'm on my feet and running again. The light in the front garden is blinding against the snow. Blades of grass catch the lamplight, reflecting eerie flashes. While all the time the wind breathes a strange kind of life into dead trees. Rocking them, twisting them, hurting them so that they groan in the grip of its brute force.

Halfway down the grass slope to the lake I see two figures.

A tall man is embracing Dain. He presses his mouth to her neck. Even from here – even in this seething mass of grave-black shadow – I can see his bottom jaw moving.

Dain's head hangs to one side. She doesn't struggle in the man's arms.

I move forward again. This time I focus on the man. The face is pure white. The hair the same.

'Ash!'

He smiles at me as I run up to him. 'Rick. What took you so long?'

That's all he says. Then he releases Dain. She drops to the ground with a soft thump, to lie motionless in the snow. More concerned about Dain than the man I know to be dead I run forward. He backs away, grinning.

I pick Dain up, holding her like a baby in my arms. When I look up from her pale face I see that Ash has vanished.

'It's going to be all right. Don't worry, I've got you now.' Repeating those words, I carry her back to the house. I kiss her cheek.

Her skin . . . it's so cold.

Wednesday. Late night.

Abby is horrified. 'Rick! What have you done to her?'

'I've done nothing to Dain. It was him.' I carry Dain to the sofa. She's pale. She feels cold.

'What's that on her throat?' Abby looks closely.

'Blood.'

'But how did she come to hurt her throat?'

'Ash did it.'

'Ash!' She shakes her head. Her eyes seem to fill her face. '*Ash?* It *can't* be Ash. He's dead.'

'I'll get the towels and the first-aid box,' I tell her.

In the kitchen is a cupboard with towels. There's a first-aid kit fixed to the wall above the freezer. Through the window I see Ash White standing on the lawn. He's wearing no shoes.

Snowflakes dance round him. He is smiling. In one hand he carries the white guitar he loved so much.

I threw it into the lake. How can he—

'Rick. Come here!'

I go through into the living room where Dain lies on the sofa. Her eyelids are fluttering. She's groaning softly.

'Rick. Look at her throat. It's been cut.'

I kneel down beside her, dabbing at the wound. It's directly above her windpipe; the skin there is torn, leaving radiating splits in the epidermis. Blood pours out. A lot of blood. I'm sure I can see the gristly hardness of her trachea through it.

'You didn't do this, did you, Rick?'

'No, of course not.' I open the first-aid box. Abby takes the largest dressing and tears open the sterile pack. She begins to tape the dressing to the wound. She talks in a rapid voice as she works on our daughter.

'I know she's been difficult lately, but you'd never hurt her, would you?'

'Abby, what do you take me for?'

'It's just that you've been so odd lately. We've both been frightened of you.'

'*Frightened of me?*'

'I know it's the pressure of finishing the album. We know you're not normally like this.'

'Me?' I'm still finding it hard to believe that my wife and daughter find me frightening.

'Rick, we'll tell them that she fell.'

'You think *I* did this? Just look at her throat. Can you believe I'd do that?'

'We'll tell the doctor she ran into a wire fence, or tripped in the kitchen.'

'Abby—'

'Let's just get her to hospital.'

'We can't.'

'If you've had a drink I'll drive.'

'It's not that. When I hit the wall in the car I damaged the tyre. It's flat.'

'We can change it.'

'There isn't a spare. I left it at the garage to have a new tyre fitted.'

'But that was weeks ago.'

'I didn't get round to picking up again.'

'You mean you didn't have the money to pay the garage bill.'

'It was the tyre or the credit card payment.' I wipe blood from where it stains Dain's collarbone. She breathes with an effort. As if she's having a bad dream. Muttering. Frowning.

I wish she'd wake up.

'It looks as if you've stopped the bleeding,' I tell Abby.

'But she needs medical attention.'

'There's no phone here, but I'm sure I can find one in the morning when it's light. I'll call the ambulance then.'

I see Abby staring at her daughter's face.

'I'm sure she'll be OK tonight.' I say it again. 'The bleeding's stopped.'

What I don't tell Abby is how my dead friend inflicted the wound. He was holding Dain while he sucked the blood from her throat. I say nothing, either, about seeing him standing barefoot in the snow. The guitar in his hand. Flecks of lake weed streaming from the strings.

It's strange, but I knew that an event like this was waiting for us here. That premonition brought me here to this forbidding house that overlooks Lazarus Deep. I wasn't ridding myself of the guitar after all. I was sending a message.

Thursday. Before dawn.

It's three in the morning. I haven't slept. I sit in the living room in a leather wing-backed chair. It's cold as hell. My stare is nailed to the carpet. The draughts have got under it again, lifting it up and down with every gust of cold wind. The floor's breathing, I tell myself, and there's nothing I can do about it. This whole godforsaken house is coming alive. Outside the night winds whoop against the roof, sending their sneering echoes down the chimney.

I hear the snigger of the wind recede into the distance. Deep under my feet, as if it is running down and down and down into vast subterranean vaults hidden beneath the house.

'Rick . . . Rick!'

I run upstairs to the master bedroom where Dain lies on our bed. Abby's face is a mask of worry; she twists a tissue in her fingers.

'Rick, I don't like the sound of Dain's breathing. It's as if she's struggling for breath.'

I look at Dain. She lies on her back on our bed. Her face is alabaster, her hands blue-white. Her lips have become a deep red – they have that swollen bee-stung appearance – and again I ask myself what happened to her down by the lakeside before I reached her.

All around that white face is a splash of her soft dark hair. The surgical dressing is held against her throat by sticking plaster. She does not move. Her condition is closer to a coma than to sleep. I crouch beside her and hear faint sighing sounds coming from those heavy red lips.

Abby touches her forehead. 'Her skin's like ice.' She glances back at me. 'She's slipping, away, isn't she?'

I rub the sides of my face, thinking hard. I'm her father. I must save her.

'Isn't there any way to reach a phone?' Abby asks. 'There must be a farm nearby.'

'I haven't seen any.'

'Or a house?'

'I wouldn't know where to begin looking.'

'Dain must have lost more blood than we thought. She's going into shock. I don't— Rick? What are you doing?'

I pull blankets from the cupboard. 'I'm going out to the car.'

'But the tyre's flat.'

'I'm going to do something. I can't just wait while . . .' I choke back the next words, then take a breath. 'Stay here with Dain.'

I have the car keys in the pocket of my leather jacket. I zip it against the driving winds that carry the snowflakes. Even if I can work some miracle with the car, will the roads be passable in this blizzard?

The garage lies some way down a slope, away from the house. I reach it and haul impatiently at the up-and-over door so that it screams as it rises. And there's the car. The headlamp is shattered and the driver's wing is buckled where I struck the wall. I'd seen Ash White in the road. I'd swerved . . .

Now the tyre has softened into a misshapen ring around the wheel hub. After switching on the garage light I run my finger across the steel rim that should hold the inside edge of the tyre in place. My fingers soon find a raised bulge in the steel edge where it had hit the stonework. So the tyre itself might be undamaged. It could be merely the steel rim that's become deformed, breaking the seal and so releasing the air from the tyre. I don't know what tools are in this garage. But I see shelves at the back. I search through them, pushing off objects that clatter onto the concrete floor.

Hammer . . . hammer . . .

The word flies through my head. I need a hammer. But there is no hammer.

Damn . . . the world's against me. It won't let me take my daughter to hospital. I think of her pale and unconscious on the bed. Think, Rick. You don't need a hammer. All you need is something hard that will—

Yes!

I find a sturdy iron bar that's thicker than my thumb. I pull it from the shelf. It's almost the length of my arm. A second later I'm back at the damaged wheel. I swing the iron bar with both hands. The first blow strikes the rubber tyre. The bar bounces back, clattering against the garage wall. I strike again. This time I catch the metal wing of the car. Paint flakes off.

I don't care. The car's no longer important. I pause. Take deep breaths. I need to improve my aim. I strike again. The iron bar hits the wheel rim. Sparks fly. I strike it another three times. Then I run my finger against the rim. The bulge has dipped inward. It's not perfect, but if it forms a tight enough seal against the lip of the tyre that's all that matters. I strike once more. Blue sparks shoot across the floor. The ringing sounds of metal on metal toll from the open garage and out across the night-black lake. It's the sound of some demon bell.

I check the rim again. It's flatter now. There's no gap between the rubber and the steel. I've married the surfaces back together. I run out into the snow to check on the bedroom window in case Abby is looking for me. She's not there. But is this a good sign? She isn't trying to attract my attention so presumably she's not in a state of panic – but then, is she having to attend to Dain?

All I can do is make sure the car is drivable. There's a foot pump hanging from a nail on the wall. I seize that, connect the hose to the valve and then start to pump. Soon I'm sweating. My skin steams in the cold night air. I tug down the zip of my jacket. My leg aches but I'm not stopping now.

Through my own panting I hear air hiss along the pump line into the tyre. But is it leaking back out again? The seal might not be good enough. I might pump here until the end

of time and never inflate it. I pause to push at the tyre wall
with my fingers. It flexes loosely. The air isn't being held.
There's a leak.

Try again. I use the iron bar to knock the rim against the
lip of the tyre. This time I don't use swinging blows but jab
the end of the bar against the damaged tyre rim. This is more
controlled. A sharp stabbing motion. After a dozen taps with
the bar I return to the foot pump. I stamp down, working it.
My heart pounds; sweat trickles down my face. In the light
from the garage I see snow flashing by outside. The ground
is completely whited over now. I think about those moorland
roads. It won't take much to make them impassable. Tearing
my gaze from the deepening snow, I look at the tyre. I can't
believe my eyes. Its rubber walls are rigid. The car has risen
again. I push at the tyre with my hand. Hard as stone. I kick
it. My God, I've done it.

Carefully, I pump in more air. There's a chance that it's still
leaking. Yet if it's only a slow puncture the tyre might still get
us to the hospital in Whitby. If I over-inflate, it might simply
rupture. Then there'll be no hope. I don't have a spare. We'll
be stranded until morning. And the rate the snow's falling, the
roads might become blocked. Then the ambulance will never
get through.

Dain needs me to get this right. I don't have a pressure
gauge so I can't check the p.s.i. of the tyre. This is going to
have to be guesswork.

Only make it good guesswork.

After a few more efforts with the pump I disconnect it and
put it in the car, just in case I need it again. Then I lick my
finger and hold it above the damaged wheel rim. I can't feel
any leaking air. But then, the breeze is gusting through the
garage door now, carrying swirls of snow.

It will do, I tell myself. It will get us to Whitby. I climb
into the car and start the engine. It runs smoothly, despite

the fierce cold. Not rushing now, not wanting to undo what I've done, I ease the car out of the garage, along the drive to the front of the house.

'Abby, wake up . . . I've fixed the car.'

Abby lies beside Dain on the bed. She must have lain down there through sheer exhaustion.

'Abby?'

She's fast asleep.

'Abby!'

I shake her gently by the shoulder. There's no response: her face is relaxed, her breathing rhythmic.

'Abby, come on, wake up.' Unease springs like a sudden pain in my chest. Why can't I wake her?

The room isn't particularly warm. I think about the old gas boiler downstairs and begin to wonder. 'Abby!' I slip the catch on the bedroom window. The moment I push it open ice-cold air floods into the room. That will drive out any toxic gas. The fresh air should revive her. Snowflakes dart swiftly between the flapping curtains to speckle the floor. In seconds the bedroom is as cold as an ice tomb. 'Abby, wake up! I've fixed the car. We can get Dain to hospital . . . Abby!'

But it isn't the gas heater, is it? The realization strikes me as hard as a slap. There's something else that's making her sleep. I touch my forehead. There's darkness behind my eyes. A gathering mist of weariness. Even though I resist, I think how pleasant it would be to lie down myself, or at least to sit in the armchair in the corner of the room. The cushions are so soft . . . so inviting.

I stick my head out of the open window, dragging in huge lungfuls of painfully cold air. I mustn't go to sleep like Dain and Abby.

'Rick . . . let me help you.'

I look down. Gazing up at me from the lawn is a figure.

'I don't want to see you again, Ash.'

'You're seeing me now, Rick. So I don't think you've got much choice.' He smiles. 'Do you?'

'Aren't you going to invite me in, Rick?'

Sheer instinct spits the word through my brain. *NEVER.*

'I've nothing to say,' I tell him. I find myself staring at his bare feet as he stands in the snow. He's wearing a shirt and trousers. The material they're made of has almost completely decayed.

A smile forms again on the flesh-and-ghost face. 'We haven't seen each other for years. The least you could do is invite me in to talk.'

I remember that I left the front door of the house open when I ran in from the car. I glance down, seeing light from the hallway spill onto the garden path. Ash looks too. He's seen the open door. He can be through it and into the house before I can stop him.

He smiles up at me. It's as if he's read my mind. 'It wouldn't be polite of me to just walk into the house without being asked.'

That's because he can't. I have to invite him in. He can't enter unless he's asked to do so.

I shake my head. 'Not after what you did to Dain.'

'Sweet, isn't she?'

'Get away from here, Ash.'

'Now, that isn't polite. We're old friends – we went to school together.'

'You're dead, Ash.'

'Do I look dead?' He held out his hands. 'Do my friends look dead?'

I've not noticed them before but walking from—

Sleep . . .

Gliding from the shadows come two figures. I look round

the garden. There are more. Five, six . . . seven. They've been keeping so still that I never noticed them. They're as white as the snow-dusted bushes. They blend in with the garden. I have to blink and then look again to focus on them once more.

Sleep.

'We're here to help you, Rick. We know that Dain isn't well . . .'

'You hurt her.'

'No, Rick, I was helping her.'

Sleep. You need sleep.

'You hurt her throat. We can't wake her.'

'Let us help.' Ash's green eyes gaze up at me. They look vast: two pools of emerald light set in a snow-white face.

Sleep. I feel drowsy. The night winds no longer feel cold against my face. They are warm, scented, wonderfully scented. Summer roses, cherry blossom . . .

Sleep now. Curl up on a bed. Sleep.

Ash has a lullaby voice. 'Thank you for returning the guitar to me.'

'How could you find it?'

'In the lake, old friend.'

Sleep. Sleep . . .

'It's too cold. You can't swim in that.'

'On the contrary, that's my home.'

Sleep in a warm, soft bed. That's what I want. To relax. To be comfortable. To breathe deeply, rhythmically . . .

I hear a laugh. I'm surprised that it's come from my mouth. 'You live in the lake?'

'With my friends, yes.'

I see that the garden is full of them now. There were barely a dozen a moment ago – now there seems to be a hundred. I look at them. They gaze up at me. They have no hair on their heads. Most are naked. The snow falls. They have such kind eyes. They care about Dain. They care about me. They only want to help.

Sleep now. Don't hide the yawn. Lie down. The beds are so soft. Curl up on your side with your knees up to your chest, pull a duvet over your head and sleep . . . Feel that warm relaxation spread through you in a sunlit glow.

My eyes are closing. The bushes, the trees the figures in the garden are pale, comforting shapes. The air gliding through the window is warm – a beautiful warmth that feels like loving arms scented with frankincense.

'Rick. There's no need for me to come in if you don't want me in the house. You could come out here.' Ash's voice is soothing. He had such a wonderful singing voice. Women loved him.

Surrender yourself to sleep now.

I look at Ash's friends in the garden. I see they have lovely faces. There are beautiful women with lively blue eyes; their lips are red and glow with health. Their teeth are so white. Everyone is so happy and friendly. I feel their warm loving gazes on me.

Sleep.

'You must wonder what happened to me.' Ash speaks as softly as a falling snowflake. 'One night, while I stayed in this house, I realized I didn't want my old life. I found a new one in Lazarus Deep. My new friends made me welcome there. We swim all day like beautifully sleek dolphins.'

I'm drowsy but manage to speak. 'It's so cold in there.'

'No, not once you come over to us. We know how to stay warm. My friends know all about life; about how we shouldn't waste it seeking material possessions or striving for ephemeral success.'

'You're dead . . .'

'We're not dead. How can we be dead? When you see us here, talking to you.'

I look down from the bedroom window into the garden full of beautiful men and women. And those women . . . their eyes twinkle. A man strokes the naked breast of a girl with long blonde hair. She smiles at me. She imagines that I'm the one running my fingers over her nipple that's as red as a berry. Sleep . . . embrace sleep . . .

Ash continues speaking, 'I know that early success has gone. Life's hard for you now. There's no money. So why continue fighting a battle you've no need to win? It's so easy. Either step out here to be with us. Or invite us in.'

'You can't just come into the house?'

'It wouldn't be polite to walk in without being asked, would it, Rick? I told you that before.'

Sleep. Relax. Warmth. Peace . . . I yawn.

'Listen to our story, Rick.' Those green pools of fire. Those eyes. They're a warming drink on a winter's day. They're a soft bed when I'm tired. They're a comforting embrace when I'm lonely. They're gentle music after a trying day. They're peaceful rest when I'm tired.

'Listen to our story,' he says again as the breeze becomes a musical sigh. 'My friends have lived in this lake for a thousand years. When their village sank beneath the water their god would not forsake them. He saved them from death. They were the last to believe in his power. He loved them. They preserved his link with this earth. So he gave them each a drop of his own blood, placing it on their lips. Now they cannot die. And they want to share this power with everyone. They can guide back those people lost to Christ. Here we can live for each other, but it's not some bland, colourless afterlife. If anything the passions we feel now are more powerful. Colours are more intense. Physical sensation is amplified beyond what you can imagine. When we make love we feel as if stars explode inside us. Will you allow us to help you? Will you invite us into the house?'

A raven glides over their heads. It's waiting for my answer.

'If I say yes, will you let Dain and Abby go?'

Ash doesn't like this. 'But all three of you can be together. Children grow up and leave their parents. Dain never has to. She can always be your daughter. You'll never lose her.'

'Let them go. Then I'll give you my answer.'

I bite my lip with such force that I feel my teeth crunch through the skin. At first there's no pain. My body is numb. All I feel is a tingle. I bite harder. The pain comes roaring in. Suddenly the air blowing through the window is pure ice again, tearing at my face and hair.

And below me in the garden are monsters. I'd seen them as beautiful. Now I see hairless heads covered by graveyard skin. Their eyes are deep-set malignant splinters of ice. Their mouths are crooked; as raw and as ugly as axe wounds. Their teeth are needle sharp. The need for sleep flies from me. I'm wide awake again. Snowflakes stab at my face.

Ash looks at his companions, then back at me. 'We want to save you, Rick. But we think you will leave us.'

'You know me, Ash. If I promise to stay here in the house I'll do exactly that. I won't leave with Abby and Dain.'

For a moment Ash's gaze goes back to the humped, monstrous forms of his companions. Then he raises his stare to me. 'I've always trusted you to keep a promise.'

I turn to the bed where Dain and Abby lie. My hands burn, they are so cold. I taste a mouthful of blood where I have bitten myself.

'Dain . . .' Dain is deeply unconscious. I turn to Abby. 'Wake up, Abby. Time to go.'

She doesn't stir. I slap her face. I am too gentle. Not even her eyelids flicker.

'I'm sorry, Abby.' I slap her harder. No response. Then harder again, knocking her head sideways.

I hate this, but I know I must wake her. I slap her again.

The sound is shocking. When a trickle of blood appears from her nose I close my eyes.

'Dain must go to hospital,' I say to Abby even though I know she's sleeping. (And those things outside are making her sleep, just as they tried to force me to lie down; maybe their power is stronger over unconscious prey; maybe they are still trying to keep Abby and Dain here. And I know why. I feel their hunger.)

I take a cigarette lighter from my pocket. Dipping to my knees by the bed, I kiss Abby on the lips. 'Abby. I love you. I don't want to do this. But you've got to wake up now. You've got to drive Dain to hospital.'

I take her arm, slip back the sleeve of her sweater, then press the lighter button. A tongue of yellow fire appears. I hold her arm higher with one hand, while moving the flame toward her wrist.

Gales scream through the ancient chimney. The elements themselves are tortured tonight.

I carry Dain to the front door that lies open to the darkness beyond. Snow settles on the hallway carpet. Abby follows me downstairs. She is unsteady on her feet, as if drunk. Beyond the door she sees the figures that glare in at us. Only it doesn't quite register. Instead she glances at the red mark on her wrist. The fine hairs are scorched away; a blister is forming. She winces when she touches it.

'Rick, what happened?' She murmurs the words, half asleep.

'You're all right,' I tell her. 'I'll put Dain in the back seat. Once I close the doors, lock them, then drive to the hospital.'

'Hospital?'

'The hospital in Whitby. Dain hurt her throat.'

'Yes.' She touches her forehead. Again she looks round as if she's not sure where she is. 'Are you coming?'

'No. I need to stay here. You drive Dain straight to the hospital. She's not well.'

I step through the doorway. The humped figures with their burning eyes move toward me, evil intent in their expressions.

I look Ash in the face as he stands by the car. He lifts an arm. 'No. Let them pass.' He gives me a faint smile. 'I trust my old friend to keep his promises.'

A moment later I've reached the car, my feet crunching on the snow. Ash opens the rear door. I slide Dain onto the back seat, then lean in to make sure she's comfortable, with a cushion under her head and a blanket over her.

'Here. Let me help.' Gently, Ash pulls the blanket so that it covers her bare feet. I look at his hands and see what they have become.

I now guide Abby to the car. She sees the monstrous figures surrounding her. She shakes her head. I realize that she doesn't know if she's awake or dreaming. Her hair flutters in the breeze. She blinks against the cold and her eyes start to water.

'I love you,' I tell Abby. 'I love you both.'

With a last look at Dain in the back seat I close the car door. Abby seems to know what she has to do. She starts the engine, then drives along the track. The blazing headlamps have physical power against Ash's vampires. In slow motion they fall back, their hands shielding their sensitive eyes. I wait out in the snow, watching the car's lights glide through the trees and out onto the main road. I stand there until I can see them no more.

Then, before Ash and his vampires can move, I step back over the threshold of Lazarus Wake. The figures react. They come forward as if to rush the open doorway. Then they freeze. I notice their ugly-eyed stares are fixed on the stone slab above the door, the slab with that ominous inscription:

Lazarus Wake
Raised by Magnus Leppington, a True Believer.
Dedicated to my god. To his FURY and to the
LIFE BLOOD of his sons.

Ash steps forward. Like his companions he stops short of the door, too. I've not invited them into the house yet. I turn to walk up the stairs. I do not even bother to close the front door.

'Rick? What about your promise?'

I don't so much as glance back at my old friend who is many years dead. 'I haven't broken my promise, Ash. I'm not leaving the house.'

'If you're not leaving the house, what are you going to do?'

I don't answer.

'*Rick . . . what are you going to do?*'

I go upstairs. I know Ash and the others will not follow me.

Thursday. Far side of midnight.

I'm safe in this house, Lazarus Wake. Although I do sense the vampires' influence. All I want to do is sleep. And the one time I did doze for a moment I woke up not knowing who I was or where I am. They have the power to steal away portions of your mind. Once you forget, you become vulnerable.

So I keep the windows open. I feel the cold air rush at me. I breathe deeply, trying to stay awake. I've not heard from Abby. I believe in my heart of hearts that she managed to reach Whitby Hospital safely. Dain will be receiving the best medical care. For the last dozen hours I've been typing at my laptop computer here in the windowless attic room. I've made disk copies of the preceding pages of this document, which I have entitled *THE BROXLEY TESTAMENT*. With as much guile and ingenuity as I could muster I've hidden them throughout the house.

Tonight, as darkness fell, I watched from the kitchen window as the beings emerged from the lake. They walked up the lawn to the house. Loathsome sodden things with bodies whiter than grave worms. Ghost-flesh faces, I told myself. Hungry mouths.

I saw some embrace each other in the snow. Ash kissed one of his vampire clan on the lips, then looked at the window. He smiled.

There's nothing more to do. I call out, knowing that my voice carries downstairs, through the open door and into the snow-covered garden. The night air glides up through the building. A cold of supernatural intensity floats through my blood, cutting loose my soul from its house of bones. It must be the same kind of cold that men and women wake to in their graves when they are buried alive.

The night winds cry from the lake and Lazarus Wake, at last, sighs its answer.

I take a breath. 'Ash. You can come into the house now.'

A moment later I hear the sound of feet on the stairs.

There's time, I know, to finish this paragraph, then slip this last computer disk into an envelope and push it out of sight.

I recognize the rhythm of the footsteps on the stair. This is my old friend. He has waited a long time for me.

Rick Broxley
Lazarus Wake
North Yorkshire

CHAPTER 10

I

I'll be damned.

Electra stared out of her room's window at Leppington's roofs. The night swamped the town in shadows, leaving the church tower to jut upwards like an arm thrust from a grave.

'I'll be damned.' She murmured the words aloud, trying to absorb what she'd just read on the computer: *The Broxley Testament,* written ten years ago in a house overlooking Lazarus Deep. Then there were the e-mails from her mystery correspondent Rowan, who appeared to suffer from a fugue state that had left him near-comatose and without a memory in the very same house – Lazarus Wake. And what of the builder of the house three hundred years ago? One Magnus Leppington who praised a god of blood and thunder who was god the father to not one son but several. Yes . . . Fingers trembling, losing their customary dexterity, Electra fumbled a cigarette from the packet and lit it.

When the lighter flared she saw her own reflection staring pensively back from the window. Her gunmetal black hair poured down over one shoulder and breast. Her eyes gleamed large beneath the twin arches of her eyebrows; their gaze held her, twin grey fires in her head.

Her heart beat hard as what had once seemed to be many separate (and unrelated) incidents and thoughts and dreams began to collide inside her brain. They were forming a pattern now. Those dreams of Jack Black taking her to Lazarus Deep. That sense of foreboding that had nagged away at her, whispering that the monstrous beings she and her friends had defeated three years ago were back.

But they've haven't returned to Leppington, she told herself. *They have made a lair for themselves in the waters of Lazarus Deep.* She glanced at her watch. Five in the morning. *I can hardly leap into a car and go driving up there myself, can I, now? Moreover, I can't do this alone.*

Despite the temptation to find out who occupied the house known as Lazarus Wake Electra knew that she must tread carefully. There was great danger there. Look at what had happened to Broxley. Also, what exactly was going on with Rowan?

And was there any way of finding out what had happened to Rick Broxley? What if the man she knew as Rowan had simply invented the whole thing? Could it be bait to lure her to Lazarus Wake?

If I go there I can't go alone. Who can I take?

Jack Black.

If only.

Jack's dead, she told herself. *You've got to let go.*

No.

Call David Leppington.

If he'll come, she told herself. He'd had a bellyful of this town and what had once haunted the tunnels beneath it. *What do I do if he refuses to come?*

2

Dylan Adams woke at five-thirty to hear the chirping tones of his mobile phone. He lay still for a second, only half awake. At this time of night the darkness in Morningdale was absolute.

The phone kept ringing.

Uh . . .

If this was a prank call from someone at college . . . Then again, it might be Vikki. The thought of Vikki eager to speak to him at this time of night made him grab hurriedly for the phone. His fingers roamed for a second among clusters of film rolls, CD cases, loose change, his car keys before his hand closed on the phone. He thumbed the illuminated button and put the mobile to his ear.

'Hello?'

'Dylan.'

He knew that voice. Although it was oddly husky.

'Luke? Shit, Luke! Where the hell are you? I've been looking—'

'Dylan. I can't talk for long.'

'Luke, you need to get your application in for a place on the HND course next year. If you don't you're going to lose it. They've only got—'

'Oh, no, no, no . . .' Luke's voice purred in a husky whisper. He sounded relaxed – in good spirits. 'Don't sweat it.'

Dylan said, 'The college won't hold the place for you.'

'It doesn't matter about that now. We're having a great party here.'

'When you sober up you'll regret it.'

'I am sober. And I'm having the time of my life. Why don't you come over here and join me?'

'Christ, Luke. Don't you know what time it is?'

'You only live once, bro.'

'At this rate you'll wind up working on the farm all your life.'

'Come over and join us.'

'Where are you?'

'Lazarus Deep.'

3

Electra Charnwood checked her watch again.

'Five-thirty,' she murmured. 'Looks as if you're going to miss your beauty sleep.'

Outside, the first milk trucks lumbered by on their way to outlying dairy farms. They were the early risers round here. Collecting milk for the big commercial dairies in the cities. Sunrise was still a couple of hours away.

I really should catch some sleep, she thought. But that disturbing piece by Rick Broxley had kept her sharply awake. She couldn't sleep now. First, she had to do a little searching. There must be a way to find out about Broxley. Starting with one simple question.

Did the man ever exist? Or had Rowan invented the whole thing while in the grip of madness?

Now, the Internet is a beautiful thing; it cuts out a hell of a lot of drudgery when it comes to a little home-brewed detective work. Electra accessed a search engine, then typed into the query box the words 'North of West'. The name of Broxley's band. Then she hit 'enter'. Seconds later a list appeared on the screen.

'Nine thousand entries. Dear God, I don't have to wade through them all, do I?'

Within ten minutes, however, she had everything at her fingertips. She saved many of the files to disk so that she could reread them later. But here was the evidence. There were several websites devoted to the cult band North of West. Over twenty years ago they'd enjoyed phenomenal success with their first album – their *only* album, it transpired. *Found Wanting* sold two million copies worldwide. It won a trophy case full of 'best first album' awards. Then, according to the official record company statement, there were 'artistic differences within the band'. Quickly, she compared the band's history on the websites with what she'd learned about it from the darkly haunting *Broxley Testament.*

OK, she told herself. *These are the points. Just tick 'em off.*

According to a North of West fan page the bassist's name was Rick Broxley. Drums: Ollie Gurvitz. Keyboards: Pete Thurstan. There were photographs of the men when they'd been barely out of their teens. The largest was devoted to the lead guitarist and singer, Ash White. He was an albino with a strikingly beautiful face. His hair matched the paleness of his skin. All the man's colour had centred in his eyes. They burned with a cold green fire.

Unearthly eyes, Electra told herself. Eyes that had seen things that no one else could see. Or so the knowing curl of the lip seemed to suggest.

And yes, it was all here, just as described in *The Broxley Testament.* After the first album, the group had spent months writing new material. A succession of record companies had hired them, then eventually fired them. One day, Ash White rented a lonely house on the edge of Lazarus Deep. That was where he'd disappeared, presumed drowned. Several years after his disappearance bass guitarist Rick Broxley rented the same house – Lazarus Wake. He was working on songs for that long-delayed final album. The band history mentioned his problems: repeat visits to rehab, a legal wrangle for unpaid song royalties, financial hardships. However, it didn't carry much detail about what happened when he stayed with his wife and daughter at Lazarus Wake. *(Not that it needs to – I've got all the detail I need to kill any desire for sleep,* Electra thought.) Briefly, it revealed that there had been a 'domestic incident'. A phrase served up by the police. The daughter had been hurt in mysterious circumstances. In the early hours of a winter's morning Abby Broxley had driven Dain to Whitby Hospital. Abby too had suffered injuries – blows to her face and a burn on her wrist. Ten years later both women refused to be interviewed by the press. Abby had moved to France. Dain had gone to New Zealand to study drama.

The biography finished with an account of the fate of the other band members. The drummer now worked as a schoolteacher and the keyboard player had become the entertainments director on a cruise liner. And as for Rick Broxley, the embittered bass player? Electra scrolled down the page, reading what was on the screen.

The night that Abby and Dain fled the house during the blizzard had been the last time that anyone set eyes on Rick Broxley. By the time Abby returned forty-eight hours later Rick had vanished. Police searched the surrounding woods and moor. Boats scoured every square metre of Lazarus Deep. No trace of him was ever found. In the final written account that the remaining band members prepared they stated that they believed that Rick had became depressed about his failure to recapture earlier success. That he'd simply walked into the lake to join his friend, Ash White.

In a postscript, years later, a coroner ruled that Rick Broxley was officially dead and that whatever assets of his remained should be vested in Abby Broxley.

Electra frowned. Now that was strange.

She read the final words aloud to herself: 'One of those assets included a white Fender Stratocaster guitar that had once belonged to the band's founder, Ash White. It was found in the attic room of Lazarus Wake on Mrs Broxley's return to the property to collect a number of personal items.'

After reading this Electra switched off the computer and went to lie on her bed. Outside, Leppington slowly came to life with the sound of car engines, and doors opening and closing. The first train of the day rumbled out of the station. She decided that she'd wait until seven-thirty and then she would telephone David Leppington. There was important news for him.

CHAPTER 11

1

Where now? What now?

David Leppington sat at the kitchen table on that rainswept Friday morning. He flicked through sheets of paper covered with telephone numbers and names. He needed to leave his flat in the next five minutes for the start of his shift at the hospital. But he also needed to continue the search for Katrina. Where she'd vanished to God alone knew.

Schizophrenia is a demon that cannot be killed. The drugs can only put it in chains. Every day that went by without medication would loosen the shackles that tied the madness down. Soon delusion and paranoia would eventually break free. They'd submerge Katrina's rational mind. What she would do then was anybody's guess.

David glanced at the kitchen clock. Time was running out for Katrina.

2

'Thank Christ it's Friday morning.' Goldi hung on to his extravagant blond dreadlocks as the gales tore across the railway station. 'You doing anything illegal this weekend?'

Dylan Adams smiled. 'I'm going to Whitby tonight.'

'Jack of Christ.' Goldi had a whole hatful of interesting profanities. 'The bright lights of Whitby, huh? There's a girl involved?'

Dylan nodded. 'Vikki Lawton.'

'Hmm . . . tasty. Hell's teeth, it's cold. Brass monkeys'll be weeping today.' He grinned. 'So what're you doing in Whitby tonight? Or is that being nosy?'

'We're going to the cinema.'

'The back row? My mother told me I was conceived there. At last!' Goldi didn't wait for a reply. 'The train. Thank the bloody Lord.' He hurried to the edge of the platform as the train rumbled into the station. Schoolkids ran ahead of him to grab the seats. Despite being over twenty, Goldi always competed with schoolchildren for a seat near the window. The train was nowhere near full, so his race for the seats was hardly worth the effort.

Dylan didn't dislike Goldi, even though the guy's childlike (some said childish) sense of humour could get wearing. He was taking an illustration course at the college and liked nothing better than to play practical jokes on the models who'd pose nude for the students. It was ten-year-old sense-of-humour stuff. Models would strip off their clothes in a stock room, then they'd don a dressing gown for the short walk to the classroom. Goldi often managed to sneak out of life drawing to put eggs in their shoes or itching powder in their pants.

Well, *he* thought it was fun.

Dylan put it down to an over-abundance of energy on Goldi's part. The guy could hardly sit still on the seat. He was pulling faces at the schoolkids when Dylan walked along the aisle, heading for an empty pair of seats at the back of the carriage. With luck Vikki would telephone. Although he found it hard to admit to himself he loved to hear the sound of her voice. He'd even saved her message on the mobile's answering service so he could replay it.

Christ, Dylan, he told himself. *Don't fall in love. Not now. Not when there's a chance of that London job.*

'Hey, Dill . . . Dill! Seat.'

Goldi pulled his holdall off the seat next to his and thumped the cushion. Dust clouds billowed.

'Thanks.' *Bang goes my privacy.*

'Hey, Dill, guess what I'm doing this weekend?' He picked up an apple core and threw it at a bunch of twelve-year-olds who were forking their fingers at him from the far end of the carriage.

'If it's you, then it's got to be white-knuckle, Goldi. Rock climbing?'

'No.'

'Windsurfing?'

'Warm.'

'Deep-sea fishing?'

'More extreme.' The apple core came sailing back through the air. Goldi caught it.

'More extreme? Caving?'

'No, you're colder.'

Dylan fired off a guess. 'Demolition derby?'

'Nice idea. I haven't tried that yet. Nope.' Goldi threw the core. It struck a red-haired boy on the ear. Some of the adult passengers glared. 'You're way off, anyway.'

'OK, tell me.'

'I'm going diving.'

'It's going to be cold.'

'Wimp.' He wiped apple pulp off his hands onto the legs of his jeans. 'It's the first dive of the year. We've all agreed that we're sick of waiting for the weather to improve.'

'You're going to dive in the sea in *this*?' Dylan nodded at the bleak landscape outside, where flurries of snow raced the train.

'No, the coastguards red-lighted us. They say the sea's too rough. Bastards.' Goldi nodded toward a stretch of dark water that extended across the valley. 'So we're going to take a shot at that.'

'Lazarus Deep?'

'Yeah, looks wicked, doesn't it?'

'You've got to be crazy.'

'Yeah, crazy like a Viking.' Goldi slapped his knees. 'You know, they say it's a thousand feet deep.'

'Christ, when are you going in?'

'First thing in the morning. Can't wait.' He stared out of the window.

Dylan saw Goldi's eyes burning with anticipation. The man loved danger. He was greedy for it. Then Goldi looked back at Dylan, remembering something.

'It's closing day for the HND applications today. Did you find Luke Spencer?'

'No.'

'He's in Shit Street, then.'

'I got a call from him. At five o'clock this morning.'

'That man can party.'

'Can he.'

'Did you tell him that he's going to miss that place on the course?'

'I did.'

'And?'

'He didn't seem that interested.'

Goldi tutted. 'That boy's going to wind up working on his Dad's farm for ever and a day.'

Dylan shrugged. 'He knew about the application deadline. If he's not interested there's not a lot I can do.'

Goldi suddenly sounded mature for once. 'But he kept talking about doing the HND course. He was mad keen to do it. So why's he changed his mind?'

'Search me. A couple of days ago it was the most important thing in his life.'

'Did he sound OK?'

'How do you mean, OK?'

'Well, did he sound as if he was on something illegal?'

Dylan shrugged again. 'He sounded relaxed.'

'And he didn't say where he was?'

Dylan's gaze strayed to the expanse of dark water. 'When he called he said he was at Lazarus Deep.'

'That's hardly the party capital of the world. I mean, apart from about ninety billion gallons of water there's nothing there but trees and sheep shit, is there?'

'You know Luke. All he needs is a roof over his head and a girl – then he's got all the party he needs.'

'Must be a hell of a girl.'

Dylan nodded. The train roared in and out of tunnels as it ran by the lake. Waves deformed the face of Lazarus Deep. The water looked as if it was fighting the gusts of wind that tore down from the hills. Despite sounding unconcerned about his friend, he had begun to wonder. It wasn't like Luke to disappear when it was such a crucial time at college.

The train plunged into another tunnel, darkness enveloped the carriages, and Dylan found his own reflection staring back at him with a thoughtful expression. The train horn sounded. A deeply melancholy note. For some reason he shivered as the words ran through his head: *Luke, old buddy, you're starting to get people worried. So where are you now?*

The train horn cried out into darkness again.

3

By nine that morning Electra Charnwood had made the call.

He's bound to have moved on or changed his telephone number, she told herself. *He was keen to sever any remaining ties with Leppington, the town that bore his name. He won't want to be reminded of it talking to me, either.*

To her surprise, however, she heard David's voice after a few ring tones.

'You've reached the voice mail of David Leppington. I can't answer the phone right now but . . .'

So you're not unreachable, after all.

The sense of relief was far greater than she'd expected. She couldn't face this alone. And in the cold light of day going to Lazarus Wake by herself would be sheer madness.

Beep.

The voice-mail prompt brought her back. 'David. This is Electra Charnwood. Can you ring me as soon as possible? I'm sorry to have to do this, but it's important.' She gave the number of the Station Hotel.

Just in case he'd misplaced – or even destroyed – it. But if only bad memories could be destroyed so easily.

She replaced the telephone.

'Good morning, Miss Charnwood.'

Electra looked up to see Katrina West walking downstairs. She was wearing black boots and a long woollen coat of pale amber. It was definitely a city coat. A beautiful one at that. There was freshness about her. She looked almost excited, too. As if she had something big planned for the day.

'Oh, we don't stand on ceremony at the Station Hotel. Call me Electra, please.'

'Only if you call me Katrina.'

'It's a deal.' Electra smiled. 'How was breakfast?'

'Wonderful. I don't usually eat much but I made a real pig of myself. I've never tasted bacon like it.' Her eyes twinkled. Electra hadn't seen anyone look so vivacious in a long while. Or so cheerful. When someone was feeling down that could be so damn irritating, but Electra found herself smiling broadly. *Hell, I haven't slept a wink all night and here I am grinning like the bloody Cheshire cat! The woman's high spirits are infectious.*

Electra watched Katrina move, her body poised as if she was about to start dancing.

Yes, I know your secret, my dear. You're in love. It's only just happened as well. Cupid's arrow just found another heart.

Katrina walked across to the hotel entrance and looked out. She seemed to be searching for someone or something.

'Katrina, if you need any directions just give me a holler.'

'I'm looking for a Mr Morrow.'

'From Morrow Autos?'

'I'm renting one of the hire cars. He said he'd bring it round at nine.'

'Mr Morrow's very reliable. I'm sure he'll be here soon.'

Katrina smiled. 'I'm like a kid on holiday, aren't I? It just looks so beautiful up there on the hills. I want to start exploring.'

'And there's plenty to explore out there. Have you got anywhere in mind?'

'I thought I'd just drive and see where I arrive.' She laughed. 'Not very well planned, I know, but I'm a great believer in serendipity.'

Electra smiled back. 'Me, too. But don't be too impulsive, will you? There's snow forecast. It doesn't take long for it to turn into a blizzard up here in the wilds. Our winters are vicious when they have a mind.'

'Oh, I hadn't realized.' Katrina looked disappointed. 'Sometimes I'm too reckless for my own good.'

'Don't worry, that's me all over, too.'

'I'll keep close to the town.' Katrina dipped her head to look through the window. 'I think Mr Morrow's here with the car now. Oh!' Suddenly she looked back at Electra as if she's been struck by a surprising thought. 'Say no if you don't want to. And I'm sure you're busy. But do you fancy coming out for a drive with me this morning?'

Electra glanced at the pile of unfinished paperwork in her office.

'I'm sorry,' Katrina said. She blushed. 'I'm being too impulsive. You've got the hotel to run.'

'I'm sure the hotel can run itself for at least one morning.' Electra smiled. 'I'd love to come for a drive.'

'That's great.'

'Be warned, I love to play tour guide, too. I'll get my coat.'

CHAPTER 12

I

'Never mind, I'll find it myself.'

Even the patient noticed the irritable tone of David's voice. The injured mechanic had a scalp laceration from eyebrow to ear where an over-inflated tyre had exploded in his face.

David Leppington gritted his teeth as he detected the sound of the streak of bad temper in his voice. In a more level tone he added, 'Finish the suture. I'll be back in a few minutes.'

The mechanic rolled his eyes at the nurse as if to say, 'Look who got out of bed on the wrong side this morning.'

Peeling off his latex gloves David left the treatment room. A&E was buzzing. Different times of the day brought different types of casualties. Weekends it was invariably children who'd fallen from bikes; there'd be the DIYers, too, injured by power tools or hurt in falls from ladders; in summer this changed to a flood of men who'd put garden forks through their feet or gashed their limbs with hedge trimmers. Now, on a Friday morning, as the last of the drunks with patched-up heads and black eyes limped home, in came the RTA casualties with a smattering of carpenters, electricians and builders (plus the mechanic with the tyre injury). So far all the injuries had been minor.

So why are you playing the bastard, David? he asked himself as he prowled the corridor like an angry grizzly bear. *Because the girl that I loved – and that I think I love again – is missing. Without her medication she's vulnerable. Even after just a few days without drugs she could start hearing voices again as the schizophrenia gets its ugly teeth into her sanity. The mind demons might tell her to kill herself. In that frame of mind she'd probably do it. And here I am treating patients with minor cuts when I should be—*

What, David? On your white charger racing to the rescue. She's not your patient. She's your ex.

But then he remembered only too vividly a couple of nights ago when he'd met her again. How she'd looked, naked in the candlelight in the bedroom. The way she'd felt when he'd stroked her skin. The smell of her hair. Burned into his mind was her expression of rapture as he'd made love to her. And he'd gone and done the crazy thing. He'd fallen in love with her all over again after all those years apart. He should be out searching for her, not stuck here for another eight hours.

Fuck this!

He'd reached the front reception desk when he realized that this wasn't where he wanted to be at all. He'd been looking for a set of X-rays for a patient brought in at the start of his shift with a suspected broken wrist after slipping on ice.

It's your own damn fault, David. You're so preoccupied with Katrina that you're letting your obsession interfere with your work.

He prided himself on his professionalism as a doctor. When he started a shift he shut personal problems out of his mind. All that mattered was the patient. Now this . . . he was like a lovesick teen. *Damn.*

Now where were the X-rays? *Think where you saw them last. They came down from radiography. I had the file in my hand. I had a few seconds between telephoning the surgical registrar and collecting the results of another patient's cardiogram test. So what would I do with a spare moment or two?*

I'd grab a look at the X-ray. To do that I'd need a light box. Got it!

He remembered he'd ducked into one of the treatment cubicles where he'd taken a look at the X-rays. Then his pager had sounded, announcing he'd got a call.

Katrina's phoning me. The thought had shoved everything else aside and he'd rushed to the nearest office to grab a phone. Only it hadn't been Katrina. It had been admin who'd wanted to schedule a meeting about staffing levels. *So that solves the mystery of the missing X-ray film,* he told himself. Now he knew which treatment room he'd used. There were more than a dozen of the rooms lining the corridor. Each had a pair of double doors that were wide enough to admit a trolley. The doors could be locked if a patient required privacy. He'd used the treatment room right at the far end of the corridor. The ones nearest reception filled up first. He pushed open the door.

'Good morning.'

'Oh, I'm sorry.' David smiled at the elderly man on the hospital trolley. 'I didn't know this room was occupied.'

'That's all right.'

'Are they looking after you?'

'I haven't got anything that demands urgent treatment. There's far more deserving cases out there.'

David smiled again. His bad mood began to fade as he slipped into the doctor role he'd practised for so many years now. 'I'm just picking up these films.' He took the file of X-rays with their shadow shapes of the wrist and splayed bones of the hand.

The old man nodded. He lay propped on a trolley with a blanket up as far as his bare shoulders. He looked relaxed. At least being in a hospital's A&E department hadn't alarmed him. And God knew they could be frightening places if you were sick or hurt.

'Fracture to the left wrist, I see,' the patient said. 'Distal end of the radius.'

'You're a medical man?'

The old man chuckled. 'Sort of. I'm a vet. I've been retired a good many years. Though I still know a fracture when I see one.'

'This isn't too bad.' David nodded at the X-ray. 'Might not even need a black slab.'

'Most of the fractures I attended to were feline or canine.' The retired vet smiled. 'Don't believe it when they say cats always fall on their feet, Dr . . . uhm?'

'Oh, I'm Doctor Leppington.' David smiled. He liked the man. The old fellow's calmness was having a relaxing effect on him too.

'Leppington? Now there's a coincidence.'

'Oh?' David walked toward the door. He needed to see the fracture patient.

'And the accent, too.'

'Ah, that's Lancashire.'

'No, it's not.' The man held up his finger. 'By the time you reach eighty-eight like I have you develop an ear for accents.'

David smiled, good-naturedly. 'I was raised in Liverpool.'

'Maybe. But there's some Yorkshire in there, too.'

'You *do* have a good ear. Now if you'll excuse me, I have—'

'Not just Yorkshire, either. North Yorkshire.'

David looked at him in surprise. 'Yes. I lived in North Yorkshire until I was six. But I thought any trace of Yorkshire accent would be long gone.'

'You don't lose those vowel sounds and inflections so quickly.' The old man smiled. 'I've lived in London forty years and there's still a bit of Yorkshire Tyke in me that just won't shift. Not that I want it to, you understand.'

'No, of course not.'

The man held out his hand. There wasn't so much as a tremor in the strong fingers. 'Sam Gotland.'

David shook his hand. 'David Leppington.'

'I'd flagged up the Leppington. I was born in Danby just a few miles up-valley from Leppington.'

Up-valley? That's a phrase I haven't heard in a while.

'I was born in Leppington.' David felt a moment's unease even admitting the fact. As if to talk about his birthplace would somehow resurrect the monsters that he'd fought three full years ago. *It's gone. It's history. All we're doing is chatting.*

'My goodness. Born in Leppington?'

'But I don't really know the place, Mr Gotland. I moved away before I—'

'Please . . . call me Sam.'

'Sam.' David acknowledged the invitation with a nod. 'My father was offered a job in Liverpool too good to refuse.'

'Needs must. Needs must.' The man's calm blue eyes looked over David's face. 'Of course, it won't be a coincidence that your family name is Leppington and that your home town is called Leppington?'

'There's an old family story that we're descended from a Viking warlord by the name of Leppingsvalt who conquered the area about a thousand years ago. He built a village that he called Leppingsvalt and gradually it became Anglicized.'

'And now it's known as Leppington.'

'Something like that.' David knew it was time to move on to see his patient. Only for some reason he felt a compulsion to stay and talk.

'My name Gotland is Viking, too. Just like your family, mine was known by the name of the valley that was their homeland. Gotland is in Denmark. It can be translated as "God Land". But of course the god referred to is one of the old Norse gods. The gods of blood and thunder.'

David's mouth went a little dry. The sounds of the hospital seemed far away, as if being in this room talking to the other man was taking him to another place. Then he had it. The man reminded him of his uncle. The resemblance lent an air of familiarity to their conversation, as if the old vet was a member of David's family.

When Sam Gotland motioned for David to sit, David sat on the edge of the table, the file forgotten in his arms.

'I'll let you into a little secret.' Sam spoke softly.

'Oh?'

'Our Viking forefathers arrived in the same fleet of ships.' He gave a friendly smile. 'Your ancestor, Leppingsvalt, was the leader. Legend had it that one of his ancestors was Thor himself.'

'The Viking god of war.'

'You know the legend too, David?'

'Yes, I know of it.' The hospital walls faded around him. He felt as if he was being drawn away to a distant place. The other man's voice was gentle. Almost hypnotic. David felt drowsy. His heart beat in a slow rhythm.

'So you know, David, that the old gods had given your ancestor an army of dead warriors in order to protect the ancient Viking way of life from the Christian invaders.'

'I know the story.'

'Not a story, David – historical fact.'

'That this army of the undead would return, and that they would feed on the blood of the living.' David grimaced. 'A vampire army.'

'One that waited for a new leader to take them into battle.' Sam's wise eyes stared intently at David. 'You knew who that leader would be?'

'It would be a descendant of Leppingsvalt.'

'Yes, one of the bloodline. Only now, of course, they're known as Leppington.'

'An interesting *story*,' David said, deliberately repeating the word he'd used earlier to describe the legend. He took a deep breath, trying to rouse himself from the clinging drowsiness. 'So what happened to the Gotland clan?'

'My ancestors settled up-valley. By the lake known as Lazarus Deep. Do you know it?'

'I've heard of it. My uncle used to take me up there as a child.'

'George Leppington.'

'You knew him?'

'I went to school with him. He was best man at my wedding.'

'Then you know he's dead?'

'Yes.'

You do know a lot, David thought as he tried to escape the man's calm gaze. Those blue eyes were hypnotic. *Do you know what happened three years ago in Leppington? When the vampire army of the ancient gods came in search of one of the last of the Leppingtons? And this son of the bloodline, who could trace his ancestry right back to the god Thor, denied responsibility for the vampire army, and destroyed them?*

David heard the restful rhythm of the old man's breathing. His own eyelids grew heavy. He was warm, sitting in the room. His arms were so heavy that he could not move them. Sam Gotland looked at him, tilting his head to one side.

The man is assessing me, David thought. *He's judging me.*

Sam continued to speak in that relaxed way. 'The Gotland clan made their home on the shores of Lazarus Deep. They fished the waters and farmed land nearby. They were famous for breeding livestock. In later years they even supplied the Australian government with their breed of sleep. The sheep were so hardy that they could live anywhere. You might say that animal husbandry ran in Gotland blood. That's why I became a vet, I guess.'

'And the Gotlands bred pigs, too.'

'Prizewinning pigs, yes.'

'Which your family sent to the slaughterhouse in Leppington.'

'I do think you're beginning to remember more of the family history, David. Both our families have been closely entwined for more than a thousand years. In fact, there is a legend that two thousand years ago Thor came to one of your ancestors in a dream and ordered him to travel to Judea, taking one of my forebears with him as a companion, in search of a boy child. A child whose followers would one day trouble our families, who'd destroy our ancient heritage. Your ancestor and mine travelled through the ancient world on a quest to—'

'I don't want to know.' David raised his head. He felt so tired now.

'No, I don't believe you do. But isn't "avoidance" a psychological trait common among doctors?'

'Avoidance?'

'Yes.' Sam Gotland's stare wouldn't let David go as the old man's eyes filled with a cold blue fire. 'Doctors often display traits typical of avoidance. They avoid conflict. They avoid having to make decisions. They avoid situations where they have to openly show disagreement with another's wishes.'

'Where's all this going?' David rubbed his face, trying to shift the black fog settling behind his eyes. Hell, he just wanted to find somewhere to lie down and sleep.

'Because, David, you avoid emotionally difficult situations. This leads to you not forming close relationships. You evade your own family's heritage. I *celebrate* mine. I know about the Gotland dynasty and Kirk Fenrir, their village on the banks of Lazarus Deep. I know how Kirk Fenrir sank beneath the lake, drowning the entire population. I've swum in the waters and seen the ruins myself. I've seen what still occupies the ruined homes—'

'I'm not interested.'

'No? You're fighting it, that's for sure. The modern, shallow part of you denies your heritage, but deep in your heart of hearts you know that it is true. And you know what destiny expects of you.'

'I'm sorry. I've patients to see.' David stood up. A sheer effort of will pushed the dark fog away from behind his eyes.

Sam Gotland echoed the words. 'I'm sorry. I've patients to see.' He shook his head, that grave blue-eyed stare still fixed on David. 'Avoidance, David Leppington. Avoidance.'

'I hope your stay here is a short one.'

'I'm sure it will be.'

David felt the weariness leave him. He blinked, feeling wider awake by the second.

'We need you, David.'

'We?'

'Your own people. The men and women of your blood.'

David shook his head. All he wanted was to get out of the room. The man's voice was like a drug.

'You had an army once. But you destroyed them.'

'What? An army of vampires?'

A third voice cut through the room behind David. 'What vampires?'

David spun round to see a confused hospital porter standing in the doorway. He looked bemused by David's outburst.

'I'm sorry,' David said, clutching the file. He felt dazed. Good cold fresh air would be wonderful right now.

'My apologies, doctor. I thought you were talking to me.' The hospital orderly stepped through the doorway and closed the door behind him. He was a middle-aged ex-soldier who was always at pains to be formally polite with medical staff.

'No, I was . . .' David tailed off, shrugging. 'It doesn't matter.'

The hospital porter wore an expression that suggested he was used to dealing with the eccentricities of doctors and surgeons. Here was a man who took such peculiarities in his stride.

David took a deep breath. A headache flared behind his eyes. He needed that fresh air more than ever. The X-ray films slipped from the file. David picked them up. The pull of vertigo nearly toppled him to his knees.

'Are you feeling all right, doctor?' asked the porter.

'I'm fine. You carry on.'

'I'll attend to this gentlemen, then.'

David straightened to see the man pulling the sheet straight up over Sam Gotland's face.

David raised his hand. 'Wait a minute – what do you think you're doing?'

The porter's expression slipped back into one of bewilderment. 'I'm getting him ready.'

'But you don't cover a patient's face like that. How long have you worked here?'

David pushed past the porter to draw the sheet back. He recoiled. Gotland lay flat on his back, his eyes closed. David saw the tell-tale blue shading around the old man's lips.

'A nurse told me to move this one out of the treatment room. See?' The porter showed David a clipboard. 'Samuel J. Gotland. He was brought in more than an hour ago. Dead on arrival.'

'*Dead on arrival?*'

'Yes, doctor, it should have the cause of death down here on—'

David pushed open the door and walked away.

'Doctor Leppington . . .' The hospital porter's voice followed him down the corridor. 'You've forgotten your X-rays . . . Dr Leppington? Dr Leppington . . .'

CHAPTER 13

I

By the time Electra returned to the Station Hotel with Katrina the threat of snow had passed. Radio reports forecast the arrival of milder, windier weather later in the afternoon.

As they left the car in the car park Electra said, 'That's me being overcautious, I'm afraid.'

Katrina smiled. 'Better safe than sorry. You know the area better than I do.'

'It can get nasty. Roads are often blocked by snow in minutes. Even locals forget how dangerous it can be on the moors.'

'I might go further afield tomorrow.' Katrina stopped as if she'd heard something that startled her. 'What's that?'

Electra looked round the hotel's small car park. 'What's what?'

'That noise.'

Electra saw that Katrina's eyes had suddenly acquired a nervous flicker. Electra shrugged. 'All I can hear is the river. After all this rain, it's— Katrina? I wouldn't go that that way. The banks are muddy.'

Katrina didn't hear. She hurried to the gap in the wall where a path led through bushes to the river bank.

What's got into her? Electra followed, her own alarm growing. *Why has the sound of the river frightened her?*

'Katrina,' Electra called after the other woman, who hurried forward, her amber coat flapping wide in the breeze.

'Katrina. It's not safe on the banks when the river's in flood.'

Electra knew she had to follow. By this time Katrina had vanished into the bushes. *Damn, this is dangerous. Swift currents tear away the earth under the bank. If you stand too near the edge the crust of turf is likely to give way under your feet, dropping you into the river.*

'Katrina . . . wait . . .'

Electra, it's dangerous for other reasons too, isn't it? Shivering, she pushed her way through the bushes. She tried to avoid looking in the direction of the storm drain where Jack Black had died.

Three years ago I stood here and watched him bleed—

Electra shoved the thought aside. 'Katrina. It's not safe here . . . *Katrina!*'

2

The gales shrieked through the trees. Branches without leaves clawed at a sky bloated with lumbering cloud. Electra called out again as Katrina leaned over the water. Just a metre beneath her the river tore by in a swirling mass of foam. The force of it was enormous. It roared over the boulders. In the shallows it fizzed white. In the deep parts it was the same liquid black as the centre of an eye.

'Katrina.'

Electra grabbed the other woman's arm. She felt firm muscle quiver beneath the sleeve. Katrina vibrated with sheer emotion.

'Katrina, come back from the edge . . . *please.*'

For a second the woman resisted, even leaning further out. The breeze tugged the curls across her face in a hazy veil. Her eyes seemed to burn through the hair so brightly that something recoiled inside Electra.

'Katrina, you'd best—'

'God, it's marvellous, isn't it? Feel that *power!*'

'It's quite something.' Electra spoke calmly but inside she was shouting, *Get back from the river. You don't know what it can do!*

'The sense of power's enormous.' Katrina had to raise her voice over the roar of the water. 'It's more than just seeing it or hearing it – you can feel its energy pounding up through the soles of your feet. Here! Touch the tree.'

With an abrupt movement Katrina seized Electra's hand and pushed it against the willow trunk. The force of the water transmitted some of its energy through the timber. Electra felt the wood vibrate beneath her hand. Katrina's body quivered in time with it as well. The wind caught Electra's hair, wrapping it across her face. All she could see were dark, rippling strands. All she could feel was the vibration of the tree and Katrina's bare hand pressing against hers.

'What is this?'

Electra heard the voice above the thunder of tumbling water but discovered that she couldn't find her own voice to reply.

With the fingers of her other hand, Katrina gently moved Electra's hair from her face. 'What's the name of the river, Electra?'

'The Lepping,' Electra said at last. 'Let's go indoors. It's not safe here.' She dipped her head to hide the blush spreading across her face.

'The Lepping? My God, it's awesome! If you were to dive in there you'd vanish, wouldn't you? There's no way you'd ever be found!'

'Come on, it's cold out here.' Folding her arms, Electra shivered deeply. 'There's still time to order lunch in the bar. Or you can have something sent to your room.'

Electra glanced down at her bare wrists as she shivered again. Katrina noticed too.

'Goose bumps,' she announced, touching Electra's bare

skin with a beautifully shaped nail. 'Someone just walked over your grave.'

Then Katrina walked quickly back to the hotel. As she did so she threw smiling glances back over her shoulder.

Electra followed, feeling the heat in her face as the blush deepened.

3

The plan was simple. Arrive Whitby on the 6:30 train. A meal at the Whitby Tandoori, then the short walk in the direction of Bagdale to the cinema.

The plan's gone all wrong, Dylan Adams told himself as they walked along the harbour pier. *But it's gone wrong in a beautiful, wild, amazing way.*

'I'm up for it if you are.' Vikki looked up at him, shifting her gaze away from the night-time darkness of the ocean surf as it glided toward the shore in gleaming, luminous lines of white. A gull hovered on the breeze overhead. And across the harbour the lights of Whitby were shining as bright as so many precious jewels cast across the hillside. While above it all on the hilltop loomed the bulk of the ancient Church of St Mary.

Vikki's statement tingled through Dylan's bloodstream. The meal in the Whitby Tandoori had been a good one . . . no, it had been a *great* one. It was more than the cuisine, too. Dylan had sensed it. Magic had sparked between them.

'Well?' She smiled, the lights from across the water twinkling in her eyes. 'Are you going to keep me waiting all night?'

He couldn't stop his gaze flitting from her face to her hair feathering in the breeze, to glimpses of her slender figure as currents of air flipped open her leather jacket.

'Seems like a great idea,' he said, smiling slowly.

'You won't blame me for missing the film?'

'Not at all.' He kissed her on the lips again. Her mouth had become a magnet. It drew him every few moments.

'So we'll marry our fortunes together, as the line in the song goes.' She laughed, touching her lips as she did so. 'I can't believe we're doing this.'

'Nor me.' Dylan pulled out his wallet. 'I've got a couple of tens.'

'Same here – and I've got my credit card, just in case.' Vikki took his hand and pulled him back toward the town, pretending that he was reluctant to move. 'Come on. Don't dawdle.'

As if I would.

'You think we'll find one?' he asked.

'What, a coastal resort in winter? There'll be hotel vacancies galore!' Her eyes flashed with excitement.

That excitement transmitted to him, too. His heart beat hard in his chest.

She kissed him again, her mouth pressing firmly against his. 'First, I'll phone my mother and tell her I won't be home tonight. Then . . .' With one finger she stroked his chest. 'Then we'll find out more about each other. Hmm?'

He slipped his arms around her. Seagulls screamed in the distance. 'I should warn you, Vikki.'

'Oh?'

'I'm a wicked man. I do wicked things.'

Her soft lips touched his. 'Hmm . . . Promises, promises.' She gripped his hand, suddenly impatient. 'Come on, we don't have to stay out in the cold now.'

Fires blazed in Dylan's blood.

God, yes, life had got so much more complicated. So much more exciting, too.

4

Straight after work, Bernice Mochardi went to the cinema alone. Something she'd never done before. But the prospect of another restless evening at home didn't appeal. Nor did a trip to the Princess Louise where the Goths flocked like ravens. Every aspect of her life made her uneasy now. Bernice felt she didn't belong in this town any more. Something new was coming into her life; some huge event. She couldn't begin to guess what it was, but it was creeping up on her with all the dark promise of a thunderstorm looming over the horizon on a summer's day.

5

When David Leppington arrived home that evening he saw the light on the answer machine flashing. He pressed the button.

'*David. This is Electra Charnwood. Can you ring me as soon as possible? I'm sorry to have to do this. But it—*'

He deleted the message. *Dear God. No way. Not after today . . .*

Immediately he went to take a shower, tearing his clothes off as if they were contaminated. If only he could peel away the memories so quickly. He couldn't shift the image of Sam Gotland's face. Those blue eyes. They'd been hypnotic.

David, you don't have conversations like that. Dead men don't talk. They don't walk.

Only you know better, don't you, Leppington? The man with the town named after him.

He scrubbed his body under the steaming power jets. He lathered soap on his face to mask the hospital smell that lingered in his nostrils. If only he could dismiss the conversation with the dead man as a common-or-garden hallucination, then *great!* He could write it off as overwork. Only he knew better, didn't he? He wondered if he should telephone Electra Charnwood in her monstrous Gothic hotel, then tell her what had happened. She wouldn't doubt him for a second. He could even imagine her husky voice saying, 'Yes, David. I expected this all along. They're back, aren't they?'

No, he wouldn't do that. Whatever Electra needed from him he didn't want to know. Doctors bury their mistakes. He'd bury all links between himself and what had happened in that Yorkshire town of Leppington three years ago. That included Electra. He wouldn't telephone her. Come to that, he wouldn't answer any telephone calls.

But what if it's Katrina? No problem. I can use the answer machine to screen them.

He rubbed his soapy hands across the back of his neck. It ached like fury. Whisky would be good right now. He raised his face to the driving rods of water. Their force stung his face but he didn't mind.

Sinking a bottle of whisky while sprawling in front of the television had its appeal all right, but he was stronger than that. A sense of duty called louder than the bottle of spirits. He still needed to find Katrina. Without her medication every day that passed would put her deeper in danger. The schizophrenia demon would soon break free of the chains that the pharmaceuticals had bound it with. *If anything happens to her, it's my fault.*

That wasn't entirely logical, he told himself as he turned off the water. Professionally, he wasn't responsible for Katrina. But emotionally he was. He'd never forgive himself if she came to harm.

'You're doomed, aren't you, Leppington?' He murmured the words at his reflection as he wiped the mirror. 'You're doomed to haul a ship full of guilt around after yourself. You always find yourself thinking that you could have helped Katrina. You blame yourself for her breakdown . . . you self-pitying bastard. Oh, and now comes the self-loathing, Dr Leppington. Yet another safety valve in your psychological make-up, eh?' He wiped the upper quarter of the mirror free of condensation. The reflection of Jack Black stared back at him. The wound in the figure's throat yawned wide.

David's heart lurched so hard in his chest that it hurt. He spun round.

Steam hung in dense clouds in the bathroom. Through it he could see shapes – the kitchen cabinet, a shelf, a framed print of dolphins.

But no Jack Black.

Dead men don't talk; they don't walk. He repeated this to himself as he went through into the bedroom to dress. It was time to pull himself together, to forget about the freak event of the day, to put Electra Charnwood from his mind. It was time to continue his search for Katrina.

6

In the middle of the night seagulls scream over the rooftops of Whitby. The raven glides through the ruins of the ancient abbey on the clifftop. Surf pounds against rocks. Boats tug at their moorings on the ebb tide. Whitby's streets and alleyways are empty. The pubs are closed. Church Lane is a windswept canyon at this time of night. The wonderfully named Arguments Yard echoes to the ghostly groan of air currents that play through the eaves of the houses and to nothing more.

The raven glides over the River Esk before soaring upward, hugging the contours of the valley side, the jumble of the town's roofs below. The bird's black-as-death wings are outstretched, running wing-tips across the dead winter sky. Beneath it is the roof of a large building.

Sensing rather than seeing, it gazes down through the tiles, through the attic piled with a century's worth of furniture, dusty suitcases and the bones of a lost cat; it peers down through the ceiling to a room where two humans lie sleeping on a bed.

These two are important. Why? The raven doesn't know. Only its master knows the reason. And far away in Lazarus Deep the waters are stirring. Pale shapes rise up; they move as slowly as the creeping iron hands of a church clock.

Soon their time will come.

7

Below, in the hotel room, Dylan heard the cry of the raven pierce the walls and drive deep into his brain. He sat up, panting. His heart thudded in his chest. For a moment he saw the furniture in the roof space as if he was looking up at it through water. His shortness of breath began to hurt.

He was eleven years old again. Six feet underwater when his flipper buckle caught in the seaweed. He couldn't swim back to the surface. His lungs tightened. He had to breathe but the moment he opened his mouth the ocean would gush into his throat and drown him. The pain of suffocation engulfed him. He needed—

'Dylan. Are you OK?'

The voice broke the evil spell of the nightmare. The hotel room was normal. He was breathing easily.

'I'm fine.' He looked down at the lovely face against the pillow. Vikki's expression of concern melted into a smile. She stroked his bare back.

'This has been nice,' she breathed. 'I've loved it.'

'*Has* been nice? We don't have to be out of the room until ten.'

He saw her gaze stray to the clock radio.

'Hmm . . .' She stretched and smiled. Her teeth glinted with amazing brightness in the gloom. 'That gives us another five hours.'

Dylan slipped his hand under the blanket to caress her naked waist. Slowly, he allowed his palm to stroke her skin as far as her hip. Vikki turned to face him and once more her soft mouth found his. The nightmare was gone. Instead, his body began to respond to her touch. First came a helter-skelter of thoughts. *London . . . I'll get that job. I'll find a flat. Vikki can join me. Every morning I can wake up . . . find her like this . . . naked . . . warm . . . a lively, beautiful woman . . .*

Then thought vanished, too, as instinct took over, and he folded her into his arms.

CHAPTER 14

I

It's sex in the back of the van. It's eight in the morning. Oh, and am I loving it . . . Bone-shaking sex . . . brain-stirring sex . . . sex making blood fizz in the veins . . .

'Yes, like that . . . that's it,' she murmured. *That's it:* round and round. *'S nicer than just* in and out. *It takes men a long time to learn that round and round is best for a woman.* And at the age of twenty-six Steff Kline celebrated her womanhood thoroughly and often. After a nerve-stripping week at the architectural practice where she headed the design team for a new international airport she knew she'd damn well deserved this. It was one thing to earn a six-figure salary, but it took experience to be able to extract maximum *excitement* from that mountain of cash.

Steff Kline lay on a blanket in the back of the dive truck parked on the shore at Lazarus Deep. She'd known Goldi for a while. She'd teased him often enough about his blond dreadlocks. Once he'd pelted her with wild blackberries on a rock climb. She'd said she'd get him for that. Now she had.

This morning they'd driven up from Morningdale together, ahead of the rest of the dive team, with the aqualung cylinders and face masks in the back of the truck. When Steff had parked she'd leaned across to Goldi where he sat in the passenger seat, pulled back his dreadlocks and whispered into his ear. 'The others won't be here for ages yet. Come into the back. I want to see how you fuck.'

God, yes, now she could *feel* how he fucked. The dreadlocks swished down into her face. He rotated his hips, groaning, panting, sweat dripping down his chest. Steff had already wriggled part-way into the wetsuit top. She loved the way the rubber constricted her. It clung to her upper half, pulling her in tight. Her bottom half was naked. She felt Goldi's stomach, groin and thighs against hers. She relished the feel of his skin rasping against her skin. She moaned as he gripped hold of the zip on her sweatsuit, tugging it down to expose her breasts that glistened with captive perspiration. Scents of sex were rich in the air.

Goldi sucked her nipples. Steff felt his teeth nip, too. God, this was good, this was wonderful. His cock worked somewhere deep inside her body. His pubic hair scraped the skin of her lower belly.

God, this boy was going for gold. *Yeee-ha!*

The side of the truck clanged. 'Hey, Steff! You in there?'

Goldi stopped dead inside her. 'Vance?' he whispered

She nodded. Then she whispered, 'Shit. He told me he wouldn't be here until nine.'

'Bloody Christ. Trust him to fuck it up.'

She giggled under him. Goldi's face was a picture.

Goldi frowned. 'It's not funny.'

'Shh.' Then, louder, she called, 'Vance. I'm just getting into my suit. Give me ten minutes.' She looked up at Goldi; his throat bulged. It was all veiny and red. She could feel more proof of his fierce arousal inside her body.

'Is he going?'

'Shh – listen.' She put her finger to her lips. From the back of the truck there was no way of looking out. The windows in the rear doors were painted over. She waited a moment, content to run her fingers up and down the crack of Goldi's arse. *Nice arse. Two mounds of hard muscle. Round as footballs, too.* She scratched a buttock hard enough with her nail for him to jerk forward.

Ooooh, felt *that, honey*.

His jerking rocked the truck. Aqualung tanks shook in their racks.

'Hey.' Goldi looked down at her. 'You'll leave a mark.'

'Don't you want me to mark you?'

She did it again.

'Steff.'

She saw that he didn't know whether to be angry or laugh.

'What's Vance doing?'

'Be patient, Goldi.'

A second later a car door slammed.

'He's gone back to warm himself,' she said. 'Now . . . you finish me off.'

He grinned. He took his weight on his outstretched hands that were planted at either side of her head. Lightly she bit his wrist as he made with those delicious limbo movements again. His hips rotated. That rigid hunk of manhood moved inside her again. Slippery as she didn't know what.

'Ooooh,' she cooed. 'Keep it like that.'

'Faster?'

'If you like.' She smiled at him. 'Don't rock the truck, though. Vance'll know.'

Steff lay back, feeling the delicious friction against her body. Then, all too quickly, it was over. With a groan Goldi shot all he had inside her. She wrapped her legs around him, pulling him tight against her while she raised her bottom, pushing up against his body.

For a few moments they lay together. Steff felt his heart beating against her breast. Sucking a middle finger with a deliberately maintained short fingernail she reached down, then jabbed the finger into Goldi's anus. He convulsed, slamming his hips against hers. *Hmm*. A man's involuntary thrusts could be nicer than the intentional ones.

'Eeech!' He gritted his teeth. 'What ya do that for?'

'Just a little something to remember me by, Goldi.'

He closed his eyes, yielding to her deeply probing finger. Wincing when it stung. Sighing when it brought pleasure.

Oh, I need more . . . That was sweetness itself. After a while Steff withdrew her finger, then whispered, 'Go through the curtain at the front of the truck. You can climb over the seats and leave by the cabin door.'

'Don't you want Vance to know what we've just been doing?'

'That pig?'

'He's that bad?'

'Worse. He'll make vulgar comments all day.'

'Where can I go?'

'Into the woods.'

'What?' Disbelief made Goldi's voice sound almost high-pitched. 'You want me to hide in the trees?'

'No, you lovable lump, you. Walk through the woods to the road, then cut back along the track.'

'Why?'

'Vance'll think you caught the bus or had a lift or something and you've just walked down from the road.'

'Sounds a bit too devious to me.' Goldi brushed his dreadlocks back, looking doubtful.

'You obviously don't know what kind of pig Vance is. Like I said, he'll keep making stupid jokes about us if he finds out you've been fucking me in the back of the truck.'

'Well . . .'

'It'll only take you twenty minutes to walk to the road and back again.' Steff stroked his testicles. 'Please . . . pretty please.'

'Seeing as it's you.' He grinned that huge toothy grin of his. 'OK.'

'You're my hero.' She gently pinched the end of his penis. 'You can do me all over again later. If you want?'

'You've got a deal.'

'Go. And don't let him see you.'

Steff Kline waited for a few minutes until she reckoned, that Goldi had reached the trees. Pulling the blanket round her waist like a long skirt, she pushed open the back door of the truck. Vance climbed out of his car, which he'd parked right at the water's edge, and walked across to her. Ice-cold air gusted up the blanket, chilling the hot cleft between her legs.

Vance was stocky, with a bulging neck like a bull's. *Or maybe that should be a pig's*, she mused. The man had the appetite of a pig. He had a brutish sense of humour. He treated women like crap. She didn't like him at all.

Steff pulled open the blanket to reveal her naked lower half; cold fingers of air stroked her pubic hair. 'Time for a quick one?'

Every man has his uses.

2

By nine most of the dive team were there. They numbered ten in all. Steff watched them heft the compressed-air cylinders from the back of the truck. On its side explosive Day-Glo lettering spelled: *Club Adrenalin!* Most of the team were shivering as they looked up at the forbidding skies. Cloud moved in slabs that were nearer black than grey. To Steff's eyes they formed the shapes of grotesque heads that had hollow eyes and mouths that yawned wide. She shivered, too.

There go the feet across my grave. Steff forced the black neoprene hood over her head; the rubber tugged at her hair. With an effort, she tugged the rim that fitted close to her face and pushed wisps of hair back inside.

Waves stirred on Lazarus Deep. They ran shoreward to

break over beachside boulders. An observer wouldn't think it was a freshwater lake. Today it looked more like an angry ocean.

'Awesome, totally awesome!'

Steff watched Goldi run at the lake. This time his golden dreadlocks were crammed inside his wetsuit's rubber hood. The body-hugging neoprene turned him into a hard silhouette against the line of cars. Whooping, he ran across the beach to throw himself into the water. He splashed there like a kid at the swimming pool.

'Come on in, you wimps. The water's lovely . . . warm as a bath!' Goldi swam on his back, shouting for them to hurry.

Vance winked at Steff. 'Warm as a bath?'

'His idea of a joke,' she replied.

Steff saw Vance's appreciative gaze flick over her figure, now embraced tightly by the second skin of her wetsuit. 'Do you want to come over to my house later?'

'Sorry.' She smiled. 'I'm going riding.'

'Riding.' He nodded. 'Energetic girl.'

'It's the weekend. You've got to let it rip, haven't you?' Before Vance could say anything else, Steff called to the others. 'OK. Everyone got a diving buddy? Everyone checked their air tanks are full? And everyone got their life jackets?' Each diver gave a thumbs-up as they helped each other to strap on the aqualungs.

'Goldi . . . Goldi! Time to get out of the water.' She turned back to the others. 'OK, we're an extreme-sports club. We love extreme things.'

'Extreme drinking.'

'Extreme copulation.'

It was the usual good-natured banter.

She laughed. 'OK, OK. But this is a freshwater dive so you're going to be less buoyant; keep that in mind if you need to come up fast. So, remember: safety first. Fun second.'

They gave the usual jeers.

'Steff, we laugh in the face of danger. That's our motto.'

'Yeah, I've got it tattooed on my butt!'

Goldi stood knee-deep in the water, giving a clenched-fist salute. 'Glory before safety. Death before dementia.'

The others applauded him. 'Well said.'

'OK. We all plan to die before we trade in our kit for Zimmer frames.' She glanced up at the cloud faces tumbling over the hills. Vaporous corpse faces. 'But not just yet, do you hear?'

'We'll be fine, Steff.' Vance buckled on his weight belt. 'You know we will.'

'We've never dived Lazarus Deep before. We don't know what's down there.'

'Of course we do.' With a huge grin on his face, Goldi lumbered out of the water. 'There's Pirate Gold down there.'

Pirate Gold was club-speak for the adrenalin buzz. That was why they were here. Pirate Gold – the rush that was stronger than an orgasm. By now, Pirate Gold was their drug of choice. Rock-climbing, bungee jumping, surfing at Sand's End on Christmas Day. Diving deeper than was safe or even sane. All Pirate Gold. Forget stimulating your favourite sex organ – this was the Full Body Fuck.

'Just be careful, do you hear? Don't take any risks. And—'

They all chorused: *'And stay with your buddies.'*

Steff smiled. 'And stay with your buddies.'

Above her the scowling mask of cloud glared down. Waves sucked at the shoreline. The sound that beasts made, feeding at a trough. And there, deep in the mix, were rivers of arctic air pulsing through branches of dead trees. She saw the gaunt sticks clawing at the air. This barren place gave the breeze a voice. It sounded like breathless laughter that mocked the people beside the lake.

And the lake itself?

I don't like the look of you at all.

Lazarus Deep looked as though it had been transformed by evil magic. It no longer seemed like water. It was liquid darkness, a seething ocean of shadow filled with noxious forms that flitted beneath the surface. Ghost sharks. Phantoms of creatures that had haunted the glacier lake in primeval days long before humans had even named their dark and monstrous gods who thundered through the sky on steeds of black lightning.

A dark mist had gathered behind Steff's eyes. She felt drowsy. The group of laughing young people were far away.

Come out of the water. We're not diving today. I don't like it. It's not safe . . . The warning tried to force its way through her lips. She wanted to tell them that the dive was off. A storm was building over the mountains. Only they'd mock her. They'd say she was too old for the club.

Grandma Steff. Go home and knit yourself a cardigan. Grandma Steff's going to bingo . . .

She adjusted the straps of the aqualung. On land it was a brutally heavy piece of steel.

So what's it to be, Grandma Steff? Cancel the dive. Then home for a nice cup of tea, you old dear . . .

She pushed the mocking voice into the back of her head. 'Don't forget your fins, Goldi . . . Right, gang. Are we ready to dive?'

They gave their thumbs-up signal.

'I didn't hear you, gang. I said: *Are we ready to dive?*'

They whooped and clapped their hands above their heads. Automatically, she counted the divers as they picked their way across the pebbles. Ten humped figures in their wetsuits and breathing apparatus. Steff stepped into the lake. Black water swirled round her calves; the current tugged at her, eager to carry her to where Lazarus Deep sank into some fathomless abyss that was colder and darker than any grave.

3

Coldness penetrated Steff Kline's rubber diving suit. She shuddered to the roots of her bones.

There go feet marching over my grave again. She bit into her breathing equipment's mouthpiece. *Now don't be so macabre. Enjoy the dive. Feel the buzz.*

She pulled the face mask down as she waded slowly into the icy waters of Lazarus Deep. Through the glass she saw the vastness of the lake stretching out in front of her. It had hardly been dived before. The club was doing what it loved to do: taking a leap into the unknown.

To Steff's left and right the dive team moved as if in slow motion, wading deeper and deeper into the water. They were faceless things now behind their masks. Their eyes were invisible. All she could see in the glass plates were reflections of the lake, the hills, the ominous cloud – now an unbroken slab nailed down onto the face of the valley.

Waves buffeted her chest. A burst of spray licked her bare skin beneath the mask and wetsuit hood. Steff clenched her teeth as the cold bit through the rubber, penetrating the layer of warmer water sandwiched between suit and skin that was intended to shield the diver from the worst of the cold. This would be a hazardous dive. The weather was deteriorating. But to call it off now would probably mean the end of her membership of the club. Wimps weren't tolerated.

A hand touched her arm. Steff glanced back to see Goldi grinning at her around the mouthpiece of his aqualung. The glass of the mask hid his eyes, but she saw the distorted reflection of herself give a thumbs-up sign. Again, she counted the divers. *Ten.* She thought of calling out one last time: *Everyone remember to stick together. The water's getting rough.*

No. That would sound weak. Especially to men like Vance.

They'd give each other knowing smiles that would say all too clearly: *Old Steff's over the hill*. And, at twenty-six, she *was* the oldest here.

One by one the black-suited figures dipped their knees, allowing the water to rise up their torsos and so bear the weight of the heavy compressed-air cylinders. Steff heard Goldi give a wild whoop into his mouthpiece as he launched himself forward into the lake. A stir of bubbles and he was gone. Around her the other divers did the same. Soon she was the only one left with her head above water. She glanced back at the shore.

Beyond the line of cars and the dive truck the trees had become a writhing mass of spikes as the wind tore at them. Even through the wetsuit hood she could hear the scream of turbulent air tearing along the valley.

Past the fringe of trees the valley sloped up to a house that stood by itself in the middle of this godforsaken nowhere. Steff had never noticed it before. It was an ugly brute of a thing, built of bone-white stone and with deep-set windows that reminded her of eyes . . . weird goblin eyes at that. Around it, trees and bushes were in ceaseless motion in the high wind, writhing, twisting, squirming, trembling. Just looking at the building made her uneasy.

What's got into you today? You're so jumpy. Your imagination is running away with you.

That vertigo she'd experienced earlier came back, catching her in its dizzying grip. Through the face mask she glanced back at the forbidding house. Water droplets had splashed on the mask's glass. Peering through them, Steff thought that the house looked even more monstrously distorted. Its white stonework seemed to blaze with white rays. While in the window—

What was that?

A face was looking out at her. A shockingly white face both

magnified and warped by the beads of water. A man was
shouting at her from behind a window-pane. He beat at it
with his fists. He looked as though he was in the grip of some
dreadful panic.

He's seen something behind me . . .

Steff twisted round, her movements clumsy under the
weight of the aqualung cylinders. Water swirled as she turned.
Waves slapped at her chest again, unbalancing her. *What in
God's name has he seen?*

Steff found herself holding her breath as she scanned the
lake anxiously. But Lazarus Deep was just the same as it
had been a few moments ago. A dozen metres away the
dive team would be swimming beneath the surface. Rain
came down across the valley in a twisting veil. It struck her
rubber suit with a pattering sound. The lake surface dimpled;
a goose-flesh effect.

Once more she turned back to the house that was white as
a skull on the hill.

There's no one there. They've gone . . . Steff wiped her
mask with her gloved hand. There was nothing for her to
be concerned about. The man in the house couldn't spook
her, could he now?

The water reached her breasts . . . and *youch!* How that
cold gripped them through the rubber. Shivers ran from
her nipples to tingle through her breasts, to spread over her
chest, and then to engulf her entire body in electric chills.
Her teeth would have chattered together if it hadn't been for
the mouthpiece grips between her jaws. Across her tongue
from the tank flowed air now flavoured with rubber from the
connecting hoses. Strangely, it reminded her of taking a deep
breath after sucking a mint. It still had that type of pristine
freshness, despite the underlying rubber odour.

At that moment Steff launched herself forward. The surface
of Lazarus Deep closed over her head. Here the water formed

a grey mist in front of her mask. Visibility was almost zero. Particles streamed by her head as she swam. Shapes appeared. They were indistinct at first, only resolving themselves into pieces of twig and dead leaves as she moved toward them. Steff slowly kicked her legs, the fins on her feet driving her deeper beneath the misty layer of surface water. When it cleared she saw the other divers had left her behind. She was alone.

4

In front of Steff the water became a pit of grave-dark shadow. She could have believed she was swimming through liquid darkness rather than cold lake water.

Where have they gone? She'd only paused for a moment when she'd thought she'd seen the man with the stark white face trying to warn her of—

No, not warn me; that was my imagination taunting me. Now everyone's left me behind. Damn. Why didn't they wait? For God's sake, they know not to leave anyone to dive alone.

Steff swam deeper. Perhaps they were just a little way ahead. She could catch them up if she moved more quickly. As she finned through the water she unhooked the diver's lamp from her belt and thumbed the switch. The light beam shot out ahead. Now she could see that although it was dark, incredibly dark, there were red tints to the water.

It's like swimming through red wine, she told herself, surprised. It was a deep, deep red that couldn't have been far removed from black. Probably natural mineral deposits carried into the lake by streams had coloured the water in this way. Steff shone the lamp downward to assess how deep it was at this point. In the distance she could make out that the lake bed had a covering of boulders roughly the size and shape of human heads. Weed trailed from them. Long witch hair. That was what it looked like. Green slimy witch hair. She estimated the lake bed to be about forty feet beneath her. She checked her own gauge. It told her that she was twenty feet down.

Steff Kline swam deeper still, guessing that the team would move nearer to the lake bed on the lookout for any interesting finds. A shoal of fish ghosted through the water. They weren't startled by her presence. She didn't recognize the type. They were perhaps a little larger than a human hand. They had long dark bodies that were oddly snakelike; their eyes bulged, round as marbles, from their heads. A moment later the fish passed from view. She checked her gauge. Forty feet deep. She glanced down. The boulders were becoming indistinct as they receded into swirling shadow. *So the lake bed's dropping.* She'd heard that it might fall away as deep as two thousand feet. That was as deep as the hills were high at this end of the valley. Of course she couldn't reach a fraction of that depth. Her limit would be a hundred feet. Now, where were the other divers?

Damn them.

She finned on, listening to the rhythm of her own breathing as her lungs drew air from the cylinder, through the valve, along the hose and into her body. Then came her exhalation. Spent air bubbled from the valve, rumbling in that characteristic muffled way as bubbles swept past her ears for the now-distant surface. Glancing up, Steff saw the layer of misty grey that lay just beneath the surface, obscuring it. A full-blown storm might be raging up there. But down here it was as silent as a grave. The water was still. There was no noise apart from her own breath followed by the bubble and rush of spent air from the valve.

Steff stared into the dark void in front of her, searching for the lights of the other divers. In the distance shapes twisted eerily in the darkness. *Maybe . . .*

No, not divers. There was no tell-tale stream of bubbles. No lamps, either. Even so, she swam toward the formless shapes that were just beyond the range of clear visibility. There was a chance that otters lived in the lake. Perhaps even a family of catfish that had grown monstrously large over the years. She finned her way through the encircling gloom. Beyond the range of the lamp there was that deep unyielding darkness. *That's the kind of darkness you find in the depths of space,* she told herself. *Limitless. Almost palpable.*

Steff strained to look. Purple blooms blossomed on her retinas with the effort of trying to see. The coldness of the water slithered through the wetsuit, into her skin and along her bloodstream to chill her heart. She shivered. The deep silence worked its way into her head, too. The ancient waters of Lazarus Deep formed a yawning gulf beneath her. It was a dark, brooding place. Its ghostly vastness left her feeling like nothing more significant – or alive – than one of those dead leaves hanging there in the water.

The pressure squeezed her rib cage. It became harder to breathe. Steff's heart thudded with a morbid, funereal beat in her chest. The melancholy spirit that permeated the water crept into her. Through the smeary darkness the shapes still twisted with eerie grace. Only now they began to swell with ominous promise . . . like those indistinct forms that flitted on the boundaries of nightmare. Never seen clearly but always terrible. Frightening shapes that weren't identifiable. But were bloated with the power to terrify.

She needed to find the others. Her imagination haunted her reason now. Alone here in the depths of the lake her mind was running out of control. Maybe those forms just beyond reach were her friends after all? If she swam closer she could check.

With an eerie sense of detachment, Steff moved through the water like a ghost . . . she was the spirit that haunted the lake now. A sleek, masked creature. Swimming hard, her thighs aching, she sped through fathomless depths.

Closer . . . closer . . .

Now use the lamp. She shone it ahead of her.

Men and women hung in the water. They floated upright as if standing on invisible platforms. Their hair floated out in goblin tresses.

Her first thought: *Why have they taken off their gear?*

But these weren't Steff's friends. A dozen men and women were floating there. They should have drowned long ago. They should be swollen corpses with corrupted eyes; their chests and limbs should have been fields of green weed.

Only these things were white. Bloodless white. Their eyes blazed at her. Eyes such as she'd never seen before. There was no colour to them. Only an eggshell white, containing a hard black dot in the centre. Their stares were fixed on her.

They're waiting for me.

A man glided through the water. Although he was young his hair was as white as that milky skin he and the others had. But his eyes were different. They were a luminous green that flashed with witch fire. He was smiling, and his teeth looked enormous behind his lips.

The figures moved forward to Steff, their hands outstretched. With the albino was another young man with a swirling mass of black hair. Behind him came monstrous figures with bald heads and humped shoulders. All those dead years in the water had turned them into creatures that were far from human. Their fingers were clawlike. Veins like purple rope wormed under their throats and bulged proud of their arms.

Steff screamed into the mouthpiece. Then she writhed in the water, turning herself completely around so that she could get away from them. Swimming hard, she glanced back. They powered after her, moving with the grace of killer sharks.

Mouths opened. She glimpsed sharp teeth. And their eyes . . . *Good God, those eyes!* White as sepulchre marble, with sharp, black points at their centres. They stared at her with utter savagery. There was something else in those eyes as well. Hunger. Greed. Lust.

Quelling the urge to rip out the mouthpiece and scream, Steff concentrated on swimming. *If I can get back to the shore . . . if I can reach the truck I'll be safe.*

Beneath her, she glimpsed a drowned car on the lake bed. Its doors were open, spread like wings. Two headlamps glinted; a pair of dead glass eyes.

Now she knew what she had to do the panic left her. She had a cool mind. She was strong-willed. She always got what she wanted.

Now I want to get away from Lazarus Deep.

Steff glanced back again. They were moving fast. But she was fast, too. They weren't gaining as rapidly as they'd hoped. Frustration mixed with fury on their faces. They hadn't expected her to be so swift. Now the lake bed ran close beneath her, while the surface layer of grey water-borne particles was just a short way above her head. In front, she saw a splash of bubbles. Waves breaking on the shore.

Nearly there . . . nearly there . . .

The white creatures were trying to swim beneath her.

Beat this! Steff thought with a sudden blaze of triumph. She reached down and unbuckled the belt that carried her diver's lead weights. The moment they fell from her hips sudden buoyancy seized her and shot her upward. She looked up to see that she was soaring toward that layer of misty grey that hugged the underside of the lake's surface.

A moment later she plunged into it. She was nearly there. Soon she'd break through the membrane of surface water into fresh air.

Then, above her, she saw a figure she recognized, its arms outstretched like some hovering underwater hawk.

Luke Spencer.

He was naked to the waist. The milk-white skin of his chest was veined blue. He was smiling down at her.

Buoyancy carried Steff up into his arms. She felt those long limbs wrap around her. His face thrust down against her face mask until his two staring eyes jammed hard against the glass, looking in at her. Then the others were on her. Two dozen hands snatched at her limbs, dragging her back down, deep into the water. Clawed fingers ripped the rubber suit; they tore it to shreds. Then mouths filled with sharp teeth found her naked body. She felt the pressure of lips, the pricking points of incisors.

Above Steff, bubbles of air from her screaming mouth were the only things to escape the night-black waters.

CHAPTER 15

I

Saturday morning. Electra Charnwood gave directions as Katrina drove. Slabs of grey cloud moved over the moor at barely treetop height. Not that there were many trees on these high plains with their covering of heather and alpine grasses. What few trees there were had grown with their limbs fabulously contorted. Twisted trunks were stunted. Leafless branches probed the air with the suggestion of insectile antennae scenting fresh prey.

'Is that one?' Katrina pointed to a mound a hundred paces from the roadside.

'A tumulus?'

'Yes. They're prehistoric burial mounds, aren't they?'

'They date back to at least five thousand BC.' Electra glanced at the forbidding rain-bearing cloud. 'I'm afraid it's not ideal walking weather today.'

'Look at the size of the mound,' Katrina said, her tone hushed. 'It's as big as a house.'

'One like this would have been the tomb of a chief or warrior hero.'

'I want to see it close up.'

Katrina stopped the car so sharply that Electra had to put her hand against the dash to steady herself. 'Whoa, tiger,' she joked as the following car swerved round them, sounding an angry note on its horn.

'You coming?'

Before Electra could reply Katrina climbed out of the car, then hurried across the expanse of heather.

In those shoes? Electra shook her head. At this time of year the moor was a sodden sponge. Someone could easily sink in black muck up to their ankles. But there was no stopping Katrina West.

Electra followed, pulling up the scarf around her neck and adjusting her woollen hat to keep her ears warm. That wind from the North Sea was biting. She could almost smell Arctic ozone sweeping across the landscape. She paused to glance back the way they had come. The road swept, zigging and zagging, into the valley. A mile away the black moor ended, yielding to softer greens where pastures climbed from the protection of the valley bottom. In the distance were the regular shapes of Leppington's buildings.

Katrina's suggestion that Electra should accompany her on another drive had seemed an agreeable one. But now she was out of the car the cold winds were nothing less than an assault on her body. She followed the path that led to the burial mound. Covered with hardy grasses, it formed something that looked like a green cone with a slightly flattened top. Katrina climbed it as if she expected to find gold at its summit. At times she even dropped forward to scale the steep sides on all fours.

In those shoes . . . and that *coat. Those are expensive clothes for scrambling up mounds of earth in winter.*

When Katrina reached the top a weird thing happened to her. Electra stared, blinking tears from her eyes as icy currents blew hard into them. Katrina had disappeared from the waist up. For a moment the bizarre sight stopped Electra dead. Then she realized what had happened. The cloud layer was so low that Katrina's top half had actually entered the cloud base. Electra sidestepped a puddle. Even so her boots (her more sensible walking boots) sank nearly as far as her ankle with a lubricious squelching sound.

I'm not climbing the mound, she told herself. *I'll stand at the bottom and wait for her to come back. With luck she'll satisfy her curiosity quickly – then we can get back to the car. There's a nice inn in Rosedale with a wonderful log fire. We can eat lunch there. This haring around the countryside's wearing me out.*

Electra reached the mucky base of the burial mound. Mud glistened in leprous patches. Above her Katrina's top half was still invisible in the cloud. What on Earth was so interesting up there? Katrina had driven round the entire area as if ticking off items on an agenda.

If I didn't know any better I'd say she was searching for something . . . Come to that, I don't *know any better. Maybe she* is *searching for something. She seemed jumpy this morning. Almost nervous.*

One of the kitchen staff had told Electra that he'd seen Katrina on the river bank again, staring at the River Lepping in flood. For a moment he'd been afraid that she was going to jump in.

Or maybe it was just high spirits. Perhaps Katrina was just giddy. Excited to be enjoying a few days' break away from London with its bustle and noise and traffic jams. Here it was incredibly peaceful. Visitors described the sheer vastness and emptiness of the moors as a drug. They gave you a high.

'Marvellous.' Katrina's eyes shone with excitement as she came running down the mound. 'Bloody marvellous!'

'Careful!'

Electra had to lunge forward to catch the other woman as gravity caught hold of her and carried her down, her arms windmilling. For a moment they were so close that they were face to face, noses almost touching. Electra saw she'd only been half right about Katrina's eyes shining with sheer *joie de vivre.* One eye looked dull, almost as if a film was clouding it.

'Oh, thank you. I nearly went head over heels then.' Katrina took a breath. 'Phew. This place is exhilarating.'

'But cold on a day like this.'

'Come on, let's get you back to the car and warm you up.'

Katrina linked arms with Electra and walked swiftly back to the car. Electra experienced a stir of unease. The woman seemed unusually euphoric. And then there was that dead-looking eye . . .

2

Leaving the warmth of the hotel room was a wrench. Dylan Adams walked hand in hand with Vikki to Whitby Station. The town bustled with Saturday-morning shoppers but he didn't notice. He still carried the night's passion as a warm infusion inside him.

'Thank you, Dylan.'

'What for?'

'Last night.'

He smiled. 'Don't mention it.'

'I enjoyed it.' She smiled back shyly. 'Maybe we should do it again sometime?'

'No "maybe" about it. It should be a *certainty*.'

She stopped and looked him in the eye. 'I was hoping you'd say that.' She slipped her arm around his back and kissed him on the lips. 'Come on – we don't want to miss the train.'

3

Electra glanced at Katrina. The woman drove quickly, as if eager to reach the next stop – wherever that would be. Excitement quickened her movements. Her head dipped and turned as she scanned the landscape. *She's searching for something, or someone. But what?*

Half an hour after leaving the burial mound on the moorland heights, Katrina drove downward into the valley bottom,
following the twisting road as it ducked under the railway line
or turned back on itself to cross a bridge.

'How did you come to be running a hotel in Leppington,
Electra?'

'I inherited it from my parents.'

'You never wanted to move away?'

'Yes. Often.'

'I'm sure you could have. You're an intelligent woman.'

'Thank you, Katrina, compliment noted. Somehow I just
wound up rooted in the damn place.' Electra made her voice
sound cheerful but she'd had enough of this crazy drive across
the countryside. Also, there was something about that dead
eye of Katrina's that had unsettled her. It hadn't been like
that yesterday. Was the woman sickening for something? *But
what would make your eye go as dull as that? Maybe I should
suggest that she see a doctor?*

Moments later, Katrina pulled such a sharp right that the
car's tyres squealed.

'Careful,' Electra warned. 'These roads can be treacherous
in winter.'

'What's happening across there?'

'Where?'

'On the side of the lake. To your left.'

Electra looked through the side window. Through the trees
she could see water. Parked close to it were half a dozen cars
and a truck. On the side of the truck were painted the words
CLUB ADRENALIN. Katrina blazed the car along the dirt
track toward the lake.

She shouted, 'What is this place?'

'Lazarus Deep.' Electra shot Katrina a look, wondering why
the other woman sounded so frightened all of a sudden.

'Lazarus Deep?' Katrina turned to look at her. 'My God,

my God . . .' One eye glittered with something like panic while the other remained dead-looking.

'What's wrong?' Electra asked, seriously concerned now.

'Something terrible's happened. Look, they're dragging a body out of the water.'

Shocked, Electra looked too as Katrina braked hard some way from the other cars. Then, throwing open the door, she scrambled out, almost falling. A second later she was running toward a group of divers who were carrying a figure from the lake.

'Wait . . .' Electra realized that Katrina hadn't even paused to switch off the car's engine or apply the handbrake. The car was still rolling forward to the water's edge. '*Katrina!*' Through the windscreen all Electra could see was the dark, glowering face of Lazarus Deep.

4

Although he was preoccupied with Steff Kline's tragic accident, Goldi still noticed the car rolling forward toward the lake's edge. He also noticed the young woman running toward them, her coat flapping. He watched a second woman in the passenger seat of the car. She must have managed to tug on the handbrake hard enough. The car stopped two metres short of the bank that ran down into the water.

'Oh God . . . oh Jesus,' Vance was saying. 'She's as cold as ice. Tony, get some blankets . . . Sasha, phone for an ambulance. Use my mobile! It's in the glove compartment.'

One of the divers ripped off his own mask. Panting, he said, 'What causes wounds like that? They look like bite marks.'

'Pike or catfish.'

'Don't be bloody ridiculous. Look at the size of the bites. They're enormous!'

Everyone was in a state of shock, shouting instructions to

each other. Goldi looked down at the woman he'd made love to barely two hours ago. They'd found her on the lake bed as they'd returned from deeper water. After pulling her from the lake they'd taken off her aqualung. Now she lay on the ground. Her face had a white powdery appearance even though it was soaked with lake water. Her lips were blue and her eyes had sunk back into her head. The skin surrounding the sockets was an ominous-looking black.

'She's lost a lot of blood.'

'Is she still alive?'

'I can't find a pulse . . . stand back . . . let her breathe . . .'

If she is *breathing.* Goldi looked at the state of Steff's body. The rubber suit had pieces torn from it. The top part had been completely ripped away at the front. Her breasts looked smaller now, as if they'd been shrunk by the cold. Even her nipples were pale. Blue veins beneath her skin webbed her chest while her stomach bore a mottling of grey-white blotches. Worse were the wounds. In a dozen places her skin had been torn open. The gashes were big enough for him to slip three fingertips into with ease. Blood smeared out from them to mix with lake water into streaky pinks and reds.

Dear God. It looked as if a pack of animals had savaged her.

Her eyes were closed. The eyelids had become blue-black. She was either unconscious or . . . He couldn't bring himself to think the word.

Vance rubbed one of her hands between both his palms. 'Steff. Steff . . .'

At that moment the stranger ran up to the group. She threw herself down on her knees and stared at Steff as if the mutilated woman was her own child.

'Oh, God . . . look at her.' The young woman sounded close to hysteria. 'I know what's happened. He's done this to her. He's tried to steal her heart . . .' She panted, breathless.

'I know. It was him. He tried to do the same to me when I was eighteen. They found me in time and took me to hospital.' One of the divers tried to help her up but she beat away his hands. 'Listen to me. David Leppington's to blame. He did this to her. He bit her. He bit me like this . . . just the other night he tried to steal my heart again.'

'Please . . .' Goldi took hold of her arm, trying to pull her away from Steff. The woman was hysterical.

'Listen to me. David Leppington did this. He'll attack you in the same way. You've got to help me . . . No, let go. David Leppington's to blame for this. He's a vampire.' The woman looked up, her face wild, her coat pulled off one shoulder, her hair messed. 'It's David Leppington. *You've got to help me to kill him.*'

5

Electra's heart was pounding as she ran up to the group huddled round the body. First Katrina had leaped out of the moving car. If the handbrake hadn't stopped it the car would have rolled forward into the lake. Now this.

Katrina was screaming at the group of divers as they stood round what looked like the drowned body of their colleague. She looked as if she was trying to tell them something important, only hysteria had scrambled her words in a nerve-stripping sound of panic.

Electra's sharp-eyed gaze locked onto the body of the female diver. In a split second she'd assessed the situation. 'Is there an ambulance on the way?'

One of the divers nodded. 'But they've got to come from Whitby.'

'That's going to be another fifteen minutes,' Electra said. 'She's in shock.' She touched the woman's forehead. The cold of the skin bit through her fingertip. 'You –' she turned to Goldi and pointed at Katrina who was sobbing, her eyes bulging as she stared at the body '– drag her back . . . by the hair if you have to. Keep her away.'

'But she—'

'Do it!'

Electra turned to another man who stood twisting a face-mask strap in his hands. 'You, start one of the cars. Keep revving the engine, then turn the heating on full when I tell you.'

He looked dazed. 'Which car?'

'Pick the most expensive, it'll have the best heater . . .' Electra nodded at another of the men. 'Help me get her to the car—'

'But she's—'

'She's alive. Believe me, she's alive.'

'But she'd lost her mouthpiece. She must have drowned out there. We—'

'She hasn't drowned. It's blood loss. She's in shock – massive shock.'

'But what can we—'

'Help me get her to the car. We have to warm her up.'

A couple of the divers pulled themselves together suffi-ciently to help Electra get the wounded diver into the back of a BMW. Another of the team now sat revving the engine as she'd instructed.

Just pray he can get warm air blowing from the heaters. This poor wretch's going to need all the help she can get. Electra looked at the woman's face, noting the blue lips and black-ringed eyes. Symptoms of acute blood loss.

I've seen this before, Electra found herself thinking. *Three years ago. When those monsters attacked.*

The rest of the dive team were too cold to offer what the woman needed. So Electra stayed with her in the back of the car. Cradling the woman's cold, wet head in the crook of her own neck, she pulled blankets over them both. Electra hoped that her own body heat would be enough to ease the severity of clinical shock. 'OK,' she told the man in the driving seat. 'Turn on the heating.'

Where was that damn ambulance? She glanced out of the window to where Katrina sat in the mud, hugging her knees to her chest and sobbing uncontrollably. And, dear God, what was wrong with that woman?

Whispering over and over, 'You're going to be all right. Everything's fine,' Electra hugged the injured woman. She felt a whisper of cold breath against her ear. The woman was breathing. She hoped it would stay that way.

6

At the end of the harrowing day Electra poured herself a huge brandy in the Jack Black bar. It was still early. The Goths wouldn't arrive for their Saturday Night Communion for another twenty minutes or so yet.

And God, do I need this brandy. She took a deep swallow. A few years ago she'd have winced and coughed as the drink carved a path of fire down her throat. Not now. She'd grown used to a drop of the hard stuff, as her mother used to call it. *But Christ, what a day. What an awful day.* She felt as if all the miseries of hell had been unleashed on her. First, she'd witnessed Katrina having some kind of fit . . . or was it even a nervous breakdown? Perhaps it was the shock of seeing what appeared to be a corpse being dragged from the lake? God only knew. Then, when Electra had realized that the divers were themselves in a state of shock at finding their friend with her suit half torn off and her body covered with bite wounds, she'd taken charge.

Those hotel management skills are transferable after all, Electra told herself dryly as she knocked back the brandy. She'd got the woman into the car with the heating on full, then warmed her as best she could with her own body heat. Then, thank heaven, the ambulance had arrived. Only then she was faced with the task of coaxing the weeping Katrina back to the car, in her muddied clothes, and driving her back to the Station Hotel.

Thankfully, Claire had still been on reception and both of them had managed to get her back to her room and into bed. At least now she'd fallen asleep. Electra had wondered whether she should call a doctor. But perhaps it was just the shock of seeing what could have been a corpse. Katrina might be better in the morning.

Now the time was just past seven. She'd spoken to one of the divers on the phone. A man who called himself Goldi. He said that the girl, Steff Kline, was recovering in hospital. Although she'd required a massive infusion of blood. 'The doctors said she'd been exsanguinated. That means—'

I know, mused Electra. It meant the poor woman had been all but drained of blood. It was a miracle that she'd survived. But now all those random events – *seemingly* random events, coincidences, chance meetings, fragments of half-remembered dream – were coming together.

Complete the jigsaw, Electra.

She'd dreamed that Jack Black carried her to Lazarus Deep. For weeks she'd felt a growing sense of foreboding. An air of impending danger that was so dense she could almost reach out and touch it. She'd received the bizarre *Broxley Testament* about the family staying in the house overlooking Lazarus Deep. The mysterious disappearance and then the macabre reappearance of the guitarist called Ash White. *Complete the jigsaw, Electra.*

And now she could. She put the glass down on the bar and picked up an envelope.

She had the final and crucial part of the jigsaw.

The white envelope bore an address in handwriting that Electra now knew was Katrina's. Electra had seen it in the woman's shoulder bag . . . and no, she hadn't found it by accident. She'd searched the bag deliberately. If the woman was on medication then she might need to take it. Electra steadied her nerves with another mouthful of brandy and then read the address again.

Yup, there it is, Electra. It was a London address. Nothing strange about that. But it was the individual to whom the letter was addressed that was the clincher. *Dr David Leppington.*

CHAPTER 16

I

For David Leppington his Saturday evening consisted of picking at a Chinese meal he'd bought from the supermarket across the road. Tonight the television didn't interest him. He wished he'd gone to the pub with his friends. Even so, he knew his heart wasn't in it. All he could think about was Katrina.

So much for clinical detachment, David told himself. But when they'd met again a few days ago after so many years something had detonated in his mind. He'd suppressed one huge FACT. The fact was that he was still in love with her. That love had been concreted over in some recess in the back of his brain but it had still been there. He knew that people whose loved ones had died must feel something similar. Only Katrina had been taken from him by mental illness. Then the miracle. She'd come back to him sane and healthy and beautiful.

But where was she now? Why had she stopped taking the medication? David stabbed a plastic fork into the meal's tray of fried rice. This stuff was choking him. He needed fresh air. After dumping the food in the kitchen he headed for the door. He knew that this walk was going to take him only as far as the corner of the street. The Red Lion wouldn't solve his problems but it would sure as hell distract him from them. He'd almost reached the door when the telephone rang.

Katrina.

Tearing the handset from the cradle he slammed it against this ear. *Please, God, let it be her.*

'Hello?'

'David. I need to speak to you.'

'Electra?'

Electra Charnwood. Good God – the last thing he wanted right now was to speak to her. Just the sound of her voice raised enough phantoms.

'David. I'm sorry to have to phone you out of the blue like this, but there's something you need to know . . .'

2

The rain fell steadily on Bernice Mochardi as she walked along Oxford Street. Despite the swarming crowds, the brightly lit boutiques and restaurants, she felt eerily alone as if she was walking across a remote mountainside. She looked down at her boots as she moved. Pointed-toe boots in patent leather. Rainwater beaded on them.

I don't belong here. I should be somewhere else.

The notion troubled her. Bernice felt settled in London. She liked it here. But over the last few days she'd felt herself becoming withdrawn. She barely talked to her friends. Instead she felt compelled to walk through the streets as if she was looking for something, or someone. When she reached Bloomsbury she cut through to the British Museum where it stood gloomily behind iron fences. It was closed now. Here it was quieter. The building brooded in the night's rain. From the top of the statue of a long-dead general a raven watched her walk by.

3

'Listen to me, David: something's not right up here.'

'Electra, what do you mean – "something's not right"?'

David intended to shut down this conversation with Electra

Charnwood as quickly as possible. He imagined her sitting in that gloomy back office of the Station Hotel in that godforsaken town with which he shared a name. It wasn't a big step from picturing Electra there with her mane of blue-black hair to recalling those things that had lurked in the tunnel beneath the building.

No, I don't want to go back there – not even in my imagination.

He'd finish this call as quickly as possible, he decided, then leave the flat for a few hours. Beer was what he needed right now.

'David, I've been having nightmares. I dream that Jack Black is—'

'Jack's dead, Electra.'

'I know, but in the dream he carries me to Lazarus Deep where—'

'It's only to be expected that you'll have dreams after what happened . . . Electra, *I* have bad dreams. I'm sure that Bernice does, too.'

'There are other things, too. I was at Lazarus Deep this morning. I saw a woman who'd been attacked by something when she went scuba diving in the lake.'

'In a lake? Then there can't be any connection to—'

'If you saw the wounds, you'd make the connection instantly.'

'Electra, I'm sorry if you're feeling down. Isn't there any-where you could take a break? Somewhere overseas?'

'David, don't patronize me.'

'Electra—'

'I don't want you to prescribe platitudes, either. I want . . .'

David heard Electra take a deep breath. *She's taking the plunge now. She's going to ask a favour . . . or even make some demand.*

He was right.

'David. I want you to come up to Leppington.'

'Electra, I can't just drop everything. I'm working at—'

'David. Please. I want you to come as soon as possible.'

He heard her take another deep breath.

'Tonight.'

'Electra, it's gone eight. It'll take five hours to drive up to Leppington from London.'

'Well, first thing in the morning, then. The roads will be quiet, what with it being a Sunday. You can be here by midday.'

David gripped the phone so hard that his knuckles whitened. Hell, what was wrong with the woman? He couldn't head off to Leppington simply on her whim.

'I can't, Electra. I'm sorry.'

'David—'

'I promised myself I'd never go back to Leppington. If you're ever in London I'll be happy to meet you for a drink but I'm not going—'

'David, I wouldn't ask you to come here if I didn't think it was absolutely necessary.'

'Electra, I'm not coming. Now, I'm due to meet a friend so I'll say goodbye now.'

'David—'

'Electra, I'm sorry. It sounds rude of me, I know. But I'm late. I've got to go. Goodbye.'

'David, wait. There's—'

'It's no good, Electra. I'm putting the phone down now.'

'There's someone staying in the hotel. A woman . . .'

David paused. He could hear his heart thumping. 'What about her?'

Electra's voice sounded as if it was coming across some dark gulf from light years away. 'She took ill this morning. I've managed to get her to stay in her room. She's been sleeping for hours. She's dead to the world. I looked through her bags in case she needed medication. I did wonder if she was diabetic.'

'Go on.'

'I found a letter, David. It was addressed to you.'

'I see.' To his own ears he sounded calm, but his heart beat painfully against his ribs.

Electra continued, 'The woman gave her name as Katrina West. I wonder if that name means anything to you?'

'Katrina West?'

There was a pause. In his ear David could hear the sound of Electra's breathing whispering down hundreds of miles of telephone line. In the distance there was a hissing sound. For all the world it sounded like rushing water. A river in spate. Instantly, in his mind's eye, he saw Electra talking on the telephone. Beyond the window lay the town of Leppington, shrouded by night. The River Lepping rushed seaward. In his imagination he sped through the darkened waters upstream to where the river spewed from a cave. Travelling deeper into the cave would take him to the heart of the mountain where a secret lake fed the river. There, David Leppington's Viking ancestors had communed with their dark and terrible gods.

'David . . . David? Are you still there?'

'I'm here.'

'Do you know this Katrina West?'

'Yes.'

'Then you should know that the letter she has written to you is disturbing, to say the least. She talks in a rambling way about blood and how precious blood is to life.' Electra paused. 'David, she ends the letter with an accusation. She claims that you are a vampire.'

4

Bernice Mochardi found herself in the legal quarter round Aldwych. Here the streets were wide and windy. They were deserted, even though it was barely nine o'clock. The winter's night had driven pedestrians into taxis or onto buses.

What are you going to do? she asked herself. *Walk round London all night? Go home. Go to bed.*

But restlessness kept Bernice moving. She had to do something that would ease this sense of edginess that crackled through her like electricity.

I'm wearing a short skirt, she thought with a sudden thrill. *I could unfasten my coat and then stand on a street corner. How long before a car stops and a stranger asks me to climb in? How would the conversation go?*

He'd ask, 'How much do you charge?'

'Less than you'd think.'

'You're beautiful.'

'Thank you. Shall we go back to my place?'

He grins. 'Right here in the car will do.' He pulls a knife from under the dashboard. 'OK, beautiful lady, say Ah.'

Idiot, she scolded herself. *I'm thinking all kinds of nonsense just to distract myself. But I feel so tense. If I went back home I couldn't sit still. What's happening to me?*

As Bernice crossed back over the street her mobile rang. Pulling it from her coat pocket she thumbed the answer button. Drops of rain fell onto the screen, obscuring the caller's name.

'Sorry . . . who's this?' She caught her breath in something closer to shock than surprise. 'David. David Leppington? I haven't seen you in months.'

'It's a good job you kept your old mobile number,' he told her. 'I couldn't reach you on your home number.'

'I've moved since then. Itchy feet, I guess. For some reason I only stay in a flat a few months before, well, you know . . .'

David sounded serious. 'I know the feeling.'

'How are you keeping?'

'Fine. But I think you know that this isn't a social call, Bernice.'

'I guessed there'd be something more.'

And now I know why I've felt so restless. They call it prescience . . . an intuitive and unconscious premonition of future events. So when he asked the question she said yes. She didn't even have to think through the implications.

'Yes, I'll come,' she told him. 'We're going by train?'

'By car. I'll pick you up from home in the morning. All I need is your new address.'

She gave it to him.

'I know the road,' he told her. 'Call it coincidence, but it seems as if we've ended up living close to one another.'

Bernice gave a dry laugh. 'Not coincidence. I think someone, somewhere, was telling us to stick close together.'

'I'll see you tomorrow morning at seven. OK?'

'No problem. Wait a minute – does Electra know I'm coming up to Leppington with you?'

'No.'

'Any reason why not?'

'She wouldn't want you to come.' David's voice grew even more serious. 'She'd claim it was too dangerous.'

CHAPTER 17

I

David thought: *OK, now for the descent into hell.*

Beside him, in the car's passenger seat, Bernice Mochardi shifted as if suddenly uncomfortable. When he glanced at her he saw that she was staring forward at Leppington where it lay sprawled out in the valley below. The hand that gripped the seat belt across her chest was clenched so tightly that her knuckles were a bloodless white.

The lady wears black, too, he mused. *As if going to a funeral.*

Rafts of grim cloud slid across the sky, while every so often a heavy single drop of rain would smack into the car. A heartbeat sound, his professional side reminded him. The sound of a diseased heart. Arrhythmic. Laboured. He braked the car as gravity tugged at it, drawing it down closer to Leppington.

'It feels as if I've never been away.' Bernice's voice sounded strained. David even picked out the nervous tremor as she spoke the word: *away.*

Good God, he felt like she did. Leppington looked exactly the same. Houses rendered bleak, like gravestones, by the dim light of a February day.

Bernice groaned. 'That church tower. I always hated the look of the thing. It always made me think of . . .' She shuddered. 'A drowning man.'

'I know what you mean.' He smiled grimly. 'Not so much

an example of medieval church architecture as a cry for help.'
He shot a sideways glance at her. The colour had left her face,
making her lipstick resemble a smear of blood on her mouth. If
she'd registered his stab at gallows humour she didn't react.

'Oh God, I never thought I'd set eyes on this town again,'
she said.

'You didn't have to come, Bernice.'

'Oh yes, I did. I felt it in my bones days before you even
called.'

'Electra said the same thing. She claimed she had pre-
monitions . . . a sense that something ominous was building.'

'Like a storm? And I'd started having dreams . . .'

'About Jack Black.'

'You've had them, too?'

David nodded. 'And I had a bizarre conversation with an
old man on Friday morning. He said he used to live round
here and that he knew my family.'

'That's a coincidence, I guess. I wouldn't describe it as
bizarre.'

David's mouth went dry at the recollection of those calm
blue eyes staring into his. 'He was a patient at the hospital where I worked. An ambulance brought him in as an
emergency admission. He'd suffered a coronary. What was
so bizarre about the conversation –' he slowed as the road
twisted back on itself '– was that when I chatted to him he'd
already been dead for more than an hour.'

He noticed that Bernice shot him a startled look.

'That's right.' A grim laugh escaped his lips. 'After all these
years as a qualified doctor you think I'd be able to spot the
difference between a live patient and a dead one.' David let
gravity pull the car toward the town again. Now he could see
the railway station with the massive slaughterhouse alongside
it; then, finally, the Gothic-roof shape of the Station Hotel.

Its quad towers – one at each corner – loomed over the street. Four forbidding sentinels in brick.

'Here goes,' he said. 'Welcome to the town of my fore-fathers.'

Sitting on the sign that simply read LEPPINGTON was a raven. It watched them pass.

'Reception committee,' Bernice said, nodding at the huge bird.

'Something tells me the guys downstairs now know we're back.'

David felt Bernice's hand close over the crook of his elbow. She wasn't trying to attract his attention. This was someone needing reassurance through physical contact. She didn't look at him but continued to gaze at the town through frightened eyes.

Poor kid, he thought. He should never have asked her to come with him, even if his instinct shouted from his heart of hearts that it was the right choice.

'Bernice.' His voice was gentle. 'Bernice. It's not too late, you know. I'll be happy – more than happy – to drive you back to Whitby. You can catch a train back home from there.'

She shook her head. He saw the way she lifted her chin, a gesture of defiance, even though the mere sight of the town frightened her. 'No. I'm not going back yet. There's a reason I have to be here.'

'They won't miss you at work?'

'I've booked the week off.'

'Me, too. It looks as if we're both prepared to spend a few days here.'

'I'm going to stay as long as it takes. I know that I'm . . .' Her voice faded as she saw what lay around the next corner. The Station Hotel loomed in front of them.

Once more David was struck by the sheer size of the place. For a small market town the hotel towered over it like a fortress. Its Gothic design dominated the surrounding buildings. Its dozens of windows were so many monstrous eyes that glared at the visitor, daring them to enter.

It has a predator's stare, David told himself. *That's not an entirely rational description. But it's the most applicable. It's a nightmare beast that has been slumbering for the last three years. Now it's starting to wake.*

Harsh winds snarled among houses at the side of the road. A poster half torn from a hoarding flapped. It showed an advertisement for a pension company. Beneath the undulating photograph of an hourglass were the words: *TIME NEVER STROLLS. TIME RUNS OUT.*

He slowed the car, stopping it a hundred metres from the forbidding structure of the Station Hotel.

'It's not too late to go back.' This time David realized he'd spoken the words for his own benefit. He could turn the car, then drive out of there fast, as if all the demons of hell were on his tail. He didn't have to stay. He could leave without even looking back.

A tremendous thump sounded against the side of the car. Bernice gave a startled cry. 'David, lock your door!'

The beggar rapped filthy knuckles against the car window. Although he was probably in his twenties, he had the pinched, fleshless face of an old man. He wore the hood of his jacket pulled up around his head. Ratty strands of hair stuck out from the gaps between his scabbed head and the material. David wound the window down.

'David, don't. Drive on.'

'Spare any change, mate?'

David scooped a handful of coins from the shallow depression behind the handbrake.

'Look after yourself,' David said, dropping the change into the outstretched hand with its odd lumpy fingernails.

The man leaned forward so that his head was level with

theirs. He stared in at Bernice, then at David. 'I've seen you two before, haven't I?'

'I don't know.' David spoke diplomatically. 'You might have.'

'You stayed at the hotel a few years ago with a big ugly bastard called Jack Black.'

'That's right,' David agreed. 'But that was a long time ago.'

'I knew Black. I did some jobs with him.'

'David,' Bernice hissed. 'Come on.'

Did she think the vagrant was going to attack them – or was there something else?

David nodded at the man. 'Take care.' He slipped the gear into first.

'Wait a minute, mate. If you see Black will you tell him Skinner's ready to work with him if he wants?' He grimaced. 'I need the money.'

David shook his head, stopping short of telling the man the truth. Instead he said, 'I don't know where Jack is. I haven't seen him for years.'

'You'll run into him before long.' The man rested his hand on the top of the window. 'I saw him walking through town last week. He's come back.'

2

As David parked the car behind the Station Hotel he said, 'Bernice, best not mention to Electra what the man said back there. You know how she felt about Jack. It'll only upset her.'

Bernice looked shaken. 'It didn't do a lot for me. What did the man mean, "*He's come back*"?'

David switched off the engine. 'Look, we both know that Jack Black is dead. You saw the state of the guy back there.

He probably does street drugs. There may be a history of psychiatric problems, too, from the way his face was twitching.'

'You don't believe him?'

'That Jack Black's in town? Bernice, dead men don't walk.'

'They shouldn't talk, either. But that didn't stop you having a conversation with one last week.'

David found himself ready with a rational explanation. God, he was good at those. He'd had plenty of practice. Instead, he merely shrugged. 'I'll get the bags. You go on ahead before it starts raining.'

'I'm not afraid of the rain,' she said. 'I'll wait for you and we'll go in together.'

3

'David? You didn't tell me you were bringing Bernice.'

'That's not the welcome I was expecting, Electra.'

Electra advanced toward him, her blue-black hair falling in a rich swathe over one shoulder. *My God, she's as formidable as I remember.*

Dressed in black. With kohled lids forming a dark line around the eyes that lent her the look of an Egyptian queen. Her aristocratic manner hadn't become diluted during the years since he'd last seen her. He saw her sharp-eyed gaze sweep over him, assessing what effect the intervening time had had on him. Then she turned her steely gaze on Bernice. David observed Electra examining her from her pointed-toe boots to the top of her head.

And Electra Charnwood didn't look happy with what she saw.

'David. Bernice. Welcome to the Station Hotel.'

The greeting wasn't just formal, it had ice clinging to it.

'Electra, where's Katrina?'

'She's sleeping at the moment.'

'If you tell me the room number I'll—'

'Go through to the kitchen first of all, please. There's fresh coffee and sandwiches.'

David guessed that Electra wanted to speak to them without being overheard. Here in the hotel's lobby an elderly couple were talking to the receptionist, while a pair of Goth girls in their late teens sat reading the Sunday newspapers over glasses of red wine.

'This way, please.' Electra held a hand out, indicating the door behind the reception area. 'You know the way.'

David caught Bernice's eye. This was like the schoolteacher taking a pair of unruly pupils aside for a scolding.

The kitchen hadn't changed. This facility was away from the restaurant kitchen that would be serving the Sunday lunches. If anything, it was Electra's private retreat. It had a lofty Victorian feel to it, with its brass pans hanging on the wall. As before, a huge table sat in the middle. Lacking any varnish, it had been scrubbed clean with such ferocity down the years that it dipped slightly in the middle where the surface had worn away. Now the wood resembled hard, white bone. On the table were some plates of sandwiches under cling film, along with two cups.

'I'll get another cup,' Electra said pointedly. 'Both of you take a seat, won't you? Here, Bernice, let me take your coat.'

David decided to get to the point. 'Electra, you didn't want me to bring Bernice.'

'No.'

'It seemed the natural thing to do.'

'It's not a good idea, David.'

'When we faced those things last time there were four of us. We were a team; we were stronger than the sum of our parts.'

'Jack Black is dead.' She put a cup in front of Bernice. 'So we're never going to be a complete team again.'

'No, but I believe three is better than two.'

Bernice said, 'I wanted to come.'

'What people *want* isn't relevant.' Electra poured coffee from a Pyrex jug. 'It's dangerous . . . help yourself to cream.'

'Thank you.'

We observe the formalities of a meal, say our pleases and thank yous, while talking about mortal danger. How English can you get? David shook his head as he put a sandwich on a plate, added a napkin, then pulled it toward him.

'All I needed,' Electra was saying, 'was for David here to accompany me on a trip to Lazarus Deep—'

'Lazarus Deep?' Bernice looked puzzled. 'What's that?'

'It's a lake just a few miles away from here. There's also an old house up there by the name of Lazarus Wake.'

David said, 'I've heard of the lake, but not the house.'

'Ah . . . I hoped you might know it.'

'Lazarus Wake? Any reason why I should?'

'According to information I received it was built three hundred years ago by one Magnus Leppington.'

'Hmm.' David had picked up the sandwich, then put it down without biting into it. 'A Leppington. So there's my family connection again.'

'Have you heard of Magnus Leppington?'

David shook his head. 'He probably belonged to an offshoot of the family rather than being a direct descendant of its primary ancestors.'

Bernice asked, 'But what's all this about?'

'A document was e-mailed to me by a mysterious correspondent I know by the name Rowan.'

'You've never met him?'

'No. All the correspondence has been by e-mail.'

David finally bit into the sandwich. Ham salad. Top-quality Yorkshire baked ham, too. Electra never stinted on hospitality.

Bernice took a sip of coffee, then said, 'This may seem almost facetious, Electra, but do you think Rowan is alive?'

'Alive.' Electra's eyes narrowed. David wondered if she thought she was being made fun of. 'Alive. Of course he's alive. What makes you ask that?'

David said, 'It's not such a bizarre question as you might think.' He told her what had happened on the Friday morning: the conversation with Sam Gotland at the hospital. 'It'd be a fair question if you asked me if I was hallucinating.' He wiped his lips with the napkin. 'It might have been something of the sort. But I don't think I'm insane, do you?'

Electra thought for a moment, then said, 'You think that this "vision," we'll call it, was imposed from outside?'

'I guess so.' He found that his appetite had become blunted. 'I imagine this calls for a council of war later. We need to compare our experiences of the last few days and decide what we should do next.'

'If we can do anything,' Bernice added. Then to Electra she said, 'Are you going to send me away?'

'Send you away?' Electra smiled and took Bernice's hand in hers. 'You make me sound like some Victorian matriarch. No, dear, I'm not going to send you away.'

'But you said I shouldn't have come here with David.'

'I didn't see the point of dragging you more than two hundred miles. And, what's more, I'm concerned for your safety.'

'I knew I had to come,' Bernice stated. 'As simple as that. I felt it in here.' She touched her chest. 'The moment David called me I knew what he'd ask.' Her dark eyes stared at them each in turn. 'And I agree with David. Somehow we're stronger if we're all together.'

'So that's settled, then,' Electra said. 'Like the old days – we three are back under one roof again. I'll have the receptionist book you in as my guests. We'll have adjoining rooms.'

'Thank you,' David said. 'What I'd like to do now is see Katrina.'

'I'm not going to pry,' Electra told him. 'Although I guess there is some history between you and Katrina West?'

'There is. We go back a long way.' He gave a grim smile. 'I guess you could call us childhood sweethearts.' He drew a breath. 'My relationship with Katrina might be relevant now, so I'd better tell you something of that history.' He told Electra and Bernice how Katrina and he had met. About Katrina's devastating mental illness, then her apparent miraculous recovery, and how she'd vanished from his life again.

When he'd finished Electra said, 'Of course you must see her, David. But first you might like to read this.' Electra slipped a piece of folded paper from her pocket. 'It's the letter Katrina was going to send you. In fact, it looked as if she'd started writing several to you. But this was the only finished one.' She stood up. 'Bernice, would you give me a hand with a poster? I'm advertising a special Goth Ball for next Saturday.' David saw her glance at Bernice's black clothes and newly dyed black hair that now echoed her own style. 'I think you might enjoy it.'

David sat at the table with the sheet of folded paper. More than ever it was like old times. Back in the Station Hotel again. In Leppington, the town of his ancestors. Outside the River Lepping roared beyond the yard wall. And just like old times he'd got a letter from the girl who was once the love of his life. Without any effort on his part he recalled those disturbing little sight-bites of mail he'd received in the past when Katrina had still been in the mental hospital.

Dear David,

   I know what you want from me. I sense your passion and determination in wanting to steal my blood. Blood is precious; it is life in solution . . . You are a vampire-hearted man, David Thomas Leppington . . .

Electra had been sensitive enough to ask Bernice to help her with the poster. So now here he was alone with the letter in the kitchen of the Station Hotel. *What are you staring at it for?* he asked himself. *It won't bite you, will it? You've got to read it sometime, so it might as well be now.*

The time was one p.m.

4

At one-fifteen Dylan Adams watched Vikki pull her T-shirt over her head, hiding her delicious nipples. With her slender figure in silhouette against the drawn curtains she looked more beautiful than ever. Soft curls of hair bounced as she reached for her jeans that lay over a chair.

'Dylan. Sorry to be a killjoy but . . .' With a laugh, she threw his shirt at him. It covered his face. She laughed even louder. 'My dad's going to be back soon.'

Dylan grinned. 'So what? I'll just tell him we've been enjoying some Sunday delight.'

'Sunday delight, my foot. If he sees you in my bedroom he'll fetch his shotgun. Come on, boy, up and at 'em.'

'I wondered who'd put all the bullet holes in the wall . . . ouch, stop it.'

'Ticklish?'

'Not my feet.' Laughing, he stuffed his shirt into his mouth to stifle the noise. 'Not my feets!'

'Ah, *feets!* We've found your vulnerable spot, have we?'

Vikki's eyes glinted with pure mischief. 'I know how to make you suffer now.'

Tears streaming down his face, Dylan spluttered, 'Sadist.'

'That's exactly what I am. And I'm going to groom you as my victim.'

'But not the *feets*.' He pulled a pillow over his face as the laughter burst from his mouth again.

'Get dressed pronto or I'll take a feather to your foot.'

'OK, OK. Now you've given me hiccups.'

'Hold your breath while you get dressed.'

As laughter alternated with hiccups Dylan started to dress. He'd just begun to buckle his belt when his mobile rang.

Grinning, he said, 'It's your dad giving me ten seconds' start before he gets the gun.'

'Don't even joke about it.'

Dylan pressed the answer button. 'Hello.'

A breathy sigh sounded in his ear. 'Long time no parler, bro.'

'Luke?'

'That's me, bro.'

'Where are you?'

'Waiting for you, old friend.'

'Are you all right, Luke? You sound—'

'Fine, fine.' His friend's voice rose over his own like a wave; a strange hissing quality. 'I'm having a party tonight with some friends. Come over and join us. We'll be at Lazarus Wake. You know where it is.'

'Luke. Are you feeling OK? Luke?' Dylan realized that the connection had been cut.

Vikki adjusted the sleeves of her sweatshirt. 'That was AWOL boy?'

'Yeah, but he sounds strange.'

'He's probably been on a bender.'

'No – he's been on some benders before but I've never heard him like that. I hope he hasn't got mixed up with—'

'Shit!' Vikki cocked her head, listening. 'My dad's back early.'

5

The river's turbulence sounded loud, even from inside the hotel kitchen. Mingled with that noise was the 'voice' of the wind that blew through the ornate Gothic carvings on the outside of the building. The sound carried from the gargoyle heads high on the face of the hotel. Deep, soulful notes that would drone at a single sustained pitch before breaking down into a noise not unlike the sound of a human sobbing. A broken-hearted sound.

David Leppington's skin crawled with that insect feeling: a thousand cold legs marched up his arms, up his neck and into his hair to irritate his scalp. It was a long time since he'd seen a letter from Katrina like this. But instantly it evoked that same cocktail of feelings – dread, disgust, sadness, impotence: a deep hatred for the evil disease that had robbed the girl he loved of her sanity and taken her from him. Instantly it reminded him of the time he'd received the message from Katrina's parents all those years ago when she'd suffered the nervous breakdown at university. At the time, of course, no one believed that she'd fallen into the grip of full-blown schizophrenia. But soon she started to exhibit the classic symptoms of delusion and paranoia. David was studying for his medical degree then. At nineteen he'd done the decent thing and visited her in hospital but that had thrown Katrina into paroxysms of panic. Her mental condition had affected her mind so much that she believed that her childhood sweetheart had become some kind of monster. That he was there only to hurt her. Soon his parents had asked him to stop visiting. But still he'd continued to receive her strange, rambling letters accusing him of drinking her blood and claiming that he was planning to destroy her.

David glanced up at the sound of footsteps. He realized that they came from the corridor that ran parallel to the kitchen. *Electra will guard the door and not let anyone in*, he told himself. She'd make sure that he had privacy while he read the letter. Sighing, he unfolded the piece of paper.

Yes, that was Katrina's handwriting. There was a spikiness to it that suggested it had been written at a time of emotional stress. As David began to read, he raised his hand to his mouth. A universal gesture of self-comfort. His medical persona registered this quirk of behaviour that was common to everyone when they were frightened and in need of comfort or reassurance. But his ordinary human side felt that same sadness of old that he'd experienced when he'd received one of Katrina's letters.

Dear David,

I know I've been unwell for a long time. The medicines I swallowed day after day weren't intended to cure me but to make me so drowsy and confused that I couldn't fight what was happening to me. But why should that have surprised me? You, David are a doctor. The men and women who forced those drugs on me were doctors, too. You had come to a secret agreement about me. You all conspired to keep me locked away.

But I did fight the evil magic. I played them at their own game. I feigned this thing they told me was 'sanity'. Once I could act in a way they deemed 'normal' they were forced to release me. Of course, they told me to keep taking those mind drugs that repressed my free will. I pretended to do that.

But once I was in a home of my own I stopped eating the poisons they prescribed. Soon my mind cleared. I could plan my life again. I could do as I chose. And as insight and analytical thought returned I began to think about you, David Leppington. I asked myself why you had done this terrible thing to me when you had always told me you loved me.

I knew that as we made love on those winter afternoons you drew blood from my veins into yours. You blood-sucked me dry, only I was so unaware at the time.

Why was I so unaware? Why didn't I have the clarity of vision to see the truth of your diabolical nature?

Then, last month, I saw a film poster in the Tube. It described itself as a romantic comedy but I knew that whoever made the poster was my secret friend because they had printed a message under the film's title. It read THIS BOY STOLE MY HEART.

Then it became clear, David. When I was nineteen you stole my heart. Without my heart I lost my power for instinctive understanding . . .

David broke off from reading the letter. The sandwich he'd eaten weighed heavy in his stomach. He felt short of breath. Outside, winds whooped and cried round the eaves of the building. Through the window he saw storm clouds towering over the town.

Come on, David. Nearly done. He read on:-

Therefore, my course of action was a simple one. I had to find you again. I telephoned hospitals until I traced a Dr Leppington. Then I waited for you by your car. I knew you would steal more blood from me when we slept together. That was an acceptable price. I had to get close. I had to listen to your chest as you slept.

And yes. There it was. My heart beats inside your body. You stole it. I need it back.

I am in the town that bears your name – Leppington.
Come and find me here. Return what belongs to me.
And yet, even as I write this, I understand fully that you
will not do that. I write, fatalistic, knowing that soon I will
die in your strong arms . . .

David folded the letter and put it in his pocket. *Dear God in*
heaven. A few days ago she'd looked so healthy and alive –
and sane. But all the time madness had been eating away at
her. She'd been concocting this bizarre plan. He took a deep
swallow of coffee. It was stone cold. Not that he noticed. He
drained the cup, then went to find Electra.

She was standing with Bernice at a noticeboard by the hotel
entrance, pinning up a poster advertising the Goth ball.

David licked his lips. They were so dry that they burned.
'Electra. I'd like to see Katrina.'

CHAPTER 18

I

'Jesus, Dylan! What are you doing to the bitch?'

Dylan Adams looked up as Vikki's father strode through the door.

'Brushing her.'

'I can see that, lad. But what on Earth for?'

'Dad, I told you last week.' Vikki walked into the living room with the camera tripod. 'Dylan, where do you want this?'

'Just stand it by the camera, thanks.'

The frown vanished from her father's face. 'Oh, your mother's birthday? Right.'

Vikki took over brushing the dog's long fur. 'Dylan's going to take the photographs, then he'll get them blown up to portrait size. After that I can get them framed in Whitby.'

The older man's powerful shoulders drooped. 'Uh, so you can hang them over the fireplace. Now I remember. Hell, those dogs . . . soon everywhere I look I'll see them. She's even got pot dogs in the bathroom.'

Dylan smiled. 'They go well with the dog's-head loo-brush holder.'

The man groaned. 'Oh, you've seen that?'

Vikki laughed. Then she shot a look at Dylan. 'You'll have noticed that my mother loves her dogs.'

'Christ,' her father said with feeling. 'You can say that again. She bought me bloody dogs' slippers for Christmas.' He watched Vikki brushing the dog. Dylan saw from the expression on the man's face that here was a husband who suffered in silence – most of the time. 'What's the plan then, Vic?'

'Dylan's going to photograph Tarka and Smudge together on the sofa, then he's going to do individual portraits. But I'm having trouble keeping the ribbon in Tarka's hair.'

Vikki's father turned to Dylan. 'You don't intend doing this kind of thing for a living when you leave college, do you, lad?'

'No, I planned on going to London. I want to get into photojournalism.'

'Good money?'

'Not bad, once you make a name for yourself.'

'You've got your head screwed on right, then.' He eyed the dogs with distaste. 'You want danger money for handling those two. I've never seen dogs like 'em. They're a pair of bloody tarts.'

Dylan smiled. 'I like a challenge.'

'You've got one there, lad.' He nodded at his daughter. 'I hope our Vic's giving you something worthwhile in return for your work.'

Dylan found it hard to suppress the grin as Vikki blushed.

'Now then,' the older man said. 'I've got a truckload of logs that won't unload themselves. See you, Dylan.'

Dylan nodded. 'Mr Lawton.'

'Vic, see that you give Dylan what he wants.'

Vikki's blush deepened, spreading down her throat to her chest. 'I'll see to it, Dad.'

When her father had gone, Vikki, still kneeling on the floor, buried her face in the armchair's cushion. The dogs decided it was the start of a game and both of them began to pull at her hair with their mouths.

Dylan grinned as he heard her muffled, '*Oh, God . . . oh, God. God!*'

He sat down himself, shaking his head. 'Phew, that was a close one.'

Face flushed, but grinning from ear to ear, Vikki lifted her head and pushed the dogs back. 'My God, I thought my dad had caught us then.'

'I've never moved so quick. And –' he pulled up the bottoms of his trousers '– I didn't even get a chance to put my socks on.'

'I don't think my heart's ever going to slow down.' She fanned her face with her hands.

Dylan couldn't help but smile at the way her eyes twinkled outrageously. Patting her calf, he said, 'It all adds to the excitement, doesn't it? Forbidden love on a Sunday afternoon.'

'But, hell, it was a close call.'

'I only hope he doesn't spot the condom wrappers in the bathroom.'

Her eyes widened. 'Dylan! You didn't!'

He chuckled throatily. 'Sorry . . . only joking.'

'You're going to give me heart failure . . . you idiot. Where *are* the wrappers?'

He patted his trousers. 'In my pocket. I'll get rid of them.'

'Discreetly, I hope. Don't chuck them on the drive on the way out.'

'What, me? You can trust me, Vikki, with your life.'

'I hope so.' Suddenly she turned and straddled his legs, kissing him on the lips. 'Now, that's going to have to last for a while.'

He groaned with disappointment as she climbed off him.

She pointed at the camera. 'Time to get those photographs, now we've gone to all that trouble of making my dad think that's the reason you're here.'

'And the truth is I only came up here to get you hot and naked.'

Vikki blushed again, her expression suddenly shy. 'I'll get the ribbon in Tarka's fur. Do you want her sitting or standing?'

'Standing first.'

The look on Dylan's face must have given him away because Vikki shot a look at him. 'What's the matter?'

'Uh . . . that call from Luke Spencer.'

'I thought it was preying on your mind.'

'It's stupid . . . I'm not his keeper or anything; he's over eighteen.'

'But?'

'There's something not right . . . he sounded strange.'

'He's probably overdoing the partying.'

'God, he's done that in the past. Only I've never heard him like that before. His voice has altered.'

'Are you sure it was Luke?'

'Yes, no doubt at all.'

'Was he using his mobile to call?'

'No, a payphone.' Dylan opened up the camera tripod legs. 'I guess I'm starting to think he's got mixed up with some heavy-duty drugs . . . he didn't even sound as if he was –' Dylan struggled for the right word '– *connected* to reality any more.'

'Has he used hard drugs before?'

'Not that I know of.'

'And earlier he invited you to a party at the house near Lazarus Deep?'

'Yeah, the one we called at the night we went looking for him . . . what was it called now?'

'Lazarus Wake?'

'Yeah, that's the one.'

Vikki nodded, her face serious. 'OK. It's a date. Tonight we'll drive over to Lazarus Deep. Then you can see what state Luke's in for yourself.'

2

The church clock sounded its dead chimes over Leppington town. Two o'clock.

David heard the chimes fade then echo back from distant buildings, altered by distance. It sounded like a brassy chuckle to his ears. A sound that had mocked the dreams and hopes of men and women for generations. And in the consecrated ground over which the bell tower loomed the church gathered the dead of Leppington into the cemetery's unbreakable grip.

Lying there on the bed, looking more dead than alive, Katrina stared at the ceiling through half-open eyes.

'How long has she been like this?' David slipped his fingers around her wrist, feeling for the pulse.

'Since yesterday morning.'

'More than twenty-four hours? Didn't you think to call a doctor?'

'I thought it was the shock of her seeing what she took to be a diver's dead body.' He saw Electra press her lips together. She thought David was criticizing her. 'I hoped she'd come out of it once she'd had some rest.'

David took his hand away from Katrina's wrist. The pulse appeared normal enough – a little sluggish, maybe, but her lying comatose for more than a day would explain that. Electra and Bernice stood at the foot of the bed in the gloomy hotel room. Electra had folded her arms across her chest.

She's defensive. She expects me to criticize her for not calling a doctor. David moved back from the bed. Katrina's face looked a bloodless grey, while beneath her eyes were dark rings. Her hair had become matted from lying in bed for so long. In this half-light her lips showed as a black line.

Electra said, 'I thought she'd simply go to sleep and then wake up perfectly normal. I assumed it was the shock. Before she freaked she seemed so . . .' She shrugged. 'Cheerful. Ebullient, even.'

'Electra, you weren't to know what was wrong with her. Don't blame yourself.' David shook his head as he gazed down at the woman he'd fallen in love with all over again. 'I mentioned earlier that Katrina suffered a nervous break-down when she was nineteen. But I didn't tell you that the psychiatrists diagnosed acute schizophrenia.'

Bernice tilted her head, puzzled. 'That's where a person develops a split personality, isn't it?'

'The Jekyll and Hyde syndrome.' David smiled grimly. 'No, that's a misconception. Schizophrenia is a disintegration of the mind. Sufferers can become paranoid – they think other people want to harm them. They might develop delusional ideas that they're kings or presidents, or they might imagine that electricity can sneak out of plug sockets at night to electrocute them while they're sleeping.' He shrugged. 'Schizophrenia is devastating. It's mind cancer. As well as outright hallucinations sufferers experience distorted percep-tions: they have difficulty making sense of things they see, hear, smell or even taste. Everything is jumbled up in a way that they perceive as frightening and disturbing. They lose interest in friends, family, hobbies. They find it hard to sum-mon up the energy to go to work or do chores that we take for granted. Their ability to speak diminishes so much that they won't speak unless spoken to. The thing is, schizophrenia isn't even rare. For example, at the last count the condition affected three million Americans. Hospital wards overflow with schizo-phrenics, so we push them back out onto the streets as fast as we can . . . Damn.' He clenched his fist. 'I'm lecturing you, aren't I? See, in times of stress I guarantee that Dr Leppington takes over, so I can hide behind the professional mask.'

Bernice touched his arm. 'Don't worry, I'm sure she'll be all right soon.'

If only.

But he smiled at Bernice, thankful for her concern.

Electra, ever the practical one, said, 'What now?'

'Now? Katrina's suffered a major relapse. Before that she must have been in what is called the maintenance phase of the illness. Her doctors discharged her from hospital; she was well enough to find work and a new home. Now she's experienced an acute episode.'

Electra said, 'Could it have been brought on by the shock of seeing the injured diver at the lake?'

'That's probably what triggered the hysterical outburst, which then led to this state of catatonia. But relapse was inevitable, anyway. She'd stopped taking her medication . . . dear God, there I go, sounding like the doctor reeling off the pat diagnosis, don't I?' David took a deep breath. 'Old habits die hard. That aside, she's entered what is called the "disorganized behaviour" stage. In some patients this can make them repeat pointless gestures like patting their chin for hours on end or drawing crosses in the air or whatever. Some simply shut down. They don't speak or move for hours or even days.'

'Can Katrina hear us?'

'Possibly, but she's not responded so far.' David leaned over the bed to look into her half-closed eyes. 'I don't think she even knows I'm here.'

Bernice looked uneasy. 'Poor woman. Are you going to call an ambulance?'

'And add to the psychiatric wards' burden? No, they won't thank us for that.'

'That's terrible.'

'Terrible but a fact of life.' David pulled a blister pack from his jacket pocket. 'They probably won't even admit her.'

Electra noticed the pack of drugs. 'You can give her something to help?'

'I brought her medication with me.'

'But it's not a cure.'

'No. With schizophrenia you can, at best, control the disease to allow the patient to lead as normal a life as possible.' He snapped a pill through the foil. 'This is an antipsychotic.' He handed Electra the packet as he eased Katrina gently into a sitting position. 'She's been prescribed one of the new class of drugs. If she hadn't quit taking them she'd probably have behaved as normally as we do.'

Electra sniffed. 'We'll use the word "normal" in a qualified way, shall we?' He saw her hold the blister pack to the light. 'Zyp—' She had another stab at reading the word. 'Zyprexa. Snappy product name.'

'It's not a miracle cure but it's reasonably effective. OK, Katrina, open your mouth, sweetheart.'

Bernice moved forward. 'Let me help.'

David saw Bernice support Katrina's head carefully.

'Swallow the capsule, Katrina.' He spoke softly but firmly. 'Come on, sweetheart. You've done it often enough before. Swallow the capsule. It'll make you feel better.'

Close up, he looked into the dark-ringed eyes. They were dull, lifeless. What was more, he could smell that character-istic faint animal odour – a goat aroma that seeped from a schizophrenic's body when they were in relapse. As diseases went this won the gold medal for pure cruelty. Patients and their families went through hell.

Katrina had taken thousands of pills in the last ten years or so. Probably the action was automatic but once she felt the shape of the tablet in her mouth, her jaw worked as she moved it back along her tongue to swallow it. She never made a sound through the entire process.

'She's got it,' David said to Bernice. 'We can lay her back down now.'

Electra regarded Katrina with sharp eyes. 'How long now?'

'Before it works? Stabilization will occur in a few hours as the drug damps down the symptoms.' He looked at Electra and Bernice. 'I should warn you, though, she's not out of the woods yet.' He pulled the bedclothes up over Katrina's shoulders. 'We can leave her now for a while. She'll sleep.'

A few minutes later David realized he should have added the superstitious phrase: *touch wood*.

Bernice and David left the room first as Electra tidied Katrina's bedding. Then Electra followed them into the hotel corridor. David blinked. After the gloom of the hotel room here the lights seemed over-bright. They'd barely taken half a dozen paces to the staircase when there was a scream. David heard the harsh tone of real terror in Katrina's voice. He ran back to the room, followed by the other two. In the hotel room Katrina was kneeling up in bed. She was pointing at shadows in the corner of the room. Her mouth worked as if she was trying to push words through her lips only they just wouldn't come, while her eyes bulged from her head, shockingly bright. They made David think of glass balls that glittered with an uncanny light.

'Katrina,' he said soothingly. 'Lie back down. You're safe. Don't worry.' He put his hands round her shoulders. Her muscles were rigid with fear. 'Lie down, Katrina. Everything's OK now.'

Bernice moved forward to help. The moment she was close to the bed Katrina lunged at her, grabbing her. For a moment David feared that Katrina was attacking the girl. Bernice flinched back but Katrina flung her arms round her, obviously merely wanting to be protected.

'You're safe,' Bernice said. 'You're with friends now. We're going to look after you.'

Katrina hissed, 'Don't leave me alone with him.'

David felt a weight plunge into the pit of his stomach. That delusion again. The belief that he'd harm her. Only she wasn't looking at him. Her stare remained locked on the corner of the room. She didn't even seem to notice him.

'Don't leave him in here,' Katrina hissed.'

Bernice stroked the woman's hair. 'We won't. I promise.'

'But you went out just then. You didn't take him with you.'

'*Who* didn't we take with us?'

'*Him.*' Katrina pointed to the pool of shadow where two walls met. 'Him in the corner. Look at him . . . with the shaved head . . . he's a monster. Why did he cover himself with all those tattoos?' Suddenly she seemed to see something that made her neck arch as she tried to pull back. 'Look at that. Oh God. *There's something wrong with his throat!*' She pressed her face against Bernice's stomach. 'Don't leave me alone with him. Please . . . please . . .'

'It's OK,' Bernice soothed. 'We'll make him go.'

It took almost half an hour for Katrina to relax. Eventually she stopped clinging to Bernice and allowed herself to be put back to bed. David checked that she was sleeping easily before he left the room and joined the others.

Electra spoke first. Matter-of-factly she said, 'The man Katrina could see in the corner. She was describing Jack Black, wasn't she?'

3

Ten minutes later they sat drinking coffee in the hotel kitchen. Winds thrummed and whooped around the building. Monoliths of dark cloud reared over the hilltops, threatening to tumble onto the town.

The town's coming adrift from the outside world. We're slipping into another reality. Here the dead talk, the dead walk, sometimes they want your blood. David gripped the cup, using the scalding heat to halt the morbid line of thought. Leppington did this to people. The sinister old town that had been one of the last bastions of pagan England had a talent for ghosting through their skin, filling their minds with macabre ideas.

A branch tapped the wall. The sound of a bone moving in a tomb.

Bernice took a deep breath. 'It's starting again, isn't it?'

Electra nodded. 'I agree, children.'

Children? The endearment sounded odd and David looked up at her face, framed by that gunmetal black hair.

Electra continued. 'Leppington has suffered a relapse, to echo David's medical phraseology. We are about to suffer an acute episode.'

'An acute episode of what?' asked David.

'Of vampirism.'

'Oh, please.' He shook his head.

'All the signs and portents are there, if you'll excuse my dramatic vocabulary. We feel a sense of dread and foreboding in our bones. We have nightmares.'

'That's hardly evidence.'

'But then I saw the woman who'd been pulled out of the lake. She must have had a dozen or more bites on her body. She'd suffered massive blood loss.'

'She's dead?'

'No. She's in Whitby hospital.'

Bernice sat up straight. 'Then she might have become one of those things?'

'Possibly.' Electra took a swallow of coffee. 'I should visit her.'

David clenched his fist on the table. 'Then – depending on your diagnosis – are you suggesting we cut off her head? That's the tried and tested cure for vampirism, isn't it?'

'David, I suggest we assess the facts before we do anything.'

He felt a vast shroud of darkness gathering around him.

His rational mind fought that black tide of the supernatural that threatened to carry him away from the civilized world.

Electra continued, 'My belief is that somehow Katrina has been drawn into this, too. After all, we know what kind of forces we're dealing with here.'

'The supernatural?'

'That's just a label, David. And let me remind you, what happened here three years ago went far beyond nature. You fought running battles with those creatures. You smelled them, you touched them. They were as real as I am.'

He sighed. 'OK, Electra. What do you suggest?'

'That we pool information. We tell each other our experiences of anything uncanny or unusual over the last few weeks. I have a document called *The Broxley Testament* that I want both of you to read. I've left copies of it in your rooms.'

'You're efficient, Electra, I'll give you that.'

'One has to be if one is to survive.'

'And then?'

'After you've read *The Broxley Testament* and freshened up we'll meet down here again for a meal to discuss our options.'

Bernice gave a nervous laugh. 'You make it sound like a council of war.'

'That's exactly what it is.'

Electra glanced at the wall clock. 'It's now almost three. I suggest that we retire to our rooms. After we've eaten and had a chance to talk we'll go out for a drive.'

'Where?' David glanced out at the gathering storm clouds.

Electra rose from the table. 'To the lake . . . Lazarus Deep. We can also check out a house called Lazarus Wake.'

'Electra, aren't you forgetting something?' Bernice sounded nervous. 'Won't it be getting dark by then?'

'Dusk is the perfect time. After all, we won't find what we're looking for in the daylight, will we?'

CHAPTER 19

I

Electra ran the Station Hotel with total efficiency. David found that not only had his room been made up for him with an array of complimentary drinks (alcoholic and non-alcoholic) but there were pens, pencils and notepads alongside a comb-bound document entitled *The Broxley Testament: a Vampiric Lament*. She'd been most keen that he should read this. He glanced at his watch. Three-thirty. If Electra was serious about driving out to Lazarus Deep she was cutting it fine. On a cloudy February day like this it would be dark by five. And roaming high on the lonely moors in darkness wouldn't be a good idea.

David's arms and shoulders ached from the drive up from London. Before reading the document he undressed and took a hot shower. The five-hour car journey had left him feeling grimy. Now he took pleasure from chasing the dirt away under the blast of hot water that filled the bathroom with steam. Even the mint scent of the shampoo refreshed him, leaving a piquant tingle in his nose.

A few minutes ago, when he'd been talking to Electra, he'd found himself rationalizing away what had happened. His conversation on Friday morning with a man who he'd found out later was dead. Katrina being somehow influenced (supernaturally influenced?) to travel up here to Leppington. The re-emergence of her delusional behaviour, of her fear that *he* was a vampire and that he had literally stolen her heart. On top of that there was the panic attack she'd suffered when she'd thought that she could see someone in her room.

That someone being Jack Black. Hallucination? Coincidence . . .

There you go again, David. Rationalizing. Deconstructing the supernatural with your clinical mind. Damn . . .

He dropped the soap. *All I need to do is step on that and slip. Hobbling round Leppington with a broken leg would put the tin lid on it.* Retrieving the soap, he straightened to look through the tendrils of steam curling in the confines of the shower cubicle. Through the frosted glass a face stared in at him. Grabbing at the sliding glass door, he wrenched it to one side.

Jack Black . . .

David caught his breath; his heart pounded at his ribs. Steam swirled. He dreaded what he'd see as it thinned beyond the confines of the shower cubicle. Rubbing the water from his eyes with the back of his hand, he looked again. *That's your ghost.* He sighed. A dark green towelling robe was hanging behind the bathroom door. It must have swung in the draught to produce the illusion of an eerily swaying figure.

So, no. There was no ghost . . . no Jack Black . . . no vampire . . . no nothing . . .

Just a towelling robe. His imagination had twisted something as innocent as that into a ghostly shape. David rinsed the soap from his skin, enjoying the beat of the water against his face and chest and back. Another twenty minutes of this would work wonders on his tired muscles . . . only he'd best quit the shower now, wonderfully reviving though it was . . . Electra had insisted that he read *The Broxley Testament*.

Switching off the shower, David stepped out onto the mat. As he began to towel his hair dry he heard the cry of the wind as it blew down from the hills to play among the ornate Gothic carvings on the building. The sound had the power to send a shiver down his spine. It was the cry of this brutal landscape calling to the living – and to the dead.

2

I can't believe I'm back here. I can't believe it . . .

Bernice sat on the bed, staring at the row of her boots and shoes along one wall. *After all these years I'm back, and it feels as if I've never been away. The heavy velvet curtains are the same. For heaven's sake, I didn't even use this room but the framed prints on the wall are the same, too. Views of horses drinking from a stream. And there's the same kind of television on its bracket. Here's the double bed with the same quilt in lush, swirling purples. There's the dark wood of the furniture. Morbid coffin wood. The décor of the room echoes the Gothic architecture of the hotel. The Gothic style of the hotel echoes the dark mood of the town.*

And there are my shoes. I saved for those shoes. The pair with the silver inlay in the heels are the most expensive I've ever bought. So why did I bring my best shoes to a place like this?

So that I can be buried in something nice?

Quickly, she moved across the room, trying to shake off the macabre line of thought. Looking out through the large window, she saw the town laid out before her. *(Same old view, too.)* Few people moved through the streets. The wind was so cold that they walked with their heads tucked down deeply between their hunched shoulders; a town populated by people without heads. A shuffling, zombie race. *Dear God, what am I doing here?*

Even though a voice in the back of her head told her to catch the first train out, Bernice knew that she couldn't leave yet. They were all back here for a reason. She had to wait and learn what that reason was.

3

Electra Charnwood got an e-mail. While David showered in his room and Bernice gazed out of the window at a town that looked bleaker than gravestones the message arrived. It had come ghosting through telephone cables that were buried as deep as a tomb beneath Leppington's streets. *And now I have it*, Electra told herself. It had come from Rowan at the house near Lazarus Deep.

I detest being superstitious, she mused. *I hate throwing spilt salt over my left shoulder, or avoiding walking under ladders, or not making journeys on Friday the thirteenth. I hate reading horoscopes in magazines. Why do I hate them?*

Because deep down I am superstitious. Try as I might not to, I believe in horoscope predictions. I fear the consequences of not throwing salt over my shoulder or walking under a ladder. And right now I have a deep sense of foreboding about this e-mail. She gazed at the sealed-envelope icon on the computer screen. A click with the mouse and it would pop open; she would be able to read the message from Rowan. *So why don't I do just that?*

Because I'm afraid of it. I feel it down to the roots of my veins. If I read this e-mail it's going to change my future.

Electra sensed foreboding hanging like a mist in the room. It crept over her skin . . . cold, goose-bump-raising, unsettling. Twice she looked back over her shoulder, convinced that she'd see someone standing there.

Come on, Electra, where's that steel will of yours? You don't get spooked. The e-mail's there in the computer. You can't pretend it never arrived. For better or worse, read it!

She did just that. Then she sat back, her eyes glittering, her fists clenched. Her instinct had been right. That e-mail had confirmed her worse fears. She looked out of the window. Late afternoon and the ocean of grey cloud flooding the sky had brought dusk early. Gloom came ghosting down the valley to invade the streets silently.

Even though Electra knew what she must do she paused, hoping deep down that . . . What? She'd receive another e-mail from Rowan revealing that it was all a hoax and that she should ignore all the messages he'd sent her as well as that disturbing document?

'No,' she told herself. 'You're turning into a big old 'fraidy cat.' She attempted a smile to try to dispel the cold blue fear that she felt creeping through her veins. But the distorted phantom mask of her reflection in the window revealed a grimace rather than a smile. Shutting down the computer, she murmured, 'Time to do the job, old girl. Anyway, what's the worst that could happen to you?'

4

David had all but finished reading *The Broxley Testament* when he heard the knock on his room door. It was one of those urgent taps that immediately sent a warning flash along his nerves. After his shower he'd dressed in jeans and a sweatshirt, but he was still barefooted when he went to answer the door.

Electra stood there, her face the bloodless white of someone who'd just received shocking news.

'Is it Katrina?' he said.

'No, she's still sleeping.' Electra handed him a sheet of paper. 'It's a print of an e-mail I've just received.'

'More reading material? I'm almost through *The Broxley Testament*. You're right, it's certainly a disturbing—'

'David. Please read this e-mail, while I get Bernice.'

'Electra, what's wrong?'

'We need to drive up to Lazarus Wake.'

'I thought we were going to discuss it first. It's going to be completely dark in an hour.'

Her face was grim. 'I know. Read the e-mail. That tells you why we have to move fast.'

David looked at the sheet of paper in his hand. With its

fierce black print, the thing had the ominous aura of a death certificate.

'I'll fetch Bernice. You'd best finish getting dressed. We might have to do some walking,' Electra said.

'It looks as if there's a storm building.'

Her gaze never left his face. 'You're right. There is.'

5

By the time he'd finished reading the e-mail David Leppington knew that Electra's remark about the coming storm didn't just concern the weather. Down the corridor he could hear her using those same hushed – and hurried – tones as she talked to Bernice . . . *Get dressed quickly . . . Wear something warm . . . We're leaving in five minutes* . . . After David had pulled on his shoes, he reread the print copy of the e-mail that had so unsettled Electra.

> *To: Electra*
> *From: Rowan*
> *Days and night ride seamlessly by me. Remember, Electra? I told you that I'm in this house lost in the barren wilderness near a lake called Lazarus Deep. Remember, I pleaded with you to come to me? I had faith in you, that you would rescue me. Believe me, I cannot help myself. I've suffered some injury or illness. My mind isn't clear. It's as if I live in a fog. Sometimes I remember a little about myself, then it all goes again. I suddenly find myself in one of the rooms of the house and wonder how I got there. I don't remember walking up the stairs or down a corridor. Other times I see an open can of casserole and a spoon on the kitchen table. I guess I must have eaten the meat cold from the can, only I don't remember doing so.*
> *And still – and still! – I'm afraid of what lies outside*

the house. I daren't go out. And I wonder why. But then I remember what I'd read in the document I found that explains so much about the house. Now I have difficulty in distinguishing dreams from real experience. Last night I found myself leaning out through the bedroom window. In the garden there were men and women. They looked up at me. I realized I'd been talking to a man with long white hair and the palest skin imaginable. He was only young, yet he had old eyes, if you know what I mean? They were the brightest green you've ever seen.

Now I realize that I must have been dreaming about the albino, Ash White. Yet the dream was so vivid. I remember the cold night air blowing against my face. Many of the people in the garden were naked. I remember telling myself that they must have walked here barefoot. Their feet were caked with dark silty mud, as if they'd waded through a stream or pond. Dreams don't usually contain that kind of detail, do they?

But I'm drifting from the point – already I can feel my mind sliding away again. Still, I wanted to tell you about this vivid dream. The man I recognized as Ash White explained that he and his friends had come from the lake to see me for a reason. They said it was very important. They had an offer.

The albino said this to me (and I remember his exact words): 'In Lazarus Deep is an army of warriors. I am here to tell you that they are YOUR army. You will command them. Your destiny is to reclaim the world in the name of the Viking gods. The Father of the Gods is Odin. He has willed it to happen. I am here as his representative on Earth to hand you the command, so that you will go forth and conquer.'

See, I remember that dream in perfect detail. Yet I can't remember what I did an hour ago. Even now I find it hard to concentrate. That mind fog is stealing through my head again. Steals my wits. Steals my memory. Steals my identity.

Please, Electra. Come and find me.

'David?'

He looked up, startled. The implications of the e-mail had struck him so hard that he'd forgotten everything else.

'David,' Electra repeated from the doorway. 'Are you ready?'

'Yes, I'm ready.' Grimly, he held out the sheet of paper to Electra. 'You know what this means?'

She nodded. 'It means a big, BIG problem.' He saw her shiver as if cold hands had touched her throat. 'It's going to be dark in an hour, like you said. We'd best go now, before we lose the daylight completely.' She glanced at the window. 'What there is of it.'

David picked up his coat and followed Electra downstairs. From the darkening skies hail began to fall. Soon a hard clicking filled the lobby as it struck the hotel's window-panes. It had the same sound as fleshless fingers tapping on glass, wanting to come inside.

CHAPTER 20

I

Bernice Mochardi shivered in the shadow-strewn yard. 'Are you sure Katrina's going to be all right? She's all alone in the room.'

David opened the car door for her. 'She hasn't taken the antipsychotic for a while, so it'll make her drowsy and lethargic for the next few days. She'll probably sleep for hours yet.'

'And I've briefed Claire on reception. She'll keep looking in on her.' Electra climbed into the driver's seat, the breeze rippling her long hair. 'OK. It'll take about twenty minutes to reach Lazarus Deep. Hang on tight.'

She started the engine, then eased the car out of the yard, along the side of the hotel to the main road where she pulled a left. David sat in the back, watching the houses pass by. With the winter's evening creeping in most had their curtains drawn early. Through some came the ghostly flicker of TV screens. There wasn't much traffic on the road; probably drivers had been warned off making any journeys by storm bulletins on the radio. Already hail was coming in great sweeps of pure white down the valley to rattle against the bodywork of the car. The noise was incredibly harsh. David found himself wondering if there would be any paint left on the vehicle by the· time they arrived at— He clenched his jaw. He hadn't allowed himself to imagine what the house, Lazarus Wake, would be like. Even thinking the name sent a shiver down his spine.

'I'm sorry to have to do this to the pair of you,' Electra said as she drove out of town. 'But all the facts are stacking up. The attack on the diver. The e-mails from Lazarus Wake.'

'Especially the last one,' David added.

Bernice shook her head. 'Let me get this straight. We know that David belongs to the Leppington bloodline, and that his family legend states that the Leppingtons have been ordered by ancient Viking gods to destroy Christianity . . .'

'And to reinstate Odin as humanity's chief deity.' David shrugged. 'That's how the Leppington myth goes.'

Electra said, 'And we know that, three years ago, David was given control of this army of the undead, so that he could conquer the world for Odin and his cohorts.'

David grimaced. 'A filthy ragtag army of vampires. Jesus, I don't need reminding.'

'And when you refused to have anything to do with them they tried to destroy you.'

Bernice added, 'But failed in the process. Thank heaven.'

'Amen to that,' Electra said with feeling. 'But you do see what's happened, don't you?'

'The monsters are back, we know that for sure.'

Bernice said, 'Only they're in this lake? Lazarus Deep?'

'What's more . . .' Electra downshifted as she took a bend. 'What's more, history is repeating itself. A man by the name of Rowan is being offered control of the vampire army.'

Bernice looked back at David. 'But according to your family legend it must be a Leppington, a son of the bloodline, who inherits command of the army.'

David shook his head. 'It's a different army this time . . . so different rules apply.'

'I wouldn't be so sure,' Electra countered. 'There's the Leppington connection, remember?'

'Lazarus Wake.'

'Yes, the house was built by an ancestor of yours. Magnus Leppington.'

'I don't buy it, Electra. Who's this Rowan? There's no one in the family by that name.'

'Maybe if we can find Rowan, our mystery man, at the house, then we can ask him some questions.'

'You really think he'll be there?'

'He *says* he's there.'

David saw Electra look back at him through the rear-view mirror. 'It could be a hoax, or it could be something else.'

'Like what?'

'A trap.'

2

'You're picking who up?' Vikki wrinkled her nose.

'Goldi.'

'Goldi's crazy.'

Dylan smiled as he climbed into the car. 'Yeah, he is a bit . . . a lot, actually.'

'So why bring him along to play gooseberry?'

'I thought we'd enjoy his company. Crazy gooseberries are hard to find.' He eased the car along the track from Vikki's house to the main road. Hail swirled along the valley – a white, nebulous phantom that lunged at houses and cars alike, rattling them hard with flinty pieces of ice. As he drove he noticed that Vikki was glancing at him.

'Dylan? There's something you're not telling me.'

'Me?'

'I can tell, there's something on your mind.'

'You sound like my mother.' Dylan kept smiling as he spoke. But Vikki had him sussed.

Vikki fixed him with a stare now. He knew that she was reading the expression on his face. 'No big deal, Vikki. We'll just drive up to Lazarus Wake and check that Luke's all right.'

'But you're taking Goldi with us.'

'He's a laugh.'

'What else is he? Back-up?'

'Back-up? I'm not expecting to meet gangsters up there.'

'Tell me what's on your mind, Dylan.'

'There's nothing—'

'Or you can drop me off right here.'

'It's a long walk back, Vikki.'

'I'm not joking, Dylan, so stop pissing me around.'

Dylan felt the smile slide off his face.

'Dylan?'

'OK, OK . . . look, when I spoke to Luke on the phone at your house he didn't sound like he normally does.'

'But he didn't sound drunk?'

'No.'

'Stoned?'

'No, he sounded lucid. If anything, more lucid than usual.'

'So why are you worried?'

'Because it just didn't *sound* like Luke. Do you see what I mean?'

'Not entirely, no.'

Dylan switched on the car's lights as the winter afternoon crept into a funereal twilight. Then he made another stab at an explanation. 'I know it was Luke on the phone. But he sounded strange. He talked in a slow, flat way. And there was something precise about it. Like he'd only just learned how to speak English.'

'Drugs?'

'That's what I figure.'

'And you think there might be trouble if we walk into a house full of toxic monkeys?'

'I'm sure Luke wouldn't be a problem. But if he's got himself in with a gang of junkies they might not want to lose him. Especially if he's been dipping into his college fund to sponsor their habit as well as his.'

'I see your point.' Vikki touched Dylan's knee. 'Luke's got a loyal friend.'

'Or an idiot friend. I've been chasing him for days. If he doesn't want to come home or go to college that's his lookout. I'm not his—'

'Dylan, admit it, you're worried about him.'

He gave her a tight smile. 'I suppose so. We've hung around together since we could walk. Looking out for each other's become a habit. Remember Rosso?'

'Oh, that big ape, who could forget him?'

'When I was ten Rosso used to beat me up every day when I was walking home from school. One day Luke found out what was happening so he went up to Rosso and said, "Why don't you pick on someone your own size?"'

'I remember that. Rosso beat Luke up, didn't he?'

'Yeah.' Dylan smiled easier now. 'In a perfect world Luke would have been the big hero and hammered Rosso. But life isn't like that . . . Hell, just listen to those hailstones.'

'I hope your paintwork's going to survive.'

'Forget the paintwork. Keeping us in one piece, that's a lot more important.' He said it in a humorous way but Dylan heard the ring of truth in his own voice.

And it wasn't only the God-awful weather that was bothering him. If the house up by Lazarus Deep really had become a drug den then things could get risky.

Dylan planned to leave Vikki in the car while he and Goldi went to check on Luke. If everything worked out he'd talk Luke into returning home with them. But if there was a bunch of addicts there who were depending on Luke's money to fund their own wacky trips through inner space then they might turn nasty.

'What happened to Rosso?'

Dylan glanced at Vikki, surprised that she was still thinking about school all those years ago. 'I thought you knew. His family moved to Saltburn. His parents ran an amusement arcade or a bingo hall – something like that.'

'No. What happened after he had the fight with Luke?'

Dylan shrugged. 'Someone shot Rosso with an air rifle.'

'That cost him his right eye.'

'I know.'

'People in my class said Luke did it.'

'There's always rumours like that flying about in schools. The police decided it was an accident.'

Vikki looked searchingly at him as he drove. 'You think Luke shot him, Dylan?'

'Luke wouldn't do a thing like that.'

'Like he wouldn't disappear from the face of the Earth and then start making bizarre calls to you?'

What answer do you give to that? Maybe Vikki was suspecting that there was a dark side to Luke.

A figure danced into the road, waving its arms.

Relieved at being able to change the subject, Dylan said, 'Well, here's Goldi.'

'Idiot's going to get himself run over, jumping in front of cars like that.'

'That's Goldi all over. He does dangerous things just for the thrill of it.'

'Jesus. Who's that?'

A second figure moved out from where they'd been sheltering from the hail behind a wall.

'Uh.' Dylan looked through the white swirl of hail. 'It looks like Hyper.'

'Hyper?' Vikki rolled her eyes. 'You don't mean Liz Fretwell?'

'Dizzy Lizzie. Hyper. Pick which name you want. She lives up to both.'

Vikki groaned. 'Dylan?'

'I didn't know Goldi was bringing her along, honest.'

No sooner had Dylan stopped the car than Goldi had dragged open the door. He bundled a girl of around twenty inside. She had gaudy orange streaks in her hair that hung in wet straggles. She slid sideways across the back seat, with Goldi brutally pushing in after her, shoving her along with his hip.

The girl gave something between a scream and a guffaw. 'Watch it – you're like a bull in a china shop.'

'Wow, great weather, man!' Goldi didn't talk; he shouted. 'God must be shitting icebergs.' He pulled down his hood and shook his blond dreadlocks. 'Christ on a vibrator. It's freezing my family jewels off . . . hey, you don't mind if I bring Liz along?'

'No.' Dylan grinned at Vikki's expression of horror. 'More the merrier. Nice to see you, Liz. You keeping well?'

'Fucking dandy. And you?'

'Never better.'

'God, it's freezing. Feel my hands.' Liz plunged them down the back of Dylan's collar. He convulsed forward.

'Typical Morningdale weather,' he managed to say as he jerked away from the woman's icy hands.

'Yeah,' Liz sang out. 'As if it'll get any better in summer. It's still cold enough in July to freeze your lugs off.'

Goldi cheerfully slammed the car's back door shut. 'Hey, know what happened yesterday?'

Vikki got one in. 'You sat quietly in a library?'

Dylan saw Goldi shoot Vikki a quizzical look. 'No way!' He leaned forward between the two front seats. 'I went on a dive up at Lazarus Deep.'

'At this time of year?' Vikki sounded shocked.

'Sure, it's more exciting. But get this. Something made a meal out of Steff Kline.'

'Made a meal out of her?'

'Yeah, man. She swam away from the rest of the team and something bit her.' Goldi leaned forward and, mimicking jaws with his hands, made ravenous biting motions at Dylan's shoulder.

Cold hands, then this. Jesus.

Dylan leaned forward again. 'Watch it, Goldi. I'm trying to keep this heap on the road.'

Vikki turned back in the seat. 'You say she was attacked?'

'Made a real mess, I can tell you.'

'So they know what did it?'

'Fish?' Liz hazarded.

'Have to be a bloody big fish.' Goldi leaned back, holding his hands apart. 'Need big jaws to make those kind of bites. Tore lumps of skin the size of my hand off her body.'

'My God.'

Liz squealed. 'I bet it was a crocodile.'

Goldi elbowed her. 'You *are* joking? You don't get crocs in Yorkshire.'

'No, I don't mean *naturally*. But you hear about people buying baby crocodiles and alligators for pets. Then, when they get too big, they dump them in sewers and rivers. What are you looking at me like that for, Goldi? I'm not stupid.'

Dylan said, 'This kind of cold would kill a crocodile.'

'Might be a shark?'

This time Liz elbowed Goldi. 'Now you're taking the piss.'

'How is Steff?'

'She's in the hospital at Whitby. She lost a lot of blood.'

'Is she going to be all right?'

For the first time, Goldi's voice dropped below a shout. 'They've had to sedate her. When she came round she started climbing the walls and screaming.'

'Poor cow,' Liz said with feeling.

Goldi added, 'Some of the guys think someone might have dumped a catfish in the lake. *They* grow into big bastards. They get vicious, too.'

'You think a catfish would attack a human?'

'God knows. Anyway, we're going back there next week. We're taking harpoon guns to see if we can nail the fucker.'

Dylan looked back at the man through the rear-view mirror. Normally Goldi was a bundle of explosive movement. Now he sat still. Troubled-looking. Steff's injury must have worried him more than he was letting on.

'This trip shouldn't take long,' Dylan told them. 'Afterwards I thought we could have a beer at the Lion.'

Goldi leaned forward again, the sparkle back in his eyes. 'Hey, Dill, I thought Luke'd invited us to a party?'

'He has.'

Liz chipped in, 'At somewhere called . . . what was it, Lazarus Hall?'

'Lazarus Wake,' Dylan supplied.

'Never heard of it.'

'It's an old farmhouse.'

Goldi hooted. 'How does Lukey-boy afford a place like that?'

'He doesn't. His mother takes care of some holiday cottages, so when they're empty—'

'Lukey-boy moves in and takes over for a while.'

'Something like that.'

'Sounds like a good move. If you get away from the neighbours and the cops you can really let it rip.'

Vikki shot Dylan a glance. 'Dylan, you've told Goldi the reason we're going up there?'

'Yeah . . . well, sort of. I said we'd drop in on Luke to check that everything's OK.'

'Now, that's a guy who knows how to party.' Goldi let out a whoop. 'Did he say if there were plenty of women there?'

Liz elbowed Goldi in the stomach. 'Hey, what about me?'

'Don't worry, there'll be enough chicks for everyone.'

'You know what I mean, Goldi.'

Dylan glanced at Vikki. She raised her eyebrows in a way that said only too clearly: *Dylan, you've told Goldi that he was going to a party, haven't you? You've tricked him?*

Yeah, but only a little white lie. Goldi would have laughed in his face if he'd suggested to the man that they should check whether Luke Spencer was all right. That he hadn't been snared into some kind of crack-cocaine orgy. When it came down to it, Goldi didn't do the 'concerned friend' bit. So you told white lies sometimes. Which was no bad thing if it prevented people being hurt.

But then, Dylan had grown up with a white lie that he'd told to stop his parents being hurt by one stupid thing he'd done. OK, it had been cruel as well as stupid, but he'd only been ten years old.

Dylan remembered the brutal way in which that big ape Rosso had kicked Luke Spencer in the back and even the neck after he'd beaten him up. Luke had been screaming for him to stop but Rosso was a thug. He wouldn't stop. And Jesus, oh Jesus, Dylan had been so scared for Luke when he suddenly sagged limp on the ground after a vicious kick to the back of his head. Rosso had rubbed his hands together. The ape looked so pleased with himself; there'd been a huge grin on his repulsive face. 'That'll teach you, Lukey-boy.'

Dylan had been convinced that Luke was dead. After Rosso had gone Dylan had shaken Luke by the shoulder for what had seemed like hours before he'd come round. Luke hadn't said anything, he'd just walked home with a moustache of blood on his top lip. Dylan had been sickened by the look of fear in his friend's eyes.

So, here was what had given birth to the lie. His uncle had owned an air rifle that he used for shooting rats that came into the chicken coops. One evening Dylan had waited until his uncle had gone out. Then he'd sneaked the rifle from the shed. It had all been straightforward. He'd planned to threaten Rosso with it. Warn him never to touch him or Luke again . . . or else.

But when he'd seen Rosso swinging on a tyre down by the

river he'd chickened out. He'd imagined Rosso taking the rifle from him and laughing in his face. Dylan had been so angry at the imagined scenario that he'd run into some bushes where he couldn't be seen. Then he'd fired the rifle, aiming at Rosso's backside. Only the kid was on a rope swing, spinning round and around. The pellet had ripped into the kid's eye. Later, Dylan heard that doctors had had to operate. They'd taken out the ruined eye and replaced it with an artificial one. After that, Rosso became withdrawn. He was no longer a bully: the aggression had bled right out of him. Comfort eating took him over. The kid lived on chocolate. He'd ballooned and all the other kids had started to bully *him*.

Dylan had told Vikki a little white lie, too. He'd been vague about what had happened to Rosso after his family had moved away from Morningdale. Because he'd heard that Rosso had got heavily into drugs by his mid-teens. Later, his parents had kicked him out when they'd discovered he'd been stealing cash from the family's amusement arcade.

But a boy's gotta feed his habit.

Recently, Dylan's mother had said she'd seen someone who looked like Rosso. He'd had this sore, weepy glass eye. He'd been standing on a street corner in York, holding a paper cup and begging for coins. Of course, it might not have been Rosso . . .

'Dylan, look out!'

'Uh.'

He braked to avoid running into a pair of sheep ambling down the road.

'Oooh!' Goldi cooed. 'Nearly mutton road-pie there, Dill, old buddy.'

Vikki looked at him with real concern. 'Are you all right, Dylan?'

'Fine.'

Another little white lie.

The time was four p.m.

CHAPTER 21

I

From **Hotel Midnight**:
Electra is in the chair, so without further ado: What vampire mythology and literature doesn't elaborate on is that, just as different ants in a nest have very different and very specific roles – such as soldier ants, nursery ants and worker ants – so vampires within their communities have specific roles, too. The ones I encountered three years ago had once been Viking warriors, or at least the bulk of them had been. These were to be the foot soldiers of an invasion force that would sweep away the pre-eminence of Christianity. Yet the passage of the centuries had atrophied the creatures' minds and bodies. Mentally they had become stunted. They operated at an instinctual level and if one could measure their intelligence it would be little more than that of a rat – albeit a very dangerous rat with a craving for human blood. A smaller number of vampires were what one could call more recent converts. These were modern men and women who had been fed upon, and who'd been 'infected' by the vampires and undergone 'vampirization'. That's an inelegant term but sufficiently descriptive.

These 'new blood' members of the vampire colony still had their intelligence; moreover, their looks hadn't yet degenerated into those monstrous visages of the ancient vampires. The new-blood recruits had a specific role. They could act as go-betweens and as such provide a link between the vampire world and the world of humanity. What was more, they acted as procurers. After all, the vampire army constantly needed conscripts who'd become new warriors for the dark cause. And so this team of 'new boys' fomented their deceits and formulated their strategies to lure men and women into their traps.

So, remember Electra's words, my dears: always be on your guard. Be wary of the stranger who is unusually kind – especially at night. Remember, vampires give little but take everything . . .

2

'Shit, that's some place, Dill.'

Dylan felt Goldi's breath in the side of his neck as he drove along the trackway to the house.

Liz whistled. 'And you say that's where Luke Spencer has been hiding himself away since last week?'

'Lazarus Wake.' Dylan nodded. 'That's the address he gave me.'

'Must be some party,' Liz said, impressed.

Dylan peered through the deepening gloom. The white stones of the house gleamed against the trees with all the lustre of a skull. 'But I don't see any lights.'

Excited, Goldi slapped the back of the headrest. 'Who needs lights, man?'

Vikki was puzzled. 'But when we checked here last week there were no lights on then, either, and no sign of Luke.'

'Hey, you think he's playing a joke on us?' Goldi sounded annoyed. 'That's a bum trick. If you invite someone to a party you invite them to a party, not for a drive across this fucking wilderness.'

Dylan glanced sideways at Vikki. She looked back at him. *She's thinking the same thing as me*, Dylan told himself. *That this is some kind of set-up by Luke. But why invite us to a party all the way out at Lazarus Wake? Unless Luke's moved out of the area and wants to throw us off his trail? Hell, but that doesn't make sense either. If Luke wants privacy then he didn't have to call at all.*

Darkness had all but buried the countryside now. Dylan Adams glanced at the clock on the dash. Five past five. It was as good as night-time now. The hail didn't help either. It came at them in swarms of ice bullets that rattled the car's bodywork. He watched ice particles spitting through the light thrown by the headlights. Ahead, he could make out the lonely house swathed in a white mist of hail. The deeply recessed windows that made him think of deeply sunken eyes stared out. He could see no house lights. No sign of life.

Maybe I should just turn the car round? This is a waste of time. No one's here.

'Look! There's Luke!'

Vikki's sudden shout startled Dylan. He dipped his head forward to look up at the house as it loomed out of the darkness and the hail.

'No, not in the house. He's on the driveway . . . there, at the far side.'

'What the hell is he doing out there?'

Liz added, 'And in this shit, too. It's freezing.'

Goldi whooped. 'Look at the crazy S.O.B. He's not wearing any shoes.'

'Or even a shirt.'

'He's on some good gear.' Liz sounded impressed. 'If he doesn't feel this kind of cold.'

Excited, Goldi thumped the back of the headrest again.

Dylan turned on him. 'Hey, Goldi, take it easy; my head's on the other side of that.'

'Sorry, man, but take a look at Luke. He's cooking on something.'

Through billowing white sheets of hail Dylan caught now-and-then glimpses of his friend. One moment he was there, waving to Dylan to drive forward, the next he'd vanished into a spinning of vortex of ice particles.

'He's waving you on,' Vikki said.

'But he asked us to come to Lazarus Wake.'

'Maybe there's another house further on?' Goldi suggested.

'As far as I know there isn't.'

'Well,' Liz said. 'He's waving you to follow him.'

Dylan drove slowly forward. High winds shook the car, hail rattled against the windscreen. He switched on the wipers to push the gravelly particles of ice aside. Ahead, in the lights, he saw his friend waving him on. Dylan had never seen him looking so excited before. The man was acting like he'd found the pot of gold at the end of the rainbow. Now he was deliriously happy and wanting to show Dylan, too.

Goldi's laugh sounded loud in Dylan's ear. 'Man, he's going to get frostbite in his tootsies.'

So it's got to be drugs, Dylan thought. *Luke Spencer's brains must be baking in some narcotic. You don't prance around stripped to your waist in this weather. The ground must be frozen, too. It must be like dancing barefoot on jagged rock.*

'He's out of it,' Vikki murmured softly so that Goldi and Liz wouldn't hear.

'Damn, he's got himself into a right mess.' Dylan shook his head. 'We're going to have to drag him into the car and drive him home. His dad's going to go crazy.'

'He'll freeze to death if we don't do something.'

'Whoa,' Goldi shouted. 'There he goes, Dylan. You're going to lose him if you don't take this thing out of tortoise drive.'

Dylan watched Luke run along the driveway, away from the house. He kept glancing back and waving to Dylan to follow. Dylan was pretty sure that there were no more houses between Lazarus Wake and the lake, but what else could he do? He'd have to follow his friend to wherever he was taking him. Then somehow get him into the car. He eased the car along the driveway, taking its speed up to fifteen miles per hour. Tyres scrunched on frozen leaves. Glancing back at the house receding into the distance, he thought he saw a face at a darkened window. Not that Lazarus Wake mattered any more. Luke Spencer was guiding them toward Lazarus Deep, that bleak expanse of water locked between two sides of the valley. Dylan glanced left and right as he drove. There was nothing but rough pasture and trees. Ahead, the pale strip of the driveway ran between twin banks of dark grass, dotted with shrubs. More hail cracked against the car roof. A tree with twisted limbs overhung the road. It trailed woody claws over the car as Dylan drove on. *Hell, where's Luke taking us? Any further and we'll hit the lake itself.*

And there, right at the edge of the dark waters, standing on a strip of pebbles that formed the narrow shore, Luke stood in the light thrown by the car's headlamps. He waited for them, his arms by his side. His smile was huge. Dylan saw that Luke was pleased that his friend had come. Luke held up his hand, signalling Dylan to stop.

Dylan stopped and climbed out the car. The wind coming off the lake was biting. He opened his mouth to speak but the force of the gale sucked the air from his lungs.

Luke stepped forward, the smile not leaving his face for a second. 'Dylan. I know this looks weird.' He indicated his bare feet. 'Before you say anything, let me introduce you to my friends. They've been waiting to see you.'

'Luke, this is crazy. Get into the car.'

'No.'

'You're going to freeze to death!'

'No, I'm not.' He nodded toward the bushes at the edge of the lake. 'Meet my friends . . .'

Dylan looked at the wind-buffeted bushes. Two shapes were unaffected by the strength of the storm. They grew larger and Dylan realized that they were the figures of two men walking toward him.

Luke continued in that pleased way of his. 'These two are Rick Broxley and Ash White. They were famous once.'

'And we're going to be again.' The man who spoke was tall, with white hair, bone-white skin and the brightest green eyes that Dylan had ever seen.

'Good to meet you, Dylan. Luke here tells me that you once recorded some songs with him. I was hoping we might join forces to work on a new project.'

Get in the car . . . get in the car . . . The voice tapped away in the back of Dylan's head. *Yes, that's what I should be doing.* Only there was something about those green eyes. Their stare held him there. A dark fog gathered behind Luke's eyes. He found that the cold had suddenly gone. The storm quietened. He never even noticed the hail striking his face. And out over the water a raven glided with outstretched wings.

Yes . . . he should get in the car . . . only he couldn't . . . he couldn't even move . . .

The albino flashed Luke a look of triumph as he walked smoothly forward.

3

By five-thirty David could see Lazarus Deep from the car – a stretch of liquid shadow in the gathering gloom – then he saw Lazarus Wake. The house was so white that it looked as if it could have been built from bleached bones. The house name hung from a gallows cross set at the end of the drive.

Electra turned along the driveway, then allowed the car to roll forward beneath the canopy of trees.

'Well,' she said, 'here goes.'

'I don't think I've ever seen a place so bleak,' Bernice added. 'Just look at that lake. I'm a mass of shivers just looking at it.'

'What we haven't done,' David warned, 'is discuss strategy.'

'Strategy sounds good,' Electra agreed. 'But what the hell we do in a situation like this God alone knows.'

David leaned forward between the seats so he could get a better view of the house with its ugly windows set deep into the walls. 'I don't think it would be a good idea for us to get out of the car just yet.'

'You're right.' Electra said, pressing a button. 'The doors are all locked.'

'So what are we going to find here?' David asked.

Electra shrugged. 'My mystery correspondent Rowan for one. And . . .'

'Vampires?' Bernice stared out at the mass of trees. Their Gothic columns marched away into the wild landscape.

'Vampires.' Electra nodded. 'We might find those, too.'

4

Dylan groaned. 'Stop that . . . stop hitting me, you shit.'

Dylan heard Goldi announce, 'He's awake. What now?'

'Keep him in the back seat until I stop.'

'You're not going to get much further. This track ends where the river runs into the lake.'

Dylan opened his eyes. He was looking up at the car roof. Two faces swam into his field of vision: they looked huge, like free-floating balloons. They were distorted with over-large eyes . . . gaping mouths.

Goldi looked down at him and slapped his face again.

'Hey, I told you. Stop that.'

'Just checking to see that you're still with us, Dylan.'

'Hell . . . what have you done to me?'

Vikki glanced back over her shoulder as he drove. 'Goldi got you away from those weirdos.'

Liz added, 'You owe him for saving your skin.'

'Christ. Let me sit up.' Dylan's head spun as he pulled himself up. He wasn't making much progress. Then he realized why. He'd been lying across Goldi and Liz's laps, with his knees pulled up to his chest. They must have folded him into the back of the car as best they could.

'Ouch. You best stay where you are, Dylan, until we stop the car.'

'God, I feel weird. What happened?'

'You conked out on us, man. You'd got out of the car to talk to Luke, then these other two guys walked up.' Goldi shook his head. 'We thought you were just staring at them but something had blown up here.' He tapped his head with his finger.

Liz said, 'You were in a trance . . . mesmerized.'

'Vikki here just yells at me to drag you back into the car by the scruff of your neck.' Goldi grinned. 'So that's what I did. Vikki jumped over into the driving seat and blasted us the hell out of there.' His grin broadened and he gave Dylan a matey slap on the cheek. 'Hey. Your girlfriend's got presence of mind, did you know that, Dill?'

'But who were those guys?'

'I don't know.' Goldi still sounded jazzed by the experience. Adrenalin was powering the blood through his veins. 'But they were weird. And you know what?'

'What?'

'They were just like Luke. They weren't wearing any shoes.'

Vikki braked hard.

'What's wrong?' Liz sounded alarmed.

'We're out of track.'

'Shit.'

Liz leaned forward, peering out at the river that rushed into the lake. Hailstones swarmed from the night sky. 'What do we do now?'

Goldi jerked his head. 'We go back that way.'

'You serious? That's where the weird bunch hang out.'

'It's the only way I know back to the road. Unless you fancy your chances walking home across the fields.'

With the car at a stop Dylan managed to turn himself round and then haul himself through the gap into the front passenger seat.

'Are you feeling all right?' Vikki asked, her eyes large with concern.

'Fine. I think my brain skipped a couple of tracks or something.'

'You feel up to driving?'

'I'm fine now, like I said. It must have been the shock of seeing Luke like that. He's got to be off his head.'

He saw Vikki staring back along the track. 'It looks clear. We can swap seats.' She opened the door, admitting a blast of cold air.

'No, you don't,' he told her. 'I'll go round the outside of the car. You slide across.'

She shot him a grateful look. 'Thanks.'

Dylan opened the passenger door. Wind tried to tear it from his hands, but he hung on tight and slammed if after him when he'd climbed out. Now he could see clearly enough that the track ended at a river that tumbled over rocks into the lake. Behind the car the dirt track followed the line of the lake right at the water's edge.

Dear God, this is an evil-looking place, he told himself. *I'll be glad to leave it behind.* Just for a second he pictured himself working in a photographic studio in London. A world of light and warmth, of streets full of people. Cinemas. Theatres. Cafés. Restaurants. Wine bars. Talk about different worlds. This stretch of land at the head of a bleak Yorkshire dale could be on an alien planet.

'Dylan,' he heard Vikki call from the car. 'Dylan. Don't stay out there.'

Glad to obey, he told himself as he moved round the car to slip into the driver's seat.

Goldi leaned forward as he closed the door against the icy night air. 'I don't know what your plans are, man, but I'd suggest you drive as fast as you can back along that track and don't stop if those freakos get in the way.'

'What about Luke?'

'He looked happy enough chumming up with the Brothers Weird.'

'I can't leave him here. This cold's going to kill him.'

Vikki rested her hand on his knee. 'Dylan, there's something strange about those three. Don't you feel it?'

'But Luke? I can't abandon him.'

'Get away from here, then call the police.'

'*Vikki*—'

'Listen, don't ask me how I know it. But I know that those men will do something to us if we stay around here.'

Liz rubbed his shoulder. She looked frightened. 'Vikki's right. You could tell by the look on their faces. They were gloating like they'd got us just where they wanted us. We were lucky to get away.'

Goldi sounded more reluctant. 'They were weird fuckers. I bet they've got some wicked medicine, but . . .' He shrugged. 'The ladies are right. They're up to no good.'

'OK.' Dylan started the engine. 'It's back the way we came. But as soon as we're out on the main road I'll call the police.

I'll spin some story about Luke being abducted or something. Then we can sort out all this shit afterwards.'

But it wasn't going to be as easy as that.

Dylan slipped the car into gear, then accelerated gently to avoid skidding on the frozen mud. In the headlights he saw the track running alongside the water. At first he told himself that the wind was churning up waves near the shore. Then he had to admit that something was moving there.

CHAPTER 22

I

Dylan Adams still drove forward along the lakeside track, only his gaze was drawn to the right. From the sudden silence of the other three in the car he knew they'd seen, too. For there, in the darkness at the water's edge, were men and women.

Men and women?

Hell, whoever had seen men and women like that? Dylan's knuckles whitened as his grip on the steering wheel grew tighter. Hailstones cracked against the car. The winter's night seemed to ooze out of those lake waters, a liquid darkness that engulfed dry land, drowning it in a morbid gloom that had the power to reach into his heart and chill that, too.

From the back seat, Liz's voice came as a whisper. 'Oh God, it's *us* they want . . . Dylan, get us out of here. Drive faster – they're coming out of the water.'

'The track's frozen.' He eased off the power as the rear end fishtailed on puddles of ice.

'Shit, man!' Goldi punched the headrest behind him. 'Get us out of here!'

'We'll slide off the track if I go any faster.'

'Christ, you can go faster than this, Dill. You're only doing twenty.' Goldi punched the headrest again.

'Hey!' Dylan fought to keep the car on the track.

Vikki rounded on the pair in the back. 'Just let him drive, will you!'

He shot her a grateful look. Then he glanced right again.

Not a good idea. I should be keeping my eyes on the track, not on those . . .

Those . . . whatever they are.

In the glare of the headlamps he saw them. Men and women, wading toward the lake shore. Some wore clothes that hung in torn shreds, some were naked. But all had skin that was blue-white. He glimpsed faces. They stared at the passing car with nothing less than a ferocious hunger. He even caught sight of their eyes. *Hell, their eyes.* He'd never seen anything like them. Wide staring eyes that had no colour. They were balls of bulging white with hard black pupils at their centres.

'Dylan, careful!'

That was Vikki; he felt her hand slam against his arm.

In front of him he saw Luke Spencer standing in the middle of the track. His arms were folded. He looked relaxed, as if this was nothing out of the ordinary and he was simply waiting for his old friend to pick him up . . . just like he'd done dozens of times before. Only this time Luke Spencer stood there barefoot on a freezing winter night. His eyes had a thousand-yard stare. They burned right through Dylan's head. Somehow they seemed to look into the depths of his mind, seeing into the store of old memories. Luke could see a ten-year-old Dylan Adams firing that air gun at the bully on the rope swing.

Luke wanted him to stop. To thank him for getting Rosso out of their lives.

Vikki's voice jabbed into his ear. 'Dylan! What are you slowing down for?'

Dylan shook his head; a black fog had formed behind his eyes, making the world a distant place. Suddenly he heard the three shouting at him to keep driving. Goldi was punching the headrest.

Shit . . . what's wrong with me? I felt as if I was falling asleep.

He pulled the car hard over onto the strip of grass at the side of the track. Then, with the wheels spinning, flinging up grass stalks and mud, he roared past Luke. And all Luke did was stand there with his arms folded to watch them pass. In the rear-view mirror Dylan saw his old friend shake his head, as if Dylan had disappointed him. As if somehow Dylan was being disloyal.

But – *oh God* – Dylan was fully awake now. His mind registered the brutal reality of it all. Dozens if not hundreds of weird figures were emerging from the lake. Hell, the water was so cold it would kill a man in minutes. So how could they—

Vikki warned, 'Dylan, watch it, they're coming onto the track.'

'I see them.' He hit the light stalk, switching the car's headlights to full beam. The powerful light struck them. They flinched before it, throwing up their hands in front of their faces.

Goldi gripped Dylan's headrest. He shook it, whooping wildly. 'Hey, did you see that? The light hurts the fuckers! Lay it on them, Dill!'

The headlamps were a physical force to the creatures. Sheer wattage had the strength to make them reel back to the water's edge, their hands held out to shield their sensitive eyes from the brilliance.

Vikki touched his arm. 'You're doing fine, Dylan. Just concentrate on getting us out of here.'

'You don't even need to ask,' he breathed. 'We're as good as gone.'

He accelerated along the track, his confidence growing as the car responded to his steering. Here the tyres could grip the dirt surface. There was less ice. Ahead of them the track turned a sharp left, then climbed across the meadow in the direction of the bone-white house of Lazarus Wake.

In another five minutes he'd make it to the main road. Fifteen minutes after that they'd be driving into Morningdale and home.

2

Electra told them straight, 'Well, my dears, we can't sit staring at the house all night.'

David looked through the car's side window at Lazarus Wake. Its appearance was grotesque. Its white stone blocks looked like human skulls. Even the deep-set windows resembled eye sockets.

He studied the area to the front of the house. 'The driveway branches off through those bushes,' he told Electra. 'I guess you could drive right up to the front door.'

Bernice shivered in the front passenger seat. 'That's better than wandering round in the dark.' She gazed at the silent groves of trees that surrounded the house. 'After all, you don't know what's out there.'

'On the contrary.' Electra started the engine. 'I think we know *exactly* what's out there.'

'Then all the more reason to get the car as close to the front door as possible. Then maybe we can talk to your mysterious penfriend.'

Electra glanced up at the darkened windows. 'If Rowan's home.'

Before she could even engage the gear and drive off the main driveway David saw ghostly lights flitting over the leaves of the evergreen bushes that flanked this section of drive. For a second he stared at them, not making any sense of what was happening. Then he understood.

'Electra, there's a car coming this way.'

'Don't worry, I'll get us off the – *Damn.*'

It happened too fast. A sudden blaze of light lit everything up, as if the whole end of the house had exploded. David saw the other car come tearing toward them, its lights on full beam. He heard the howl of the motor. *My God, the driver must be crazy to drive at that speed on a gravel driveway like this.*

He heard Bernice shout, 'He's going to hit us!'

Electra's car was flooded with light from the other vehicle's headlamps. David caught a glimpse of the silhouettes of Electra and Bernice in the front seat. Both had flung up their arms to protect their faces. David braced himself for the collision.

Then the lights vanished as quickly as they'd arrived. No collision. No shattering concussion as the other car hit them. Instead, sudden darkness. Sudden silence apart from the murmur of their own car's motor.

'Hell, that was close,' Electra said at last.

Bernice took a deep breath. 'He was driving like a madman. He could have killed us.'

'But where'd he go?' David looked through the rear window of the car. He had a clear view of the driveway as it ran up through woodland to the main road. Only there were no receding tail lights. So how could a car vanish into thin air?

He leaned across the car seat to look out of the side window. *Damn.* 'It's gone off the drive.' He opened the rear door.

Electra shouted, 'David! Stay in the car! You don't know if—'

'Electra, the car's crashed.' He climbed out. 'Stay here with the doors locked.'

'David, get back into the car. It might be a trick. They might—'

'I'll be all right. Just stay put, OK?'

Slamming the door, David headed for the gap in the evergreen bushes where the car had ploughed through. Glancing back, he saw Electra's anxious white face illuminated by the dashboard lights. He knew that she was furious at him for leaving the car. But so what? This wasn't a trick. He was sure of it. That car had come off the track at one helluva speed. People might be hurt. His professional persona kicked in now. Automatically, he touched the hard shape of his phone in his coat pocket. Depending on what he found in the next five minutes he might need to call an ambulance. Darkness closed in. He could no longer see the lights of Electra's car, screened as it was by dense bushes. Instead he moved through the gloom, his hand held high in front of him, feeling for tree trunks, or even for the car itself.

Damn. The darkness was like a blanket over his eyes. He could barely see a thing. Cold night air fingered his bare hand and wrist. At any second he might suddenly touch a face in the darkness. A face that might not even be human. As David moved forward as quickly as he could he began to imagine the touch of skin as smooth and as cold as marble. *Eyes, nose, lips, teeth . . .*

No, concentrate, he told himself. *Find the crashed car. There might be people who need your help.*

Within moments his eyes started to adapt to the little light there was under those stark winter trees. He began to see the Gothic columns of tree trunks marching into the distance. The white flecks of hail spiralling down from the sky. The humped forms of bushes shivering in the breeze from the lake. *And, dear God, the cold. It bites you to the bone.* He paused to blow into his hands. He should have gloves. He should have his medical bag as well. What if he needed to give emergency treatment?

More hail came down in a twisting swirl of white. It ghosted through trees, tapping branches, clicking against bark before striking David in the face. He paused while he turned his face away from the stinging rush of ice particles. As he did so he caught sight of the frozen grass beneath the trees. By now his eyes had adapted sufficiently to register individual blades of grass, clumps of thistle, the corpse of a rabbit with its throat torn out. He also saw twin lines of tyre tracks. They swerved through a gap in the trees. Now he saw flattened clumps of weeds, the smashed remains of saplings. He paused to touch the white gouge mark in a tree where something hard had struck it. Speckles of blue paint.

David moved faster into a darkness that swirled with hailstones. The sobbing cry of the wind roamed through the forest, shaking branches. Bushes trembled before it.

There's a storm coming, he told himself. *You've got to find shelter before it breaks. These winter blizzards in North Yorkshire are killers.*

The urgency of trying to find wherever the speeding car had careered drove out of his mind why they'd driven up to Lazarus Deep in the first place. For ten minutes Electra and Bernice and he had sat there in the locked car, fearful of what might lurk in this godforsaken stretch of countryside. Now that was forgotten. He was a doctor. People might be hurt. That was what dominated his mind now. The woodland started to run downhill. He saw more trees with pieces of bark clipped from them, and branches sheared off at waist height. That driver had been damn lucky or uncannily skilful. David realized that so far he or she had managed to avoid hitting a tree head-on.

But why hadn't they braked? He could see the tread of the tyres imprinted on the earth. Whoever had been driving the car hadn't even tried to stop when they'd crashed off the access drive. They'd kept going, powering the car through the wood. Or at least that was what it looked like.

Two points of red burned out of the darkness in front of him. He started to run toward them. Now he saw that the twin lines scarring the turf had converged and crossed. A classic sign that the car had begun to skid out of control. A moment later he saw the hard outline of the car. It had come to rest side-on against a tree. The car lights were still on, revealing an expanse of dull green grass. Falling hail showed as silver sparks as it flew horizontally in the rush of air.

He saw figures in the car. Three . . . four? For heaven's sake, why didn't they try and get out? Despite car designers' best efforts vehicles still sometimes caught fire.

David ran forward and gripped the rear passenger door. Pulled hard. He'd expected to find injured passengers. Shocked passengers. He didn't expect what happened next.

With a scream, a man in the rear seat exploded outward in a mass of waving limbs. He launched himself at David, who fell back, his arms in front of his face to protect himself.

'You think you'd take me without a fight? You think I wouldn't fight you?' The man screamed the words over and over as he tried to grab David by the throat.

'Hey! I'm trying to help . . . Listen, I'm trying to help!'

But the man with the blond dreadlocks fought like a demon. He roared so much that all David could really see was the red of his mouth and the white of his teeth and the saliva flying from his tongue.

'You'll not take me. You'll not—'

Then a pair of hands – or was it *pairs* of hands? – grabbed the screaming man and dragged him back.

David heard a female voice. 'Goldi . . . Goldi! Leave him! He's not one of them!'

'How can you tell?' the man yelled. 'It might be! How can you tell . . . shit, let go of me . . . let go!'

David had come here to help the occupants of the car. Now *they* seemed to be saving *him*. He climbed to his feet before the screaming man could attack again. He saw that a girl and a man, late teens perhaps, had dragged the raging man backward until he sat down hard on his rear end with his back to the car. He still kicked and shouted.

'Goldi, shut up! Hey . . . I'm not letting go until you calm down.' The guy reinforced the word by jabbing the toe of his shoe against the struggling man's hip.

'Hey, Dill, that fucking hurt.'

'Good. Now sit still, or I'll do it again.'

David took in the scene. The pair who had saved him from the attack were now moving back from his assailant. The guy was holding his finger up at the attacker who now sat still. The raised finger was a 'Just you stay there' gesture; the kind you'd give to a mischievous dog. Emerging now from the back seat of the car was a fourth figure. A girl with a wild mop of hair, streaked with orange, and wearing vivid make-up. She rubbed the side of her neck.

David took a deep breath, then he plunged in again. 'Is everyone all right?' he asked.

'No,' the girl with the mop of hair said with feeling. 'My neck's sore.'

'That might be whiplash. Anyone else hurt?'

The other girl shot him a clear-eyed look, appraising him. 'Who are you?'

'I'm a doctor. My name's David Leppington. I was in the car you nearly rammed.'

'Stupid place to sit in a car,' the girl said.

David shrugged. 'We didn't expect another car tearing up the driveway on a night like this. Now, is everyone all right? No one hurt their heads when the car hit the tree?'

'Jesus, look at the car.' This was the guy who'd pulled the madman off him. 'Jesus . . . That's going to cost.' He shook his head over the dents and scraped paintwork.

David told him, 'Count yourself lucky you didn't ram a tree trunk head-on.'

'The wing's completely busted . . . shit, look at the door.'

'The main thing is that no one's injured.'

'My neck hurts like hell.' The girl with the mop hair rubbed it with a sullen expression. Then her expression changed to one of wide-eyed shock. 'Hey, we can't hang around here. What if those weirdos come up from the lake?'

'Liz is right,' the other girl said. 'We've got to get away from here.'

'The car—'

'Forget the car, Dylan.'

The girl called Liz fixed David with a searching look. 'Hey, doctor, you've got a car?'

'Yes, but—'

'We need a lift away from here. There's—' She suddenly paused, as if unsure how to finish. 'There's some people we'd rather not meet, you know?'

An icy sensation prickled across David's back. 'Who?'

'Shit,' the guy with dreadlocks spat. 'We haven't got time to debate this. Come on, before they get here.'

David stepped forward. 'You say some people tried to attack you?'

'Weirdos, just weirdos,' the tall girl muttered, suddenly uncomfortable. 'But we can't stay here.'

'And neither should you,' the other guy said.

'Wait . . . wait just a minute. Is this why he attacked me?' David pointed at the man with dreadlocks. 'Did he think I was one of them?'

The guy stood up, brushing the back of his trousers. 'You still might be, for all I know. After all, Luke Spencer still looked—'

'Hang on.' David held up his hand. 'Let me get this straight. You say that there are people down at the lake?'

'Weirdos.' The girl spoke with feeling. 'They were standing in the water. In *this* weather.'

Hailstones rattled against the car's battered bodywork.

'They tried to attack you?' David prompted.

'If you ask me, that's what they intended,' said the tall girl.

'That's why we need to get the hell out of here.'

'And not stand here debating,' added the guy with dread-locks.

'Look, my name's David Leppington. My friends are wait-ing in the car back there. We need to get back there as quickly as possible.'

'Then what?' The guy with dreadlocks sounded suspi-cious.

'Then we need to find a way of getting you all away from here as quickly as possible.'

David saw how all four of them frowned and looked from one to another. The tall girl must have been thinking the fastest because she suddenly asked, 'You know something about those people, don't you?'

'Yes, I think I do,' David admitted. 'Now, let's get out of here.' Then, as an afterthought, he added, 'And if you do see anyone, just run. OK?'

CHAPTER 23

I

David realized that the four teenagers he led back through the night-time wood were dazed by what had happened to them. It was more than the shock of the near-crash. It was what they had seen in the lake. Repeatedly, he glanced back to make sure that the four were still with him. The cold winds, the stinging hail and the dark made it difficult to see. More than once he glimpsed pale figures following them, only to dismiss them as silver birch tree trunks. He glanced at his watch. Six o'clock. Still early evening. But the February night had plunged them into near-instant darkness. It could have been midnight in this frozen landscape. The rush of air sighed through branches. Tree trunks groaned as they shifted. A sense of restlessness infected the forest.

David urged his group to move faster. Out here he felt all too vulnerable. No knowing what lurked around the next bush. Or what might already be on their trail.

An animal screamed off to his right. *A fox has killed a rabbit,* he told himself. *That's all. Now concentrate on getting these people away from here. But how? Can you cram seven people into Electra's car? Maybe. If we rip out the parcel shelf . . .*

A rush of hail crackled through the branches. Everyone shielded their faces against the stinging blows.

'Nearly there,' he told them as his dark-adapted eyes made out the break in the evergreen bushes. The driveway and Electra's car would just be a few seconds away. He glanced back when no one replied but he could see their troubled expressions. They were trying to figure out what they'd seen down by the lake. There hadn't been time to give him a description. But David had automatically supplied the word that identified the 'weirdos', as the girl with the mop hair had described them.

Vampires.

2

From the lake they came, surging from the depths with all the menace of sharks. For more years than they could count they had lain there in the cold silt in the lake bed, locked in dreamless sleep. Now they'd been called from the depths to the world of air and night shadows. One instinct drove them now. The urge to feed.

They were the undead . . . vampiric.

3

David gaped at Electra's car, not daring to believe what he saw. The wind blew hard. Twisting veils of ice particles moved with the speed of vengeful phantoms, spattering against the bodywork of the Volvo. Bushes trembled before the blast of air. Spiky branches clawed the night sky above them. *And there's the car* . . . David's chill sensation burrowed deeper into his bones. *It's been moved close to the front of the house. Only one problem. It's empty.*

He looked round, half expecting Electra and Bernice to be standing on the driveway. But there was nothing but dead leaves tumbling across the gravel. There was no sign of them in the garden. All he could see were bushes writhing in the wind. Here and there the rotted face of a statue peered bleakly through a shroud of ivy. Had the women gone to look for him?

The forest looked vast, stretching up as far as the moors on the hilltops. Had they got lost in the dark? He glanced at the four teenagers he'd brought from the car. They stood with their arms hugging their bodies against the bitter cold. Their eyes were dull-looking, as if the low temperatures and shock had robbed them of their vitality. They wouldn't be able to stay out here for long before they began to suffer from exposure, perhaps even frostbite.

And what if those figures they spoke of should walk around the corner? David's gaze turned back to the house. *That's as good a place to shelter as any.*

'Come on,' he told them. 'This way.'

They followed without comment. The cold was eating into them now. He saw their lethargy. How they dragged their feet; how their heads hung forward until their chins almost rested on their chests. The cold was biting deeper than he'd anticipated. He crossed the driveway and walked onto its offshoot that led to the front door of the house where the car now stood. He glanced up at the mean, deep-set windows beneath heavy lintels of stone that gave it such a brooding quality. There were no lights. No movement. Even in the near-dark, he noticed the inscription above the door:

1727
Lazarus Wake
Raised by Magnus Leppington, a True Believer
Dedicated to my god. To his FURY and the
LIFE BLOOD of his sons

Magnus Leppington? It had to be some ancestor. No doubt some guardian of the Leppington dark secret, too, the one that had been passed down the Leppington bloodline since Viking times. Glancing back, David checked that all four teenagers were keeping up with him. They were, but they were slowing. Each walked with a hand to their eyes to shield them against the spitting hailstones. *Get them out of the cold. They need shelter.*

With the thought beating urgently in his head he moved forward to the front door – a huge thing banded and studded with iron. As he raised his fist to beat on the timbers it suddenly swung open to reveal a white face, with shockingly wide eyes.

'Bernice?'

'David, come inside – quickly!'

'Bernice, how did you get into the—'

'David, hurry up. There's something you must see.'

4

Dylan Adams stood back to allow Vikki, Liz and Goldi in first. Shock at seeing the figures in the lake, shock at seeing what had happened to his friend, shock at the car crashing off the driveway into the wood, and then the mad drive to find his way back before sliding into the tree had left him numb both inside and out. That and the cold, too.

He found himself walking into the house on autopilot. Dear Christ, it didn't feel much warmer in here. Like walking into ice water. Dazed, he looked at the stone floors, the oak wall panels, the staircase that went spiralling up into darkness. A voice in the back of his head warned him that this wasn't a good place to be. The dimensions of the hallway and the way shadows clung to the corners like crouching beasts made his skin crawl. The way it would if he touched a dead rat.

The girl with glossy black hair who let them in had shoved the door shut against the force of the wind, then locked and bolted it. Damn it, she looked scared, too. No, not scared – terrified. The blood had fled from her face, leaving her with a livid red gash of a mouth and eyes that glittered in an unblinking stare.

'David,' she said, all jittery. 'Are these the people from the car?'

The man who'd told them that he was a doctor glanced back. 'Yes, as far as I can tell no one's seriously hurt.' His voice altered. 'Bernice, what did you want me to see?'

'He's upstairs. Electra's with him now.' The dark-haired girl climbed the stairs, the doctor following.

No one told Dylan what to do. Still dazed and numbed from cold and shock he stood in the shadowy hallway. Vikki and the others did the same, all looking like they were in a trance.

5

As Bernice lead the way, David heard her say, 'We didn't think it wise to stay in the car. Especially after you'd been gone for so long.'

'Their car had travelled a long way before it hit something.'

'When we reached the house we found the door was unlocked.'

'So you just walked in?'

'I don't think we had an option, do you?'

'It could have been a trap.'

'It wasn't, thank God. Of course, Electra went to look for the man who'd been sending her e-mails.'

'Rowan?'

'Yes. He's here.'

They reached the top landing. From the slope of the ceiling David realized that they were about to enter an attic room. Electra came to the door. But instead of standing aside to admit them she stayed there.

Why's she blocking the doorway? he thought, puzzled. *What doesn't she want me to see?*

'You've found Rowan,' David said at last. 'He's in there?' He nodded at the room that lay in darkness behind Electra.

She nodded. Her face was hard, as if emotionally she'd steeled herself against unpleasant shocks. But instead of talking about the man somewhere in the room behind her she said, 'You found the car that nearly hit us?'

He told her that the occupants were shaken but unhurt.

'Where are they now?'

'Downstairs. I couldn't leave them out there.'

'Absolutely. I think we're in a dangerous place here.'

He nodded. 'From what I can gather the people in the car were running from something down by the lakeside.'

'Something?'

'OK, I won't split hairs,' he told her. 'Vampires.'

'So this *is* a dangerous place,' Electra said, her face tight with muscle tension. 'It's also a place full of surprises – if that isn't too gentle a word.' She inclined her head, her gaze searching David's face. 'Shock revelations might be a more apt term.'

He watched as she glanced back over her shoulder to look at something inside the room. 'David, I'm not going to split hairs either. Rowan's in the room. He's lying on the bed. I can't wake him up . . . at least, not properly.'

'I'd best see him, then.' David stepped forward but Electra put her hand to his chest to stop him.

'I should warn you, you're going to have a shock when you see him.'

'Electra, I *am* a doctor.'

'I know, Doctor Leppington, you are. But I don't mean the shock of seeing his condition . . . whatever that might be.' She took a deep breath. 'Come on, you'd best get it over with.' She stood back so that he could enter.

The room had little furniture apart from a single bed in the centre of the room. Walls sloped inward to meet above

David's head. The single bed in the centre lent the room the appearance of a chapel of rest where the deceased lay before the funeral. Nevertheless, he didn't know why Electra had warned him. He'd seen all kinds of sickness and injury in the past. After years of experience in a hospital he was hardly likely to—

He stopped dead when he saw the man lying flat on his back on the bed, his arms straight by his side. David's eyes took in the detail of the darkly arched eyebrows, the colour of the hair and the shape of the jaw. Chills cascaded down his back as his muscles clenched tight.

Before he could stop himself he found himself voicing the shock realization. 'Oh, my God . . . *it's me.*'

CHAPTER 24

I

David thought: *That's me lying on the bed. I was Rowan all along.*

They were mad thoughts, crazy thoughts. But when David Leppington stood in the attic bedroom of Lazarus Wake that was the only conclusion he could reach. That somehow he and the stranger who'd been e-mailing Electra were one and the same. The walls of the room pulsated inward at him before receding out to a vast distance.

'David . . . David.'

He felt Electra pull at his coat sleeve.

'David, I think you could do with a sit-down.'

Feeling the pull of vertigo, he gratefully sat at the foot of the bed, while all the time staring at the figure that wore the same face that he saw every day in the mirror. Somehow the vampires were twisting his senses. He wasn't seeing this; he *couldn't* be seeing himself lying there half dead.

Where Electra had got it from he didn't know but she moved toward the head of the bed with a lit table lamp. 'It's not what you think, David. Look closer.'

A hand rubbed his back. A simple act of affection. He glanced back to see Bernice standing there, her anxious eyes peering into his.

'Here,' Electra said. 'Look at his face in the light.' The man stirred a little as she brought the lamp down beside his head. 'It's an uncanny resemblance.'

David stood up again, his knees shaking almost uncontrollably. Hell, this he hadn't expected. Vampires, yes. Duplicates of himself? No. *A thousand times no.*

'See,' Electra whispered. 'His hair's longer than yours. The shape of his nose is a little more pointed. He's gaunt, incredibly gaunt – malnourished, I guess. But the same colouring and, as I said, the resemblance to you is uncanny.'

Bernice added, 'He could pass for your brother.'

'But I don't have a brother.' He shook his head. 'I have a sister, that's all.'

'Look at his face, David.'

'And apart from my father there are no more male Leppingtons. I'm the last of the bloodline.'

'So you've been told.' Electra's voice was gentle, little more than a whisper. 'But I don't think you even need to conduct a blood test to confirm what you're thinking right now.'

David was stunned. 'So my father's got a secret.'

'Maybe.'

Bernice breathed deeply to steady her voice. 'That explains what Rowan said in the e-mail. That he'd dreamed – or thought he'd dreamed – that a group of strange visitors had stood in the garden and told him that he was to be given command of an army.'

'And we know what kind of army,' David whispered.

'There's something else to consider.' Electra nodded down at the sleeping man. 'You not only have a new brother . . . you have a new rival, too.'

It was 6:48 p.m. Dawn was a long way off yet.

2

They held a council of war on the stairs. Or at least they tried to.

Bernice thought that David Leppington still looked dazed

from the shock of finding what appeared to be his doppelgänger lying in the bed. Through the landing window, she could see only darkness. The wind thrummed and whooped around the house. Draughts came sobbing through the gaps in the old window frames. A rattle of hail against glass had the rattle of bones in a grave. Bernice shuddered. *God help us tonight*, she thought. *God help us. We're stranded in this damn house. And who knows what's outside watching us. Waiting for us to try and leave. Then they'll*—

'Bernice.' Electra's voice was sharp. 'Are you all right?'

'I'm fine.'

'You looked distant.'

'No, honestly, I'm—'

'David, are you with us?' Electra's voice was even sharper.

'By that, do you mean am I firing on all cylinders?'

'You've had a shock, and . . .'

'And?'

'And we know that those creatures can exert an influence on our minds.'

Bernice saw David digest the words. 'You think that's happened to . . .' He jerked his head back at the door. 'My long-lost brother.' His expression was grim.

'Absolutely.' Electra sounded in gear. She'd got this sussed. 'All those e-mails he sent me. They were nebulous, to say the least. He complained of being afraid to leave the house. Of being so forgetful that he didn't know where he lived. Most of the time he spent sleeping or semi-comatose.'

Bernice nodded. 'So in effect they were keeping him here while they worked on his mind?'

'Yup,' Electra said. 'Whether by chance or design our old vampire friends realized that they had a blood Leppington right in their own backyard.'

'Which couldn't have been a coincidence?'

'Maybe, maybe not.'

Bernice glanced back through the doorway at the comatose figure on the bed. 'So it has started again.'

'Only this time they have another Leppington.' Electra shot David a look. 'And maybe this time round a different Mr Leppington might be more amenable to their plans.'

'I don't think so.' David shook his head. 'He's been resisting their influence. That's why they only made direct contact with him a few hours ago.'

'But my guess is that they have been softening him up while he's been in that state for what must have been two or three weeks at least.'

David frowned. 'But why hasn't anyone found him like this?'

'We have.'

'But surely he must have family or friends who've missed him.'

'Maybe he came here for peace and seclusion to compose a symphony or write a book. We know Rick Broxley came here to work away from the pressures of his day-to-day life.'

'With tragic results. I know. I read his account of what happened.'

'So . . .' Electra placed her fingertips together. 'We need to summarize some of the facts. And we need to be fully aware of our own position.'

'I'd say our own position is precarious,' Bernice said, her voice suddenly tense. 'Look down there.'

Bernice watched the pair of them look down through the window as a pallid figure ran across the grass.

'Friend or foe?' Electra asked.

'Foe.' Bernice heard the certainty in her own voice. 'Definitely foe.'

As hail stormed down on roof tiles in a roar that nearly drowned her voice, Electra added dryly, 'It's a shame our monsters don't feel the cold. What I wouldn't give to see them suffer.'

'Electra,' David said, 'we were going to assess our position.'

'Ever the professional, David, aren't we? Examination followed by diagnosis?'

He gave a grim smile. 'Blame all those years of working in A&E.'

'David's right. We need to understand what's happening here.' Anger flushed through Bernice's veins. 'So don't fuck him around.'

Electra's aristocratic features coloured. 'I wasn't *fucking* David around. Just a little light teasing to ease the tension.'

'Well, don't. You can play the haughty bitch to your heart's content once we're out of—'

'Well, who asked you to come here, anyway, Bernice?'

'I felt it was only right to come.'

'Only right?'

'Yes.'

'You only came, Bernice, because you wanted to get your hooks into David here.'

'Rubbish!'

'Because you missed out first time around.'

'That's idiotic, Electra.'

'Not only did you fancy the size of his professional salary. You fancied a fuck with someone with divine blood in their—'

'Electra—'

'—veins. Fancied yourself as queen, with a house full of Leppington brats.'

Bernice lunged at Electra, grabbing a handful of blue-black hair.

3

David didn't believe what he was seeing. From talking reasonably to cat fight in less than five minutes! He pushed himself between the two women, nearly knocking Electra downstairs in the process. As she teetered on the top step she shot him such a look of shock. From her expression he reckoned that she believed he was trying to push her down the steep flight of stairs to the entrance hall with its floor of uncompromising, bone-shattering stone. He lunged out with his right arm, getting his wrist behind her neck. Then he dragged her back to him, holding her tight against his side. He could feel her breasts heaving against his ribs as she fought to catch her breath. Glancing at Bernice, he saw that she'd moved back. Her face had become a grey mask. She seemed stunned by the turn of events.

Then it struck David. 'Listen . . . listen, both of you. Those things are out there. They're already working on us. We know that they try to influence how we think. They insinuate strange ideas into our heads. They have the power to muddy our ability to read events as they really are. They can influence our decision-making.'

Bernice's look of shock intensified. 'You mean they were inside my head?'

'That's about the size of it.'

'I'm sorry, Electra.' Bernice was gasping as if her chest had grown painfully tight. Tears glistened in her eyes. 'I didn't mean what I said. I just felt this anger . . . this totally unreasonable anger. I didn't mean—'

'Hush, child.' Electra smiled and reached out to hug Bernice. But Bernice had frozen herself into the corner. 'It's not your fault.'

'But I just let them walk straight into my head. I didn't fight them. I let them fill me with anger; I didn't—'

'Listen, Bernice,' Electra told her gently. 'It isn't your fault. If anything, it's a good thing. We know their mind games now. We can be vigilant from now on.'

David glanced downstairs.

The hallway's empty. So what's happened to the people I brought in from the car?

He felt a pang of unease. 'We're going to have to warn everyone to be on their guard.'

'You're right.' Electra nodded. 'Those young things who were in the car are going to be especially vulnerable.'

David said, 'If we're going to discuss what's happening, and the dangers, we'd best involve our young friends down there, too.' He looked down into the hallway again. 'Wherever they are.'

4

Through the woods they came, bare feet pressing down on frozen ground. Lake water dripped from hair and fingertips. Above them cloud rolled through the night sky. No moon. No stars. A raven glided overhead, watching all the time. Reporting back what it saw to its master.

Ahead lay the house. A house made from stones as white as bone. They sensed people inside as a dog senses rabbits deep within their burrows. Hunger flared in their veins: they'd waited so long for this. Sheer need burned inside them. A need that was hotter, more intense than lust.

Thoughts reached them from the occupants of the bone-white house. . . . *State of the car. It's going to cost to have that repaired . . . looks as if the entire wing's gone. Hell, I need that job in London now. And I need out of Morningdale. If I ask Vikki to move to London with me I wonder what she'll say? She looks so cold. Frightened eyes . . .*

More thoughts from a different mind: *What came over me? Why did I feel so angry with Electra? Could those monsters really . . .*

More: *This is worse than I anticipated. Why on Earth did I allow Electra to bring us out here at dusk? And – Christ Almighty*

– now it looks as if I've found a brother I never knew I had. If only I could phone Dad and . . .

And more: *When David stopped me from falling down the stairs and held me tight I felt such electricity. No, stop it, Electra, sweetheart, don't go down that road. Nevertheless . . .*

The closer the vampires moved to the house, the clearer the thoughts became. And the traffic wasn't all one-way. All it needed was for the vampires to catch one strand of thought, to concentrate on it, then coax it back down that line of thought . . . to push inside that mortal head. Take control.

Rick Broxley, with his wet hair forming brilliant white flashes of ice in the north wind, moved in closer. Stray thoughts came free and bright on the air, like blossom falling from a cherry tree in spring. He caught an anxious thought: *If they've left the house, they're dead . . . no, worse than dead.*

5

If they've left the house, they're dead . . . no, worse than dead. The understanding came only too keenly to David as he descended the stairs with Electra and Bernice following him. There were monsters out there in the freezing darkness. Maybe he should have warned the four more forcefully when he'd led them back from the car to the house. He glanced at the front door. *Still locked and bolted, thank God.* It was a formidable piece of timber. He only hoped it could hold up to a battering, if it came to that.

The moment he stepped into the lounge the light and heat pressed against his eyes. He blinked.

The guy with blond dreadlocks looked up from the huddle of people round the fireplace. 'We lit the fire. I hope nobody minds?'

'Fuck them minding,' the girl with the mop hair said. 'I wasn't going to sit here freezing my butt off when there's a pile of logs there.'

David regarded the four young people from the car. They were more animated now. The colour had returned to their faces. 'We don't mind,' he told them as Electra and Bernice came to stand at either side of him. 'In fact, we're trespassers here ourselves.'

The other guy looked at David and his companions, appraising them. 'So you're not renting this place?'

'No, but we came to visit the man who is.'

The mop-haired girl had a sullen curl to her lip. 'Great, you've made the duty visit. Now, how about getting us home?'

Beside him Electra spoke. 'That wouldn't be wise at the moment.'

'How'd you mean not wise?'

'I mean that—'

'Just what kind of stunt are you pulling?'

'Liz, let her speak.' That was the taller of the two women.

'Thank you,' Electra continued. 'I'm sorry. But for tonight we must stay here in the house with all the doors and windows locked.'

'But your car – it's only—'

'I know, it's five seconds' walk from the house,' Electra told them. 'But believe me, boys and girls, you wouldn't want to risk walking even that far on a night like this.'

'On a night like this?' The dreadlocked youth laughed. He was wondering if this was a leg-pull. 'Yeah, it's pretty cold outside but we're used to this stuff.'

Bernice said, 'My friend isn't referring to the weather.'

David nodded. 'You told me you saw some people – and I use the word "people" loosely – down by the lake. They frightened you.'

The dreadlock guy was feeling braver now that he was warmer. 'Not frightened, no way. Surprised, yes.'

'Bunch of weirdos, they were,' said the mop-haired girl.

'Probably out of their brain pans on head gear.' The dreadlocked guy slapped his thigh. 'They were so out of it that they didn't feel the cold.'

'No, they wouldn't have felt the cold, that's for sure,' Electra said. 'But for altogether different reasons.'

The tall girl said, 'I know it's nothing to do with drugs. Something's happened to those people, hasn't it?'

Hail tapped the window-pane. Or was it frozen fingertips trying to attract their attention? David noticed that the curtains were all closed. Best they stayed that way, too. He glanced round the room with its pair of large sofas and its antique chairs. A clock on the wall had stopped at twenty past two. To lend it a rustic air the walls were decorated with horseshoes and a pair of large wooden malt shovels.

'I think we should make ourselves as comfortable as possible,' he told them. 'There's something we've got to tell you.'

'We'll skip it thanks,' the girl with the mop hair said. 'If there's going to be no party we're going home.'

'You can't leave.'

'You're going to stop us?'

'Yes, if we have to,' David said, his voice grave. 'And when I've told you what you need to know the last thing you're going to do is step outside through that door tonight.'

CHAPTER 25

I

From **Hotel Midnight**:

'BELIEF' – the dictionary definition? 'That which is believed; full acceptance of a thing as true. Faith. A firm persuasion of the truth of a body of religious tenets.' The dictionary doesn't do a word like BELIEF justice, for BELIEF is the engine that drives humanity. In the ancient city of Constantinople its people believed that if they were under attack all they needed to do to repel the invaders was to walk the city walls, holding up portraits of their saints. Their BELIEF in the power of saints was absolute. Did it work? Well, the city survived for more than a thousand years and became the capital of a vast empire. It is vital to have a BELIEF in something; it matters not whether it is BELIEF in God, Socialism or Technology.

Several years ago, Subject A, as I will call him, inherited the power to change the world. But he refused it, and did everything he could to destroy the gift. With the benefit of hindsight I believe he made a huge mistake. Now I realize that he suffered from the worst lack of BELIEF of all: SELF-BELIEF.

And yes, children, this is Electra speaking, and if you are wondering where this essay in human behaviour is taking you I am still talking about VAMPIRES . . .

2

Electra's mind went back to what she had written for the Hotel Midnight website just a few weeks ago. Now she stood next to her Subject A, David Leppington, who was talking to the bunch of teenagers he'd rescued from the car wreck . . . and rescued from whatever walked the night outside these stone walls. Electra shivered, despite the heat from the fire. She took a step toward it, grateful for the waves of heat and brilliant golden light flooding from the fireplace. Her eyes were drawn by flames leaping from logs that popped and cracked as they burnt. The stone fireplace was huge . . .

. . . Why, it's certainly large enough to spit-roast a child. Perhaps even two if you're lucky . . .

As always her sardonic humour came to the rescue at times like this. She glanced back at David. He was telling it like it was to the youngsters. Not to leave the safety of the house.

Safety, huh? Safe as a straw house when the big bad wolf comes to town.

The fire drew Electra's gaze back. Such a huge fireplace. *Why, I'm sure you would get three whole children in there. They'd be all lovely and toasty, turning on a spit, with a tray underneath to catch all that sweet fat as it bubbled out . . . Yummy, yum, yum.*

The heat and the light of the blazing fire made her want to close her eyes. Subject A's voice – *oops, slip of the mental tongue there, Electra dear* – Dr David Leppington's voice was firm but gentle – a perfect bedside manner. Perfect in most other things, too – charm and looks, for instance. *And don't forget he has the divine blood of his Viking ancestors driving through those silky veins.* But he'd made that single huge, HUGE mistake three years ago. When he'd been presented with the vampire army and had had the opportunity to lead it. *He should have accepted. He could have been king of the world.* Instead he'd remained a humble doctor. Treating mangy men and women for trivial injuries.

Instead he could have been the *master* of humanity, not its repairer when little Johnny fell off his blessed trike or little Sarah caught her finger in the toy-cupboard door.

A thought struck Electra. One that was as surprising as it was pleasing. What David Leppington needed was a strong woman to guide him. *With me at his side he could have commanded that army of the undead and done great things. He just needed me to advise him. To help shape and support his decisions. Yes, that was the problem all along. His lack of self-belief. His lack of* me.

The fire's heat stroked Electra's face. Warm air currents caressed her neck, feathering her hair of gunmetal blue-black. She was pleased she'd made the decision: *I have the power to seduce David Leppington. Once I have him I will persuade the good doctor that his view of those beings he calls vampires is entirely mistaken.*

3

'We've got the message about not leaving the house. Now must be as good a time as any to introduce ourselves.'

David looked at the tall girl who'd spoken the words. She appeared self-assured and he found himself liking her far more than the mop-haired girl who'd gone from making flippant comments to the sulky demeanour of someone who usually got their own way, only this time they'd been thwarted.

'Good idea,' David said. 'Events have been moving so quickly that we haven't had time to get to know each other.'

'Like who'd want to?' the girl with the mop hair said.

Bernice sounded conciliatory. 'We're going to spend the night here so we might as well make ourselves as comfortable as we can, and at least be on first-name terms.'

David watched as Bernice extended her hand to the nearest of the group, the tall girl in the amber coat. 'My name's Bernice Mochardi.'

'Vikki Lawton.'

David watched the introductions. Bernice had made the wise move of shaking hands. That initial physical contact, no matter how formal-seeming, was important. There was the possibility that they might have to trust each other with their lives before the night was out. He repeated their names mentally as they introduced themselves. David shook their hands, too. Mop-hair was called Liz Fretwell. Handshake: reluctant, as if she didn't want to be bothered. The tall girl: Vikki Lawton. Attractive, clear-eyed, high-cheekboned, with shortish curly hair. Handshake: firm, sincere.

The guy with blond dreadlocks: Emil Milani. 'But call me Goldi.' He touched one of the shining locks. 'Everyone does.' Ferocious handshake but good-humoured.

The last one was tall, late teens: Dylan Adams. A firm handshake. Sincere as Vikki's and he looked David in the eye as if to say, *OK, we're in this together. I'm going to trust you.*

Electra joined in the round of handshakes. 'My. It's turning into quite a palm-pressing fest, this. My name is Electra Charnwood.'

Electra could play the haughty aristocratic type when she met people for the first time, but David noticed that this time she let her shoulder drop a little. It softened her stance, made her seem warmer, friendlier.

Vikki said, 'I've seen you somewhere before.'

'Oh? Not anywhere disreputable, I hope.' Electra smiled.

'No. You run the Station Hotel in Leppington, don't you?'

'Guilty as charged, my dear. And come to think of it, I saw you and Dylan there a few days ago. Weren't you looking for someone?'

David saw Vikki shoot her a surprised look.

'Don't worry, Vikki dear. My bag of tricks doesn't run to telepathy. More a case of what BIG ears I have. I just happened to overhear what you were saying.' She smiled broadly. 'Hoteliers are natural eavesdroppers.'

Dylan nodded. 'That's how all this started. We were looking for my friend, Luke Spencer. The last I heard he'd gone to one of your Goth parties.'

'Then he disappeared?'

'Into thin air. I checked all the usual places where he might be. Then I started getting some telephone calls from him that were just plain weird.'

David listened as Dylan told him about the strange late-night calls, about his sudden change in behaviour, the invitation to the party here at Lazarus Wake. Then the chilling encounter with his old friend at the edge of the lake just an hour ago.

Liz tutted. 'What a cheap trick of Luke's. There never was a party.'

David shrugged. 'There was a party of sorts. Only you were probably going to be the snacks.'

'Shit, man.' Goldi began to pace the lounge floor. 'Are you telling us that Luke and those other weird fuckers really *are* vampires?'

'I could go into detail about their anatomy,' David told them. 'They are vampire-like – they'd drain you of every drop of blood if they got the chance.'

'You mean like Dracula?' Gold: slapped his thigh again. 'Shit. We've got Count Dracula living in Yorkshire – can you believe this guy?'

'No, not like Dracula. Think of them as human beings reconstructed by forces we don't understand.'

'But they drink blood?'

'They do. Just as vampire bats, leeches and mosquitoes ingest blood.'

'Why don't we whack them with crucifixes, then put a stake through their hearts?'

'Because, Goldi, they won't stand still and let you do that. Religious symbols don't faze them. And while you're standing there with your hammer and piece of pointy wood they're going to rip you to shreds before you can even use it.'

Electra added, 'That's what happened to your friend yesterday, the diver.'

'Steff? You know about her?'

'I arrived just after you pulled her from the lake. In the heat of the moment you probably don't remember me.'

'Jesus, it was fucking chaos.' Goldi slapped his forehead, remembering. 'You were with that crazy woman.'

Electra winced. 'She was distraught.'

Goldi's mouth hung wide in astonishment before he added, 'You mean Steff had been attacked by those things?'

'She was lucky to survive.'

'Lucky? Hell, woman, you saw the state of her.'

'She didn't die. So yes, she was damned lucky.'

Bernice said, 'And if she *had* died – she would have become one of those monsters. She'd be out there in the woods, waiting to do the same to you the moment—'

'Hey!' Dylan looked as if he'd been slapped. 'You mean that's what happened to Luke? That they killed him?'

'And now he's one of them. I'm afraid so.'

'Hell.' Dylan rubbed his face.

Vikki looked David in the eye. 'It seems to me that you know a lot about these vampires.'

'*Vampires!*' Liz snorted. 'They're nothing but a bunch of junkies who've taken some bad gear. This time tomorrow they'll be back to normal.'

'Sweet Jesus, I wish you were right,' Bernice said with feeling.

'You just wait,' Liz said. 'Just you wait and see them in—'

'Liz.' Vikki sounded calm, controlled, but David saw that

she wasn't going to let the mop-haired girl keep interrupting. 'What I'm going to do is make a hot drink. Then we're going to hear what Electra, Bernice and David have to tell us. So, who's for coffee?'

Liz returned to the sulky tone again. 'I'll have something stronger if there's anything. My neck's starting to hurt again.'

4

Electra thought: *Isn't this cosy? All of us sitting here by the crackling log fire, with big steaming coffees, listening to old Uncle Leppington tell us a bedtime story. Gather round closely, children. This is going to get scary . . .*

She stifled what she knew would be an inappropriate giggle. She couldn't stifle the sudden revelation she'd had a few moments ago. That it was time for David Leppington to accept his divine inheritance. And that she would be instrumental in him doing just that. But she knew she had to tread carefully. She had to appear to be on their side until she'd won David over. Then the rest of them, including that bitch Bernice Mochardi, could be junked. They had throwaway lives anyway. Who'd miss them? Just for a second as she gazed into the fire a tiny voice in the back of her head warned: *The vampires are getting to you, Electra. You've let them in without a fight . . .*

Then the thoughts were crushed by the image of her lying naked beneath David as he pounded into her. *Oh, how I'd dig my nails into his back and tear and scratch until there was blood on the sheets.* Thoughts of crimson splotches on white cotton were strangely appealing . . . the taste of it . . . *I wonder how his blood will taste if I—*

A crash from the doorway made her look up.

Rowan, David's gaunt doppelgänger, stood in the doorway. He leaned against the frame with his hand supporting his weight. After looking round the room at each face he snarled, 'How the hell did you lot get into the house?'

5

David's stare locked onto the man. Again, he was shocked by how much alike they were. The man noticed, too. He moved forward, using his hands to steady himself with the chair backs. Rowan looked into David's face. They were so close that David could see the tracery of veins in Rowan's eyes. Smell the stale saliva in the other man's mouth. He must have slept for days.

David heard Rowan whisper, in something close to horror, 'Who on Earth *are* you?'

'Rowan. You'd best sit down. I've got a lot to tell you . . . Bernice, can you bring a jug of water and a cup? Not a glass. He's badly dehydrated.'

Goldi stared with fascination. 'Say, have those things been at his blood?'

'No, but they've been working on him.'

'But he resisted their influence.' Electra smiled. 'Leppington blood is powerful stuff.'

David saw that he'd been right to ask for a cup, not a glass. Rowan drank thirstily, cup after cup, but it was all he could do to grip onto the thing. Water trickled down his chin to soak his shirt-front.

After the fourth mugful his eyes cleared a little more. 'You still haven't told me what this is all about. Why have you broken into the house?'

'We haven't broken in.'

'Are you the owners? Because if you are I paid two months' rent on this place up front.'

Electra knelt down beside him as he sat in the armchair. 'Do you remember me?'

'No. Why the hell should I?'

'My name is Electra.'

'Electra?'

'You've been corresponding with me on a very regular basis over the last few weeks. You sent me the—'

'*The Broxley Testament.*' Rowan suddenly came alive and rubbed his face violently. 'The Broxleys. Yes, I remember now.' He looked at his thin hands with their protruding veins and odd, untrimmed nails. 'But, dear God – what's happened to me?'

'You've been ill.'

'No, not ill. I know that much. Something strange has been happening.' His voice grew stronger. He looked round. 'And it's just got stranger. For weeks I've lived in a kind of dream. Last night I saw a weird bunch of people in the garden. I tried to e-mail you this morning but the telephone line's been torn down. Now I find people have broken into the house and he—' Rowan pointed at David. 'And he looks like me. If that doesn't get the Nobel Prize for weirdness, I don't know what does.'

David was impressed by the man's recovery. From coma to lucidity inside twenty minutes. What was more, David recognized a forceful personality leavened with a robust sense of humour. *He reminds me of my Uncle George,* he thought, surprised.

Rowan held out his hands. 'Isn't anyone going to tell the idiot what's happening here?'

David smiled. 'You're no idiot, but I think you might be a Leppington.'

'A who?'

'I see we've got more to talk about than I thought.' David held out his hand. 'My name is David Leppington and I think we both realize that we're related.'

For a while the people in the room broke up into smaller

groups. Bernice talked to Goldi, while Electra spoke with Vikki and Dylan. Liz sat by herself. The sulky pout of her mouth wasn't going to change in a hurry. Most of those in the room tried to use their mobile phones but no one could receive a signal in this out-of-the-way place.

David pulled up a stool so that he could talk to Rowan. He was pleased that a twinkle had surfaced in the man's eye. David told him a little of himself, mentioning his own family. 'Now the question is, if I can get personal here, Rowan, who are *your* parents?'

'I've a feeling you're already leapfrogging ahead to the right conclusion. My mother is – was, rather – Joy Harper. She died on Christmas Eve.'

'I'm sorry to hear that.'

'A brain tumour at the age of fifty. No one knew she'd got cancer until the week before. She thought she was suffering from vertigo, that's all: no headaches, nothing. She was admitted on the Tuesday. I sat and watched her die the following Monday.'

David saw that the memory still ate into him; the man's eyes had lost their focus as he stared at the wall. Then, just as quickly, he snapped out of it.

Rowan said, 'But you're interested in hearing about my father – even though I think you've already guessed. It took a long time to work out myself.' He smiled, the lines on his face deepening. 'By the age of eight I was toying with the notion of immaculate conception but by the time I was ten I'd reached the conclusion that the angels of the Lord don't visit the northern parts of England much, especially Sheffield where I was born and grew up.' His thin shoulders gave a little shrug. 'I never knew who my father was. I can pitch a few scenarios at you, but your guess is as good as mine. All I do know is that my mother raised me herself. She never mentioned my father.' Another shrug of the shoulders. 'I never asked.'

'Then we have to accept the possibility that we might be brothers,' David told him. 'And that my father had a secret affair with your mother.'

'Think that's likely?'

'It's a possibility.'

'What was your father's name?'

'Gordon Leppington. And he's still alive.'

'He looks like this?' Rowan touched his face.

'Very much so. My mother always said that all Leppingtons look like peas out of the same pod.'

'Sounds an interesting family.'

'If only you knew the half of it.'

Rowan smiled. 'I'm hoping you're going to tell me about this Leppington clan.'

'Don't worry, I will. But first there's a more pressing problem.'

'Which is the reason you're all here?'

'And why we can't leave just yet.' David looked at the man's deeply etched face. He was painfully malnourished. 'We also need to get you looked at.'

'I'm fine.'

'I don't think so. You've been slipping in and out of a coma for days, if not weeks. Although we don't have to worry any more about you being dehydrated. You've downed a couple of litres of water without any problems – but you do need to eat.'

'You sound like a doctor.'

'I am.'

'A long-lost brother who's a doctor.' Rowan grinned. 'This has got to be my lucky day. And he brings the beautiful Electra Charnwood to me as well. You know, she's just as I imagined. Tall, aristocratic . . . she's smart, too.'

David couldn't help but smile. 'I'm going to check your pulse, but I'd say there's nothing wrong with your health.'

'You mean my libido's firing on all cylinders?'

'Couldn't have put it better myself.'

Rowan sat still while David checked his pulse. 'I'm right about your physical state. Despite what you've gone through your pulse would put an ox to shame.'

'And just what have I gone through? Why did I lose my memory? Why was I afraid to leave the house?'

'I was just going to talk to everyone about what's been happening here.'

'And that ties in with my rather pitiful condition?'

'Yes, it does. That's why it's important to—'

'Hey, Doctor.' Liz suddenly looked up from where she'd been brooding over the fire. 'If those things from the lake are supposed to be so dangerous, why haven't they tried breaking in here?'

It was Electra who answered. 'It's because we're on holy ground.'

'Huh? Say again?'

'Don't let the physical appearance of the monsters put you off. They have certain rules that they must obey.'

'But you said holy ground, Electra.' David looked round. 'It's just a house.'

'You might not have noticed as we came in but there's an engraved tablet over the door that dedicates the building to what, presumably, must be the old Norse gods. Moreover, the builder of the house in the seventeen-hundreds was one Magnus Leppington.'

'Hey, there's the family connection again,' Rowan chimed in. 'We Leppingtons are popping up all over the place.'

'What's more,' Electra said, 'I wouldn't be surprised – if one was to look closely enough – to find Viking runes carved in all kinds of hidden corners of the building. There'll probably even be Viking religious artefacts embedded in the walls. The stonework could, just possibly, be recycled from the temples of Thor and Odin. And see how the timber mantelpiece has been cut. The shape represents a hammer . . . Thor's hammer, undoubtedly.'

'So the house was designed as a pagan temple?'

'Absolutely. One dedicated to the Viking gods, yet disguised sufficiently so as not to attract the attention of the Christian authorities.' Electra patted one of the massively thick stone walls. 'Remember, when this little beauty was built it was only a few decades on from witches being burned at the stake by zealous Christians.'

'So, history lessons aside,' Liz said, 'that means those bozos from the lake aren't going to bust their way in, right?'

'If my theory's correct – that this place *is* sacred to those *bozos*.' Electra gave a grim smile. 'But it wouldn't hurt to say a little prayer to your god of choice.'

For a moment the people in the room fell silent. David heard the cry of the wind sounding down the chimney. Hail rattled against window glass. And suddenly he was aware of jets of air blowing up between the flagstones that formed the floor. They felt like jets of cold water around his ankles. He saw Bernice and Vikki shiver as if the cold had touched them too.

'OK,' David said. 'It's coming up to eight. We've still got a long night ahead of us.'

'Yeah,' Goldi said. 'And we're prisoners, too, aren't we? We can't even phone out.'

'It isn't pleasant but we should be safe.'

'What happens in the morning?'

'Then we can leave.'

Liz snorted. 'Are you telling us those things have to crawl back to their coffins or they turn to dust?'

'No, they avoid the daylight. Their instincts will make them return to the lake.'

'But what if—'

'Liz.' David held up his hand. 'I don't claim to be an expert. An hour ago I told you that I was going to try and explain what's happening here. I think this is as good a time as any, so if you want to grab a seat I'll make a start.'

'Yeah, doesn't it begin "Once upon a time"?'

'Liz, button it, will you?' This one came from Goldi. Even he was getting tired of hearing the girl. 'Just let David tell us what's happening.'

David nodded his thanks at Goldi. 'Liz has guessed right. It's going to be a long story.'

Rowan smiled from deep in his armchair. 'Like you said, bro. We've got all night. You take your time.'

David glanced at Bernice and Electra. 'I'll begin, but jump right in if I miss anything important.' They nodded. 'OK, you've all heard of chemical spills where a pipe in a factory bursts and toxic material leaks into a river and pollutes the water. Well, in essence, what's happening now is a kind of toxic spill. For some inexplicable reason the past is leaking into the present. It's polluting it, too.' David Leppington did indeed almost find himself using the words 'once upon a time' when he started at the beginning. 'This is the story. Centuries ago, the Leppingtons, my – *our* – family –' he glanced at Rowan '– were then known as Leppingsvalt. Before they came to England in the Viking longships our family were blacksmiths. Legend has it that Thor, the Norse god of thunder, loses the legendary hammer that was the source of his great power. He searches across the whole world for centuries and never finds it. By chance he arrives at the house of Leppingsvalt. The blacksmith is an unhappy man. His wife can't give him a son and he knows the Leppingsvalt line will die out. This is a terrible calamity for a proud Viking. Anyway, the legend tells that Leppingsvalt, on hearing about Thor's loss, makes him a new hammer, which he called Mjolnir – it's known by that name today. The hammer is better than the old one and Thor is so pleased that he lies with Leppingsvalt's wife so that she will bear a male heir and so continue the dynasty.'

'So you're saying we have divine blood in our veins?' Rowan's eyes widened. 'Some claim.'

'That's the family legend,' David said, looking round at the faces of those in the room. They were listening intently. 'Later the Leppingsvalts became warriors and joined the Viking invasion of England. They settled not far from here, building a town once known as Leppingsvalt and which eventually became the Anglicized Leppington. But the legend didn't end there. Leppington became one of the last bastions of the pagan Viking religion. And as Christianity swept away all pagan rites so the ancient gods retreated into the deepest rivers and lakes. However, my ancestors received an order from Odin, the patriarch of the gods, that it was the Leppingtons' blood destiny to restore the old faith. They were to topple Christ and reinstate Odin, Thor and their divine family. By this time the Leppingtons were suffering a social and economic decline. They had no warriors to fight the Christian armies so the god Thor summoned the Valkyries – these were the warrior maidens of the gods – and he commanded that they should fly to the battlefields of the world where they would collect the bones of dead Viking warriors and bring them back to these valleys.

'And it was here that the old god placed a drop of his own blood into the jaws of the dead warriors and raised them from the dead. And down through the centuries the army has waited for a blood Leppington to lead them into battle against Christianity. You'll have guessed by now that this supernaturally resurrected army sustain themselves on the blood of animals and human beings.' David paused, the fire crackling in the background and the sobbing cry of the wind surging about the house. A door creaked loudly in the draught, then slammed.

'I see.' Rowan nodded, digesting what he had heard. 'A vampire army. That is one hell of a story.'

'It's a hell of a *legend*,' Electra added. 'Which isn't quite the same thing as a story.' She nodded at David. 'Go on.'

'Well, that's the family legend. Now, what I'm going to tell you next is what happened to me – and to Electra and Bernice here – just three years ago.'

David was no longer relating a family legend. This was personal experience. He told the story in plain terms and as clearly as he possibly could.

CHAPTER 26

I

Dylan Adams sat on a sofa next to Vikki. Oddly, despite the circumstances, he felt relaxed. The log fire filled the lounge with heat and light. That and the hot coffee chased away the near-paralysing cold he'd felt on the walk back here to the house after the crash. Even the anguish of wrecking the car had receded now. A warm buzz spread through his veins. He allowed his head to rest back against the sofa. The pressure of Vikki's thigh against his was delicious. His mind repeatedly went spinning back to the night in the Whitby hotel where they'd spent hours making love. Even his tongue moved in his mouth as he remembered licking her nipples and kissing those soft lips. The stir came in his groin. He wanted to hold her now; to run his hands up her long back, enjoying the supple curve of her spine . . .

Hey, Dylan, he told himself, *you're supposed to be listening to what David Leppington has to say.*

He listened to the man speaking. The voice was soft, and there was a slow, dreamy rhythm to his words. David explained that he and the two women had encountered these creatures before. Vampires, he called them. David told how he and another guy had fought these creatures in tunnels under Leppington town. He said that the only way to kill them was to behead them. That the other guy, whose name was Black, had been killed. And that eventually they had destroyed the vampires . . . Dylan's eyes strayed around the room again, taking in the rural décor, the beamed ceiling where flickering firelight sent shadows to scuttle playfully from one end to the other and back again. The storm had dropped to a breeze that sighed through the trees out there in the night. All the curtains were tightly drawn over the four windows in the room. With the whispery rise and fall of the breeze the yellow fabric of the curtains moved backwards and forwards. It was only a small movement. It was the same as the rise and fall of a person's chest when they slept.

Dylan, drowsy now, watched the curtains. They moved in and out; they inhaled and exhaled; the house was a living thing that breathed. Nerves and arteries ran through the stone walls. It sensed they were there, this ancient house built by the ancestor of the man who stood there talking now. Nearly three centuries ago Magnus Leppington had cleared the forest here. Perhaps he'd dug away the earth to reveal the ruined Viking temple. With the care of a priest conducting a holy rite he eased the stones from their resting place, lovingly cleaned them until their bone-white lustre was restored. Then, binding them together with bird lime, he had built the walls of the secret pagan temple he called Lazarus Wake.

Did the house have a heart and a mind? Because Dylan could sense its personality. He'd registered its sinister aspect, with its deep-set windows beneath brooding lintels, when he'd walked here in the dark. Even drowsier now, he turned his half-shut eyes to a wall of raw, bulbous stone blocks that were the size of human skulls. In parts they even had hollows suggestive of eye sockets.

And does the house see us? Drowsily comfortable, his imagination spun out lazy lines of thought. *Can the walls and hearthstones and timber ceiling beams see the people in the room?* In his mind's eye Dylan pictured the people gathered there in front of the fire that pumped out so much heat and flickering light into the room. *From which viewpoint would*

Magnus Leppington's house see us? Yes, there in the corner above the fireplace; from the top of the wall where it reaches the lumbering ceiling beam. There's a hunk of the stone wall that looks like a human skull. There's a crease at the bottom of the stone that looks like a grim mouth; there's a protrusion that suggests a nose. And in the upper half are two deeply gouged hollows.

Those are the eyes of this old house, he mused, drifting into sleep. *Two big misshapen eyes where the spirit of Lazarus Wake watches us. So what does this pile of stones see?*

In the dancing, golden light of the fire it sees David Leppington talking; his hands move slowly, making hypnotic passes in the air. Sitting by the door are the two women dressed in black – Electra Charnwood and Bernice Mochardi. The house notes Electra's aristocratic air, the way she holds her chin up. Red flashes from the firelight run along her long hair; pulses of energy that are as vivid as they are erotic. Bernice Mochardi is the shyer of the two women. She is vulnerable. Although she is extremely pretty with those fathomless dark eyes, she'd make men want to put a protective arm around her rather than seduce her. Even so, her choice of long calf-hugging boots in black leather hints at smouldering fires deep down inside . . .

The house watches us. Examines us. Judges us. Dylan's mind swam between sleep and wakefulness. In his mind's eye he found himself seeing the room's occupants through the stone eyes of the house. The same enduring stone eyes that had watched generations of people come and go.

Now he imagined that he was looking down at himself from high in the corner of the room. *I'm half sitting, half lying on the sofa, my fingers knitted together on my chest. Beside me is Vikki, her eyes catching the firelight, her cheeks flushed from its heat. Beside her, in that loose, languid sprawl of his, is Goldi; drowsily toying with one of his blond dreadlocks. Goldi's gaze rests on David's face as he talks. By the fire, hunched on a stool, is Liz. Her face, framed by the mop of hair, holds no emotion. Rowan sits in his armchair, keenly attentive. And there we all are. Eight people, ranging in age from late teens to late thirties. We're basking in the heat of the log fire. We're listening to David's bedtime story. The breeze sighs down the chimney. Draughts slipping through the four windows in the lounge gently push the curtains. The yellow material bulges ever so slightly, as they move in and out with a sleepy rhythm. Four sleepers' chests,* Dylan thought, now more asleep than awake. *The sofa and the heat from the burning logs are so comfortable that I could close my eyes now and sleep until morning.*

He was still listening to the pleasant rise and fall of David's voice when—

'*Hell, you expect us to believe that!*' As Liz spoke she leaped to her feet with an explosive rush of breath that came out with a startlingly loud pop. Dylan felt Vikki jump with shock. Wide awake now, Dylan saw Liz's eyes glitter with anger.

'What do you take us for? Idiots?' Liz kicked the stool away from her. It clattered against the wall. 'Is this your idea of fun? Roaming round until the three of you find some fools to unload your stupid stories onto. Jesus Christ, you should be locked up!'

'Liz, I've been trying to explain what—'

'Explain? Weirdo mind games, more like!'

Vikki said, 'Liz, sit down. There's no point—'

'Shit to this!' Liz zipped up her jacket. 'I'm not staying here any longer. If you won't drive me home, I'll walk!'

David said, 'You can't leave. Listen to me. It's dangerous.'

'Dangerous – ha! This is just some power trip for you.'

'Liz—'

'And I'm not falling for it.'

David held out his hands. 'Liz. You're not going out there. I won't let you.'

Furious, she plunged her hand down to the fireplace. When she straightened Dylan saw that she was holding an iron poker. 'OK. Are you going to stop me?'

No one moved. With the snap of burning logs came the whispering sigh of draughts ghosting down the chimney.

'Yes,' David told her in something near a whisper. 'I'm going to stop you.'

Liz raised the poker, pointing it at him like a sword. David moved fast. But instead of approaching her, he walked from window to window, sweeping back the curtains with a slashing movement of his arms.

'There. Tell me you're going to walk out of that door right now!'

Dylan heard the collective gasp fill the room. Everyone stared at the windows. He felt Vikki shudder as if grave-cold fingers had trailed down her back. For there, visible through the window-panes, crowding closely together, yet still as stone, was a mass of faces. The light blazing from the fire revealed them with shocking clarity.

Dylan saw the bone-white faces. Eyebrows were thick, black, coarse; they bristled outward; clusters of spider-leg loathsomeness. As for their eyes, those terrible eyes, they had the power to blast their way into the back of someone's skull. Dylan sensed everyone in the room recoiling from that massed stare. He wanted more than anything to look away but those malignant, gleaming gazes held him. They had a dark, bruised quality that made the whites of the eyes stand out and shine, as if fires blazed inside the mass of hairless heads. As his own gaze was drawn into the dozens of eyes to drown in the vastness of those sockets he saw that there was no colour in the eyes; no irises. Each eye had a pupil that fixed its stare on him with an intensity that mated ferocity with lust.

2

As quickly as he'd opened the curtains David closed them again. With the curtains shutting off that mass of staring eyes, the spell within the room was broken. Yet even when the last pair of curtains had been firmly closed, sealing off those naked white heads from sight, no one spoke. Liz's face drained of colour until it was a bloodless grey. Still unable to take her gaze from the curtained windows, her mouth open in shock, she sat down on the arm of the sofa.

David didn't feel the savage satisfaction he might have done at his brutal act. Even so, he thought: *They believe now . . . oh, do they believe . . .*

3

Time crawled. David glanced at the grandfather clock as he walked through the hallway from the kitchen to the lounge. Still twenty-five minutes to midnight. It was more than three hours since he'd swept back the curtains from the four windows to reveal those monsters staring into the room.

Flimsy though those yellow curtains might be, they now closed off the sight of the faces that must still have been out there.

How many are there? Twenty? A hundred? A thousand? One thing's for sure, I'm not going to look out again. Opening the curtains was a reckless act triggered by Liz brandishing the poker. But then, how did I know the vampires were outside with their faces at the windows, waiting?

That thought made him uneasy, too. Maybe he'd sensed them there, or worse, they'd implanted in him that mad impulse to open the curtains. Because to look those things in the eye rendered someone even more vulnerable. Their stares held their victims powerless.

The eight people in the lounge were silent. Most stared at the fire. Liz, on the other hand, still had her gaze fixed on the curtains. The image of those white faces with blazing eyes must be seared on her mind. At least she wouldn't suggest hiking back to town now.

'Are you sure no one wants coffee?'

They shook their heads. Rowan, however, pulled himself to his feet. David saw that the man still looked shaky. 'I'm going to find something to eat. If anyone wants to join me they're more than welcome.'

'I will.' Dylan stood up. With a backward glance at Vikki still sitting on the sofa he asked, 'Coming?'

'Not for me . . . I couldn't.'

'Fear affects people in different ways.' Rowan stretched his arms. 'I heard of a comedian who was so affected by stage fright that he had to eat two whole roast chickens before every performance. Then, the moment he left the stage, he vomited them right back up.'

Dylan gave a grim smile. 'A sandwich will be enough for me.'

Rowan examined his thin wrist and near-skeletal fingers. 'I don't know what kind of hex those monsters put on me but I don't look as if I've eaten in weeks.'

'They were trying to weaken you,' David told him. 'So you'd lose your will to fight them.'

'They shouldn't take on a Leppington, eh? Not with the blood of Viking warriors in our veins.'

'Even so, take it easy when you eat. I'd suggest something light for your stomach.'

'Soup it is, then. Lead the way, Dylan. Kitchen's the first door on your right.'

Again, David marvelled at the resemblance of his own face to Rowan's. They certainly did look like brothers. Remarkably, they even shared some of their mannerisms. David had noticed that when Rowan was thinking he frowned so that one eyebrow seemed ready to climb above the other. At the same time he'd rub his temple lightly with the tip of his index figure. One thing

David did notice (a touch of sibling envy?) was Rowan's air of easy charm. *Sweet Jesus, Dad's got some explaining to do.*

Vikki sat up straight on the sofa. She looked wide awake. 'What now?' she asked. 'Do we try and sleep until it's light?'

'You can if you want,' Electra told her. 'But it's important that we don't all sleep at the same time.'

Bernice added, 'We can take it in turns. I think half of us should stay awake.'

'You mean to stand guard?' Liz glanced round, scared. 'You said those things wouldn't try to get in. Holy ground, you said.'

Electra nodded. 'That's true, but I wouldn't want to rely on that theory one hundred per cent.'

'I'm too wired to sleep,' Goldi said. 'I'm going to try the mobile phone again.'

Liz groaned. 'How many times do you have to try?'

'Better than just sitting here.'

'You still won't get a signal. We're trapped here until those things get it into their skulls to go back to the lake.'

Vikki rubbed her forehead. David saw that she was thinking hard. 'David?'

'Uhm?'

'You told us that as a blood descendant of these Viking warlords – the Leppinvahl?'

'Leppingsvalts.'

'The Leppingsvalts.' She blinked as she committed the name to memory. 'You told us that the surviving blood Leppingtons are expected to lead these vampires on a crusade to destroy Christianity.'

'So the family legend runs. Why?'

'Then you're likely to be safe from attack.' She looked round. 'After all, you have a divine mission . . . well, not to put too fine a point on it, you are the boss of those things out there.'

David gave a grim smile. 'Now that's one thing I wouldn't put to the test.'

'But you are a blood Leppington. Why would they harm you?'

Electra fielded that one. 'Because they might feel betrayed. David rejected his divine right of leadership and eventually he destroyed the comrades of those creatures outside.'

'They might not be very forgiving,' Bernice added.

'So it's wise for me to stay put.' David put the coffee on the mantelpiece, then set about building up the fire with more logs. A chill had started to creep back into the room as the fired died down. *Only there's more to it than that, isn't there, David? You're worried about Rowan, aren't you?* The thought sneaked up, catching him by surprise. *If Rowan's your brother then you, David, might be expendable; at least in the eyes of the vampires. If they do kill me in revenge for what I did to their kind three years ago, then they'd still have another blood Leppington to lead them.* That was why it would be nothing less than suicidal to go striding out of the house. The fire began to blaze again as the logs caught hold.

Electra rubbed her hands on the arms of her black lacy blouse. 'I'm sure these walls suck the cold right into the house.' She reached out to touch one of the walls between the windows (curtains still tightly drawn, thank God). The second her fingers pressed the stonework she tugged her hand back. 'Ouch. They *are* cold.' She ran her thumb across her fingertips. 'Believe it or not, boys and girls, touching the wall just took the skin off my fingertips.'

David walked forward. 'Let me take a look at that.'

Electra let him take her hand in his so that he could examine her fingertips. 'Painful?'

'Stings a little,' she said.

He noticed her eyes scanning his face as if looking for something there.

'Classic freezer burn,' he told her. 'It's pulled off the surface skin.'

'So will I live, doctor?' She gave one of her wry smiles.

'I'll see if I can find some antiseptic cream.'

'I noticed a first-aid kit in the kitchen,' Vikki said, rising. 'I'll fetch it.'

Goldi walked up to the wall and looked at it without touching it. 'But, hell's bells, it can't get *that* cold, can it?'

'Oh, but it can,' Electra told him. 'When you stir those darlings out there into the mix.' This time she addressed the vampires through the wall. 'You can meddle with people's minds. You can drain them of their blood. You can even suck the heat right out of rock, can't you?'

If they couldn't hear her voice, David wondered if they could hear her thoughts. Sometimes Electra's cynicism could veer into dangerous territories.

'Sit down by the fire, Electra.' It would be best to deflect her from any action that might antagonize the vampires. 'I'll check your hand again. There's a chance of frostbite.'

'I'm sure I'll be fine, David.'

The smile she shot him was different somehow. Besides the warmth, there was an erotic, sultry quality to the curl of her red lips.

Liz snorted. 'Well, if you guys are going to play doctors and nurses I'm going to bed.' She held out her hand to Goldi. 'Come and tuck me in. You can help me say my bedtime prayers as well.'

David saw that the alluring flutter of lashes she shot Goldi needed no explanation.

'Hey, Liz. We don't have bedrooms, remember? We're just visiting this shithole.'

'Oh, I'm good at finding a bed for the night. You coming?'

With a grin, Goldi took her hand.

When they'd left the room, Electra rolled her large kohled

eyes up at David. 'And so the young lovers retire to bed. Are you sleepy yet, David?'

'Me? No.' He glanced to his right. 'Ah, thanks, Vikki.'

'I found two tubes. Both are for grazes, stings and burns.'

'The purple tube should be best. It's got a local anesthetic.'

Electra smiled. 'You're so sweetly considerate, doctor.'

David detected the fine balance between flippancy and tenderness. As he unscrewed the cap he avoided looking into her face because he knew she was trying to catch his eye.

OK, Electra, what's your game? With the question going round inside his head he squirted a small pyramid of pink cream onto her fingertip.

4

Electra hadn't been this deliciously happy in years. *Why haven't I seen David Leppington in this light before? He really is good-looking.* She should move quickly to stake her claim before that bitch Bernice Mochardi tried to snatch him. *Oh yes, we could be so right for one another.* She would see to it that he accepted that gift of the gods that was waiting so patiently outside the house for him.

For a second she rebelled against the line of thought. Then a dark mist settled behind her eyes again. It left her content to sit there by the fire and enjoy the sensation of David's gentle fingers smoothing the antiseptic cream into the tips of her fingers. So cool and soothing. Then – how odd – she felt a growing heat inside her veins.

When Electra looked up at David's face she knew exactly what that pulsing heat meant. What's more, she knew she couldn't delay. She had to act tonight.

CHAPTER 27

I

'So why are we down to six?' Rowan asked as he walked into the lounge carrying a bowl of soup and, incongruously, a plate full of mashed potato with wedges of cake on the side. Dylan followed, bringing more cake.

Bernice answered. 'Goldi and Liz have gone to bed.'

'Really?' Rowan shrugged and smiled. 'Well, if it helps take their minds off those guys outside then they can be my guests.'

David saw the potato steaming in a great mound on the plate. 'Seeing as you haven't eaten for so long I'd take it easy. Solids might make you nauseous.'

'I'm sure I'm going to be all right, Doc. I'm so hungry I could eat a hippo.' He stuck his fork into the potato. 'It's only light stuff, anyway – mash and soup.'

Dylan said, 'There's not much in the way of fresh food. Milk and bread's gone off. There's plenty of packs of microwaveable mashed potato.'

'Hey, I like mashed potato.' Rowan gave a good-natured smile. 'But you're all welcome to my stash if you get peckish.'

'Thanks,' Electra said. 'I'm going to fast tonight.'

David finished off applying the cream to Electra's injured fingertips, wiped his own fingers free of the balm, then tossed the used tissue into the fire. As the flame touched it, the updraught caught the flimsy paper and carried it up the cavernous chamber, a ball of brief-lived yellow flame that would emerge from the chimney pot, casting an uncertain flicker of light on the vampires massed around the house.

Electra examined the pink marks at the end of her fingertips. 'They feel better already, David. Thanks – you're my hero.'

'Hardly.'

'Now.' Electra slapped her knees, suddenly businesslike. 'Sleeping arrangements.'

Back to that again, thought David. The way she's been . . . well, for want of a better phrase, 'making eyes at him'. Was it just her flippant sense of humour again? Maybe she was simply teasing him? But here and now that was hardly appropriate.

Rowan spoke between hungry mouthfuls. 'I've had enough shut-eye to last a month. All I've done is sleep for twenty hours a day.'

David said, 'You still might be weak. Those creatures were trying to break your will-power – you do realize that?'

'Yes, I do. But, believe me, I'm wide awake now.'

Electra said, 'You certainly seem alert now compared with – what? – six hours ago.'

'I feel bright as a new blade . . . ha, my mother's expression. She worked as a knife polisher in a factory where they made cutlery out of Sheffield steel. Hardly glamorous work for the mother of a descendant of the great god Thor, was it, bro?'

David saw Rowan's gaze meet his. For the first time David detected an undertow of bitterness behind the affable smile. Rowan was still grieving for his dead mother. Then again, such an underlying bitterness toward life in general might be dangerous in these circumstances. For a split second David pictured the massed vampires outside, waiting so patiently in the darkness, their hairless heads gleaming eggshell white. He also pictured the sudden blaze of excitement in those menacing eyes as they picked up Rowan's bitter strand of thought. *A blood Leppington with a grudge? Yes, that's a useful tool for the coming battle . . .*

David fired off the question before he'd even thought it through. 'Does anyone know you're staying here in Lazarus Wake, Rowan?'

'Nobody.'

'You don't have any other family?'

'Do dead mothers count?'

Again the purple edge of bitterness. David pressed on. 'But surely your employer will miss you?'

'I'm self-employed.'

'And you have no employees?'

'None.'

'What made you rent a cottage out here in the middle of winter?'

'None of your business.' Rowan started eating the cake.

The man's retort was good-natured enough but David could see that he didn't relish such close questioning.

Bernice spoke to ease any tension. 'At least you're feeling better, that's the important thing.'

'And I'm still hungry as a horse. Dylan, do you find the cake stale at all?'

'No, not me. Anyway, it came out of a sealed carton.'

'It's probably me.' Rowan munched a hunk of cake. Swallowing, he added, 'When we were children, and we'd fallen asleep during the day and we'd got that strange taste in our mouths – you know the one? – we'd always say we had "monkeys in our mouth". Anyone familiar with the phrase?'

He's being deliberately chatty to divert the topic of conversation away from why he's holed himself up here, David told himself. *I wonder if he—*

'David, penny for them.'

'Hmm?'

Electra's eyes twinkled as she smiled up at him. 'I said a penny for your thoughts.'

'Sorry, I was miles away.'

'Sleeping arrangements? I was just saying that we should work out some rota.'

Dylan looked uneasy. 'Damn right. I don't like the idea of all of us sleeping when those things are standing just outside the windows.'

Rowan finished off the cake. 'As I said, I'm wide awake. I don't think I'll sleep for days.'

Vikki said, 'I don't think just one of us should stay awake alone.'

'I agree.' Electra stood up and stretched, yawning. 'With Goldi and Liz otherwise occupied that leaves six of us.'

'So.' Bernice shrugged. 'Three sleep while three stay awake?'

'If anyone *can* sleep.' Vikki shuddered. 'With those things out there.'

'Unless anyone objects,' David said, 'I suggest two hours on, two hours off.'

'Who's for the first watch?' Electra asked.

Rowan brushed crumbs from his fingers and put up a hand. 'I'll be on first. I'm feeling pretty hyper anyway.'

Bernice was next. 'I'm not ready to sleep yet.'

Vikki shrugged. 'Me neither. So that makes us three night watchmen for the first two hours.'

'And so to bed.' Electra yawned again, her whole body relaxing into a catlike suppleness.

'There's plenty of rooms upstairs,' Rowan told them. 'Take your pick. Sweet dreams.'

2

Dylan followed Electra and David upstairs. Between yawns Electra suggested that they should place candles and matches by the bed. 'You never know about the electricity supply in these parts.'

Dylan almost found himself uttering the words: *Are you sure we're going to be safe? Those things aren't going to break in?* But then, these two people couldn't be sure of that. And to even ask the questions would put him on the level of a child constantly seeking reassurance.

'First bedroom's out,' Electra noted, nodding at the door.

Dylan clearly heard the sounds of fucking. Goldi and Liz weren't going to let something like this stymie their recreation.

'Eeny, meeny, miney, mo.' Electra used the children's counting rhyme to choose a bedroom. 'This one.' She pointed at a door at the front of the house.

David spoke almost brusquely. 'I'll take this.' He opened the door to a bedroom at the back of the house.

'I guess I'll go for the attic room,' Dylan told them. 'See you later.'

'Try and sleep, dear.' Electra told him, smiling. 'And don't worry. Everything will be fine in the morning.'

3

Bernice watched Rowan place more logs on the fire. Then she turned her attention to her boots. Some mud had splashed onto the leather. She wiped it away with a tissue. As she did so, she noticed Vikki looking at her.

Bernice smiled. 'You find yourself doing anything to take your mind off . . .' She nodded toward the curtained windows.

Vikki smiled. 'Right now a bottle of brandy seems a good idea.'

'There's whisky and vodka in the cabinet across there,'

Rowan said as he raked away dead ash from the heart of the fire. 'You're welcome to help yourself.'

Bernice said quickly, 'I wouldn't recommend it. We need to keep our wits about us.'

'Quite right, too,' Rowan said.

'I don't think I could stomach it, anyway.' Vikki rubbed her midriff. 'I've got butterflies like you wouldn't believe.' She gave a nervous smile. Bernice found herself liking the girl. Vikki seemed a little on the shy side, she thought, despite her deliberate air of self-confidence. What was more, she reminded Bernice of herself when she'd first encountered those creatures. *I felt as if I had a whole jungle of winged things in my stomach. I was scared to the bone.*

Perhaps Rowan noticed Vikki's jumpiness at the slightest sound. 'Right, all the doors and windows are soundly bolted. We're safe as houses.'

Now there strides an optimist. Bernice found herself shooting a glance at the window as tapping came from beyond the curtains.

'Hailstones,' Rowan murmured. 'Now . . . I don't know what we're supposed to do during vigils like these. Play cards? Swap jokes? Exchange life stories?'

'Drink lots of coffee, probably.' Vikki rubbed her stomach as if the abdominal twitching was growing stronger. 'Lots and lots of coffee.'

'I'll make some more,' Rowan said.

'No, let me.' Bernice stood up. 'It'll help if I move around.'

'Feeling tired?'

'No, not at all. More cake?'

'Yes, please.' Rowan smiled. 'Now my long-lost brother's not around I can let my hair down.' He brushed his fringe away from his eyes. Bernice saw the boyish twinkle there. 'I'm sorry there's no television, but we'll find plenty to occupy ourselves for the next two hours, won't we?'

4

Luke Spencer knew that he was different from everyone whom he'd ever known before. As he stood, bare-chested and barefoot, in winds so cold that they would kill any human being, all he could feel was the hungry fire that burned inside his belly. That fire flooded through him like a great tide; it had the power to sweep his mind from his body and to carry it away, so that it soared like a raven across the face of Lazarus Deep. Down through the water he could see more of his kind. Thousands upon thousands sleeping deep in the mud at the bottom of the lake. They were waiting for the call to join the rest of them who now stood motionless outside the ancient and holy stones of Lazarus Wake. Inside the house were both strangers and people he'd once known as his friends.

Once more the tidal flow of hunger and lust blazed through Luke, catching up his mind and carrying it toward the house. Even though he never moved so much as a finger his mind's eye raced low across a lawn salted white with hailstones. Then he raced not over or around the car but *through* its steel shell. After that his mind ghosted right through the door of the house itself.

In a blurring rush of speed Luke found himself in the lounge. Three people were there, sitting in front of a log fire that burned so bright that it seemed a part of the sun had fallen into the hearth. Even though his eyes, which had once been mortal flesh, weren't physically there in the room he recoiled from the barrage of incandescence. As he whirled away, flitting as lightly as a bat through the air, he saw his old school friend Vikki Lawton. Sitting beside her was a girl dressed in black. Even though he didn't recognize her a voice whispered to him from the depths of the earth: *Bernice Mochardi. Foe.* And then there was the man whose blood he could smell from here. Leppington blood. Soon the Leppingtons would get one last chance. But which Leppington? This one, whom they'd been holding here comatose for weeks? Or the one lying on the bed upstairs? There could only be one leader. The remaining Leppington would be expendable. But which one?

That wasn't for the thing once known as Luke Spencer to say.

In the room opposite were two more people he recognized. Goldi, and Liz Fretwell. Both were naked. Goldi knelt on the bed; Liz reached up, curling her fingers round his bleached dreadlocks. Dark sheets made a striking contrast with their ice-white nakedness. She looked up into Goldi's eyes.

'Come on, Goldi, you can do it. One more time.'

'Christ, Liz. I thought *I* was a machine but you win that gong.'

'Come on, Goldi. I know you can.' She turned over so that she was on her hands and knees on the bed. *'Please, Goldi.'*

'I can't.'

'Shit, Goldi.' She reached back and slapped her own buttocks. 'Use your fist if you have to but I want to feel you inside me. *Now.*'

In the adjoining room was the older woman with long dark hair that tumbled glossily down her back. She'd stripped to the waist. Now she sat on the bed, rubbing skin cream on her arms, stomach, and into the soft swell of her breasts. She sang softly to herself. Her nipples tightened and darkened as she worked with her fingers. Her gaze was faraway and she was smiling.

Electra Charnwood, Station Hotel, Leppington. A lifetime ago, or so it seemed, Luke had met her there at a Goth Communion. His brothers and sisters from the lake had worked well tonight. They'd found a route through her protective shell of cynicism into her cache of secret hopes.

Now his people spun their puppet strings that would guide her actions in the coming hours.

The woman didn't even pause in rubbing the cream into her skin when she heard Liz's explosive cry through the wall as his old friend Goldi forced himself into her. And speaking of old friends . . .

Ghosting up through the ceiling, Luke saw on the bed the figure of the young man who'd been his closest friend of all. Dylan Adams. They'd been planning to be musicians together but a passion for photography had won Dill over. He wanted to leave Morningdale as soon as he possibly could. Of course, he never would now. His future lay here. For ever and ever . . .

Luke's mind's eye hovered close to the ceiling. It gazed down at the single bed in the centre of the room. His old friend lay on his side, his face turned away from whatever nebulous cloud of consciousness hung there with its power to see the occupants of the house. One of the sleeper's arms was folded at the elbow, so that one hand covered the exposed throat. Dylan's eyes were lightly shut. His hair curled against the pillow.

Dylan.

Suddenly Dylan sat up in bed, looking straight up at the ceiling as if staring at Luke. But Luke knew that Dylan could see nothing but the pale expanse of ceiling. *A dream; that's all.* Luke could almost read his friend's mind. As the surge of panic subsided Dylan lay back down on the bed again. *Soon, old friend . . . we're going to meet face to face again . . .*

As was its primeval nature, the tidal flow of voracity swung back. The bedroom where Dylan lay fell away. Walls whirled by in retreat. A view of Electra massaging cream onto her throat momentarily filled the vision of the fleeing mind's eye, then shrank into distance. Another wall. Goldi and Liz grunting on the bed. Cotton sheet smeared with blood. The outer wall. Then a fall back through the night air. Grass, trees, pathways, statues; the raven on the roof.

Luke Spencer was back in his body again. Standing beside his bloodless companions.

5

Air currents whispered in the chimney breast. Draughts stirred the yellow curtains. From the hallway came the tick-tock of the grandfather clock. Bernice sat with her head resting against the wing-back of the sofa. She watched the updraught run its ghostly fingers through the grey ash in the hearth.

No logs. No flame. Only cold, cold ash.

From the hallway the grandfather clock began to chime. One . . . two . . .

Good . . . time to wake the others; we can sleep now.

Three . . . four (the shimmering chimes continued) . . . five . . .

Dear God! Bernice sat up straight. Beside her, Vikki lay with her head on the sofa's arm, her eyes closed. Across the lounge Rowan, the uncanny double of David Leppington, sat with his head lolling to one side. His eyes, too, were closed.

'Wake up . . . *wake up!*' Fear jolted Bernice with the power of lightning. 'I said, wake up! We've been asleep!'

CHAPTER 28

I

Bernice shook Vikki by the shoulder. Vikki's head rolled but her breathing continued as rhythmically as before.

'Rowan!'

She went across to where he was sleeping in the armchair. 'Rowan!' His face didn't even give up so much as a tremor. *'Rowan! Wake up!'* She knew her voice must have been piercing but he didn't hear her. She touched his face that was such an eerie replica of David Leppington's, right down to the strong arch of his eyebrows and the broadness of his cheekbones – although Rowan's skin retained the deep lines left by days without food. His temples felt cool and Bernice ran her finger down to the pulse in his neck. Nothing amiss there. Strong. Steady. She did the same to Vikki. Her pulse pumped steadily beneath Bernice's light touch. Nothing outwardly wrong with the pair of them – but why wouldn't they wake up?

Even as Bernice asked herself the question she knew the answer. Broxley. In his account of what had happened to him here he had written about how his wife and daughter had slipped into this kind of coma. Rick Broxley had only roused his wife to semi-consciousness by burning her exposed arm with a cigarette lighter.

'Vikki . . . Rowan!' She raised her voice to a shout. 'Come on. You've got to wake up!'

No amount of shaking was going to rouse this pair.

Damn . . . Bernice glanced at the curtains; they still pulsed in the draughts oozing through the gaps in the frame. At just after six in the morning in February it would be dark for a while yet. Even longer, if this godforsaken wilderness stayed shrouded in dense cloud. A rattle from the fireplace startled her. Gasping, she saw an object fall into the hearth. Surely it was only a piece of mortar that had been dislodged during the gales?

Or was it one of those monsters climbing down the chimney?

No, surely not. Her imagination was running away with her, that was all. Even so, Bernice found herself staring into the fireplace, expecting at any moment to see a face with two white glaring eyes appear in the dark mouth of the chimney.

Then the light went out. Now a scream *did* escape her lips. She stood there by the fireplace, panting, her heart beating rapidly in her chest. It beat so hard that she tensed her muscles, hurting inside. A hand from the fireplace tugged at her skirt. With a squeal, Bernice backed away, moving in total darkness. A second later her heel banged against Vikki's outstretched legs and she tumbled back onto the other girl. Even though she landed hard enough on Vikki to send a spasm of pain up Bernice's spine Vikki didn't even whimper.

Oh, God . . . Oh, God . . . What now? What the hell do I do? I can't see . . . The hand that caught hold of me . . . there must be one of those things in the room. But I can't even see if it—

Oh!

Light sprang from the darkness so suddenly that she flung a hand in front of her eyes.

It's just the lamp, Bernice told herself. *The electricity's back* . . . Her gaze darted round the room as her panic mounted. Looking for one of those loathsome white figures.

Only there was no one there. *Behind the sofa? Hiding in the hallway?* Her heart pounded.

Then she glanced back at the fireplace. A scrap of cloth had caught on one of the ornamental points on the knee-height fireguard. Quickly, Bernice lifted the bottom of her skirt in one hand. The hem had been torn down, leaving a ragged cleft where a fragment of material had been ripped away.

So . . . no hand had reached out to her. Even so, her face felt clammy with shock. Her heart refused to slow its mad clamouring pounding. Once more the lights flickered. Only this time they held. *But for how long?* She looked at the table lamp in the corner. The bulb burned a dull yellow instead of white. Could the monsters from the lake slow down the flow of electricity through the cables to this remote house? Or maybe it was simply ice forming on the pylons. Still, the whole place might be plunged into darkness at any moment. Quickly, Bernice went to the coffee table where Electra had had the foresight to lay out candles already set onto plates with their own wax. Fumbling matches from the box onto the table, she picked one up and struck it against the box. In seconds she'd lit four of the candles.

Just in case, she told herself. *The last thing I want is to be left in the dark again. I couldn't bear it . . . I know I'd scream. And once I started screaming in the dark I could never stop.*

The electric lights flickered again. As if in collusion with the dimming bulbs, jets of air once more started to ooze through gaps between the flagstones of the floor. Bernice could feel the damp coldness reaching up to her thighs under her skirt. Shuddering, she bit down hard, grinding teeth until her jaw ached.

The coldly probing tongues of air worked their way into her bones. She hated the sensation.

Taking a candle, she held it close to the faces of the two sleepers. It occurred to her that she could play its flame against Rowan's ear. Surely that level of blistering pain would wake the man? She moved the candle closer, her stare locked on his face. The ear lobe would blacken, bubble. She imagined his scream of pain as he snapped awake. It had worked for Broxley . . . But Bernice knew that she couldn't do it. Not yet. Perhaps she might have more luck upstairs?

She'd made it as far as the grandfather clock, now showing 5.20 when the lights, without any fuss or flickering, smoothly dimmed, faded . . . went out. For whole moments she stared at the bulb inside the ceiling shade. It looked as dead as the eye of a corpse. Five minutes went by, measured so slowly, so painfully by the tick . . . tock of the big clock. Still no electric light.

'It looks as if the power's not coming back.' She spoke the words aloud, hoping to find reassurance in the sound of a human voice, if only her own. 'Come on, Bernice, let's go and wake the others.'

The sound of something like fingernails scraping down woodwork made her glance back at the door. The noise ended as abruptly as it had started. Maybe a twig blown by the wind?

As Bernice slowly climbed the stairs, the candle throwing twisting shadows of the banister on the wall to her side, the wind returned. She heard the wail coming from far off in the distance, rising louder and louder through the forest until fierce gusts once more seethed around the house. Thin cries sounded from the eaves outside the windows. The wind swept under the door with enough power to set the door mat undulating with something of the menace of a mass of rodents scurrying across the floor. Hail tapped at the glass panes. Quickly, Bernice climbed the remaining stairs to the bedrooms. Shivering, she couldn't help wondering what she might find there.

2

First room on her right. Moving through darkness, the candle casting shadows that ballooned and mutated into monstrous shapes on the walls, Bernice stepped into the bedroom at the back of the house. There on the bed lay David Leppington. Apart from his shoes and fleece jacket he was fully clothed. Placing the candle on the bedside table, she tried to wake him. He slept on as soundly as the two downstairs. After five fruitless minutes of shaking David's shoulder and calling his name she retraced her steps to the landing. The candle formed a ball of light in front of her, both dazzling her and lighting her way. Behind her, darkness rushed in to fill the illumination vacuum.

In the room opposite the first thing to hit her was the smell of sex in the air. Its blend of perspiration and musky odours filled her nose. There, lying on the bed, were Goldi and Liz. Goldi lay on his back, dreadlocks splashed across the pillow. Liz lay face down. Both were naked. Shocked, Bernice saw that blood had soaked the sheet. Moving closer, with the candle held high, she saw that more blood had dried in smears across the full mounds of Liz's buttocks. Still more stickily coated her thighs, while Goldi's hand looked as if he was wearing a glove. Then she realized that the hand and wrist – as far as the forearm – was coated in blood, too.

Just what, in God's name, had happened here? For an instant Bernice imagined the slug body of a vampire oozing through the window to attack Liz and Goldi as they slept. From experience, though, she knew that the creatures licked bodies clean of blood with gluttonous pleasure. There was still plenty of blood here. What was more, she could see no bite marks on their bodies (if, that was, she discounted the love bites bruising Goldi's neck and shoulders).

With a trembling reluctance she touched their faces. They were still warm. They breathed steadily. Their pulses were strong. Whatever had happened here wasn't directly attributable to vampires. Bernice grabbed the blankets that had been kicked onto the floor in what must have been the heat of passion and pulled them up over the naked pair.

I don't even want to try and wake these two. Both had a wild streak that could put them all in greater danger than that which they already faced. In the next room she found Electra.

'Electra?' This time Bernice didn't shout. 'Electra?' she repeated. But she was already resigned to the fact that she wouldn't be able to wake the other woman. The vampires' influence was too strong. Just as they'd done with the Broxley family, just as with Rowan Harper, the monsters had managed to invade the sleepers' minds and bury them deep in coma. Electra's dark eyebrows formed perfect arches above her kohled eyes. Even the red lipstick hadn't smudged. For some reason she'd stripped herself bare before slipping beneath the duvet. There was nothing Bernice could do but pad silently from the room. Checking Dylan Adams in that weird attic room was just a formality. He slept on his back, facing the ceiling. With his curling hair and compelling delicate features he had a youthful beauty rather than a maturely handsome face. His lips still had the fullness of adolescence. That and his perfect skin made Bernice think of portraits of sensitive poets doomed to die young. With a sigh that was more sorrowful than disappointed at not having been able to wake Dylan she turned away and left the room.

3

Bernice Mochardi didn't so much walk as glide to the stairs. Something more than gravity pulled her down, step after step. Below, in the stairwell, an impenetrable depth of darkness drew her in. The candlelight didn't illuminate very much now.

The shadows are thickening, she told herself. *They're seeping up from the cold grave-soil beneath the house. Darkness is filling the rooms. A black, liquid dark that will pool within the walls . . . rising higher and higher. Veined with ultraviolet, it will reach me, drown me . . .*

The candlelight dimmed still further. Its radiance no longer even splashed the walls. Before the pressure of darkness it folded in on itself until all that remained was a little scrap of light gathered about the wick. Now it seemed to Bernice that she followed a single faint star through the black heart of the house. She reached the ground floor. Cold fingers of air touched wherever her bare skin showed.

Drowsiness stole over her.

For some reason I was spared, Bernice told herself. *I woke up.* But they were reaching into her mind now, damping down her nerve endings, triggering sleep patterns, slowing her heart; replacing her scared intakes of breath with a slow, slow, rhythmic in . . . out . . . in . . . out . . . Fear was leaving her now. How pleasant it would be to lie down on one of the beds. Or right here on the hallway floor. Even the stone slabs didn't appear so forbidding. Sleep would take her. She wouldn't know any more . . . she wouldn't *fear* any more until the dawn came. Then everyone would wake. They would be safe . . .

But a voice flickered defiantly for a moment in her head. *If you sleep now, you'll never wake . . .*

Dreamily, Bernice glided through into the kitchen. The meagre light that the candle cast barely revealed the scene. Half a cake on a plate on the table. Cups upside down on the drainer. Cold soup with a whitening layer of fat covering the bottom of a pan. Now, barely awake, she moved slowly, step by step, across the kitchen to another door. The back door? More than anything she wanted to open the door. To step through. It was important that she do that. *But why?*

She remembered that David had told them not to leave the house on any account. Surely there could be no need now for that prohibition. They'd be free to walk outside in the pleasantly cool air. Reaching forward with her free hand, she gripped the handle, turned, pulled. The door whispered open. No . . . not outside. Another room. An annexe to the kitchen, where food was prepared on a butcher's block, a big one. Rows of pickle jars stood on shelves. Bunches of herbs hung from hooks fixed in the wall.

A cool breeze reached her. This one was more forceful than the others; the single spark that was the candle quivered, almost dying. Glancing round, Bernice saw a window consisting of just six panes, each of which was no larger than a book. One of them had been broken. The break showed as a star-shaped opening. Resting the candle on the butcher's block, she moved closer. The breeze feathered her hair.

How hot she felt. It would be so beautiful to put her face close to the hole. That cool play of air against her burning skin would be heaven. Still drowsy, still moving as if in a dream, Bernice leaned against the side of the recess in the wall that housed the deep-set window. Then, shifting her balance, she allowed her face to move closer and closer to the broken glass. Here the breeze washed in. So cool against her skin. She loved it. It sent a sexual thrill through her veins. Maybe if she unbuttoned the top of her blouse? Instantly, tongues of refreshing air licked across the upper part of her chest.

This *was* good. This *was* wonderful. *I could stay here all night.*

And when the face appeared at the far side of the glass – a man's face with the most beautiful green eyes she'd ever seen – she wasn't shocked in the least.

'Hello, Bernice.' His voice was a soft purr. 'My name is Ash White. Won't you open the door and let me in?'

CHAPTER 29

I

Bernice Mochardi gazed at the face that appeared to hang there in the darkness outside the broken window. There was no light, so how could she see him?

Ash White?

Was that what he'd called himself? She'd heard that name before. Ash White? *Why do I associate it with guitars, stars and blood?* Drowsily, Bernice rolled her head. All she wanted to do was sleep. The darkness seeped inside her now. It ran inward through her fingers, her toes; it filled her limbs. Soon it would pour through the main arterial thoroughfares of her body to her heart . . . what then?

'Hello, Bernice. My name is Ash White. Will you let me in?'

'You've already asked that,' she murmured.

'And will you?' He smiled. 'It only takes a little turn of the key.'

She shook her head. Even so, those green eyes intoxicated her. And that pure white hair of his was amazing. It wasn't grey hair. The face in front of her was young and strikingly handsome in a way that she'd never seen before. White hair, white face? That means he must be—

'Please, Bernice. I need to talk to you. It's important.'

—must be an albino.

Ash White. She remembered now.

Unable to move her head, feeling so sleepy that all she could do was murmur the words: 'North of West.'

He smiled his beautiful smile. 'Ah, you know my little secret. I used to be in a band called North of West. I played guitar.' The smile showed amazing teeth. 'I was pretty good.'

'Broxley . . .'

'Yes, he was in the band, too. In fact, he's somewhere close right now. But just between you and me, he played the bass guitar with all the finesse of a monkey knocking nuts out of a tree.'

'Oh?'

'But I know talent and beauty when I see them, Bernice.' The eyes burned brighter. That astonishing green . . . a clear tropical ocean of deep luminous green. *Tides of incredible power sweep through there* . . . 'Won't you let me in, please, Bernice? It's so cold out here.'

'No. Sorry.'

'Why not?'

'David told me not to open the doors.'

'David Leppington . . . ah . . .' He nodded. 'I really need to speak with him, too. A conversation between us is long, long overdue.'

Bernice's head sagged. A dark mist rolled in waves behind her eyes. She could barely stand.

'I won't trouble the others; just you and me. Then a chat with David Leppington. It's time for him now, you know?'

'I'm sorry.' She shook her head. 'Can't.'

An expression of fury crossed Ash White's face. The green in his eyes suddenly shrank until all that remained were twin black pupils. And, just for a moment, all the ferocity and violence in the world seemed to be concentrated there. Then they softened; the hard edges blurred, the beautiful green returned to shine there warmly. The green irises lazily expanded again, sending a warm flush through Bernice's body. She gazed at the snow-white face framed by hair that shone with the same luminous hue.

'Well,' he said gently. 'There's no point in my begging you to open the door. You've made your decision. I respect that.'

Drowsy, eyes barely open, Bernice nodded. Warmth suffused her blood. Sexy warmth.

Ash White's voice breathed through the broken windowpane and into her ears. 'There is *one* favour that I'd ask.'

'Oh?'

'Your hair. It's so rich and it shines like you wouldn't believe. May I touch it?'

Bernice didn't reply. A voice tried to reach her through the dark mist behind her eyes.

Ash White smiled his warm smile. 'Say no if you wish. I won't be offended. It's more important to me that we stay friends.'

'You like my hair?'

'Don't *like*. I **love** your hair, Bernice. I've never seen hair so beautiful. The way it falls around your face is incredible.'

'You can touch it if you wish.' The smile on her face felt as if it was due to some narcotic rather than to genuine pleasure. The undertow of drowsiness tugged hard now. The urge to sleep ran through her nervous system. That darkness that seeped up from the floor pressed toward her lungs and heart. Overwhelming pressure that left her light-headed.

Through barely open eyes she saw Ash reach in through the broken window. Her gaze took in the long fingers. They were slender – as bloodless white as his hair. His green-eyed stare touched her soul and she felt her heart open up to him. Her breath came in deep gulps; her skin tingled; heat flushed through her – an erotic heat. She wanted his touch now.

And the man had such beautiful nails. Pure white nails. The palms of his hands were soft, flawless.

With an incredible upwelling of pleasure Bernice drew a deep breath as Ash White's fingertips lightly touched her hair, then caressed it. So gentle. Caring. He curled strands of her hair round his fingers. Gradually he worked his fingers deeper into her tresses and all the time his green-eyed gaze burned into her soul. His fingers snaked round the back of her head. Once his fingertip brushed bare skin and such a flush of exhilaration ran through her that she tingled with an electric intensity through and along the length of her thighs.

Now Ash moved his hand behind her head. She felt the flat of his palm press there before closing into a fist that clutched her hair. But it felt so pleasant. His grip wasn't violent, but it conveyed a kind of passion suppressed so that it burned in a way that was positively *subterranean*. A muted power that would be released at any moment now. Slowly, he eased her head forward. Bernice saw the hole in the window-pane grow larger. At the same time his own face moved closer to hers, so that their lips might meet at the invisible boundary between the inside of the house and outside. His mouth opened as he tilted his head to one side, just inches away now; soon she'd feel the touch of his lips against hers.

An arm thrust violently into her field of vision. Hugely thick, bulging with hard muscles, tattooed in blue swirls from fingertip to elbow, it sliced through the air in front of her eyes. As that hand gripped Ash White's wrist, another hand grabbed Bernice's arm above the elbow and jerked her back so hard that her spine slammed against the butcher's block. She cried out with mingled shock and pain. The spell was broken; she was now wide awake.

Then the shock deepened to absolute terror. For there, moving like a dark god of vengeance and blood, was Jack Black.

He's dead . . . The words spat through her head. *He's dead; he can't—*

Stunned, Bernice could only watch as the tattooed giant with the shaven head gripped Ash White's arm, forced it down against the jagged spikes of glass and then dragged it back and forth in a sawing motion. She saw the flesh of White's forearm torn open by the razor-sharp glass. No blood came from the wound, but a cloudy, pale ooze smeared both White's arm and the broken edges of the window-pane.

Ash White howled. A raw sound charged with agony and anger and frustration. Instantly the candle blazed brighter. Bernice saw Jack Black gripping White's arm in his massive fist and continuing to saw the forearm against the broken glass. Only now she saw that what had once seemed like the flawless skin of White's hand was wormy with thick purple veins. The fingernails were misshapen, ragged, mottled with brown specks. And as for his face . . .

Bernice stared in horror at the mouthful of sharp teeth that were more sharklike than human. The foul mouth gnawed at the air in fury. Lake weed flecked the white hair with strands of toxic green. While the man-creature's eyes pulsed from blazing green to tiny black dots as the pupils contracted to twin fierce points.

Jack used the broken edge of the window-pane to shave flesh down to bone that was revealed as a grey hardness in the forearm. With a howl of fury so piercing that it cracked another pane Ash White wrenched his arm from Jack's grasp. A second later he was gone.

Icy winds blew through the shattered window. Beyond it, the hostile dark. A second blast of air killed the candle's flame, plunging the room into darkness.

2

Before Bernice could react, Jack Black – a huge masculine form that she sensed rather than saw – picked her up in his arms. She spun through the air as he lunged back through the doorway, into the kitchen . . .

He's going to take me outside, she thought, her heart clamouring. *He's going to take me into the wood where no one can see or hear what happens next . . . But then, why did he save me if—*

Bernice's racing thoughts stopped as Black moved into the hallway and the candlelight from the living room revealed his face. He gazed over her head, not even noticing her. His eyes, fixed and staring, appeared to be focused on something a hundred miles away through the walls of the house. Yet still his arms held her as firmly as steel bands. At first sight, his appearance had seemed the same as of old: the aggressive expression; the hard muscle beneath tattooed skin. And yet . . . the tattoos? The tattooed blue birds at the corner of his eyes swirled and morphed into winged snakes before reverting to birds. The red tear etched on one cheek shrank, then expanded. Only it wasn't a tear but a woman's face. Yet the second Bernice saw it as such it dissolved into a wash of pink that flooded his face like a blush before re-forming into the tear again.

He carried her into the lounge. Turning her head in his grasp she saw that Vikki and Rowan were still sleeping. A second later Jack dumped Bernice none too gently on the sofa beside Vikki. When Bernice tried to stand he put his hand on her shoulder and pushed her down.

Stay there. She recognized clearly enough what he meant by that shove back onto the cushions. Then, with a hard glance at her that seemed to penetrate the bones of her face to look deep inside her soul, Jack Black walked across the lounge and out through the door.

CHAPTER 30

I

David Leppington knew that something had happened the moment he woke. He checked his wristwatch. 6:15. Outside it was still black as Hades.

Why hadn't Bernice woken him at two a.m. for his turn at standing guard? There were fierce currents of air flowing through the house, too. They came shrieking under the closed bedroom door. Something was wrong – badly wrong . . .

He'd slept almost fully clothed; all he needed to do when he swung himself from the bed was to pull on his jacket and shoes. A moment later he ran downstairs to the lounge. When he threw open the door Bernice let out a squeal of fear. From the look in her eyes she'd expected to see someone else.

'Bernice. Why didn't you wake me?'

She sat on the sofa, clutching a cushion to her stomach. Her gaze darted toward the hallway.

'Bernice?'

'I tried. I couldn't wake anyone. I was the only one awake. I don't know why they . . . like a coma. I couldn't get through . . .'

Poor kid was so scared she could barely speak. David glanced at Rowan and Vikki. They both appeared to be deeply unconscious.

'OK,' David said, more gently. 'What happened?'

'I . . . I tried to wake you. I tried to wake everyone. It must have been the things outside. They'd put everyone into a deep sleep. You . . . You were . . . like dead. I—'

'Did the vampires try to get in?'

'They cut the electricity somehow. That's why I lit the candles. And in the little room off the kitchen they broke a window. When I went into the room I saw Ash White. He talked to me.'

'Ash White?'

'The man that Broxley wrote about. He was staying here when—'

'He vanished. Well, now we know what became of him.'

'He asked me to open the door and let him in. He said he had to speak to you.'

David shook his head. 'Then thank God you didn't.'

'The thing is, I nearly did.'

'Nearly?'

'I couldn't help myself.'

'Those things can reach into our minds. They do it well, too.'

Bernice grimaced. 'And, dear God help me . . . I let him touch me.'

'How? You didn't open the door, did you?'

Bernice gave an emphatic shake of her head. 'He put his hand through the broken window. I know he planned to grab hold and pull me so that he could reach me with his mouth.'

'But you managed to escape.'

'No.'

David's gaze searched her face and throat for a wound.

'No,' she repeated in a level voice. 'Jack Black saved me.'

'Jack Black? Impossible.'

'Believe me, David. It *was* Jack Black. I saw—'

'Jack's dead.'

'I know. But he's back.'

David saw her tear-filled eyes watching him closely. She seemed to be waiting for him to accuse her of dreaming, or hallucinating, or even allowing the vampires to implant the scenario in her mind. Instead, he crouched beside her to take her hand in his. 'What's important is that you're unharmed.'

'But you're going to write off what I saw as delusion?'

'Bernice. Not three days ago I had a perfectly rational conversation with a man who, I learned later, had been dead for several hours. There are people out there who lived and died more than a thousand years ago. Now they want the blood from our bodies. They can exert their influence on our minds.' He gave a grim smile. 'So you think I'm going to tell you you're mad for seeing a man who's been dead for only three years?'

'But why is he back?'

'I don't know.'

'He was on our side but he died a vampire. So why did he attack Ash White, then save me?'

'It sounds trite to use the phrase but the old Norse gods move in mysterious ways.'

'You mean they brought Jack here to dupe us?'

David nodded. 'It could be part of their strategy to confuse us. They might have conjured something in the form of Jack Black. Or they might have simply planted those images in your mind.'

'Like a dream?'

'Perhaps.'

'And I was really lying asleep here all night after all?'

'As I said, who knows?'

Bernice's expression hardened. She stood up quickly and tugged up the bottom of her blouse to expose her back. 'Then how would you explain this?'

David saw a fresh bruise forming a black line flecked with red. It ran across the lower half of her back.

She said, 'Jack threw me back against a butcher's block when he pulled me away from Ash White. Or can you dismiss a bruise as stigmata?'

'Bernice. I didn't mean that I doubted you. All I do know

for sure is that *I don't know* what the hell's going on here. If anything, I sense we're being manipulated like pieces on a chessboard. For all I know, whatever forces brought us here and whatever raised those things from the dead aren't in complete agreement among themselves.'

'You mean there's war in heaven?'

'In Norse heaven, perhaps.' He shrugged. 'Viking mythology is rife with stories of their gods falling out among themselves, and petty jealousies, and trying to outmanoeuvre rivals. It's possible that's what is happening now.'

'And we're the puppets on their—'

A groan interrupted her. David saw Rowan stirring. He yawned, glanced at his watch. 'Dear God,' he said. 'We were never supposed to fall asleep.'

David looked at Bernice. 'You'd best tell them what happened. I'll check the others.'

Taking one of the lighted candles, David went into the hallway as the grandfather clock chimed the half-hour at 6:30. The dawn should only be minutes away now. Swiftly, he climbed the stairs. He'd start with the top of the house, then work down. He glanced into the attic room where Dylan sat on the edge of the bed with his head in his hands. He still seemed drowsy but he was coming out of it.

'Dylan, come downstairs as soon as you can. It'll soon be light.'

Yawning, Dylan said, 'I thought we were supposed to be woken up at—'

'I know. We underestimated the power of Luke Spencer and his friends.'

With that, David went down to the next floor. Electra lay face down on the bed, her upper half almost hidden in the swirl of her blue-black hair. The sheet had slipped right down to expose a few inches of bare skin between her hair and the bedding. Her eyes were open. Whatever had exerted its influence on them and had pushed their minds down into a comatose state had weakened.

Perhaps it was because of the coming of the daylight?

But David was going to be contradicted in that supposition with brutal force.

2

When David reached Liz and Goldi's room Goldi was already standing there in the doorway, wearing nothing but a pair of jeans. Puzzled, the younger man rubbed his fingers through his bleached dreadlocks.

David saw him glance into the room, then look back at him. 'Hey, has anyone seen Liz?'

'She was with you.'

'She ain't no longer. Must have taken herself downstairs for something to eat.'

'I didn't see her downstairs.' David looked back up toward the second floor. There was only the attic room up there.

'Maybe she's in the can,' Goldi said, yawning again. 'Or taking a shower.'

'We need to check that she's safe.' The note of urgency in David's voice brought Goldi fully awake.

'You think she might be in trouble?'

'Hopefully not,' David said, hurrying downstairs. 'But check the rooms and the bathroom up here. I'll check the kitchen.'

3

Electra woke in a languorous mood. Through one half-open eye, she'd seen David standing the doorway, carrying a lighted candle.

I'm going to make you mine, she thought with delicious anticipation as she sensed him looking at her bare back.

Together we will rule . . . we will make this miserable world suffer for the disappointments it has inflicted on us . . .

The fog bloomed behind her eyes. With her will-power gone, memories that she'd deliberately suppressed came whirling back. The name-calling at school because she looked different and didn't act the way Leppington's other children behaved. History interested her. Pop music and comics didn't. The life stories of aristocratic Roman ladies and their intrigues and romances fascinated her. This led to the other children saying she was weird. Not just once or twice or over the course of a week but year after year at school. And year by year she built up her armour-plating of erudition and her protective force field of sardonic humour. *Sticks and stones may break my bones . . .*

Dreamily, Electra let her gaze wander round the room. She saw the deep brown ceiling timbers against white paintwork. On the far wall, the painting of trees in winter. A shelf with books and a blue crystal vase. Only it all seemed far, far away . . .

Soon David and I will be together. We will deal with Bernice Mochardi; she will not be a rival for his affections. And we must deal with Rowan, too. The mysterious brother. He's—

With a jolt Electra pushed herself up from the bed with her hands. Her skin crawled with cold. Her entire body felt stiff from lying in the same position for so long.

What on Earth's been happening to me? she thought. *Why was I thinking those mean thoughts about Bernice? Haven't I always counted her as a friend and ally? And was I really going to persuade David to accept that sick inheritance? That he should lead the vampires on their crusade?*

Electra shuddered, knowing only too well what had happened. Immediately she began to dress, feeling a sense of urgency. She had to warn David and the others. Especially David. These creatures had far stronger minds than the ones who had haunted the caves beneath Leppington had possessed. They could exert their influence over mortal minds as easily as one could change channels on a TV. If they didn't find a way to stop those loathsome monsters before night fell again then the battle would be lost. The vampires would take control.

4

It took David less than three minutes to establish that Liz Fretwell had left the house.

'But why on Earth would she do that?' Rowan asked as David headed back into the hallway. 'You saw that she was terrified of the things.'

'She might not have had any choice.'

'Any more than we chose to go to sleep,' Bernice added.

'You mean they might have got into her mind and ordered her outside?'

'Something like that.'

David paused in the hallway. 'Damn.'

'What is it?' Bernice asked from the doorway.

'The front door. Look.' David pointed. 'She's gone through it and closed the door after her.'

'How can you—'

'It's unbolted.' He tested the key. 'Unlocked, too.'

'The door's been unlocked all this time?' Rowan's eyes widened. 'Then they could have just walked straight in here.'

'Not if Electra's right,' Bernice told him. 'If this is holy ground to them the vampires won't enter the house without being invited.'

Goldi came downstairs at a run. 'You found her?'

'I'm sorry,' David said. 'It looks as if Liz has left the house.'

'Jesus Christ.'

David saw the guy's worried face. 'Are you sure you don't remember anything?'

'No . . .' Goldi shrugged. 'Well . . . it's nothing really.'

'What isn't?'

'I had this weird dream. This big, BIG man came into the bedroom, picked Liz up in his arms, then just walked out again. Like I said, it was just a—'

David snapped out the words, 'What did he look like?'

'I don't know . . . uh . . . big, like I said. Shaved head.'

Bernice fired the next question. 'Tattoos?'

'Yeah. Loads of tattoos. All over his arms, neck; he even had tattoos on his face . . . but how the hell can you know that? It was a dream, just a stupid—'

'Jack Black.' Bernice looked at David.

'He took her.' David nodded.

Goldi looked stung. 'Jack Black. Who the hell's he?'

'Someone from way back.'

'But how did he get in here to—'

'David. Liz is out there.' Bernice's voice assumed a note of anguish. 'We've got to get her back.'

Goldi still wanted answers. 'This Jack Black. You mean he's one of those vampires?'

Rowan shook his head, bewildered. 'David. You just said vampires couldn't enter the house?'

David saw the scared faces in front of him. 'Jack Black is dead. But he's no vampire. He's something else entirely.'

'Hey, but what, man?' Goldi became angry. 'You're talking in riddles, Leppington.'

'David . . .' Rowan held out his hands. 'If this Black isn't a vampire, what is he?'

Bernice moved to the door. 'We can stand and debate this or we can try and find Liz. She was naked when Black took her. Even if he doesn't harm her she'll freeze in—'

'Bernice is right.' David pulled a wool coat from the peg on the wall.

'Hey, David.' Rowan sounded appalled. 'You can't go outside.'

'Yes, I can.'

'With those monsters out there?'

'It's getting light. They'll be returning to the lake.'

'You a betting man?'

'It's as good odds as I'm going to get.' He folded the coat over his arm.

'If those things pounce you won't stand a chance.'

David found a grim smile twist his lips. 'I'm a blood Leppington, remember? They need me in one piece.'

'That's some gamble,' Rowan said.

'Hold on.' Goldi came down the last few stairs. 'I'll come with you.'

'No, you won't,' David told him, his voice uncannily calm. 'They'd tear you apart. Bernice?'

He saw her step forward, her face bloodless with fright.

'Bernice, when I'm through the door, shut it, lock it and bolt it. OK?'

'OK.'

'Hey, brother.' Rowan stepped forward. 'Don't run out on me just yet.'

David said, 'Rowan, you're these people's insurance. Stay here and look after them.'

He opened the door on a dawn that was colder than an ice tomb. 'Bernice, lock the door as soon as I'm through. Don't open it again until I say.'

From upstairs he heard a clattering of feet on stairs. Electra called down, 'David, don't go out there! There's something I've got to tell you!'

Sorry, Electra. It'll have to wait. He stepped through the door. 'Now, Bernice.'

He paused while the door closed behind him. He heard the bolts shoot home. Then he turned to face whatever lay outside.

CHAPTER 31

I

The garden of Lazarus Wake lay dead in the grip of winter. In the dreary half-light David took in the entire surrounding landscape at a glance. Bleak hilltops swept by cloud. A forest black with deciduous trees long since stripped of leaves. The driveway stretching away to the road. Evergreen bushes with leaves like flayed lizard skin. A lawn still whitened here and there with swathes of hailstones. A statue with its face gouged and ruined by decades of frost and rain. And there, standing just beyond Electra's car, a line of three men – what had once been men – with ice-white skins and torn clothes that exposed yet more bloodless flesh. David saw the tracery of blue veins beneath their skin. Shading that made it look as though the skin tissues were bruised surrounded their eyes. Nevertheless, it made the eyes look more prominent. Even in this gloom of a winter's dawn those orbs blazed as if fires burned within the beings' skulls.

With the coat folded over his arm David stepped onto the driveway. He approached the three figures. They watched him, without moving. Immediately he recognized the albino with the white hair and green eyes. Somehow he had the face of a young man that had been blended with the features of something a lot more ancient.

David's stomach fluttered but he willed himself to show no fear to these creatures. 'Ash White.'

The albino gave a single nod.

'And these two must be Luke Spencer and Rick Broxley.' Closer now, David noted the sick mottling of greys on their skin, the traces of lake weed flecking their hair. 'Am I correct?'

'Correct.' Ash White nodded again. 'You are David Leppington.'

'So you know who I am?'

'Of course.' White leaned forward a little and inhaled. 'We can smell the blood of a Leppington even through stone walls.'

'Then you know you must not touch me.'

Ash White twisted his face into a smile. David saw the cluster of pointed teeth. 'The word, I believe, is inviolate.'

The creature that had once been Rick Broxley spoke. 'We have been waiting to put a proposal to you.'

'I had a feeling you might. But first I must find my friend from the house.'

'The naked woman.'

'You've seen her?'

'Yes.'

David sensed that the vampires wouldn't attack. Not yet, anyway. 'Don't let me keep you,' he told them.

'Why's that?'

This time it was Luke Spencer who'd spoken. As a recent vampire convert, his body language was more human. There was also more inflection, more colour in his voice. It wasn't as flat and formal as those of the other two who must have crossed from humanity to vampirism a decade ago.

'It's getting light,' David told them.

'So?'

'Then you'll be wanting to slither away and hide where it's dark and wet.'

'Think again, Leppington,' Luke growled. 'We're different from those cunts you wiped out way back when.'

A shiver of unease ran down David's spine. He didn't let it show. 'For you, maybe. But the rest of your clan seem to have returned to the lake.'

'No. You're wrong.' Ash White inclined his head at the forest behind him. 'Our people were distracted by the bait.'

'Bait?'

'Liz Fretwell,' Luke said. 'The big ugly guy carried her into the wood.'

'And your wolf pack followed?' David began to understand. 'And they were distracted enough to stop exerting their control on my friends in the house.'

Rick Broxley grinned the sharks'-teeth smile. 'They're merely out of practice. Don't rely on the same stunt working twice.'

'I'm going to bring Liz back to the house. You won't stop try and stop me, will you?'

Ash White shrugged. '*We* won't.'

That sounds like a warning, David told himself as he walked past the three vampires.

2

David walked quickly to the wood. Maybe it was too late? There'd been hundreds of vampires out here last night. They'd have pounced on Liz the first chance they got. But if they had done, they wouldn't be waiting in the wood. They'd be back at the house, gloating. If Luke Spencer was right, daylight didn't faze these monsters.

David glanced back at the house just before he plunged into the bushes that lined the driveway. The building stood there in the cold morning light. The three pale figures were still maintaining their vigil. Waiting for what? Any more escapes? Beyond the house he glimpsed the meadow that ran down to the dark waters of Lazarus Deep.

His stomach muscles tightened as he crossed the driveway into the woodland where Dylan's car had crashed just the day before. If the vampire horde had carried Liz off they might be miles away by now. But he'd barely run the scenario through his head when he came across a clearing in the trees. There, crowding around a pair of figures, were dozens of vampires. These were the ancient ones, with hairless heads and eyes that contained hard, dark pupils and nothing else. Most were naked. All had their attention fixed on the figures in the centre of the clearing.

One of the figures was large, brutish. It held the second figure. This was Liz. She whipped her head from side to side in obvious terror. He heard her shout.

But was that larger figure Jack Black? A shadow seemed to have fallen across him. David couldn't be sure. He ran forward, weaving round the vampires, doing his best to avoid physical contact with them. He relied on the fact that he was a blood Leppington, that his divine ancestry as conveyed by family legend would protect him from attack. Only he couldn't guarantee it. He could only hope.

For some reason the vampires hadn't rushed the couple as they stood there. Something had been holding them back. Something as formidable as Jack Black. In any event David would soon see if—

He stopped abruptly. There was Liz Fretwell, shivering, naked, dried blood on her thighs. But where was the second, larger figure?

The ground's swallowed him. The phrase flashed into David's head. He guessed he might be close to the truth. If Jack had finished the task he'd been given by whoever, then his dark and brooding presence would no longer be required. This was confirmed by sudden movement from the vampires. They ducked their heads. Their entire body language changed. They were getting ready to attack. Some individuals took a jerking step forward as if to gauge their target's response.

David strode forward. 'Wait!' He stood in front of the naked woman who folded her arms in front of her and hunched her shoulders with her head down, trying to look as small as possible. 'Stay back!' he shouted at the vampires, and tried not to flinch in front of those faces that mated hunger with savagery. 'You know who I am. You know you can't touch me.'

Prove it, David thought. *Show them*. He took an aggressive step toward the nearest one: a huge buck vampire with a hairless head and black arteries that traced a pattern like netting across his chest and face. For a second the twin pinprick pupils set in eyes of ice glared into his. David sensed it coiling its muscles, ready to spring.

Then it suddenly dropped its gaze, avoiding eye contact. Its shoulders lowered. David took another step toward it, staring it down. Without hesitation now it took a step back; a gesture of submission.

'Now . . . listen to me.' David moved back to Liz where he slipped the coat around her shoulders. 'I'm walking back to the house. This woman is coming with me. You will not attack her; you will not touch her. Understand?' His gaze swept over the dozens of monstrous faces there. 'She is not to be harmed.' David pulled the coat around her bare throat. 'OK,' he whispered to her. 'Walk back to the house. Stay directly in front of me.'

'But I—' Her voice was a croak.

'It's all right. I'll be right behind you. Just keep walking. Don't look back. You'll be fine.'

As Liz started to walk, her bare feet almost blue against the frozen grass, David followed, sweeping his gaze left to right, staring the vampires down. They parted in front of him, their powerful, humped shoulders sagging. When he looked them in the face they broke eye contact and turned their heads aside.

David walked steadily behind Liz through the wood. Ahead, he saw the line of bushes that marked the driveway. The house was perhaps a thirty-second walk beyond that. Liz's frightened breathing showed as puffs of white vapour.

Keep walking, keep walking, he mentally urged himself as well as her. *Not far now.*

When they were a dozen paces from the driveway, David saw a raven land on a branch. He noticed that it angled its head to one side, watching them intently. It seemed to be actively considering the image of the two figures that presented itself to its glassy eyes.

This is no ordinary raven, David told himself. Immediately a spasm of dread hit him. The bird opened its beak and let out a screech of such volume that David had to half turn from the force of it.

And that was where it ended.

The vampires surged forward in a tsunami of white flesh, bald heads bobbing, arms stretching out, fingers hooked. Not one of them touched David. They didn't even brush against him as they rushed their victim. He could do nothing.

Except watch. White claw fingers shredded the coat from Liz's body, then they ripped into her bare skin. Screaming, she was caught by a dozen powerful arms and tossed head high as they passed her across the ravenous mob whose jaws were snapping voraciously. There wasn't much to satisfy their hunger.

But what there was they shared.

CHAPTER 32

I

Two hours had elapsed since David Leppington's return to the house alone. Dylan found him sitting to the kitchen table, his head to one side as he stared at the coffee cup in front of him. Dylan realized that the man probably wasn't even seeing the liquid in the cup whose contents must have been long cold by now. He must be replaying over and over again the events of that morning when he had tried to save Liz Fretwell.

Dylan asked, 'Can I get you a fresh cup? There's still some in the pot.'

The man's eyes had that no-one-home glaze.

'David?'

'Hmm?'

'Coffee? There's some left.'

'I've got a full cup. Thanks, Dylan.'

Dylan watched as David Leppington woke from the daydream . . .

No, not daydream. A wide-awake nightmare, more like. David took a swallow of the beverage, then reacted with displeasure. He couldn't have noticed that he'd sat there watching it grow cold.

'I'll get you a fresh one,' Dylan told him. He took the cup, rinsed it, then refilled it from the pot on the hob.

'How's Goldi?'

'Down, I guess.'

'It's a wonder he's not climbing the walls after what happened to . . .' David shrugged, not finishing the sentence.

'He and Liz weren't dating or anything. As she would have said, she didn't get serious, she only fucked for fun.'

'Well, she's fucked now . . . I'm sorry. I didn't mean to say that.' David took a deep swallow of coffee, this time wincing as it scalded his lips. 'Stupid thing to say.'

'You've been through hell this morning. No one's going to blame you.'

'But have you ever wished you could turn back time . . . take another run at things?'

'Always.'

'You know, I really thought I had those monsters under control. I was certain that if I'd ordered them to jump in the air they'd have done it like that.' He clicked his fingers.

'They didn't try and attack you?'

'No, but there was damn-all I could do to save Liz.'

Dylan had been thinking about a question that he hadn't been able to ask until now. 'What happened to Liz?'

'I told you. They ripped her open with their teeth, then they shared her out like you'd pass round a . . . a fucking spliff.'

'Or holy wine at Communion?'

'Maybe it was a bit of both, huh? A sacred rite.'

Dylan took a deep breath. 'But what I really meant, David, is what happens to her *now*?'

'Now? She becomes one of them. She's vampiric.'

'Hell . . . there's no cure?'

'The cure's death. Or more correctly, seeing as she's now only dead flesh walking, the cure is annihilation.' He flicked his fingers under his chin. 'Beheading's the only sure way.'

Dylan found himself recalling his visit to Lazarus Deep just a few nights ago. He remembered the strange, female-sounding cry that had sent him on the midnight search through the trees at the edge of the water. There he'd found the injured fox. Later he'd wondered why the animal hadn't bled from its horrific wounds. In fact, there hadn't been so much as a drop of blood in the creature. Now he knew why. The vampires craved the lifeblood of every living thing, even a humble fox. He moved to the kitchen window where he eased aside the curtain so that he could look out. A one-second glimpse was enough. He pulled the curtain so that it covered the window again.

'Still there?'

Dylan nodded. 'Still there.'

'And it's, what? Getting on for mid-morning?'

'I thought they didn't like the daylight?'

'These vampires don't. It won't kill them but it makes them uncomfortable, probably even makes them feel vulnerable.'

'It could be the weather. The cloud's so dense it's only half light out there anyway.'

'Or . . .'

'Or? You've another theory about them?'

David sipped his coffee. 'Or, as your friend Luke Spencer told me, they really are evolving.'

'If daylight doesn't worry them, then we're screwed.'

'Looks like it.' Dylan saw the man wince again. This time at the flippant response. This really was a man who cared about people. If he made a comment that later seemed – to him – flippant or rude you could see that tremor on his face as if he was mentally kicking himself for talking in such a careless way.

'It does present a real problem,' David said, this time more thoughtfully.

'They have us under siege?'

'For the time being.'

'They won't try and break in here?'

'I don't think so. They might try to starve us out.'

'*No. You're wrong.*'

Dylan turned round to see who'd disagreed with David's statement. Electra stood in the doorway. Dressed in black, with that wash of gunmetal blue-black hair and armed with a formidable aura Dylan guessed that not many people disagreed with her.

He saw that David was more interested in her statement than annoyed by it. 'Why do you say I'm wrong, Electra?'

'Because we've underestimated the vampires.' She went to the jug to pour herself a coffee. There were only a few silty grounds in the bottom. 'Empty.' She tutted. 'Life's like that, isn't it? All promise but no delivery?'

'I know *I* underestimated them.' Dylan recognized the bitter tone in David's voice. 'I didn't anticipate they would attack the woman when I was bringing her back here. I didn't think they'd stay here in the daylight, when by rights they should have slithered back to the fucking lake.'

'David isn't to blame—'

'I know he isn't, Dylan. None of us are responsible for what has happened here. But we *will* be to blame if we don't stop the vampires doing whatever they're planning to do.'

Dylan looked from face to face. 'And for that they need David, a blood Leppington, right?'

'Or Rowan,' David corrected him.

Electra continued, 'The vampires need a human from the Leppington bloodline who is alive in the natural sense rather than like that bunch of dead meat out there that's been reanimated through supernatural trickery.'

'Some trickery.'

'But they are still limited. They need a human being, albeit with the divine blood of Thor beating in his veins, to lead them. They need the human ability to plan forward, they need human insights, human intelligence – something that the vampires don't have an abundance of.'

'So they operate through instinct rather than through intelligent thought.'

'Correct, Dylan. That's one of the reasons they will have recruited – for want of a better word – the likes of Ash White, Rick Broxley and Luke Spencer. Although they are now vampiric themselves they should retain for months if not for years those human assets that the creatures most clearly treasure.'

'And now they have Liz, too.'

'Yes.'

David held out his hands. 'But what I don't understand is this: if Jack Black was really here, why did he save Bernice from the vampires but then take Liz Fretwell out to them as some kind of offering?'

Electra gave a grim smile. 'Now that's what I've been pondering for the last couple of hours. When you think about it, it's quite simple.'

'Go on.'

'Jack saved Bernice because he remembered that three years ago he and Bernice were on the same side against a common enemy.'

'OK, why did he throw Liz to the vampires?'

'Because, David, we have underestimated the bad guys. They are able to exert their will so strongly that they can render us unconscious. They can also implant ideas into our minds; in fact, they're not far short of controlling us like puppets.'

'That doesn't explain Liz—' Dylan began.

'It does, Dylan, dear,' Electra explained. 'Jack knew that the vampires controlled our minds. He also knew that it required their total concentration to maintain that control.'

David whistled. 'So he broke their concentration by distracting them with—'

'A tasty treat, if that doesn't sound too callous.' Electra's gaze was hard.

David added, 'Ash White and his cronies suggested that something like that happened.'

Dylan was appalled. 'You mean this Black character, whatever he is, deliberately sacrificed Liz?'

'That's how Jack works,' Electra told him. 'He never did agonize over moral issues. He just did whatever was necessary to save us.'

Dylan could only shake his head in horror.

'So you realize now why I disagreed with your observation about Ash White and his cohorts starving us out?'

'They're going to come back again with that mind-control thing?' Dylan nodded toward the window.

'Yes, gentlemen. Without a doubt.'

'Why don't they try it now?'

'You'll notice, if you watch them from the window for any length of time, that they don't stand in the open for long.' Electra gave a little shrug of her shoulders. 'The darlings don't take kindly to daylight. Most return to the shadow of the forest for a few minutes to recuperate before coming back.'

'So they *are* weaker during daylight hours?'

'A little.'

David stood up. Dylan could see the man was thinking hard. 'Which means they can't get inside our heads for a while yet.'

'Probably not until nightfall.' Electra shot a glance back at the grandfather clock in the hall. 'Only that isn't a long time away. Another seven hours. Seven and a half at most, depending on cloud cover.'

2

'So that's the current situation,' David told them as they sat in the lounge. He'd just spent half an hour rerunning the conversation that he'd had with Electra and Dylan in the kitchen. Sundown was maybe seven hours away. The tick of the grandfather clock in the hallway seemed to be racing faster, speeding along the minutes until darkness.

Rowan shrugged. 'But we should still be safe here in Lazarus Wake. If Electra's right, then it's holy ground. Our enemy won't dare violate it by breaking in.'

'*If* I'm right,' Electra said with feeling.

'I believe she is,' David said. 'But tonight they're going to come back and they're going to congregate out there, put us back into a coma, while they focus on each of us in turn to try and take control of one of us.'

Vikki sat forward on the sofa. 'And you're saying that might just entail persuading one of us to open the door and invite them in?'

'That could be enough.' Bernice nodded. 'And once they are inside . . .' Pointedly, she didn't finish the sentence.

Goldi spoke angrily. 'Shit, what we have to do is either get ourselves right away from here or call in help.'

David shrugged. 'Mobiles can't receive a signal here. They've ripped down the telephone cable so we can't use e-mail. We can't even *see* another house from here, never mind reach one.'

'We could just make a run for the car.'

Bernice made a *No-no-no* sound as she shook her head. 'You haven't seen how fast those things move. You wouldn't even make it from the front door to the car.'

Electra gave a grim smile 'And believe me, boys and girls . . . our foe is legion. If you were lucky enough to get into the car they'd simply tip it over, then start working on the windows. We're safer here. For now.'

Vikki came to the point. 'But only until tonight. Until sunset. That's when they will be strong again.'

David agreed. 'So we can't deal with this in a passive way.'

Goldi frowned. 'What do you mean?'
'First rule of defence. We must attack first.'

3

From **Hotel Midnight**:

Electra here. My dear friends, some of you have criticized me for alleging that the past not only affects our present (and, therefore, all our futures), but that the past is something akin to a tide that with uncanny regularity sweeps up the beach of our here-and-now. Right, you've all seen model aircraft operated by remote control. The boy in the meadow stands there with the radio control unit; he makes the airplane climb or dive or turn. He does not touch the model plane but he nonetheless steers it.

Events in history become the radio control unit that affects the course of our lives today. Before you flame me with your e-mails permit me, boys and girls, to present my case. First a simple example. As you read this, what day is it today? Monday? Tuesday? Wednesday? I'm writing this on Thursday. And Thursday is so named after the Viking god of thunder, Thor, which gives us Thor's Day. Wednesday is Odin's (or Othin's) Day: it is named after the patriarch of the Viking gods. Friday is named after his wife, Freya, goddess of love. Don't you see? Such was the power of the pagan gods and of our ancestors' belief in them that we still invoke their names every time we mention these days of the week.

Now, my dear children, I'll elaborate on this hypothesis that events in ancient history possess the power of remote control over our lives today. In the English city of York seventeen hundred years ago a young man by the name of Constantine was crowned Emperor of the Roman Empire, and so become that most elevated of beings THE MOST POWERFUL MAN IN THE WORLD, just like the American president today. If on the day that Constantine became emperor he'd taken to his bed with a fever and died the world you live in today would be a very, VERY different one.

Why is that? I hear you clamour. Because the Emperor Constantine, born a pagan, chose to become a Christian. What's more, he decreed that the Roman Empire should became a Christian organization. That's why what we call 'the West' has been Christian for a thousand years or more. By replacing pagan beliefs with a Christian belief system Constantine pressed a button on his figurative remote control panel and reprogrammed the minds of his own people and those of Western culture for ever.

These 'one-day' events in history that became the remote control over our lives today are numerous. Hitler saved from death by an Allied soldier in the First World War. The assassination of Kennedy. The Fall of the Berlin Wall. The Twin Towers, September 11.

You never know when another single-day event will transform world history. It might happen today.

4

They'd been silent for more than ten minutes in the lounge of the remote house that overlooked Lazarus Deep. The wind cried across the rooftop. Outside, the forest was stirring. The night was just six hours away.

At last, Rowan looked round at the six remaining people – David Leppington, Bernice Mochardi, Electra Charnwood, Vikki Lawton, Goldi, Dylan Adams.

'OK,' Rowan said. 'What are we going to do?'

CHAPTER 33

I

Good question, David told himself. *What are we going to do?* It was late morning. Dusk was only six hours away. That was when the vampires would mass again outside the house and exert their will on its occupants. The tick-tock of the grandfather clock sounded louder than ever. Already he hated the noise. More than anything he wanted to smash the damn thing into silence. *Only that won't stop time, will it?*

These thoughts passed through David's mind in a single moment as he scanned the tired, drawn faces of the people in the room. The lounge held the gloom of the winter's day tight to itself. Dark cloud rolling over the sky sealed the valley in a grim half-light. Draughts once more whispered through the cracks in the floor. It didn't take much to picture the lips of corpses whispering dark prophecies from beneath the ancient stone slabs, their cold, cold breath playing around the ankles of those who sat waiting so anxiously.

The slow tick and tock of the old timepiece. The sound of a heartbeat in a tomb. A sound from the grave that chilled David to the roots of his bones.

What do we do now? Rowan's question still hung on the air, unanswered.

What can *we do now?*

The chiming of the clock was enough to startle everyone.

'Damn thing,' Electra muttered.

David crossed the lounge, heading for the hallway. Silencing the bloody clock would be a start. The sound its mechanism made wore at everyone's nerves. If he could—

Jesus . . . sweet Jesus . . .

In the doorway of the lounge he stopped dead with shock. The front door of the house was wide open. Beyond it on the driveway stood the vampires. They stared into the house with those piercing eyes.

Dear God in Heaven, who opened the door? Sensing another presence in the hallway, David spun round. A shadow loomed over him as it moved forward. Without a word, it reached out its arms, seized him with its hands and threw him bodily from the house.

2

David landed in a sprawl of limbs at the feet of the vampires. Impassive, they gazed down at him, their naked skulls the colour of wet clay in this grim half-light. They were naked. Arteries bulging against their skin formed patterns. Random shapes, but chance formed them into barbarous runes, swastikas and gallows crosses.

Winded from the impact of the fall, David rolled sideways, expecting the monstrous figure that had lobbed him so easily from the house to attack. What he saw froze the breath in his lungs. There, looking larger than life, and far more brutal than he remembered, was Jack Black.

You're dead, David told himself, frozen with shock. *You died three years ago.*

Just for a second his mind sped back those long-dead years to the tunnel beneath Leppington town. Jack Black had been killed by the monsters that had haunted the labyrinth. He was vampiric. And David had destroyed him.

Now Black was back. But David had dismembered the body. Black could no longer be a vampire. Was he something else now? Had some other force returned him to this remote house? Clearly he'd been resurrected for a purpose . . . whatever that was . . .

To hand me over to the vampires? To kill me? To make me one of them? David saw the bestial man close the front door of the house. He saw the gleam of the meagre light on his shaven skull. He saw the bare arms covered with tattoos, and when Black turned David saw the face. That, too, had been rendered even more menacing by tattooed birds at the corner of the eyes, a tattooed tear on one cheek, and tattooed daggers at either side of this throat.

Jack Black's stare swept down at David. Then, with an expression of absolute ferocity on his face, he bent down, seized David's arm and yanked him to his feet. David expected to be pushed into the arms of the waiting vampires. Instead Black ignored them. His massive hands came up and he shoved David along the driveway.

David rounded on his one-time ally. 'Jack. You can't do this. You can't touch—'

Black didn't hear. Or he didn't listen. He pushed David again. That blank cold stare looked right through him. The actions were robotic. He merely pushed David forward, then walked up to him; pushed again.

When they reached the frozen grass David slipped, falling flat on his back. Jack Black bent down, grabbed him by the sleeve and hoisted him to his feet as effortlessly as if he'd been a feather-filled pillow. Then it started again, pushing him away from the house, down the meadow toward where the lake lay like a slab of lead beneath the cloud.

From the tops of the hills came the growl of thunder, so low it could be felt rather than heard. An icy wind tugged David's hair, so sharply cold that his eyes watered. All he could see now through blurred eyes was the monstrous shape of Jack

Black pushing him downhill to the lake. And each shove was like a blow. It knocked the breath from his body. His chest and back already ached wherever the meaty paw had crashed against him.

'Black, what do you want?'

No reply.

'Do you want to show me something?'

No words. Not even the sound of the man's breathing.

But then David doubted that whatever was pushing him, whatever had assumed the shape of Jack Black, needed to breathe.

'You're not Jack Black, are you? You're a— Uph—'

Another brutal shove sent him crashing through the branches of a bush. Twigs scratched his face and hands. He stumbled. Fell.

'OK, what do you want to show me?'

The shape loomed forward, seized David by the front of his sweater and lifted him to his feet. Then the brutal pushing started all over again.

'What is it, Jack?'

Shove!

'If you really are Jack—'

Push!

'Can't you speak?'

Shove! David fought to keep his balance. He wiped his eyes, trying to bring the blurred world back into focus. But his entire universe seemed to have been reduced to this march down to the water's edge with him being driven forward by pushes that had the ferocity of hammer blows. His ribs ached. He could hardly breathe. Then hands gripped him again. This time the air roared in his ears as he was propelled furiously forward. For whole moments the ground beneath his feet vanished. Blurred shapes swirled around his head. Then he collided with the ground. This time it crackled and shifted under

him. Jack Black had thrown him onto the shingle beach of
Lazarus Deep.

3

David pulled himself into a sitting position, wincing when he
moved his bruised knees. Just an arm's length away, Lazarus
Deep rolled its dark waters against the shore. A wet, gluttonous
sound. Even the lake seethed with its own hunger, sucking hard
at the earth surrounding it. Drawing the life-force from plants
and trees so that they rotted at the shore's edge.

He found his gaze drawn to the lake. Somehow it no longer
looked like water. It became monstrous . . . alien. What he was
seeing formed the image of a mammoth gelatinous eye that
that stared from its skull of rock. A bloated body of poison six
miles by three miles . . . pregnant with ominous intent. Its dark
waters swirled; hundreds of waves shivered across the face of
the lake to hit the shoreline, morphing the hungry sucking
sounds to something that sounded like laughter to David's
ears. Mocking laughter that rose from its lightless depths,
where cold shapes writhed and mated and gave birth to monsters that were as ugly and as loathsome as a rotted carcass.

Muted thunder rumbled again. David looked up to the dark
despair of those remote hills that had gazed down on the face
of Lazarus Deep for an eternity. Cloud as morbidly grey as
coffin lead weighed down overhead, threatening to drown this
dead landscape for ever.

'For ever and ever, world without end, Amen . . .' David
found himself uttering the words as he knelt there, feeling
that he'd become the sacrificial offering before the altar. The
upswelling of water hypnotized him. He found he couldn't
stop looking at it. There were more than vampires in the lake.
Something about Lazarus Deep terrified him . . . it whispered
a wordless yet monstrous prophecy. It knew his future . . .

With an effort David tore his stare from the lake. He looked up at Jack Black as the huge figure towered there on the shore. The tattooed brute was staring into the lake too. Only his formidable gaze had the focus of someone who saw deep into the lake's dark heart.

'What is it? What do you want me to see?' Thunder swelled as if to drown his words so that the man-shaped creature would not hear them. 'Is there something in the lake? *Something else?*'

Jack Black's eyes burned with spectral fires. He turned from the water to stare into David's face. Slowly he raised an arm. Pointing into Lazarus Deep.

David looked at the evil waters. 'The lake? I don't see anything there.'

Black pointed, his arm outstretched like the limb of a huge tree.

David shook his head. 'I still don't see anything. Can't you tell me what it is you're trying to show me?'

Still the man pointed. Eyes blazing, peering intently into David's face.

David shook his head. 'Whose side are you on, Jack? Are you trying to help me . . . and – and Bernice and Electra? Or are you with the vampires?'

For a moment the man didn't react. Not even a flicker of emotion passed over that stone face. Then he did move. Reaching down, he picked David bodily from the ground and raised him over his head.

David saw the swirl of earth, sky and water. Thunder sounded.

'Jack! No . . . Jack, you can't—'

Then, with a jerk hard enough to wrench his neck muscles, David found himself flying through the air. Icy wind tugged at his hair, his clothes.

A second later he struck water. Instantly the savage cold of the lake stabbed through his clothes to scour his skin. Shock exploded along his nerves to detonate even more fiercely in his brain. He'd never felt cold like this before. When he opened his mouth to scream water gushed into his throat. He felt himself swallowing the toxic liquid by the pint. Its cold presence felt like frozen iron in his guts.

Even though David wanted more than anything for his eyes to remain closed the sheer agony of the cold forced them open. He found that he could see through the water with an uncanny clarity. Beneath him, rounded stones ended at the edge of an underwater cliff. As he tried to swim back to the surface lake currents tugged him further out. Seconds later he was past the cliff edge. Now the lake bed lay at some unknown distance beneath his kicking feet. Particles of silt glinted bright as stars in a watery cosmos.

A moment later he saw men and women. Or what had been men and women a long time ago. Silently, the lake's vampires glided up with alien grace from the gloom below to hang suspended in the water, their arms held out at either side. Some were hairless, some had weedlike mats of hair that floated poisonously around their heads.

Closest was Liz. She stared at him as if fascinated. Her naked body had a near-Dalmatian mottling of bites and bruises. Even her breasts were marked with puncture wounds. Not that she minded now that she was vampiric like the rest of these aquatic creatures.

She was smiling.

4

From **Hotel Midnight:**
Electra's here, boys and girls.

The Gods of the Vikings are as capricious as those of the Romans, Greeks and Egyptians. Those celestial families might be divine. Their lives are anything but. They plot. They intrigue. They're in eternal conflict among themselves.

Now, as I promised earlier, my dears, here's your bedtime story. The Norse god Loki is the bastard offspring of God and Monster. Thor and Odin are friendly toward him when they need his cunning. When they do not they ignore him or are openly hostile. But Loki does not forget. Norse sages prophesize that when Ragnarok comes – the day of Doom – Loki's demonic children will topple Odin and Thor, and then they'll bring about the end of the world . . .

5

Liz moved slowly through the water, using her bare arms to almost stroke her way through it. Her smile had sensual warmth; her eyes were bright; her body still held that youthful eroticism. David looked away, then tried once more to swim to the surface. His lungs burned. He needed air. Yet the current tugged him further from the shore. All around him now vampires hung suspended in the water. Whatever the protection being a blood Leppington offered, it seemed fragile now. They might not attack him, but they might just float there like men-shaped jellyfish and watch him choke on this evil-tasting lake water.

Heart thudding in his ears, he swam for a surface that wrinkled in an ever-shifting ceiling of light. As he swam he kept glancing down to make sure that the vampires kept their distance. Liz smiled, turning so that she presented her naked body fully to him.

And yet, below her, another shape was rising from the darkness. David's eyes widened. When he believed he couldn't get any colder his veins flooded with a deep winter chill. The shape was long, torpedo-like. At this moment it revealed itself as a shadow against the deeper darkness. It moved swiftly, smoothly . . . up, up, up . . . David knew it was heading toward him. Even though he couldn't identify the thing that moved with the predatory menace of a shark he sensed its threat. Somehow this potent shape enshrined the sense of foreboding he'd felt earlier.

By now he'd forgotten the urgent need to breathe. He had to see what was rising so silently but so swiftly from the black gulf beneath his feet.

CHAPTER 34

I

The shadow that was the shape of a torpedo glided upward. A ghostly comet of the deep that had swung in its orbit through that Gothic darkness ever since this abyss had been engulfed by water six thousand years ago.

David's eyes blazed down through the lake as he hung suspended there in the centre of the shoal of vampires. The object rose smoothly. *And I just know that you're bringing me a nightmare,* David told himself. Just exactly what kind of nightmare eluded him. But like that ominous torpedo shape below him, realization floated in the back of his mind, just beyond recognition. But it was coming. Whatever it was, that shape somehow contained the answer to the question: *What do I do now?*

Here it comes. The dark, forbidding engine that will drive the events of my immediate future.

Breathe!

Blossoms of purple expanded in David's mind as oxygen starvation threatened to overwhelm him.

BREATHE!

How long he'd been underwater since Jack had thrown him into the lake, he didn't know. It seemed like hours, yet it could only have been moments. But now . . .

BREATHE!

His heart pounded. He needed air in his lungs. Already unconsciousness was rising over him like a tide. Lungs burning, head aching so much that it felt as if it would explode, he swam upward as fast as he could. The sheet of silver that was the under-surface of the lake filled his vision. Then he was through. Vicious streams of cold air struck him in the face. His limbs seemed as if they were encased in concrete but he forced himself to tread water while he held his face skyward and sucked in deep lungfuls of air. For two minutes, three minutes, David kept himself afloat. All the time he breathed hard, drawing oxygen down into his body. On the shore twenty metres away stood Jack Black. He stood there, arms at his side, moving not so much as a muscle. All he did was stare in David's direction.

With fresh oxygen racing through David's bloodstream, sensation returned to his body with a vengeance. His lungs tingled, while his entire skin surface suffered the onslaught of the brutal cold.

Ten minutes of this and I'll die of exposure, he told himself. Common sense told him to swim to the shore, then get back to the house as quickly as possible. Thunder muttered darkly in the distance again. Above him the sky had darkened. Hail began to fly through the air once more. *OK, time to get out of the water . . .* Only he knew that he couldn't. Not yet. He had to see what was swimming up toward him from the depths.

2

Taking a huge lungful of air, David dived back down under the surface. With his eyes open wide he looked down. There were the vampires again, hanging naked in the body of the lake. While beneath them rose the shape.

Now he saw that its skin was brown, while the body had resolved itself into something more like a snake's. David forced himself to stare into the icy depths, willing his eyes to identify the object that seemed so laden with the potential for terror. Seconds later he saw a pair of round eyes that were black as engine oil.

It's a fish, he realized, surprised. *A giant catfish.*

More than six feet long, with pulsing gills and long trailing barbels, it swam slowly up through the figures that hung below him. David was surprised to see how the vampires reacted. They flinched. They hadn't expected to see the catfish. Somehow it also held significance for them, too. For a moment it circled David, slowly moving its powerful tail fin to drive it forward. Soon he felt the need to breathe again as the oxygen in his lungs became exhausted. But he couldn't leave yet. There was something about this giant fish . . . something he should see . . .

This is what Jack Black wanted me to find here. But had he thrown David into the lake so the fish could attack him? If not, then the creature must be significant in some other way.

At that moment the fish turned on its tail and swam down toward the underwater cliff. Gritting his teeth, David swam after it, knowing he could not catch it but knowing that he had to follow. He knew this was why Black had brought him here. Ahead of him the fish passed into the mouth of a cave high in the submarine rock face and vanished. David tried to follow but the cave narrowed swiftly to a dark passage little wider than his fist. Then where was the fish? White lights blazed inside his head. This must be oxygen deprivation. The fish had to be a hallucination . . . nothing more . . . but then perhaps forces beyond his comprehension had conjured the illusion of the fish – one that he'd been compelled to follow with a near-lunatic tenacity. *Dear Christ* – he needed to breathe now . . . and this cold water bled the body heat from him. Making a decision to get out fast, he took one last look into the underwater cave. Then he saw a black stump protruding from the silt on the cave floor. Probably it was an ancient tree root, perhaps even a fossilized one that stood proud of the lake mud. *Surely this isn't what Black wanted me to see?*

But it was as if a voice whispered into his ear with supernatural clarity. *That root-like growth is important to you. It's vital . . .*

Breathe . . .

I've got to examine it close up.

Breathe!

Before his need to swim back to the surface overpowered him David had to see what was growing from the bottom of the cave. As the strength in his body faded he pushed himself forward with as hard a swimming stroke as he could muster. This was his last chance. After this, he'd have to quit the lake or die from the sheer cold.

Gripping the edge of the cave mouth, he pulled himself close so that he could see the blurry stump.

The pommel and hilt of a sword . . . The moment David identified what the stump really was he understood. The Leppington family myth was crystallizing into real events. With his free hand he grabbed the sword's hilt, then tugged.

With the ease of drawing an oiled blade from a scabbard he pulled the weapon from the cave floor. Lake mud misted the water darkly.

David held the sword. The blade was longer than his arm. Between the blade and the handle was a formidable crosspiece in curling iron.

But then came the inevitable. The weight of the sword dragged him downward, just as the burning need to breathe became stronger than ever. He knew what the sword was. He knew, also, that he could not drop it because then it would be lost for ever in the thousands of feet of water beneath him. Then again, he could not hold onto it. Its weight would pull him down into the depths of the lake.

His lungs burned; his heart raced, pumping through his

veins blood that, starved of oxygen, was turning poisonous. He had, he guessed, twenty seconds to decide what to do. Release the sword? Or hold onto the weapon of his ancestors and drown?

You've got to decide, David told himself. *Time's running out . . .*

3

From **Hotel Midnight:**
My Internet darlings, this is Electra speaking.

Viking legends can concern an entire race of people or an individual tribe or even a single family. I have spoken before of my friend, a very modern man, with an ancient ancestral line that traces its forefathers back to the god Thor. Or so the legend ran. It spoke of the family's ownership of a sword with supernatural powers. This weapon went by the name of Helvetes, which is Norse for 'bloody' or 'blood-soaked'. The magic sword was the source of the warrior family's power. It made its owner invincible. And like similar weapons that boast mystic powers its owners found it in a strange place after a quest. King Arthur drew Excalibur from a stone. One Roman legend has a mythical hero finding a magic spear embedded in a tree at the centre of the world. Hou I of Taoist mythology fashioned ghost-slaying arrows from the hairpins of a river goddess. The Celtic heroine, Boann, found her axe of invisibility in the funeral pyre of its previous owner that had been burning for millennia. In the Bible's *Book of Revelations* we discover the sentence: *And the remnant were slain with the sword of him that sat upon the horse, which sword proceeded out of his mouth . . .* The Viking ancestor of my friend drew the sword Helvetes from the body of a gigantic fish. And on that Jungian note . . .

4

In retrospect it was foolhardy, but when Electra heard the crash from the kitchen she ran from the lounge to see what had caused it. After what had happened to David Leppington just minutes ago, who could foretell who Jack Black's next victim would be? A wall cupboard lay on the floor in a mass of shattered crockery. Behind her the others crowded into the kitchen.

'Hell, what caused that?' Goldi stared at the wrecked wall cupboard.

Dylan shook his head. 'It's not fallen, it's *jumped* off the wall. Look how far it's travelled.'

'They're playing with us,' Rowan said. 'Trying to scramble our nerves.'

'They're doing a good job,' Bernice said, a tremor in her voice.

'It's more than that.' Vikki examined the wall where the cupboard had been. 'Look.'

Electra moved nearer to the wall, her feet crunching on broken china. 'There was plaster on this wall. Even that's been torn away.'

'And there's writing, too,' Vikki added. 'Someone's chiselled words into the stone.'

Electra studied the lines etched there in the ancient wall. They were clean, as if the stone itself had shrugged off not only the cupboard but all the plasterwork as well.

Outside thunder grumbled . . . a dark voice promising monstrous events.

Tilting her head to one side, Electra began to read. '"On this day of Thor in one thousand seventeen hundred and sixty-two Helvetes was brought to Lazarus Wake where it was consigned to rest in the waters below. Its purchase made possible by popular subscription by free men and women of Leppington, Morningdale and Castleton.'''

'Helvetes?' Goldi shook his head. 'What the fuck is Helvetes?'

'A sword that once belonged to the Leppington family,' Bernice said.

Electra nodded. 'A sword with god-given powers, at that.'

'But does that mean what I think it does?' Vikki leaned forward to read the chiselled words. 'That they put the sword . . . Helvetes . . . into Lazarus Deep?'

Rowan rubbed his jaw. 'It looks as if the locals who were still loyal to the old gods clubbed together to buy the sword. But why they decided to chuck the blessed thing into the lake heaven alone knows.'

A shiver ran along Electra's spine. 'They knew what they were doing. The Leppingtons lost the sword to Christian knights hundreds of years ago. Somehow the locals who were loyal to the pagan way were able to buy it back.'

'But they still chucked it into the lake,' Rowan persisted.

'Yes, but they weren't throwing the sword away. You have to think how they think. The sword was consigned to Lazarus Deep as part of an elaborate pagan rite. Just like we press a key to activate a computer program, their act of giving the sword to holy waters was a way of activating some supernatural or even divine software that would eventually –' she shrugged '– produce the end result they desired.'

'Whatever that was,' Dylan said.

'I think we can guess,' Bernice muttered.

When Rowan spoke it was almost as if he were thinking aloud. 'The destruction of Christianity.'

5

Cold . . . incredible cold . . . that sensation, fused with exhaustion, gnawed at his bones. David struggled from the water, barely able to stand, never mind carry the sword. Instead, he dragged the ancient iron weapon behind him through the shallows. Hail struck his face. Winds sliced through his sopping clothes. Thunder brooded in the distance, a forbidding background music to his state of near-collapse. Step by step he plodded through the shallows. With an effort he summoned the strength to cough lake water from his throat.

David Leppington knew he'd been only seconds from drowning. As he'd sunk beneath the weight of the sword, he'd swum in the direction of the shore anyway, even though he must have been nearly ten feet underwater by this time. By luck, or perhaps with the helping spirit hands of his ancestors, he made it to the edge of the underwater cliff where the rock face plunged down into the abyss. Grabbing the lip of rock, he'd dragged himself forward, kicking his legs as he did so. He couldn't swim upward as the sword was too heavy. Even so, he knew he must not let it go. With a final surge of strength he'd used the boulders to haul himself forward to the shallows. Before his head broke the surface, air had begun to escape his burning lungs in noisy spurts of bubbles. Now he dragged his hundred-ton feet to the shore. Wiping his eyes with his free hand he saw Jack Black still standing there. Motionless. His arms hanging by his side.

'This is what you wanted me to do, isn't it?' David raised the sword in front of him. 'You made me find this.'

Jack Black turned to face David. His eyes were as dull as those of the long-dead. The man himself had shrunk. Whatever had given him life couldn't sustain it. He was weaker. Even the tattoos seemed to be losing their sharp edges; bluebirds and daggers blurred, the ink running under the skin like a picture left out in the rain.

'Jack. I found the sword. That's why you brought me down here, isn't it?'

For a second a flicker of recognition sparked in the eyes. Then it was gone. The light vanished from them. They become as dull as paste. The man's head turned wearily, as if he'd heard his name being called.

'What now, Jack? What do I do with this?' David lifted the sword so that Black could see it. Only Black turned away now and began to walk.

Dead man walking . . . The phrase came to David.

Dead man walking. That was what it looked like. There was no real animation, no life there. Jack Black moved his feet. That robotic action carried him away across the lakeside field to disappear amongst the dark Gothic columns of the trees.

'Jack! What now?' David raised the sword above his head.

At that moment lightning flashed through the sky. Its blue-white light exploded against David's retinas. Thunder roared, a titanic sound that buffeted him like a fist.

This was it. The storm had begun.

CHAPTER 35

I

Dylan heard the furious knocking on the door as they stood in the kitchen.

'Here they come again,' Rowan said grimly.

Electra grimaced. 'Well, they can huff and they can puff, but they're not coming in.'

The pounding on the door sounded again.

'I'll check that the door's bolted,' Dylan said, moving through into the hallway.

'Bastards.' Goldi looked furious. 'There's an axe in the storeroom. I've a good mind to cut one of those things up.'

'Don't,' Electra told him. 'There's too many to try that particular game.'

Dylan checked that the door's bolts were pulled across. He tried to ignore the pounding on the door, but he saw the way the old timbers shivered. The sound of the voice from the other side startled him.

'Let me in!'

Dylan looked back at the others. 'It's David.'

'*Was* David,' Electra corrected him. 'He's vampiric now.'

Bernice started. 'Electra, we can't be sure if—'

'Trust me. David's gone. Whatever's out there is no longer him.'

'Electra! Rowan! Let me in.' Again the pounding from the other side. 'Let me in!'

'No,' Electra shouted through the door. 'We're not letting you into the house.'

'For crying out loud, Electra.' David's voice rose in frustration. 'You *must* open the door. I'll freeze to death out here.'

'No.'

Lightning flashed.

'Electra, there's a storm breaking. It's all I can do to stand up, I'm so cold.'

Electra looked back at the others. 'He's a vampire now. We mustn't let him get to us.'

Pounding on the door. 'Electra . . . Electra!'

'He sounds cold,' Vikki said.

'And he's got to be human to feel that.' Dylan glanced at the window. 'Because the vampires sure as hell can't feel it.'

David's voice sounded weaker. 'For God's sake, Electra . . . please . . .'

Dylan watched as Bernice moved forward. 'Open the door, Dylan. If he's vampiric I'll know.'

'Bernice, you don't—'

'I know what I'm doing.'

'Bernice.' Rowan stepped up. 'I'll open the door. You stay behind me while you take a look at him.'

'I'm sure that—'

'Bernice,' Electra said firmly. 'Do as Rowan says. He's a blood Leppington, after all.' She gave a grim smile. 'His ancestry will protect him.'

Rowan quickly unbolted the door and turned the key. Dylan watched while he opened the door just as a flash of lightning lit up the sky. At any moment he expected a rush of the monsters, running at them, with their mouths open wide, hungry for that first bite into mortal flesh.

As Rowan eased the door back, Bernice and Electra moved

close behind him so that they could see out. David Leppington stood outside in the breaking storm. Hail swirled. Thunder roared with a vengeance. Dylan saw that the man was leaning forward, taking his weight on what looked like a sword, using it like a walking stick. What was more, he was soaked. Water dripped from his hair, his face, his clothes. It pooled on the stone slabs around him.

Furious, David said, 'What the hell kept you from opening the door?'

Dylan saw Bernice looking at David's face, searching for something there.

'Well? Are you going to let me in? Or you going to damn well stand there and watch me die of frostbite?'

'Show me your hand,' Bernice told him.

'What?'

'Show me your hand.'

Exhausted, he raised his hand.

'No, the other one . . . the left.'

'Jesus Christ.'

'Do it, David,' Electra ordered. 'Or we lock the door in your face.'

He smiled wearily at Rowan. 'Don't worry. They're always like this. Twin dominatrices.' With an effort he managed to raise his left hand. The knuckles were grazed. Running from the wound was a trickle of blood. Dylan saw a hailstone fall on it and stick there. A speck of white against deep, *deep* red.

Bernice glanced at Electra. 'He wouldn't bleed like that?'

'No, he wouldn't, dear. Those monsters would have sucked every last drop from him.'

David was bone-weary with cold and exhaustion. 'What?'

Electra rested her hand on Rowan's shoulder. 'You can let him in now. And make sure he brings the sword.' She nodded at the weapon. 'It's Helvetes.'

2

David sat so close to the fire that his fringe steamed. The blaze of firelight ran in through his eyes to warm him inside. That immersion in Lazarus Deep . . . he'd never felt so cold.

'I can get you another pair of socks, if you want?' Rowan handed him a glass of brandy.

'No, these are fine.' He shuddered. 'I just want to climb into the fireplace to get warm again.'

Rowan dropped another log on the fire. 'As well as sharing the same DNA it's lucky we also share the same size in clothes.'

Bernice added, 'Yours should be dry by this evening, David.'

This evening . . . No one wanted to be reminded of nightfall. David glanced at the others in the room. *They're all here. At least, what's left of us.*

Electra held the sword in her slender fingers. He saw her examine the weapon with its runic markings. Stamped into the blade was the symbol of Mjolnir, Thor's hammer. When David had drawn the sword from the underwater cave he'd have sworn that it had been pitted with rust, but now it looked as if it had been made yesterday. The iron blade reflected a bloody light in the red glow of the fire. The leatherwork covering the hilt was freshly stitched. The round pommel, inlaid with gold and electrum, glinted bright.

David had told them how he'd come to discover the sword in the lake and Electra had shown him the inscription carved into the slab in the kitchen. The facts were beginning to fall into place.

'Formidable hunk of weapon,' Rowan said.

Goldi looked animated. 'I bet you could take their fucking heads off with that.'

'It's sharp, too.' Bernice touched the edge of the blade as Electra held the sword.

'So this is the original Helvetes.' For the first time Electra looked awed. 'This is the source of Leppington's power.'

Dylan frowned. 'And you say the man you call Jack Black helped you find it.'

'So he might be on our side?' Vikki asked.

'We'd hope so,' Electra said. 'But you can never tell.'

'But it wouldn't make sense. Black wouldn't have helped David find the sword if he was an ally of the vampires. He would have thrown us to them.'

'Like he did with Liz.' Goldi sounded angry.

'He sacrificed Liz to them to break their hold on us. If he—'

'Wait, children!' Electra handed the sword to David. 'This isn't as straightforward as you think. It isn't as clear-cut as good guy versus bad guy. It sounds brutal but you must consider us as chess pieces in a game played by the gods. Some of the pieces are the vampires. Some of the pieces are us, here in this room. Jack Black is yet another chess piece. And, like chess players, the gods use devious strategies – they aim to bluff their opponents, they dupe them into thinking they're using strategy A when in fact they're using strategy B. Do you follow?'

'You said they were capricious.' Rowan stamped the blazing log down into the fire. Gold sparks shot up the chimney. 'So what Black did to help David retrieve the sword might have been a way to deceive us?'

Dylan frowned. 'But we know the vampires are the bad guys, right?'

'Yes, without a doubt. The only question for us right now is: is Jack Black working for us or for them?'

The grandfather clock chimed twice. Darkness would fall three hours from now.

3

David drained the glass of brandy. Already it and the fire's warmth had all but driven the cold from his blood. The tingle in his fingers and toes became pleasant.

'The sword is important,' he told them. 'When I was in the lake – half drowning – I knew right then that it was vital to bring it back with me.'

'That was the voice of your ancestors in your ear.' Electra wasn't being flippant; she was making an observation. 'Because with the sword it makes you and your comrades invincible.'

'If anything, they wanted you to have the sword so that you could lead those monsters out there to war.' Bernice shivered. 'Now you have it there's nothing to stop you.'

'Only your conscience,' Electra said.

'So it's a stalemate.' Dylan stood went to the window; lightning flickered across the hilltops. 'You won't command the vampire army. And they won't let us leave here.'

'They're going to keep working those mind games on us, aren't they?' Goldi gestured. 'When it gets dark and they start getting strong again.'

Vikki stood up. 'And there's something else that needs to be added to the equation. Rowan Harper.' She looked at him. 'If those things asked you, would *you* command the army?'

'Me?' Rowan blinked. 'I guess I qualify, seeing as I have Leppington blood. But the answer's no. I don't see myself as a general, do you?'

Dylan nodded. 'So it *is* stalemate, then? We're stranded here?'

'Looks like that.'

David rested the sword across as his lap as he sat by the fire. Just for a moment it vibrated. There was a life-force in the ancient weapon. He could feel it . . .

Electra broke the silence that had settled on the room. 'This situation is a dangerous one. But it's still important that we eat and we sleep when we can. We have to be strong and alert when the next crisis comes. I suggest that we divide ourselves up into people who need to sleep and those who'll stand guard.'

'It didn't work last time,' Goldi grunted. 'We all fell asleep.'

'Because those walking cadavers could exert their influence on us. They can't do that in daylight. Right, who wants to sleep first?'

Electra had taken charge again. As she organized the sleep rota David gazed at the sword blade. It caught the dancing lights of the fire. The rune marks seemed to march along the ancient blade. Once more it vibrated, the same sensation as when someone stroked a purring cat. Yes. There was a life-force in the sword.

It's coming alive, he told himself. *When it does, I'll know what to do next.*

With a tingle running down his spine David knew events were coming to a head.

4

In the kitchen Dylan Adams offered Vikki a slice of cake. She shook her head.

'Vikki, you should eat something, you know.'

'I'm not hungry.'

'It's best to try. You never know when . . .' He shrugged.

'I might need the energy?'

'Electra said—'

'I know what she said, Dylan, but if it comes down to it I don't think I'll be able to outrun those monsters outside. No one will.' She gave a weak smile. 'Thanks for trying.'

Dylan felt her hand go to his cheek as she stood behind him.

'It shows you care,' she whispered.

Dylan glanced down at the wrecked cupboard and shards of plaster on the floor in the corner. 'Maybe I'm more domesticated than I thought but I've got the urge to clean that mess up. It'll give me something to do, anyway. Vikki?'

He glanced back when she didn't make a comment. Her eyes were dull. She swayed, looking faint.

'Here,' he said quickly. 'Sit down.' He guided her to one of the chairs at the kitchen table. She dropped into the chair rather than sitting in it. Her head went forward to rest on her arm on the table.

'Vikki . . . Vikki? Can you hear me?'

A surge of panic rose inside him. Were the vampires exerting their mind control again? She'd been speaking lucidly enough just a moment ago.

'Vikki. Talk to me.' He rubbed her back between her shoulder blades. 'Vikki?'

Thunder rolled across the sky. Windows rattled. Ice-cold draughts swept through the house. They made the sound of a child sobbing in the dark. Doors slammed. Those cold fingers of air ran up the back of Dylan's neck. He saw that even though she was unconscious Vikki was feeling the chilling effect. She gave a deep shiver. The skin of her exposed forearm came up in bumps of goose-flesh.

At that moment Vikki sat up straight, fixed Dylan with a stare that looked right through him and said: 'I'm in the ground . . .'

5

Something about that stare – and those words, spoken in a breathy kind of sigh – chilled Dylan through and through.

I'm in the ground. The voice was Vikki's, only there was some quality to it that sounded so alien. As if she had breathed the words to him from a place far away in space – or time.

Within moments of making that eerie statement Vikki's head tilted forward. Then she lifted it again, as if she'd simply woken up. Instantly a look of alarm flashed across her face. She stood up, pushing the chair back so that it screeched across the stone floor.

'Hey, Vikki, take it easy.'

'Where was I?' She looked round, frightened. '*Dylan – where was I?*'

'You were here with me. You fainted on me, that's all.'

'Fainted?'

'Clean away. Sit down, you still look groggy.'

She allowed him to help her sit. He saw an expression of confusion replace the fear on her face. 'And I was here all the time?'

He tried a reassuring smile. 'I never let you out of my sight.'

'But it felt so real. I could feel the cold and damp. I could even smell the soil.'

'*What* felt so real?'

'I'm sorry.' Vikki pushed her hair back from her eyes. He noticed that her hands were trembling. 'I'm not sure what happened. It's just that for a moment I thought I was . . .' Her voice faded, as her eyes assumed the glaze of someone recalling a powerful memory.

'Vikki? Are you all right?'

'Yes, I must be overtired, that's all.'

'You were just about to say where you thought you were.'

'It's nothing.' She gave a twitchy shake of her head.

Dylan felt for her. She was still scared. 'Maybe you should lie down and try to grab some sleep.'

This time she didn't disagree with his suggestion. 'Good idea.'

'Come on, let's find a spare bedroom.'

She forced a smile. 'Thanks.'

She stood up without any sign of dizziness.

'OK?' he asked.

'Fine.'

With Dylan following, Vikki walked to the door, up the stairs to the first bedroom. There, Goldi slept on the bed with the woodcutter's formidable axe by his side. He must have got it from the storeroom after all. Dylan realized that the man was retrieving some of his old chutzpah. He didn't plan on going without a fight. The other bedrooms were full. Bernice was sleeping in the room adjoining Goldi's. Rowan lay in the room opposite.

Dylan said, 'That leaves the one in the attic. Are you sure you want to be up there?'

'Right now, I think I could sleep in the tool shed.'

She climbed the stairs, going up in front of him. The bedroom was how it had been left earlier. The single bed stood in the middle of the otherwise sparsely furnished room. He lit the candle beside the bed.

'Do you want me to stay?' he asked. 'I mean, not for—'

'No, I know what you mean. You are being a gallant gentleman.' Vikki smiled, drowsy. 'Besides, I think I could hibernate now, never mind sleep.'

'I'll be right downstairs. Call if you need me.'

'I will. Thanks.'

He turned to leave.

'Dylan.' She looked searchingly at him. 'When I fainted . . . passed out, whatever it was. Did I say or do anything?'

'You said: "I'm in the ground."'

'Nothing else?'

'No.'

'It was . . .' She trailed off as if finding it hard to get the words out. 'It sounds strange, but this feels like something I have to get off my chest.'

'Don't worry.' Dylan spoke gently. 'Tell me whatever you want.'

'When I blacked out in the kitchen, I remember opening my eyes. Somehow I knew I was lying in the ground. I could feel damp soil under my hands. I could smell it. And there's something else.' Vikki took a deep breath. 'You were lying beside me.'

CHAPTER 36

I

David woke to hear the clock in the hallway strike three. Another two hours until nightfall. Minutes were haemorrhaging now. He looked down, sitting in the armchair, to see his ancestors' sword Helvetes still across his lap. Firelight sent blood-red tints dancing along the blade. He rested a fingertip on the keen edge. Once more it hummed.

Dear God, he thought, *this is more than dead metal. This thing has a life of its own.* Perhaps a distillation of the life essence of all those dead Leppingtons right back to the time when they had been Leppingsvalt and had ruled over this bleak enclave of Yorkshire. Just as the vampires outside would suck blood from a human being, this ancient weapon drew the souls from dead Leppingtons and held them inside it. A cache of warrior spirits that would once more flow back into the wielder of the sword when the time was right. Taking his gaze from the rune pattern on the blade, he looked round the room. He was alone apart from Dylan Adams who sat hunched on the stool by the fire, staring into the flames.

'Dylan? Where are the others?'

He saw that Dylan's eyes looked troubled. 'Oh . . .' He threw a stick onto the fire. 'They're all asleep.'

'Probably for the best.'

'So what now, Doc?'

'Apart from the waiting? I'm not sure.'

'But something's got to give soon, hasn't it?'

'Eventually.'

'I mean, we can't sit here while that lot out there wait until hell freezes over.'

'I wish there was something we could do.'

Dylan looked at him. The skin beneath his eyes was so dark with exhaustion that it looked bruised. 'You could walk away. There's something in your blood that will stop them from harming you.'

'Now that I doubt.' David sat up straight in the chair and laid the sword on the coffee table. 'They won't attack me while they think there's a chance that I'll give in to their demands and become their leader . . . or general, or whatever.'

'But if you refuse? Or try and run?'

'Then I become fair game.'

'You could go along with them. Take control.'

'And what? Go on the rampage with my vampire army throughout the world? You know, Dylan, in my imagination I can see these old Viking gods who have resurrected their own warrior dead. And I know exactly what they're like. Because Odin and Thor have been deprived of power and worship for so long that they have become psychotic. They have an insane lust for revenge. They crave the destruction of Christianity and its worshippers. That's all they care about. But what happens afterwards? There'll be no new order to replace Christendom. There'll only be a derelict planet populated by those vampires out there. And, believe me, vampires are a mouth and a gut and nothing more. They're walking leeches. And presiding over the ruin? Psychotic gods.'

Thunder crashed against the house. *Maybe something in Valhalla disagrees*, David thought. *So what? Let them try and do their worst. While we stay here we are safe. Their plans are thwarted.* David saw that Dylan was watching him, perhaps surprised at what came close to an outburst of anger.

'So you see, Dylan. We can't let them win.'

The grandfather clock chimed the half-hour. David could have sworn that time had begun to accelerate. Soon it would draw down the early night of winter. Even now, only a miserly half-light lit the lake, hills and forests. Cloud settled deeper and deeper, threatening to smother anyone who ventured out into the bitter cold. Only flickers of lightning produced anything close to a shadow on the landscape. And always the rumble of thunder that had all the dark potency of some dark and vengeful god that muttered its evil curses into the aether.

2

David thought: *Here comes the storm.*

Thunder rumbled more loudly. Lightning cast its electric blue flicker against the curtains. A gale rose from the lake to roar through the trees. Soon wind thrummed in the chimney. A sobbing sound rose from the roof eaves as icy winds swirled there. Draughts jetted up from the gaps in the floor. Curtains billowed as more draughts found their way through the spaces between the window frames.

This is a symphony for the devil, all right.

David saw Dylan turn to look into the fire as pieces of mortar rattled down the chimney to fall onto the burning logs. Sparks flew out into the room. Dylan batted away one that landed on his leg.

The wind became a human-sounding cry . . . calling . . . Then David realized it was calling his name.

'*David . . . David . . .*'

It rose and fell like the sound made by the wind in the surrounding trees.

Dylan moved away from the fire that still threw sparks out onto the hearth.

The voice came again and this time David noticed that Dylan heard it, too, making him turn to the hallway.

So it wasn't my imagination . . .

Dylan glanced back at him. 'They're calling you, Doc.'

'They can call.' David shook his head. 'I'm not going to engage those things in conversation.'

'*Daay – vid . . .*'

Wait. That's a woman's voice. Liz? Or maybe—

Suddenly he knew.

'*David . . .*'

'That's Katrina.'

'Who?

'Katrina West.' David crossed the room to the hallway, heart banging against his ribs. 'I know her.'

'But how did she get—'

'I left her in the Station Hotel in Leppington.'

'She must have followed you.'

'No, she was in no state to get here by herself. Those bastards must have brought her here.'

David paused in the hallway. His first instinct had been to fling open the door and bring her into the house. But he knew that the monsters had a motive for bringing her here.

'*Dayvvv-vidd . . . David, dear . . .*'

Dylan heard the strange drawl to her voice. 'They must have done something to her . . . can you hear the way she's speaking?'

'Katrina's a paranoid schizophrenic. She's on powerful antipsychotic drugs. She may be experiencing a hallucinatory episode or she might be suffering from exposure – both result in confusion; they might have . . .' David stopped short of putting her fate into words. 'Bastards,' he hissed. 'Why couldn't they leave her alone?'

'Dr Leppington.' The voice sounded uncannily close. This time it was male. 'It's time to negotiate some important contractual terms.'

'Ash White,' David whispered to Dylan.

'Dr Leppington,' came the voice from just the other side of the door. 'We know you're there. What's more, we know that you know, to quote the line from the song, that Katrina West is out here as our guest.'

'Go away.'

'You don't mean that, Doctor.'

'Yes, I do. Just go.'

'It's awfully cold out here for Katrina.'

David clenched his fists. 'I'm not interested.'

'Oh ho, but you are.' White almost sung the words. 'And do you want to know a little secret?'

David couldn't bring himself to answer.

'Out here we all know . . .' The vampire's voice came as a whisper. 'We all know that Katrina loves you . . . and you, Doctor . . . you love her.'

'Bastards.'

'Temper, temper.'

David punched the door, half hoping that his fist would go right through it and smash White's jaw.

Now White sounded amused: 'Of course you hide your temper well behind the good Dr Leppington mask. But we all know that the blood of your ancestors is fiery stuff. Your forefathers were Viking warriors who'd think nothing of slaughtering every family in a village or wrecking a church and crucifix-fucking the priest.'

'Shut up.'

'Shish-kebab a clergyman. Maybe that early form of surgery, warrior-style, somehow found its way down the genetic highway to you?'

'Listen,' David said through gritted teeth. 'I know what you will have done to Katrina. But it's not going to make me change my—'

'But we've done nothing to Katrina. Why should we?'

'Because I know what your kind are like.'

'True, we're hungry. But we're demonstrating admirable self-denial.'

'Wait. You mean you've not harmed her?'

'Not a hair.'

David groaned. His stomach muscles tightened until they hurt him so much he had to turn from the door. He saw Dylan look at him, the young man's eyes large with concern.

'They're going to use Katrina as a hostage. Use her to lever me into agreeing to lead them.'

At that moment David knew that he had to see Katrina. All that old love he'd openly felt for her when they'd been together, and the love that he'd harboured secretly, deep down, all the years she'd been in the psychiatric ward, flooded back into him. His blood flamed in his veins. Now he couldn't stop himself. He turned the key, snapped back the bolt and swung open the door.

He heard Dylan shout in disbelief at the action. 'David. *Don't!*'

3

Beneath cloud that was darker than the roof of a tomb stood the vampire, Ash White. Beside him was Rick Broxley. Their stark white bodies were thrown into glaring relief by the seething mass of black trees behind them. Lightning flashed, transforming their skin into a dazzling electric blue before it reverted to a white that was as bloodless as graveyard marble.

Thunder clashed against the house. David recoiled before the cold wind that rushed through the open doorway.

'OK,' David shouted above the rising storm. 'Where's Katrina?'

'Right here.' Ash White stared intently at him with those green eyes of his. 'You'll want to see for yourself that she's safe.'

'I'm taking her into the house.'

'You can. Once we've agreed terms.'

'What terms?' David spat the words.

Rick Broxley grinned. The lips slid back to reveal sharklike teeth. 'You will lead your ancestor's army over the moor to the coast.'

'Never in a thousand years.'

By way of response White and Broxley stepped apart so that David could see between them to the lawn. Standing there were a dozen vampires. These were the ancient ones – naked, hairless, their white skins displaying that random patternwork of veins. It looked as if black worms had crept beneath the surface of their skin. They moved forward. With a jolt he realized that they were carrying a body. No, not a corpse. He saw that they bore Katrina above their heads. She lay on her back as if relaxing on a bed, her head hanging down at the front of the pack of bearers. She was still wearing the nightdress she'd been sleeping in and her face was flushed with excitement; her eyes carried the druggy leer of medication. Rolling her head from side to side, she smiled at David, even though she was seeing him upside down from where she lay on the upstretched arms of the vampires.

'I know all about you.' She almost sang the words. 'I know all about you, David Leppington. My friends here have told me everything. I know that you have family in high places.' She chuckled. A gurgling, drunken sound. 'And I know a big secret. You are to be king, and I am to be queen.' Her expression grew licentious, lustful. 'We're going to be together again for ever and ever, amen.'

'White,' David spoke quickly. 'Katrina's not well. She'll die of cold if she's not brought into the house now.'

'Brought in?' Broxley sounded interested. 'You mean we can—'

'No. You're not coming into the house.' David held up his

hand just in case they were in any doubt. 'You're not invited in here. Bring her to the edge of the lawn; I'll get her inside myself.'

'Ah.' White lightly touched his chin as he thought through the implication. 'You do know the deal here, don't you? In return for us handing the woman you love over to you, you must give us your solemn oath that you will lead your people.' White waved a hand to encompass the vampires. The monster didn't want David in any doubt who his 'people' really were.

'David . . . Dayvv-vid . . .' Katrina smiled at him and licked her full lips.

David shook his head. 'I don't accept.'

Broxley tilted his head, his expression disbelieving. 'You know what will happen to Katrina?'

'No deal.' David could hardly speak. His throat burned as grief constricted it. 'No deal. Go away . . . I'm not—'

The rest of the sentence never left his lips. The blow to the back of his head didn't seem connected to the pain he felt. A blaze of agony seared his eyes. For a split second he thought the door had somehow slammed shut against him, but he found himself toppling back through the open doorway. He fought to regain his balance but all coordination had been shattered. Even before David Leppington fell onto the hallway floor he'd crossed over into a dark world haunted by monstrous things that screamed his name.

4

The first that Dylan Adams knew about the sneak attack was seeing the figure stride up behind David and strike the man on the back of the head. For a second he didn't know the identity of the attacker or what weapon he'd used.

The moment that David reeled backwards Dylan grabbed

him to make sure that he toppled back inside the house, and also that a fall against a hard stone floor didn't injure him even more. Once he had lowered David safely to the floor Dylan looked up.

There, looking down with an expression that mixed disdain with mild curiosity, was Rowan. In his hand, the sword. Helvetes.

'I don't know how badly he's hurt,' Rowan said. 'I've never struck anyone with a sword before. Baseball bats and snooker cues, yes, but never thousand-year-old ironwork like this.'

Dylan looked up; fury swept through him. 'What the fuck did you hit him for?'

'It's time I saved my own life. As for his – or yours . . .'

Dylan saw the man smile as he turned away and stepped outside, the wind tugging at his open coat. 'White. Broxley. You know who I am.'

They nodded.

'And I think you can guess that I'm here to replace my reluctant brother.' With a theatrical gesture Rowan held the sword up, so that the vampires could see it. 'I'm a blood Leppington. And I'm here to claim my divine right to lead you. Now, what do you say?'

CHAPTER 37

I

David's first experience of consciousness after Rowan's blow was a throbbing pain beating through his skull. The next was a sensation of wetness trickling down the back of his neck. When he opened his eyes he found himself sitting in the hallway with the door open in front of him.

A voice sounded close by. Dylan Adams. 'Take it easy. Don't try and get up yet. He's cut the back of your head with that—'

'Rowan.' David looked outside where the wind seethed through the trees. Lightning splashed the cloud an electric blue. 'Rowan!' David realized what had happened. 'Rowan attacked me.' A statement, not a question.

Dylan said, 'He used the sword. Not the blade, the hilt.'

'Dylan, close the door! Lock it!' It was Electra who'd called out as she hurried downstairs. She shouted again, 'Dylan, the door!'

'No, I'm going to talk to him first,' David growled. 'The bastard.'

Following Electra were Bernice and Goldi, their faces masks of shock. Their gazes darted from David sitting in a pool of blood to Rowan standing with the vampires outside.

David pulled himself to his feet. Then, using his hands, he steadied himself against the door frame. 'Rowan. You don't know what you're doing. These things will—'

'These *things*?' Rowan took a step toward the doorway, but kept a distance of a dozen paces between himself and the house. 'These *things* are my only inheritance from the Leppington family. That and the blood in my veins.'

'Rowan, come back into the house.'

'David, I heard what you called me. *A bastard.* That's right. I grew up with my single mother. And I grew up a bastard. With all that entails – like the name-calling from other kids. Evading the homework essay where you've been told to write about your mother and father.' Rowan grimaced. 'Shit happens, huh?'

'Come inside. We can talk. But don't give in to those monsters, they'll—'

'End the world as we know it?' Rowan shook his head. 'So fucking what? I don't owe this world anything. All it's done is pile grief on me since I was born.'

'No, Rowan. People don't deserve what you're going to inflict on them.'

'Don't they?'

'These monsters are working on your mind, don't you realize that?'

'No, David. That's where you're wrong.' Rowan glanced at White and Broxley. 'I'm doing this all of my own free will, aren't I, guys?'

Ash White nodded his albino head. 'There's no other way. For a Leppington to lead the army it has to be a voluntary act on their part.'

'Voluntary?' David took a deep breath. 'Rowan has a chip on his shoulder. A grudge against society that's so deep-rooted it's cancerous. He's neurotic, and it's that neurosis that has made him your ally. But that isn't the voluntary act of a rational man.'

'He's here of his own free will,' White insisted.

'Free will?' David grunted. 'He's got as much free will

as if he'd been brought to you in chains. His screwed-up childhood's forcing him to do this.'

'Is that an example of the Dr Leppington bedside manner?' Rowan smiled. 'Trying to talk me into accepting your diagnosis? My God, you'd hidden your streak of arrogance well.'

David touched the back of his head where a ragged sting had started. He saw his fingers tipped with red. Immediately the vampires became interested.

'So that's the colour of Leppington blood,' Rowan said, pointing with the sword. 'To me it doesn't look any different to anyone else's. But then, what is divine blood supposed to look like?'

David said, 'I'm warning you. Come back into the house.'

'Warning me? I'm the one with the ancestral sword and the vampire army. I figure *I*'m the one with the power to warn.'

Electra moved up close behind David. 'Rowan. What on Earth do you stand to gain, setting these monsters loose on the world?'

'Gain?' Rowan's face blazed in the lightning flash. 'Gain? You don't get it, do you, Electra? You, with your great shining intellect.' Thunder underscored his words. 'Surely you, and perhaps even our physician here, know what psychologists have been saying for years?'

'Tell me about it.'

'Didn't Dr Laing proclaim that the whole of Western society had become psychotic? That it's self-destructive and for the last hundred years it has been working towards species suicide.'

'That's just one man's hypothesis, Rowan. It's not scientific fact.'

'No?'

'No.'

'But you don't have rely on Laing's words. Do you remember Oppenheimer?'

'Yes – he invented the atom bomb.'

'Do you know why he invented it?'

'To help the Allies win the Second World War.'

'Wrong ... *Wrong!*' Rowan's eyes blazed with a weird kind of glee. 'When I read Oppenheimer's words where he explained *why* he'd devoted years of his life to developing the first atomic weapon he said, and I quote: "Well, it was so *sweet*; the capacity to do it was so sweet it was *irresistible.*"' The vampires picked up on the emotion in his voice. They lifted their faces to the play of lightning in the sky, lips drawn back, exposing sharp teeth; they tasted the promise of feasts to come on the winter air. 'So you see, Electra, David ... Oppenheimer wasn't being patriotic. Just like my friends here can influence our minds, so the suicidal madness of humanity twisted Oppenheimer's. It infected him with the desire to create a weapon so powerful that it would destroy not only the enemy but its user as well.' Rowan grinned. 'See? Species suicide. The desire for self-destruction is in *everyone*'s blood.'

Anger blazed inside David. 'So that's your motive for leading that vermin.' His gaze swept over the vampires gathered in a noxious mass on the lawn, hairless heads flickering in the lightning. 'That's your justification? That this is inevitable? That you've become the tool of the human instinct for suicide?'

Rowan stroked the blade of the sword. 'As the man said, "the capacity to do it is so *sweet.*"'

Fury surged through David. 'You bastard!' He lunged through the doorway, his fists clenched, ready to batter Rowan's smug face.

'David!'

Hands grabbed him. He realized that both Electra and Dylan were hauling him back through the doorway. Not a moment too soon. Vampires from left and right leaped at him, their heads thrust forward on the ends of necks that were so taut that muscles stood out through the bloodless skin. Their teeth snapped together as they tried to bite him.

Electra and Dylan didn't stop tugging until David was back in the hallway. For a moment he thought the creatures would rush into the house. But as if there was an invisible barrier across the open doorway they suddenly stopped, faces still straining forward, eyes blazing, mouths snapping and snarling, strings of drool dripping down from their jaws.

Bernice slammed the door shut. Locked it. They could no longer see the monsters. Yet within a moment a triumphant roar swelled outside. A wordless yell of exultation. The monsters had got what they wanted.

2

From **Hotel Midnight:**
The Viking prophecy of the end of the world is a detailed one. Ragnorok, the day of doom, begins with the phantom wolf, Fenrir, slipping his chains to devour the sun, leading to an age of ice and darkness. The battle of Ragnorok will see countless warriors raised from the dead to march against Fenrir and the enemies of the gods . . . In the legends, Odin, lord of the gods, meets a mysterious visitor whose name cannot even be uttered. Odin asks the visitor the question: 'And how shall this day end?'

3

'Sit on the sofa. Don't worry about getting blood on it.' Goldi lowered David onto the cushion. 'Hell. There won't be anyone left to complain about the mess anyway.'

David's head ached. Blood trickled down the back of his neck.

I couldn't care less about the furniture either, he thought. More than pain it was sheer fury that almost overwhelmed him. How could Rowan do that? Knock David down with the sword, then so coolly walk out to join forces with Ash White and his mob of two-legged leeches. Did Rowan so sincerely believe in that theory about humanity's instinctive drive toward species suicide? Maybe the man was so neurotic that he actually believed that. In fact, could Rowan's urge to lock himself away in this remote house in winter be a symptom of some mental health problem? After all, David had only known him for a few hours. Rowan might have discharged himself from rehab or slipped away from a psychiatric ward.

Dylan dropped more logs onto the fire. Sparks flew up the chimney in a rush. The noise distracted him from thinking about Rowan. Instead: *What's going to happen to Katrina now?*

Electra leaned over him. She held the first-aid box. 'First we're going to take a look at that cut.'

'I'm all right.'

'No, you're not, David. It's still bleeding.'

'We need to stop Rowan.'

'I know that . . . David, sit down.'

'But there's—'

'If you're going to be any use to us, you've got to let me take care of this wound.'

He finally assented, shrugging and sighing.

'It's hard to see the damage,' Electra told him. 'There's too much hair in the way.'

'Don't worry about that. The main thing is to stop the bleeding.'

He saw Electra give a grim smile as she opened the box. 'Physician, heal thyself?' She tore cellophane from a bandage. 'Not this time, David. Bernice, can you give me a hand?'

'There's sterile water. I'll wash out the cut.'

'There's no need for that,' David said. 'It'll only slow the wound's congealing.'

'David. Hands down by your side.' Electra sounded cool and in control. 'They're getting in the way. Right, I plan to apply pressure to the wound with this sterile pad, then fix it in place with a bandage.'

'Make sure the bandage is tight. The pad needs to press against the wound.'

'Yes, doctor.' She gave a grim smile. 'Don't they say doctors make the worst patients?'

'And I must be the worst of the lot.' He smiled back. 'Thanks.'

'Also, we need to make sure the blow didn't do any more damage. Do you think you were concussed?'

'I've got a rotten headache.' David winced as Electra applied the dressing. She wasn't pussyfooting around. The sting became full-blooded pain once more. 'But concussion?' He gritted his teeth as she started to bind the bandage around his head. 'No symptoms. No nausea, memory loss . . . no convulsions or loss of vision. *Eee-tch* . . . Yes, I think that will be tight enough.'

In the hallway the clock chimed four. An hour of daylight remained.

4

As the fourth chime faded away Dylan Adams suddenly realized that someone was missing. He'd been so caught up with helping David and watching the two women bind the head wound that he'd not noticed.

He glanced at Goldi who sat by the fire with the wood-cutter's axe across his lap. 'Goldi? Have you seen Vikki?'

'No, I thought she was—'

Dylan didn't hang around. He hurried from the lounge and

then ran up the stairs. From the window of the next floor he glanced out, noticing that the garden had been abandoned by the vampires. They'd got themselves a Leppington to lead them to the promised land.

But what had happened to Vikki? The commotion when Rowan had struck David with the sword and the aftermath of that attack had brought everyone else downstairs.

With shadows leaking into the house as the day died Dylan raced up the last flight of stairs to the attic bedroom. Now his heart clamoured against his chest; already his imagination was conjuring up grotesque images of what might have happened to Vikki. He shouldn't have listened when she'd said she'd be fine by herself. He should have sat on the floor outside the bedroom door. Or, even better, sneaked back in when she was asleep.

I could have kept watch to make sure she was safe. What would happen if Luke Spencer somehow got in? He'd always fancied Vikki. Although he'd become vampiric he might have forced her to—

Panting, mouth dry, Dylan pushed open the bedroom door. When he saw what was in the room with Vikki he stopped dead, his heart pounding.

His voice rasped through dry lips: *'Take your hands off her.'*

CHAPTER 38

I

Dylan Adams grasped the frame of the doorway. Pure shock at what he saw locked him tight; he stared so hard that he could even feel the moisture evaporating from his eyes. His heart thudded.

How did it get in here? He took a step into the room. *The vampires can't enter the house without invitation. This place is sacred to them* . . . But then Dylan saw that this was no vampire.

This was the man – or what had once been a man – known as Jack Black.

Dylan had seen the man shoving David brutally down to the lake. For a while they hadn't known whether Black was friend or foe. Dylan knew now, all right. The huge beast of a man, with his shaved head and fearsome tattoos, had thrust one of his giant paws under Vikki's chin. He gripped her lower jaw while pushing her head back so she couldn't move as she lay flat on the bed. Her limbs were limp. She didn't move. As he held her he stared into her face. Her eyes gazed back into his. They were dull-looking. Dead . . .

He's strangled her . . .

But then Dylan heard her irregular breathing. He moved forward. Black hadn't heard him walk into the bedroom. Acting on sheer instinct, Dylan padded across the floor and flung himself at Black. Without even looking back the man's huge tattooed arm lashed upward. Dylan flinched, expecting a blow. Instead, Black's outstretched fingers covered Dylan's face . . . then they gripped hard. The force stopped him dead. He couldn't move forward to help Vikki. He couldn't move back to escape. He couldn't even shout a warning to the others downstairs.

What was more, Dylan no longer had the strength to raise his arms to try and fight Black. He felt as if he was a paper man. Hollow, bloodless. A flimsy shell. As he stared through the fingers that now formed something like the bars of a cage across his face he saw Black's shaved head slowly turn until he was looking along his own tattooed arm into Dylan's eyes. The face held no expression. Tattoos of birds hovered at either side of the man's eyes, making them look even fiercer. On one cheek a tattooed tear. And those eyes . . .

They were too large to be human. They had become twin caves covered with a bulging membrane that glistened . . . Two pinprick pupils stared intently into his. The fingers pressing on Dylan's face were as cold as the rock in a polar cave. The tattooed birds blurred. They stretched into blue lines to frame the eyes.

Black's not strangling Vikki . . . it's something else. He's here for some other purpose.

As if he were falling asleep the world around Dylan became distant, lost in a slow accretion of shadow. Thunder faded away into silence.

From far away, it seemed, he heard Vikki whisper, 'I'm in the ground . . .'

2

Darkness flooded from the walls. Dylan's eyes closed as the floorboards flew apart beneath him. For a moment he was falling. Cold air blew in his face, tugging his hair, roaring past his ears. He gritted his teeth as he plunged down faster and faster.

The ground didn't strike his feet so much as press against them. Stumbling forward, Dylan landed on his hands and knees. When he opened his eyes he found himself some-where he knew. This was Don Flint, one of the ancient Iron Age grave mounds at the highest part of the moor. Cloud rolled overhead, cold winds tugged at his clothes; they sent a low sighing across the heather. Despite the cold there was no storm. Climbing to his feet, he saw that he wasn't alone. Jack Black stood little more than an arm's length away from him. The giant of a man was pointing at the burial mound that rose like a pregnant belly from the earth.

I'm dreaming . . . Dylan told himself this as the cold wind cut through his clothes to set his teeth clicking together. *I'm dreaming. I'm back in Lazarus Wake. I've dozed off by the fire. This isn't—*

Without uttering a sound, without a ghost of an expression on his face, Black pointed again at the mound.

'What do you want me to see?'

No reply.

'I know Don Flint. I've been here before.'

Black's finger pointed into the heart of the mound while the man's stare seemed to cut right through the front of Dylan's skull.

Dylan shook his head. 'I don't know what you want me to see. You have to tell me . . .'

Black pointed.

'You can't speak, can you?'

As if to speak for Black there came the phantom cry of winds across the moor. Dylan looked back down into the valley. He saw the lake but none of the houses or even the village of Morningdale in the distance.

Why? I should be able to see that. There should have been street lights, roads. Only there were no roads. *But this is a dream. Dreams play whatever tricks they want.* They could even conjure him back two thousand years into the past when the landscape would have looked so different. Dylan looked at Black. Once more the man's tattoos melted to swarm in shoals of blue across his skin.

'I'm sorry, I don't know what you're trying to—'

Then, in a repeat of what had happened to David Leppington, Black gripped a fistful of Dylan's shirt between the shoulder blades, then swung him toward the burial mound. Its covering of rough grass filled his vision. Dylan flinched, expecting his face to slam into the earth. Instead, he plunged into the membrane of vegetation, passing through as unhindered as a ray of starlight shining through a pane of glass.

Dreams have the power to do this . . . In a minute I'll be awake, and then . . .

With eerie similarity, just as David had plunged through the surface of Lazarus Deep into its depths, so Dylan swept through the surface vegetation and boulder layer to swim inside the ancient grave itself.

'An Iron Age grave . . . three thousand years old . . . the sacred resting place of prehistoric men and women . . .' It was the voice of his history teacher ghosting down long-dead years. 'Buried with their weapons and food for the afterlife, they were sent by their loved ones on that great mystic journey to meet their gods . . . Here, in the Esk Valley, the Iron Age people were the descendants of Bronze and Stone Age people; their ancestry went back further than we can know. Their bloodline extended far back to when their forebears hunted mammoth before the glaciers came and tore these valleys into the face of the Earth . . .'

Dylan Adams tumbled end over end through grave-soil. He smelled damp earth. Plant roots showed as milky veins against black. And still he continued down. Deeper and deeper until he saw an orb that shone with misty light. Faster now, he plunged toward it. And at that moment he experienced a pang of horror.

I don't want to see what's in there. I know there's something terrifying inside. I don't want to see . . . I don't want to see!

Only he still fell toward it. A subterranean astronaut in free fall, descending toward a tiny glowing world that contained the secret that he feared most . . . Wanting desperately to close his eyes, yet finding that he couldn't, Dylan plunged into the sphere of light. And when he saw what it contained he began, at last, to understand.

CHAPTER 39

I

'Dylan . . . Dylan?'

He felt Vikki's fingers stroking the side of his face first before he opened his eyes.

'Dylan.' Her voice was a gentle whisper. 'Dylan. It's time to wake up.'

When he opened his eyes the clock downstairs began to strike the hour. One . . . two . . . three . . . four . . . five . . . the chimes ascended the stairs with an uncanny resonance.

The night is here.

'It's time to wake up.' Again Vikki's gentle fingers stroked his face. Realizing that he was kneeling by the bed with his head pillowed on her chest, he looked up. Still lying there, she looked relaxed. The fear he'd seen earlier had gone. What he saw now in her eyes touched his heart: *acceptance*.

'Black was here,' Dylan said. 'He showed me something up on the moor.'

'I know.' She gave a sad, sweet smile. 'I saw it, too.'

'But we were—'

'Shhh.' She touched his lips. 'Come on, you know what we've got to do.'

Together they moved through the near-darkness to the stairs and began to descend. Outside the wind rose in a cry. A single note that lay suspended outside time. A call in an ancient tongue.

2

David touched his head as Electra finished taping the bandage.

'There,' she said. 'How does that feel?'

'Better. You could—'

'Wait.' Bernice held up her finger as she glanced toward the closed door of the lounge. 'Did you hear that?'

Goldi was on his feet, gripping the axe. 'It's a car! I can hear a bloody car!'

David's head swam as he stood, but it didn't stop him running. He followed Goldi as the younger man flung open the front door.

'No, keep it shut. You don't know if—'

David's voice died away. There were no vampires. There was no car, either. David saw the lights of Electra's vehicle gliding away from the house along the driveway toward the main road. *Damn.* It was going too fast to catch on foot. But who'd take the—

A thought occurred to him. 'Has anyone seen Vikki and Dylan lately?'

3

Dylan drove. The powerful Volvo swept along the driveway, its lights cutting through the darkness.

'We could have brought the others,' Dylan said. 'There's room.'

'But not enough time.' Branches clawed at the car's flanks as they passed. 'We might be too late even now.'

As Dylan drove onto the main road and began the uphill climb to Don Flint five miles away, his mind went back to the house. It had been easy enough to take the car keys from Electra's coat hanging in the hallway. The vampires had vanished from the garden. Without trying, his memory took him further back, barely fifteen minutes ago, when he had dreamed that he'd plunged down through the tomb to the orb of light shining beneath him.

He glanced at Vikki, seeing her clear eyes gleaming in the light of the dashboard instruments. She was intently scanning the road ahead.

'Jack Black showed you the same thing?' he asked.

'Yes.'

'Bones in a grave?'

'Only they were more than old bones, weren't they?'

Dylan's hands gripped the steering wheel as the images came pouring back. He'd have given anything not to descend into that ancient tomb. Because deep down he knew what he'd find there. Fleeting images of it had haunted his dreams since childhood. What he'd feared hadn't been the unknown but the *known*. The vision of the tomb had triggered . . . what? A race memory? A description whispered by a ghost into his ear as he'd slept as a child?

He couldn't say for sure. Only that he'd plunged into the grave where the bones glowed luminous in the dark. He'd seen two skeletons lying on their sides, one facing the back of the other, their knees raised, one hand pillowing a skull, the second arm of the male skeleton resting on an arm of the female. A post-mortem gesture of affection. The female wore a necklace of amber beads. The male lay with a spear beside his back.

Then came the shock of recognition. Suddenly he wasn't seeing bones. He was seeing a man and woman. They looked to be sleeping rather than lying dead in a grave. Even their position was that of lovers asleep in their bed. Now Dylan knew why Black, in that vision, had brought him to the desolate spot high on the moor. Black had shown him the occupants of the tomb. The female had a beautiful face framed by rich hair plaited in a style he'd never seen before. Even so, he recognized her. It was Vikki. The male face he knew as well. It was the same one that he saw every day in the mirror.

Then came the sight that sent a billion shivers down through his bones. Lying at their doppelgängers' feet was the body of a dog arranged in a sphinxlike way, head high, as if protecting the huddled figures of two small children. They appeared to be sleeping with their arms round each other.

So now I know. Dylan turned the corner and pointed the car's nose toward the highest part of the moor. Lightning played across the tumuli, those swelling mounds in the earth, with their strange names: Don Brow, Don Flint, Don Nether Adder. *I know that a long time ago I faced a danger like this one. Only that was another life I lived. And yet I lived it with this same woman who is beside me now. Here it comes again. A moment of crisis. Similar – yet separated by thousands of years.*

4

From **Hotel Midnight**:
OK, OK, my boys and girls, Electra here. Some of you have asked for more information about Viking ancestry. How can you know if Vikings were your ancestors? If you look in the mirror you might see blonde hair and blue eyes. If you do, or if either of your parents have this colouring, then your ancestors might have sailed the seas in dragon-headed ships beneath the banner of Odin's raven.

Now, dear children, let's begin at – where else? – the beginning. The beginning of time. Two giants turn the millstone of the gods producing, not flour from wheat, but the essence of the universe itself. They have done this since the birth of the cosmos. And as the round millstone turns like a vast wheel the marks smeared on its surface are historical events. And as it goes round and around what appears to be receding into the distance (or the past) is simply following a curving path that will return that point – or event – back to the present again. There you have it, my dears, just as astronomers will confirm: time and space are curved. Whatever our ancestors did in the past some of us will repeat in the present. And what you do today will be replayed by your descendants in some far and distant future.

5

'They've gone,' Bernice told them as she came down the stairs.

Goldi shook his head. 'Christ Almighty. I can't believe they drove off like that without us.'

'Well, that's what they've done.'

'Hell, I knew Vikki and Dylan from school. The fucking cowards!'

David saw the angry way in which Goldi was gripping the handle of the axe. He was ready to cleave skulls.

'It's dark now,' Bernice said. 'The vampires will be stronger. Maybe they planted the notion in their mind to—'

'Run out on us?' Goldi shook his head. 'I reckon they saw it was clear of those freaks out there so they took their chance with the car.' Then he added bitterly, 'Without telling us.'

'We're jumping to conclusions,' Electra said.

'I agree.' David pulled back the curtain. It was too dark to make out much, even so. 'I can't see Rowan or any of his cronies.'

'That's because they'll be heading for Whitby.' Electra spoke dryly. 'Don't you know it's almost suppertime?'

Goldi's eyes widened. 'That's where all the monsters will be headed?'

David nodded. 'Probably. It's the nearest town with a large population. For the vampires that represents both food and new recruits.'

'Jesus.'

'So we need to move quickly.' Electra slipped her coat from her peg. 'I'd suggest we wrap up warmly; it's blowing a storm out there.'

David's skull pounded. 'Electra, I was the one who took the blow to the head. It's me who shouldn't be thinking clearly. What makes you believe that we can tackle Rowan and an entire vampire army?'

'We don't. Not yet, anyway. But we must find them.'

'On foot? In this weather?' The wind rose in a scream across the house. 'The cold will kill us before we even find the—'

'David. Through there in the kitchen . . .' She gave a grim smile as she looped a scarf around her neck. 'There's a set of car keys hanging from a hook. Maybe my powers of deduction aren't what they used to be, but the presence of car keys suggests that the car itself might not be very far away.' She unlocked the door. 'Grab your coats. Then we'll start looking.'

6

Vikki saw them first. A tide of white scum rising up the side of the valley toward the Whitby road. Dylan heard her voice that was devoid of any emotion.

'Dylan. There's hundreds of them.'

They were perhaps a mile to his right, crossing the upland meadows to where grass gave way to heather. Even though night had fallen that never-ending flicker of lightning in the clouds revealed them.

'They're a disease, aren't they?' Vikki's voice was still a

monotone. 'If we don't stop them they're going to infect everyone.'

If we *don't stop them?* Faced with an army of vampires that numbered in their thousands that would take a miracle.

Let's pray that's exactly what we get, Dylan told himself as he drove the car uphill along the snaking road. *We need a powerful miracle tonight.*

The road took one of its sharp turns that almost folded it back on itself before continuing to run uphill parallel to the line of the valley. The car's lights blazed against stunted trees, stone walls, fences, road signs, glimpses of livestock in fields – sheep, cows, horses. And all the time the incline reared up in front of them so steeply that Dylan could have been driving the car into the sky.

'This road's going to bring us close to them,' Vikki warned.

'It's the quickest way to Don Flint.'

Vikki nodded, accepting the answer. They both knew that Black had revealed to them what they must do. They had to go to the ancient tombs. What would happen when they got there she didn't know. But whatever it was it would need their presence.

Maybe we're nothing more than some damn trigger mechanism. Dylan downshifted as the hill in front became steeper. *We're the trigger that detonates the supernatural device our ancestors implanted in the tombs.*

'Dylan.' She rested her hand on the back of his wrist, a signal to stop.

He pulled over at the side of the road. Looking downhill, he could see the vampires approaching. Countless white shapes that had once been men and women. Most were naked or dressed in shreds of clothes. Now that they were closer, Dylan could see the witch manes of hair tumbling from the skulls of the women, while most of the men were hairless. Their naked skulls reflected the lightning shimmering through the heavens above. Even from this distance Dylan could make out the way in which their eyes burned with an uncanny fire. It was more than hunger. There was lust, too, that had grown poisonously malignant during their confinement to Lazarus Deep. There they'd gestated with all the venom of witch spawn. At that moment another doorway of understanding opened in Dylan's mind.

When they get to Whitby they're going to do more than devour blood. The vampires had old scores to settle. They would torture and destroy until their craving for revenge was satisfied. At least for the time being. Then they would move on, their numbers multiplying as they turned more and more men and women vampiric. An old Viking word came to him as if someone had whispered into his ear. **Ragnorok – the Day of Doom.**

And here they come. The instruments of Ragnorok. Dylan watched, hypnotized by the sight of the legion of figures; no longer human but dead flesh on the move.

'And here's our vampire king.' Dylan nodded toward the head of the swarm. 'Rowan Harper.'

The man stood on a farm trailer as if it were a war chariot. He held onto the rail at the front as dozens of his foot soldiers hauled it up the meadow.

'And if I'm not mistaken that's Katrina West beside him.'

'Katrina West?'

'David Leppington's ex.'

'It looks as if she's got a new love in her life.'

Dylan watched with a chill growing in his blood as the procession approached. The trailer bounced across the meadow, but there in the front, standing proud, were two figures illuminated by lighting bolts. And Dylan had to admit to himself that they had the body language of a conquering king and queen. Behind them, the vampire warriors fanned out across the fields, spreading like a repellent white, leprous mould creeping across a loved one's face. Across the fields sheep gathered in frightened bunches. In a meadow in the midst of the army he saw a horse flailing across a wall in panic.

'Listen to that.' Vikki rolled down her window. 'They're killing all the animals.'

As thunder drowned out the agonized screams Dylan drove away. The tombs were only moments away. It was time to execute the final act.

CHAPTER 40

I

They've gone. Rowan's taken all the vampires away. Instead of a modern-day Pied Piper leading the vermin away to destruction he's become their chieftain, guiding them toward the last war this world will ever see.

These thoughts ran through David Leppington's mind as he lead the way to the garage behind the house. He shone the flashlight ahead of him. It revealed bushes, tree trunks . . . swathes of grass that still held pockets of ice in their hollows. But no vampires. They had all gone. No doubt greedy for the first taste of human blood on their tongues. Rowan hadn't thought it necessary even to bother leaving a few to guard the house. But then, what did it matter now? The army would soon run amok to wreck the entire world.

Behind him came Electra and Bernice, then Goldi carrying the woodcutter's axe in one hand and a candle lantern in the other, its flame flickering in the fierce rush of air roaring off Lazarus Deep. Incredibly cold air at that. He heard Bernice's teeth click as her body shivered from head to toe.

'David? What now?' Electra asked.

'Somehow I've got to take the sword back from Rowan.'

'How do you propose to do that?'

His reply faltered as a fiery snake of lighting darted across the sky. Thunder followed with a crash loud enough to make his injured head throb mercilessly.

He looked at her in the reflected glow of the flashlight. 'I don't know. I only know that I've got to try.'

'Maybe you can talk some sense into your long-lost brother,' Goldi suggested.

David saw the look in Electra's eye that said: *Some hope.*

Yeah, it's an option. But David shared Electra's pessimism. He turned to Bernice. 'Have you got the keys?' David glanced at the padlock. 'It's probably one of the smaller ones.'

David watched Bernice sort through the keys. She didn't even need him to direct the light onto the lock now. Lightning lit the sky in a constant pulse of incandescence. The landscape came alive in that blue-white flicker, as if somehow they'd been transported into an old silent film. Trees were transformed into demon shapes with claws that reached out to them, while their shadows writhed on the ground; dark cobra shapes, laden with the threat of something venomous.

'Got it.' Bernice pulled open the padlock hasp.

'Your powers of deduction haven't failed yet, Electra.' David walked along the side of the car. 'I guess Rowan's not going to care one way or the other if we take it.'

'I'll drive,' Electra told him.

'No. *I'll* drive.' Goldi stepped forward. 'I've been riding motorbikes along these lanes like a madman since I was fourteen.'

'Then I'll put my faith in you.' Electra handed him the keys.

As Goldi backed the silver BMW out onto the driveway David moved deeper into the garage, sweeping the flashlight's beam along the walls. Thunder morphed from a crash to something closer to a scream – the sound iron girders make when they're torn in two by a titanic force.

Bernice had already climbed into the back seat of the car. Electra stood behind the open passenger door. 'David, come on, get in.'

'Wait – I need something.'

'Then hurry up. There's not much time.'

I'm not going without a weapon, David told himself. The shaft of radiance from the flashlight picked out a scythe hanging on the wall. Its sharp blade was as long as his arm . . . curved like an Arabian scimitar.

'*David?*'

'I'm coming.'

Now he was ready.

2

From **Hotel Midnight**:

This is from something called the *Anglo-Saxon Chronicle*, written by a monk over twelve hundred years ago. *'Here terrible portents came about over the land of Northumbria, and miserably frightened the people: there were immense flashes of lightning and fiery dragons were seen flying in the air.'*

3

Hail swirled out of the darkness at them, striking their exposed faces. Dylan and Vikki tried to protect themselves. Those spitting shards of ice stung with a ferocity that was hard to bear.

But we have to stay here, Dylan told himself. *We have to do whatever's necessary to stop those things.*

Forty paces away Electra's car stood at the side of the deserted road. They'd walked hand in hand across tough moorland grass that was being tugged by the gale; they'd helped each other over outcrops of stone and earth mounds. Even though they'd not spoken the name since leaving the car they both knew where they were going. Primeval instinct guided them. Ahead stood the cone-shaped tumulus now known as Don Flint – although in prehistoric times it would have had another name entirely. Perhaps it would have been named after the man and woman who slept in the folds of earth beneath it. The couple who'd had the same faces as the two young people walking toward the tomb now beneath a sky where lightning bolt chased lightning bolt. Thunder roared. In that landscape of exploding silvers and dazzling electric blues they were within twenty paces of the burial mound when Dylan saw the figure of a near-giant being. A head razored clean of hair reflected the lightning flashes. A pair of shining eyes watched them approach.

Dylan felt Vikki's hand tighten around his; yet she didn't pause. She moved through the storm to the mound.

The figure stood there as if it had been extruded from bedrock. Black had beaten them to the mound. But then, he no longer had the restriction of conventional travel. Dylan knew that powers beyond his comprehension had willed Jack Black there. Also, he knew now that the man was there to help. Perhaps it was the sight of that immobile giant with the impassive face, whose alien eyes gazed at them as they approached, that triggered the revelation. The doors of perception flew open one after another in Dylan's mind. His nerves tingled. He knew the truth now.

Electra had been wrong. She'd talked about the Viking gods arguing, and scheming against one another. But that wasn't so. This was a conflict between the Vikings' deities and the divine spirits worshipped by the prehistoric people who had lived here before the first Viking warrior had ever set foot on the land. What was more, these ancient spirits who had been forgotten for more than a thousand years had been benevolent guardians of fertility: they had safeguarded for their people life-enhancing elements – harmony, sunlit meadows, spring water, summer breezes and abundant harvests. They were nothing like the Viking gods who were soaked in blood and death. Somehow, the old ones had held Odin and Thor and their vampire army in check for centuries. Only now that ancient equilibrium had been upset. Those psychotic gods that David Leppington had described were free to wreak carnage again with their vampiric warriors.

Dylan glanced at Vikki. Her faraway eyes told him that the same revelation flooded through her. Perhaps that agent of ancient divinities was feeding the understanding to them.

Black looked at both of them in turn, then inclined his head to nod at the mound.

'We're to go there,' Vikki said, pulling him by the hand.

What now?

The wind blew hard; lighting exploded the full length of the sky, to illuminate the whole world with a brilliant flickering blue. At the base of the mound Vikki and Dylan turned to look back. The giant figure remained where he was. Beyond him an expanse of moor ran to the road where the car stood. Beyond that the moor rolled on for half a mile before plunging down the side of the valley.

'*They're here.*'

Dylan followed the direction of Vikki's gaze. A grey line appeared over the edge of the valley to move in a pale surge toward them. He sensed dead flesh eager for food. The creatures had even abandoned the trailer now. In front of the vampire battalions Dylan could make out Rowan and Katrina striding across the moor. Helvetes, the sword of the Leppingtons, had lent them some dark power. They moved tirelessly. Nothing would stop them now.

And the only thing in their way is us. Dylan put his arm round Vikki. A gesture of affection as much as protection.

'This is where we stand,' she told him. 'We're not going to retreat from here.'

How can we stop those things? The question crackled inside his head. There were thousands of them. Each one more

powerful than him. Then he glanced at Vikki. Her eyes shone
with wonder.

She knows more than I do, he thought. *It's as if she can hear
a voice telling her marvellous things. She knows what's going to
happen next.*

4

Goldi wasn't wrong, David realized. The man really did know
the roads. *I only hope his experience of driving powerful cars
matches his knowledge of the area.* To spin off into a ditch now
would mean disaster. He glanced at the younger man's profile
with the shadowed face contrasting with the blond dreadlocks.
Goldi's gaze was locked on the road ahead, anticipating
every turn, every humpback bridge, every sudden dip into
a gully.

'All I can think of is that we somehow get in front of Rowan,'
David said.

'I'm ahead of you on that one.' Goldi floored the accelerator pedal. The car seemed to chase the light of its own
headlamps.

From the back Electra said, 'You're taking the high moorland crossing to the Whitby Road?'

'Yup, the good old A171. I can do that one blindfold.'

'Twenty-twenty vision's good enough me,' she remarked
dryly.

Bernice leaned forward from the back seat to look through
the glass at the blur of passing walls and farm gates. 'David.
Have you thought it through about Rowan?' she asked.

David nodded. 'I'm going to have to kill him, aren't I?'

Nobody replied. The question haunted the car with all the
dark intensity of the words themselves. There was another
question, too. Equally potent. David couldn't even give voice
to that one. But he couldn't stop himself from thinking it.

And when I've killed Rowan. That's when I've got to kill myself, haven't I?

Thunder buffeted the car with a wall of sound. Outside, darkness returned with a vengeance once the flash of lightning had died. *I'm a blood Leppington.* David gazed forward at the blur of road. *If I destroy myself then it pulls the plug on the vampires.*

Goldi reached a stretch of straight road that ran up to the highest point of the moor, rushing them all to their final destination.

5

As the wind raged, flinging grass and sticks at them, Dylan held Vikki tight to him. He saw her lips move. Not praying. He knew that. She was speaking to someone . . . some presence he could neither hear nor see.

Above him a raven glided through the night sky, a hell-black silhouette against the sheet lightning. He knew that it was watching them.

6

'There's my car!' Electra gripped David's seat-back as she pulled herself forward to see better. 'That's my bloody car!' Something like a note of triumph sounded in her voice. 'Goldi, pull over behind it.'

'Are you sure?'

'Sure I'm sure! Vikki and Dylan must be close by.'

David saw earth mounds rising against the lightning-ripped sky. Hail clattered against the car. 'This cold's a killer. It'd be suicide to stay out there for long.'

'They've got to be here.' Electra's head turned as she scanned the moor.

'Seeing as they ran out on us maybe they should stay here,' Goldi said, slowing the car reluctantly.

'No,' Electra countered, a tremor of excitement in her voice. 'They must be here for a reason.'

'Hell . . . what reason? These are old burial mounds. There's nothing else here.'

'Exactly!'

David looked back. 'You mean they drove up here just to visit old graves?'

'There's no "just" about it. Call it intuition but I'm getting a buzz from this place. This is where we're going to find the solution to our problem.'

Goldi shook his head. 'Solution? What on Earth's up here that can help us?' He was talking to Electra's back; she'd already opened the door and swung herself out of the car. A moment later she ducked her head back inside.

'I can see them. They're up on the mound. Come on!'

CHAPTER 41

I

My name is Bernice Mochardi . . . this is my destiny. My name is—

Bernice struggled against the tsunami of wind and hail that struck them like arrowheads, battering exposed skin. The cold, the lightning flashes, the scream of thunder battered her senses. She found herself repeating her name, simply to prevent her senses from being smashed from her. *My name is Bernice Mochardi . . . my name—*

'Nearly there!'

She glanced up to see David's face. He made himself smile to reassure her. She tried to smile back but there was more than the cold and the storm reaching her now. It seemed as if a shadow had crept from the ground beneath her to slip through the soles of her boots. She sensed its darkness rising up through her ankles, sliding along her bones, up her thighs, chilling her to her very heart's blood. As it crept up inside her body she felt an immense dread.

Something's going to happen, she thought with such a powerful sense of horror that she thought her body would erupt. *I've never felt this way before . . . even three years ago when we first fought the vampires . . . this time's it's going to be different.*

She forced herself to open her eyes against the driving hail. They were almost at the foot of the mound. Vikki and Dylan stood on the side of the tumulus, perhaps halfway up. The mound itself, she guessed, was perhaps as tall as a house. It looked like a stunted pyramid there in the stuttering light of the storm. Another figure towered at the base of the tumulus.

She recognized it instantly. Jack Black.

2

The five-minute walk from the car to the foot of the burial mound had been a battle in itself. David's heart pounded against his ribs. He was out of breath. The vicious lightning bursts dazzled him. Thunder set his head pounding. Once more he felt the trickle of blood down the back of his neck. Moving through these storm conditions must have reopened the head wound. In his hand he gripped the scythe by the handle, its scimitar blade reflecting the electric storm in flashes of blue, silver and gold.

Shielding his eyes against the hailstones, he glanced back. Electra was there, right behind him, her long hair drawn out into a blue-black banner that rippled in the mad rush of the hurricane. Goldi moved forward with the big axe in his hands. He stared up at Vikki and Dylan, obviously wondering what the hell they were doing standing there on the mound's steep sides. David checked that Bernice was with them. Her gaze looked beyond the pair on the mound. She appeared to be seeing something else there in the distance.

One thing he couldn't miss was the gigantic figure of Jack Black. He looked even taller, even more formidable than before. His biceps bulged. He didn't even flinch as the hailstones dug into his bare skin.

But that's not surprising, David told himself. The tattooed beast of a man was no longer mortal. Then an astonishing thing happened.

David could see that Jack's expression was impassive, as if his face was carved from rock. But just for a moment he saw Jack meet Bernice's eye. He smiled at her – a warm, caring smile that transformed the beast-man's expression into one of gentleness. Bernice smiled back. And some secret understanding passed between them.

Lightning burst, filling the landscape with such brilliance that it seemed to burn through the burial mound. It must have been a trick of the light, only David thought he saw silhouettes of figures within the heap of earth and stones. Thunder tore at his eardrums. Both Electra and Goldi put their hands to their ears, their faces twisting with pain.

David moved forward. 'Vikki . . . Dylan?'

Why are you here? The question he'd planned to ask remained unspoken. There was no longer any need. They'd run out of time. Dylan had been staring toward the horizon. For a second his grave gaze settled on David. Then he pointed back toward where the moor plunged down into the valley.

David looked in the direction of the pointing finger. There, flowing in a mass of noxious white, came the vampires. Thousands upon thousands of them. They were perhaps a few hundred paces away. In a minute they'd reach the road and the cars. *No running away now. Not even if we wanted to.*

David saw the figure of Rowan with Katrina at his side; both strode like conquering warriors ahead of their army. His heart leaped in his chest. Whatever the outcome, it was time to confront his brother.

3

David took a pace forward to stand squarely facing the advancing vampires. Now he could see White and Broxley and Spencer and Fretwell. The bulk of the vampires were ancient creatures, the corpses of Viking invaders raised from the dead. Their skin hues flashed from white to blue as lighting seared through the cloud that rolled across the sky like boulders to seal the tombs of people not yet dead.

Only too visible now were those thousands of pairs of eyes. They had no colour, only the vicious pinprick pupils. Their mouths opened to reveal the mad profusion of teeth that were barbed like those of sharks. Their collective expression was one of exultation. The things radiated power. They were hungry for victory now.

In reaction to this sight David felt his own strength drain from him. It was all he could do to remain standing with the scythe in his hand. The gale pushed him back. Then, with a savage switch in direction, the wind shoved him forward. Even the elements wanted to throw him to the vampires, like a man throws a bone to a dog. From just across the road he saw Rowan pause. The man had seen his brother standing there with his little band of human allies. David could see the man's mouth form a leering grin. At that moment Rowan lifted the sword above his head; the signal was brutally clear. Sheets of lightning rocketed across the sky. But this time instead of thunder David heard the battle cry of the vampire army.

They began their attack. David glanced at Electra and Bernice as they flinched before the sight. Thousands of monsters swarmed across the moor. The women sensed their hunger and their predatory power. David looked to Black. The giant figure did nothing. Merely stared forward. Impassive. Wooden. Maybe he could do nothing? Maybe the thing masquerading as Black was a messenger of some ben- evolent – but ultimately impotent – spirit and nothing more.

Then David heard a thrumming on the air. As if riding the wind came indistinct voices chanting a song. Glancing back at the mound, he saw Vikki. Her eyes were wide open as she stared above the heads of the approaching vampires. This wasn't fear. She was seeing something wonderful. At that moment she opened her mouth. Her shout even overwhelmed the thunder.

'NOW!'

Lightning crackled from the sky in salvo after salvo. It struck the burial mounds, exploding against the earth around them, sending forked rivers of light through the grass. That force surged downward through the soil and stones, deep into graves that held the bones of the sons and daughters of these valleys who had lain in dreamless sleep for three thousand years or more.

Everyone – with the exception of Black – shielded their eyes. David expected to feel the burn of electrical discharge eat into his skin, but a moment later he realized that the lightning strike hadn't harmed them. When he opened his eyes he saw that they were no longer alone. With them, their skins fresh and new, shining with health and strength, were dozens of people. No, not dozens. Hundreds. Men and women dressed in clothes that were dyed in rich purples and deep woodland greens. Finely worked brooches, or gold pins, held cloaks in place. Their hair was braided with wild vines. For a second David wondered if the vampires had rushed their small group during the time they'd been dazzled by the lightning. But he knew instantly that these folk weren't vampires.

These people had their origins way back in time, long before the Viking invaders that made up the vampire army. The gazes of these men and women were locked onto their monstrous enemy. Dazed, David watched the figures blur as they ran forward. Soon only he remained with his five mortal friends by his side. Black watched: motionless as a pillar of rock.

4

From **Hotel Midnight**:

A mysterious Hermetic cult that flourished seventeen hundred years ago recorded this verse on their fabled Emerald Tablet: *'Whatever is below is like that which is above, and whatever is above is like that which is below.'* This means that man is the mirror of the gods. That on Earth he duplicates the actions – and the events – of his deities. In short, my dear boys and girls, if nations in our world fight one another down here on terra firma, then there is war in heaven, too.

5

The men and women, citizens of Morningdale's prehistoric past, raced across the moor to meet the vampires head-on. Dylan watched it all in those incandescent explosions of lightning. The men and women raised from the graves beneath his feet were armed with axes and weapons of flint or bronze or iron. Many of the women carried spears that were as tall as them.

The two armies clashed on the moor. Strangely, there were no shouts or cries. It was as if he was watching a silent film. The images moved in strobing flickers. Faces blazed with an uncanny light. Vampires lunged forward, jaws yawning wide, teeth glinting.

Morningdale's people struck with devastating force. Female spear-holders impaled the vampires through their ribcages, holding the thrashing creatures out of harm's way while stocky men armed with axes and swords hacked off the vampires' heads – David Leppington's avowed way of dispatching the monsters.

Our people are fearless in the way—

Our people? Dylan repeated the phrase he'd used. *Our people . . . Yes, they* are *our people. The men and women fighting the vampires are* my *ancestors. They have passed their genetic essence to me. I have their blood in my veins.* He glanced at Vikki. She watched her ancestors battle in silence, her gaze locked on the spectacle.

Dylan climbed down to level ground where David and the rest stood. Goldi grabbed him by the arm.

'Hey, Dill! What the hell's happening?'

Dylan found himself grinning. 'We're fighting back . . .' He slapped Goldi on the shoulder. 'We're fighting back!'

David turned. 'These people, I take it, are *your* ancestors.'

'Electra's, too. And Vikki's.'

Electra said, 'It's time to choose which side you're on, David.'

'Don't worry. I know.' David put his hand on Dylan's shoulder. 'You knew this would happen, didn't you?'

'No . . . at least, not consciously. He had to show me first.' Dylan glanced at Black.

David nodded. 'He did the same for me.'

'Seize your moment and witness this,' Electra told them. 'The classic battle between good and evil.'

'Between the Norse gods and the gods of the people buried here.' Dylan tilted his head back at the graves.

'So my theory wasn't entirely correct,' Electra admitted. 'So, let that be a lesson to us all. Don't trust a hypothesis without supporting evidence.'

Vikki gave a cry. They looked up to where she stood on the mound. 'There's too many – we're not holding them!'

Goldi moved forward, holding the shaft of the axe in his hands.

'Wait just there!' Electra's voice came as a scream. 'What do you think you're doing?'

Goldi's eyes were bright. 'You heard, Vikki. Our guys need a hand!'

'But there's too many to—' Electra stopped when she realized that Goldi wouldn't be halted. He ran across the moor to where the battle raged.

David ran after him, the scythe gripped in his clenched hands. Dylan was about to follow, too, but he stopped when a tight grip closed over his elbow. He turned to see Electra, her face flashing blue-white in the lightning.

'You mustn't follow them,' she told him. 'You and Vikki have got to stay here. I don't know how but you've brought these people here to destroy the monsters.' She fixed her gaze on him. 'You're not expendable. We are.'

Then Dylan watched Electra turn and follow David and Goldi as they ran to join the battle. He noticed that Bernice was moving toward the conflict, too.

CHAPTER 42

I

David saw that Vikki had been right.

He thought: *We are losing. There's too many of them. We can't hold them back much longer. A few more minutes and the vampires will burst through the line. And once they have beaten us there's nothing to stop them marching on the rest of the world.* He peered through the spitting hail to where Rowan stood behind his line of vampires as they advanced. The man's expression was one of smug self-satisfaction. Katrina was at his side, a look of lunatic delight in her eye. She was swaying, caught up in the rhythm of the battle, as if she was hearing unearthly music.

'Heads you say, Doc?'

David shot a look at Goldi. 'What?'

'Heads. If you take off the bastards' heads, then it kills them, right?'

All David could do was nod. There was no point in trying to talk the man out of it. He was wired. He wanted a great, steaming slice of the action. With a whoop, Goldi threw himself against a break in the line, swinging the woodcutter's axe. One blow ripped off the face of a vampire. Of course it wasn't enough. The monster kept coming, its hands clawing at Goldi. One of the female warriors drove her spear deep into the side of the vampire, releasing a gush of clear fluid. As it used both hands to pull out the spearhead, Goldi stepped forward and with a neat sideways slash of the axe decapitated the monster. Instantly, its body fell to the ground. Goldi whooped again, shaking his fist above his head. The man was on the adrenalin ride of his life.

And long may it last, David prayed. *We're going to need all the help we can get.*

He moved along the line of men and women as they struggled to hold the vampires back. A futile effort. They were being pushed toward the road now. Soon they'd have their backs to the burial mounds. There had to be a way through the line. He had to reach Rowan. He must take the sword from him. Because, without a shadow of a doubt, it was the sword that made the vampires so strong. Its energy ran into their bodies, powering them on to attack with even greater ferocity.

Gaps would appear in the vampire line as they surged forward. But the spaces only lasted a second. Then another vampire would step forward to replace a fallen comrade. *Damn, damn, damn* . . . Each time David readied himself to leap through in an attempt to get his hands on Rowan the gap would snap shut.

This happened once, twice, three times. Four, five . . . David could have howled with frustration. Then, just paces to his right, a heavily built man swung his bronze sword, felling a vampire.

A gap . . .

Only David wasn't fast enough. A second figure leaped through from *behind* him. Goldi? No, Goldi was still swinging his axe to David's right.

'Bernice!' The cry erupted from his throat. 'Bernice . . . move back . . . move further back!'

He was still shouting. He couldn't believe what she'd done. She'd made it through the ranks of vampires. But she wasn't even armed. And there were hundreds of the fucking monsters. How could she fight them? What could she do to—

No. Dear God, no. Bernice, please don't do this.

Storm winds screamed. Lightning bathed the scene in flickering electric blue.

'Bernice! Don't you dare! I'm telling you, don't you—'

His cries were so desperate because David knew what she was planning. She ran back a dozen or so paces to a mound that reached not much higher than her slender waist. David watched her climb it; his blood crept like ice through his veins. He held his breath. Nothing else mattered now but the scene unfurling before him.

Bernice's voice came clearly – almost uncannily so – through the thud of weapons on flesh and the rumble of thunder.

'This is what you want!' she shouted. 'This is it, isn't it? You don't have to wait. Look!' She reached up and tore the neck of her blouse, opening it to reveal her skin beneath. Her neck was swanlike, luminous in that mad flicker of lightning. 'This is what you want! *Come and take it!*'

Bernice reached up again and ripped the side of her neck with her fingernails in one nerve-powered sweep that opened her skin from the bottom of her ear down to the top of her chest. Blood beaded through the torn flesh.

David watched with a dread-filled fascination. Lines of red stood out against that perfect skin. Instantly the vampires twisted their heads. Predatory animals sensing warm, living blood on the night air. David heard Rowan's furious yell.

'Ignore her! She's trying to distract you! You've nearly won. Soon you'll have as much blood as you want. Keep fighting. Destroy the—'

They had the teeth of sharks; they had the bloodlust of those predators, too. The vampires turned back. In a wave of surging grey they rushed Bernice. David saw her standing there. Arms straight down by her sides. Fists clenched. Eyes closed. There was no fear on her face. Just before the mob swept over her, dragging her down, David recognized her expression. *Acceptance.*

2

Where there had once been a five-deep line of vampires now there were none of the monsters. David raced toward where Rowan was cursing the creatures. The vampires must have realized instantly the threat against their human master. Some detached themselves from the feeding frenzy centring on Bernice's body. These monsters were the recently dead who weren't slaves to their post-mortem instincts. Broxley, White and Spencer ran to stand between Rowan and David. Other vampires were starting to leave the blood orgy, too, as the danger warning worked its way into their brains.

'You're not going any further,' White told David, his green eyes gleaming. 'You had your chance . . . you blew it.'

The thing that had once been Luke Spencer leered. 'Now you're going to join the party.'

White moved forward. 'Me first, boys. I think I've earned this one.' Opening his mouth to reveal the forest of spikes that served him as teeth, he closed in.

Then Jack Black moved between David and the vampire in a blur of ferocious speed and strength. Black seized the vampire as if White was nothing more than a rag doll. Holding him by his albino hair Black drove two fingers into his throat so they passed either side of the windpipe. Then he pulled upwards.

Images came to David of a child pulling the head off a plastic doll. Only this was no toy. With a meaty crack loud enough to be heard a hundred metres away, Black snapped off the creature's head. With contempt he tossed the head to one side while allowing the body to fall.

With a yell Goldi appeared, slashing at Luke Adams. With

what remained of his human instincts Luke raised his arms to protect himself. The axe cut through his wrists to drop the hands, twitching and clenching, into the grass. The next swipe cleaved away Luke's head. Spurting clear liquid from the neck wound, the body slumped down.

Broxley turned to run but Black seized him, then effortlessly twisted the head from the body with his massive tattooed hands. Screeching, Katrina backed away, holding her hands out in front of her. Panic convulsed her face. Behind him, David sensed a presence. He wasn't wrong. The army that Vikki and Dylan had raised from their graves rushed forward again. This time they were stronger.

A fleeting thought passed through David's mind: *Maybe this is Bernice's doing. It's more than her distracting the monsters. This new empowerment is due to her self-sacrifice . . .*

Screaming with rage, Rowan hurled himself forward. Calm now, experiencing a sense of detachment – the same emotion he felt when surgically excising dead tissue from a wound – David sidestepped Rowan. Using the momentum of the movement, he swung the scythe. Its point buried itself deep under the other man's ribcage. With a look of absolute dread on his face Rowan stumbled forward, trying to pull the blade from his stomach. David saw that all the effort produced were gashes to the man's fingers and palms.

The vampire line broke. The pressure from the men and women battling the monsters was irresistible.

Rowan looked up at David. Fear burned in his gaze. 'David . . . David. Please help me. I didn't mean to hurt you. I—' He writhed in pain. 'They drove me mad. It wasn't my—'

Then servant turned on master. Milling around in mindless panic, the vampires saw the blood that was soaking the dying man. They picked him up bodily to suck at the cuts. He screamed as sharp teeth broke open new wounds; none of the creatures wanted to lose their share. Screaming, kicking, he was carried shoulder high away from the battle.

The vampire force was dissipating. Jack Black punched at white, hairless heads with so much force that they burst in a spray of grey meat and jelly. Then the headless bodies would drop to shiver in the grass as whatever counterfeit life they possessed left them.

Helvetes. It lay shining in the grass. David picked up the sword. When the vampires ran at him, the weapon thrummed in his hand, its power flowing into his arm. Again and again he struck. Vampires fell headless as the sword sliced through their necks. Beside him Goldi fought, too, his face blazing with a near-superhuman energy. Maybe the spirits of his own warrior ancestors were guiding his blows, too, as the axe blade flashed in the lightning bursts. Behind the warrior line Electra urged them on.

With the destruction of hundreds of vampires, and the loss of their leader, some crucial point had been reached, some critical mass achieved. With a ragged stutter of thunder the storm ended. Moonlight shone through clouds that dissolved with uncanny speed.

All around David the ancient defenders of Morningdale (who were now also defenders of the world beyond) grew stronger and more numerous by the moment. And there, crawling toward him, limbs and body torn, the blade of the broken-handled scythe still protruding from his belly, was Rowan. David couldn't tell whether he was still human or had crossed over that dark abyss to become vampiric. Not that it mattered.

David gazed down at the man who resembled him so closely. Rowan looked up at him through heavy-lidded eyes that had grown dull. Once the pair could have passed for twins.

Imploringly, the man held his torn hands up to David; three

fingers hung back against his lower knuckles where they'd been torn free of their joints.

David shook his head. 'It's over, brother.'

Gritting his teeth, he swung the sword down; the blade's edge sliced through Rowan's Adam's apple, neck muscles, arteries, spinal column. The head rolled over and over in the grass; the body sagged. Lifeless flesh. Cold.

With a sound that mated a cry with the hiss of an indrawn breath the vampires that were still standing bowed their heads. They were shrivelled things now. There was no sense of vitality to them. Their eyes and skin grew dull. Their arms withered. Bellies became shrunken hollows.

Without any fuss, they simply melted: their limbs lost definition, their heads became nothing more than distorted fungus shapes. One by one they slopped to the ground where their bodies were reduced to some dull grey fluid that ran down slopes into gullies from which it would flow into streams, which in turn would bear the slick of pus back to the valley bottom. There it would eventually find dissolution in Lazarus Deep.

Goldi loped across to David. He was panting furiously and perspiration soaked his face; yet even though exhaustion weighed him down there was a look of fierce pride on his face. 'We've done it.' He shook the axe above his head. 'It's over!'

David gave a grim shake of his head. 'Not quite.'

He walked across the moor. What he was looking for would be easy to find now that the vampires had melted away. Even humanity's allies were fading now. They had become misty. More like memories than physical beings. One by one they were returning to their womblike hollows in the earth beneath the burial mounds. Time to return to dreamless sleep.

He noticed that Electra had reached Katrina where she sat on the grass. Beside Katrina stood Jack Black. He must have protected her from the vampires during the battle for she appeared physically unharmed. Even so, she was still in a daze, almost as if she was only half awake.

David glanced across at where Jack Black stood, statue-like once more. Within seconds the giant's body blurred, softening into a twist of vapour that floated away to disappear across the moor.

A moment later he found Bernice. A bloodless white, she lay on her back against the dark swathe of grass. For the moment, she reposed in true death. He raised the sword above his head, judging the best place on her throat to land the blow.

David Leppington was determined that Bernice's sleep should be dreamless, too.

WINTER'S END

1. Station Hotel. Noon.

With the wedding party under way in the main function room of the Station Hotel, Electra collected her laptop from the office and then left the hotel by the back door. She crossed the yard, then passed through the gap in the wall to the river bank. This first Saturday in May was a warm one. The sun had defeated the last crust of snow on the hilltops. The River Lepping roared by, engorged with melt water. While along its willow-lined banks the new growth of grasses and wild flowers was so fresh that she could taste as well as smell the air laden with the piquant scents of new life springing from Leppington's soil. Layered among the green of new leaves were the creamy whites of hawthorn blossom. Bird song drifted on the afternoon air. A kingfisher moved in flashes of electric blue across the foaming waters.

Electra sat down on a tree stump close to the water's edge, then opened up the laptop. Switched it on. Felt it hum on her lap as it came to life. The opening screen showed a sepia-tint photograph of Whitby's abbey ruins. She opened the Hotel Midnight file and began to type.

Electra here. Thank you for all your e-mails. I've not updated the Hotel Midnight site for a while (as so many of you have reminded me!) I've been busy. An old friend died. Two new friends got married. They moved to London. The bridegroom works for a photographic studio. His bride is a publicist at an art gallery.

*As you know, boys and girls, I've kept the identities of people
featured on this website anonymous (and, no, Mr Siwel, offers
of cash will not entice me to name names in* Nemonymous,
*cherishable though your magazine is). Someone once said that
grief is the price of love. Painfully, I've learned the hard way
that this is true. And although I've written about vampires and
other dark legends of the past I'm starting to realize that those
colourful myths of gods and monsters and fabulous faery lands
are often picturesque reflections of what you and I experience
in our day-to-day lives. We all fall in love, we all move from
childhood into adulthood (and what a hair-raising journey that
is!) and we all suffer setbacks in our lives; sometimes our dreams
are shattered, and inevitably we have to endure tragedies. Just to
step into Viking legend again, their greatest tragedy is Ragnorok,
the day of doom when the giant wolf, Fenrir, swallows the sun.
Odin, lord of the gods, is killed in the final apocalyptic battle.
And yet, even though both Heaven and Earth lie in ruins, the
legend ends on a note of optimism. It suggests a new world will
be created, complete with a new generation: –*

Through the grass of dawn shall the golden figures come,
And the sacred ones will be found again,
As they were in olden days.

*I guess what that verse echoes are our own phrases that we trot
out to the newly bankrupt or freshly bereaved:* Every cloud has
a silver lining . . . The darkest hour is just before dawn.

*There you have it, my dears. It's time for me to take a break
from the Hotel Midnight site for a little while. I'm just about to
open a new chapter in my life. However, if you should ever find
yourself in desperate straits, if you're ever forced to confront danger
of the kind described here in Hotel Midnight, then drop by the little
out-of-the-way town of Leppington, North Yorkshire. You can
find it by going straight on from Morningdale in the direction of*

Castleton. In the middle of Leppington is the Station Hotel. Enter through the main doors and go to the reception desk. If you leave your message there, then it's sure to reach me.

Ciao for now, old friends.

Electra switched off the laptop and gazed at the river tumbling down the valley toward Whitby on the coast. Some white blossom floated by. She found herself watching it as it glided around rocks and skipped over cascades until it vanished into the distance.

With a sigh, she stood up and returned to the Station Hotel.

2. Robin Hood's Bay. Dusk.

Katrina West sat dangling her legs over the bows of the motor yacht that David had chartered for the whole of June. On this perfect summer's evening the sun was setting behind her over the cliffs of Robin Hood's Bay. The boat rose and fell gently on the swell. Ahead of her the ocean, glinting with golds and reds, stretched out to the horizon beneath a cloudless sky.

Katrina was the happiest she'd been in years. The medication was working fine; her schizophrenia had dwindled away to a pinprick as tiny as that star now appearing in the night sky. Like that star the condition would always be there. But, again like that star, it would be (to her) tiny; it would be invisible for most of the time, and more importantly her schizophrenia would not affect her everyday life in any shape or form.

David called cheerfully from the yacht's cabin, 'Ice and lemon?'

Smiling, she replied. 'Please, and plenty of tonic.'

'Thirsty?'

'Like you wouldn't believe.'

'It's not surprising,' he called. 'It's been hot enough to fry eggs on the decks today.'

'Chop chop, cabin boy,' she called. 'The captain's mistress needs her gin and tonic.'

David's voice came from the depths of the cabin. 'Aye aye . . . shouldn't be long. Only the ice doesn't want to come out of the tray.'

Still smiling, Katrina admired her tanned legs. How they ran sleekly down to her toes with their nails that were varnished an erotic red. It was just four months since her chronic relapse in February. Then the hallucinations had raged out of control. She'd fled on some weird, irrational errand to a place called Leppington where she'd stayed in the Station Hotel. After that everything became blurry in her memory. All she could recall now were strange psychosis-powered dreams of herself walking across the moors in the company of thousands of monstrous figures with mouths full of sharp teeth. Of course, all delusional. What could you expect when you stopped taking your medication? Schizophrenia was like a caged beast always straining to break free. But enough of that. The doctors had it licked. She was taking a new super-breed of antipsychotic that, thankfully, had no troubling side effects. In fact, she'd even lost weight. She felt healthier; she was a fully functioning member of the human race again. And, miracle of miracles, she was living with David in his London apartment.

'Are you ready with that gin and tonic yet?'

'Uhm, not quite. It's this ice . . . *Damn.*'

He could be lovably clumsy at times. Now he sounded cheerful and carefree, even when the ice trays wouldn't yield their prize.

'David?'

'Uh-huh?'

'Need any help?'

'No, nearly done.'

'Don't cut yourself.'

'Don't worry. There's a doctor in the house.'

Smiling, Katrina shook her head and looked at how the water swirled languidly around the anchor chain. It was so clear out here in the middle of the bay, away from the fog of sand stirred up by tidal surges, that she could see a good fifteen feet of chain as it strung out deep into the water. Tiny silver-sided fish darted at the chain as if the bright, glittering links fascinated them. *Some marine version of moths drawn to the light*, she mused. Far away in the distance a gull called. Above, more stars pricked through the deepening blue of the sky.

Then David's voice came again. Almost shy-sounding, as if he'd been building up to this. 'Katrina.'

'Yes?'

'I've been thinking,' he said.

'Oh?'

'We've forgotten something.'

'No, we've got all we need.'

'We've not got everything.'

'What haven't we got?'

'We haven't got married.'

'Funny.' She smiled. 'I was just about to mention the same thing.'

'So what do you think?'

'To marriage?'

'A good idea?'

'A very good idea.'

Katrina could almost hear the smile in David's voice as it came from the cabin. 'I'll take that as a *yes*, then.'

Her own smile broadened; she felt a pleasant tingle as her blood warmed her veins. This wonderful transformation in her life, from being a profoundly sick woman to full health and happiness, was nothing less than a miracle. True, she still had those delusional glitches. But all she had to do was to jokingly tell the phantom 'voice' that muttered in her ear or the ghostly shadow manifesting itself on the wall to 'take a hike' and they always did as they were told. Those little glitches in her state of mind were of no consequence now. Oh, there were some days that were more bothersome than others.

Just yesterday, for example. David had been keen to take the boat far out to sea for a hundred miles or so to where he'd heard from local fishermen that he could find one of those invisible highways of the ocean that carried migrating pods of pilot whales. They'd found no whales but David hadn't seemed that concerned. And when, after they'd made love, Katrina had lain dozing on the bed in the motor yacht's cabin and she'd heard David moving around on deck she'd gone to look for him. She'd peeped out of the cabin door to see him standing on the prow of the boat. Of course, it must have been one of the mischievous tricks sometimes played by her schizophrenia, for she'd thought that she'd seen David standing there with a sword in his hand. It was a huge thing, half as tall as the man himself, with an elaborate hilt and pommel. Even though yesterday afternoon had been gloomily cloudy, the sword had blazed with all the brilliance of sunlight striking it. For a second David had held the sword high above his head, as if showing it to someone whom she could not see. But who *could* have seen it, with the exception of the solitary raven that had circled overhead? They'd been a hundred miles from the coast. Just the two of them on a boat, with no other shipping in sight. Then David had hurled the sword. It had flown up into the sky to an impossible height before falling back down to the ocean. Even then it hadn't splashed into the water as one would have imagined. The sea had opened up like a huge liquid mouth, ringed by raised glistening lips. The sword had simply vanished to plunge down to the seabed hundreds of fathoms below. No splash. No sound.

Like I said, she told herself, *just one of those minor aberrations that pop up every now and again. I imagined it. It was nothing more than one of those dying flickers of hallucination that'll soon never bother me again.*

She gazed down into the water, at how the links of the anchor chain slowly faded away into the deepening green of the sea.

'Yes, all imagination,' Katrina murmured to the white faces with pinprick eyes that stared up at her from just beneath the surface. 'Imagination . . . just like you.'